The Little Universe

Jason Matthews

Pismo Beach, California USA

Also by Jason Matthews

Jim's Life - the sequel novel

Better You, Better Me - for a happy life

How to Make, Market and Sell Ebooks All for Free

How to Make Your Own Free Website: And Your Free Blog Too

Get On Google Front Page

Find more at the websites:
TheLittleUniverse.com - your-own-free-website.com

This book is dedicated with appreciation to all who have helped along the way.

To Edgar Cayce, his family and the A.R.E. for your contributions to psychic wisdom, which influenced Whitney's trances and the teachings of the Thetans in the story.
To Carl Sagan, Stephen Hawking, Einstein and the people of NASA for your insights to the universe.
To my family who read early versions.
To Mom, for everything.
To friends who read and advised.
To my psychics for life direction.
To Jana, Shelby and Devan.
To Shep.
To the creative energy within every atom—the essence—the I AM THAT I AM!

"WE HAVE SOCIETY! Pinching myself. Yesterday they were primates. Grooming parasites, eating reeds. Today they're driving! Just fifty thousand orbits? How could they evolve so quickly? I need to know. We looked for the link but nothing yet. Possible I missed something, but what? Jim's going over the logs, maybe he'll find it. Mind's a blur—thoughts won't stop—could go on all night. Need to rest, hope I can. Wish Rose could have seen this."

- from p. 66 of Webster's journal.

The Concept

MY LEGS LABORED TO TURN the pedals on the bicycle as frigid winter air bit into my cheeks and knuckles. I cursed myself for leaving my hat and gloves at the bar the night before. I rode slowly, steering with one hand while warming the other in my pocket until frostbite forced a switch. It didn't matter how cold it was. I needed the work. My stomach reminded me that it needed food, real food. It was tired of stale crackers and cheap beer. I rode on through the frost.

I rode my bicycle everywhere. I even fashioned leather saddlebags over the front and rear tires to carry essential tools. I was the only carpenter I knew without a truck. Yet with two bags of basic tools, I could accomplish almost any job. From that, I felt some pride. I pedaled quickly past a busy construction site and endured the jeers from workers dressed in expensive coveralls, laughing at me as they leaned against new trucks, sipping their hot drinks. The aroma of fine coffee made my stomach grumble. I thought of my situation and felt a bit angry.

I wondered if I was a loser. Success meant having things like a good job, a wife and home, kids and pets. I was over thirty and had none of those. I didn't even own a car, but I took pride in limited needs and thought the world would be a better place if more people were like me, common and somewhat content. T-shirts and jeans filled the closet in my apartment, and I liked it that way.

Certainly I wasn't a success. Was I really a loser? It was a good question. The thought was going through my mind as I pulled up, hungry and half-frozen, to his driveway for my first meeting with Webster Adams.

Adams hired me as a handyman. He got my name from his neighbor, an elderly woman who had employed me in the past. He came out to meet me in the driveway, walking quickly in the brisk air, wearing a collar shirt and slacks. He was taller than average, thin and appeared to be late fifties with wavy black hair mixed with streaks of gray. He had very blue eyes.

Adams smiled awkwardly as he surveyed my bicycle. Then he stuck out his hand and shook mine.

"Your hand is freezing," he observed, gripping mine harder than I wanted, not sensing the pain of near frostbite I was experiencing.

I smiled and replied, "Pleasure to meet you, sir. I'm Jon Gruber."

"Interesting transportation, Mr. Gruber. Especially in this weather."

His look was one of admiration and concern. I suspected he was deciding whether he had made a mistake in hiring me.

"Gets me from point A to B," I said, disconnecting the front leather bag. I slung it over my shoulder, hoping to instill some confidence in Adams.

He led me into his house. The entry had a cathedral ceiling with stained glass windows that filled the downstairs with an array of colors, like walking through a rainbow. The wooden floor was finely polished. My footsteps echoed softly as I followed him down the hallway.

"Should I take off my shoes?" I asked. Adams shook his head no.

Dozens of framed pictures hung on the walls of a happy family: man, wife and pretty daughter. The girl instantly caught my eye. Auburn hair, easy smile, the girl-next-door look that I was naturally attracted to.

Adams jogged up the first flight of stairs and I followed. The stairwell contained paintings of planets, nebulas and constellations. Things I knew nothing about back then. Adams paused briefly on the second flight as he passed the largest of the paintings, a massive planet with a purple body and half-finished blue rings around it. It was a lovely piece of work though I wondered why it was unfinished. He stared at it for a moment then continued up.

The top floor was immaculate with marble counters, leather couches and a plush carpet leading to a stone hearth and fireplace where a small fire crackled. I looked around at the trophies of a successful man and wondered if I would ever have those things.

"I want to tear down this wall that separates the kitchen from the great room," Adams explained. "The idea is to make it one big space."

"I can do that."

"Everything?"

"Yeah."

"How would you get the materials here?"

"Delivery."

"What would you recommend?" he asked.

I imagined the finished product and said, "I'll rip out the wallboard and the studs to here, then frame a bar that stretches toward the middle. Then I'll rewire the electrical, texture, paint and whatnot."

He ended by saying, "I want it to be done well, Jon."

I answered with a promise that never failed. "Sir, if you're not delighted with the finished product, you don't have to pay me."

Adams laughed at my guarantee, but a look of ease came to his face. Then he pointed at the counter to a plate full of cookies. "Help yourself," he said. "The neighbor brought them over."

Once he looked away, I took three and stuffed them in my mouth. Fuel for good work, I thought.

I jogged downstairs and grabbed the remaining bag of tools from my bike, anticipating the ride home without the heavy tools or the bitter morning cold. I reminded myself to stop by the Star Bar and pick up my hat and gloves. Samantha would hold them for me. Then I headed back upstairs and began demolishing the wall that enclosed his kitchen. Adams watched me briefly before going to his office.

After destroying the wall, I hauled the debris down to the garage. The place was full of circuits and devices, like a high-tech machine shop. I guessed that Adams was an inventor. He came down and saw me staring at things. He showed me an oscillating microscope and tried to explain how it worked but the concepts were mindboggling. I nodded along dumbly as if I understood what he was saying. Adams didn't seem to realize the information was beyond me as he went on and on with the explanation.

I worked for him for a week. He had a quiet but pleasant nature, introverted. He often seemed absorbed in thought as he came and left frequently during those days, preoccupied with his latest project. Sometimes he would jot notes in a little brown booklet. I heard him mumbling to himself as he read over the notes, complex fragments I could not begin to understand.

"That can't be? Portal from ct over zero at y parsec?" Adams said once in passing.

"Excuse me?" I asked with a paintbrush in hand.

"Sorry, Jon. Just thinking out loud."

"No problem. Let me know if I can help with anything."

He grinned slightly, appreciating my joke.

We couldn't have been much more different. Adams was highly educated and used to wealth while I wasn't. At first we began with the usual chat about weather and sports. Eventually we talked about most anything, especially at lunch, which he preferred to be delivered. We made an odd couple, but we had good talks and laughs and over time I sensed we were becoming friends.

3

As the job came to a close, I could tell he had something he wanted to ask, but never did I expect what he was about to say. I remember how clueless I felt when he first brought up the subject.

"Jon, have you ever wondered how the universe began?" Adams asked on the final day. He was holding a panel for the bar in place as I set the nails.

"What do you mean?" I asked, continuing to pound away.

"The origin of the stars and planets. Does that *stuff* interest you?"

"A little." I knew we were on a sphere going around the sun once a year and that space was really huge. Beyond that, what was there to think about?

"What do you know about The Big Bang?"

"You mean when the universe started?" I hit the nail but bent it sideways.

"Right," Adams said, staring at me. His directness made me slightly uncomfortable, but it was just his way, intense and passionate about his ideas.

"Why do you ask?"

Adams became excited as he spoke. "Imagine watching the universe begin. What if you could go back in time about twenty billion years and see it all happen? Do you have any idea what that would be like?"

"Not exactly."

"It all began with a piece of matter that was infinitely small and infinitely dense." Adams pressed his fingers in a tight spot to convey his message. "Then it exploded in brilliant light! Everything that exists came from that tiny piece of dense matter. Everything! Stars, planets, entire galaxies came from that pinpoint of matter."

"Sounds logical," I said. It didn't, of course. How could everything have started from one tiny spot?

I pounded the last nail and made sure the panel was secure.

"Jon, what would you say if I told you I'm attempting to reproduce The Big Bang? In miniature, of course."

"What do you mean?"

"I'm recreating The Big Bang. Simulating a universe."

"For real?"

Simulate a universe? I knew Adams was an inventor but this seemed impossible.

"Would you like to see the project?"

"Maybe."

"You can stay on the clock if it makes a difference."

I put the hammer down and took off my tool-belt. We left the house and hopped into his truck, a new machine with only a few scuff marks in the bed. Adams drove as he explained the origin of the universe. I listened carefully, but the lecture was way over my head.

We passed the last of the buildings and houses in our town and continued into the countryside for a few minutes. I sat silently, wondering where this project would be and what it would be like. Adams let the silence extend. Finally, he turned onto a dirt path. We followed it until it ended and arrived at the only dwelling in sight.

"Here it is," he announced.

The Project

IT WAS AN ODD BUILDING way out in the middle of nothing but fields and forest. The structure looked newly built yet it was totally nondescript, unlike anything I had seen in my construction career. The building was three stories high and primarily elliptical, like an oval-shaped frame placed over a rectangular frame. Though it had no windows, it looked finished with a light brown plaster coating the whole thing. There was no paved driveway, just the dirt pad left from the construction vehicles.

Adams swiped a magnetic strip key and pressed buttons for a security code. The tall, heavy doors opened slowly, making a slight creaking sound. I breathed in the scent of new carpet. Large boxes placed on top of the rolls clogged up the entry.

We entered the cool room, leaving the doors open to let in light. The lobby appeared the same as the overall building. It was finished structurally but still needed texture, paint, carpeting and fixtures.

"There's work to do here," Adams said, as he showed me around the lobby. I nodded, thinking the entry alone could use many hours of my services.

Adams flicked a light switch then walked down a corridor to the center of the building. I followed slowly. My attention was drawn to large photos on the walls, dozens of images that must have been taken from a gigantic telescope. Star dust, planets, moons, entire galaxies. They were breathtaking pictures such as I had never seen and in far more detail than the paintings at Adams' home. The matter exploded out from the frames in amazing color. My first impression was that the galaxies were not just rocks and matter, but living things.

"Are these artists' paintings, or are they real?" I asked, tracing my finger around a stellar explosion. The label said it was a supernova.

"They're all real. These are parts of our universe. Except for this one." He pointed to a photo labeled a spiral galaxy. The stars were tiny points of bright light swirling in dark space. "This one's a computer simulation of our galaxy."

"Why a simulation?"

"We don't have cameras far enough out in space to shoot it from this perspective."

"Oh." I felt stupid for asking and reminded myself to keep quiet.

"That's our sun," he added, pointing to a secluded dot way out on a spiral arm of the galaxy.

"That's our sun?" I asked, mesmerized by it.

"That's it."

"What about all these other lights?"

"They're other suns. Some of them are stars you see on a clear night."

Adams opened a door to the main room on the lower floor. We entered a command central with desks, chairs, computer equipment and dozens of large monitors. Some were attached to the walls, and some were still in boxes. Packing foam, shipping plastic and empty cartons littered the floor. On the desks, papers were scattered about. I looked at them and saw handwritten equations. Chemistry or physics, I guessed. They were light years ahead of my understanding. I walked around the cool, dimly lit room, sensing something very unusual was going on.

"Have a seat," Adams told me.

I sat in a swivel chair that was still in its shipping plastic. I found the chair comfortable and used my feet to spin around in circles.

"Jim, this is Jon Gruber," Adams said. I looked around, still spinning. The room was empty except for Adams and me.

"Who are you talking to?" I asked, stopping my spins.

Adams didn't respond. He continued speaking, it seemed, to the room in general. "Jon will be doing a lot of handyman work, but if you need help with simple things, you can ask him."

"Am I missing something?" I asked.

Adams waited patiently through the silence.

Then a quiet voice asked, "What if I blow a circuit switch?" The voice spoke with honesty and calmness like that of a child, and it filled the room.

"That I'll need to fix for now. In time, I'm sure Jon can handle things like that as well."

"Cool. Are you talking with a computer?" I asked, standing up from the chair.

"Yes," Adams said. "Jon, meet Jim. And he prefers not to be called a computer."

"Sorry, Jim." I looked around the room, wondering where to direct my voice. "Which way do I speak? Can you hear me okay?"

After a pause, Jim answered with a shy, "Yes." I noticed a green light on the wall over the largest desk. It glowed more brightly as Jim spoke.

I asked, "Is that your light, Jim?" He didn't answer, but the light pulsed gently.

Adams said, "It's an indicator of how much Jim is thinking."

It was my first conversation with a computer, and I felt a little awkward about what to say. Then Jim started asking me questions.

"Why are you here?" Jim began.

"I'm here to help."

"With what?"

"I don't know," I answered, letting my words trail off, still trying to grasp what was going on.

Jim's light stayed green for a while.

I looked around and made a mental list of what needed doing. I was happy to be offered more work, but I was especially excited to be talking with a computer.

"What do you think?" Adams asked me.

"When can I start?"

"Today I took on an assistant. I wanted to do this alone, but that was just me being stubborn. Familiar, eh Rose? A young man with a strong back and good hands. Mr. Gruber will do fine. Jim's taken a liking to him and vice versa."

- from p. 12 of Webster's journal.

A New Routine

FROM THAT AFTERNOON ON, I rode my bike to Webster's house in the mornings and caught rides with him. He told me to spend the first days doing general clean-up to get the place workable. I pulled the remaining equipment out of containers. I dragged the cardboard, plastic and foam outside, then loaded it into the truck for many trips to the dump.

I helped Adams receive the final deliveries and used a dolly to move heavy things in place. Over the next few days, I finished the drywall, textured and painted. Then I placed lighting fixtures and rolled out and tacked down the carpeting.

Once the place had some order, I helped Adams install the wiring for the electronics that would be involved. I didn't know what I was doing but just followed their advice. During that time, I spoke constantly with Jim. He sounded so human it was hard for me to think of him as a machine.

I asked Adams as we drove home one night, "How can Jim sound so much like a person?"

"Didn't think a computer could talk?" Adams asked, his eyes fixed on the road.

"No."

"Neither did I when I was your age. Jim represents forty years of A.I."

"A.I.?"

"Artificial intelligence. He has the ability to learn, not just perform tasks."

Adams explained he had spent his career working for a company called Maxwell Enterprises. One department there worked solely on figuring out ways to get computers to think. Jim was designed to be able to control his features yet he had no programmed way to know how. Originally he just watched Adams work. Eventually he repeated sounds and then engaged in dialogue with Adams. Then he listened to training tapes.

"The growth rate of Jim's understanding is about a hundred times faster than humans," Adams told me.

By the time I met Jim, he was an expert on mathematics, chemistry and astronomy, at the age of three months. He was also becoming ever more knowledgeable about his hardware and the equipment that would be connected to him.

"Yet you'll need to be patient with him," Adams warned me. "Emotionally, Jim is still a child."

So many things were new to him, he constantly asked me questions. When I first started working there, Jim would perk up as we arrived. His green light would intensify as he'd ask me what I had done each night after work.

"I went home," I'd answer without interest.

"What else did you do?" No details were too boring for him.

"I ate dinner."

"What did you eat?"

"I can't remember," I'd say, trying to end the conversation.

Then the "why" questions would start. "Why did you do this?" and "Why did you do that?"

"WHY are you so interested?" I asked.

"Because... I just am."

How could I explain that my private life was just as boring as his?

Many nights when Adams and I began to leave the lab, Jim would beg us to stay. He'd yell and get angry, not understanding our schedules. He had training discs and games, videos and music, but he preferred our company. Sometimes Jim used sleep mode to zone out until the next morning though it appeared he needed very little real sleep.

I figured Jim liked me for two reasons. For one, I was someone other than Adams, someone who spoke differently and used slang. Then, as Jim realized I was the low man at the jobsite, he enjoyed a sudden sense of superiority.

"We need those secondary monitors hung right away," Jim said once, like a drill sergeant.

"I'm working on it."

"Not those, the ones for the far wall."

"Have you been watching army movies?" I asked.

"Your job isn't to ask questions. It's to follow commands."

I let him have his fun. He liked to bombard me with directions and then interrupt whenever I asked a question. For weeks, I humored him.

I spent much of my time following his wiring directions for the video set-ups and recording devices. We had over a hundred video monitors to install. Adams showed me their design and layout. They would be placed on the walls in the control room, covering nearly every square inch. They would also be hooked up to internal cameras and to Jim's hardware. We installed them one at a time while relaying them to the cameras within the egg-shaped cavity—the huge, empty space chamber where the simulation would take place. Adams checked and rechecked every connection in a painstakingly slow operation. After days of setting up monitors, we had a sea of screens covering the walls of the lab.

"Why do we need so many viewing screens?" I asked.

"A monitor for every camera," Adams said.

"Why so many cameras?"

"Hopefully, we're going to have a lot to look at. Solar systems, moons, comets..." I felt like Adams was going to add, "If it works." Those were three words we rarely said, but I thought of them frequently.

"How *exactly* is this going to work?" I phrased the question.

"Are you familiar with subatomic particles?"

"Not really."

"There are pieces of matter much smaller than atoms or their components. These quarks and leptons are fascinating little things."

Adams told me his wife, Rose, had done as much experimentation with subatomic particles as anybody. The more she studied them, the more she realized that quarks and leptons were bizarre entities, and they possessed intriguing abilities. Over time, she discovered a function within one type of quark—the ability to copy itself. She constructed the outline for an experiment run on hydrogen, a way of super-copying quarks that would multiply almost infinitely. The outrageous explosion of pure matter would be, in her theory, a reproduction of the great singularity that began our universe.

"The great singularity?" Jim asked.

"The point of time we believe the universe started," Adams said. "At that moment, there was only a pinpoint of infinitely dense matter."

I set the pliers down and raised my hand in objection. "But this whole concept doesn't make any sense! Everything in the world was as dense as a pinpoint?"

"Everything in the universe," Adams corrected me. "This is The Big Bang Theory."

"I guess I'll never get it," I shrugged.

Adams asked me, "Can you imagine a grain of sand?"

"Of course."

"Double it."

"Okay," I said. "Two grains of sand."

"Double it again, and keep going." Adams leaned against the wall and checked my math.

"Four, eight, sixteen, thirty-two—"

"Sixty-four," Jim interrupted. "One-twenty-eight, two-fifty-six, five-twelve, one thousand twenty-four..." Jim continued with speed and enthusiasm.

"Showoff," I said.

"Forty ninety-six, eighty-one ninety-two, sixteen three eighty-four, thirty-two seven sixty-eight..."

Jim quickly got into the millions and Adams interrupted him. "Hold on, Jim. Now imagine those grains of sand sharing the same space."

"That's what makes it so dense?" Jim asked.

"Density like one trillion, trillion, trillion, trillion, trillion, trillion tons per cubic inch," Adams said.

"What?" I asked.

"A one with seventy-two zeros behind it, tons per cubic inch."

"In a tiny little spot?"

"Yes."

"But that's the craziest thing I ever heard!" I argued. "I'm sorry, maybe I shouldn't be saying this in front of Jim."

"Jim's going to be hearing about it from now on," Adams said.

Jim let us speak without interrupting though his green light pulsed. Sometimes the only way to get Jim to be quiet was to talk about him.

I had to explain to them, I really did not get it. The Big Bang Theory made absolutely no sense. How could all the matter in the universe, every planet and star, all the zillions and zillions of tons come from a microscopically tiny spot? What could be more farfetched? I couldn't even imagine the contents of the lab fitting into a microscopically tiny spot, let alone the contents of the universe.

"I'd sooner believe in people flying," I said.

"What about space?" I asked Adams later, as we stood in the egg-shaped cavity placing and wiring dozens of camera set-ups. The cameras were like piercing rods. They could extend or contract while also moving sideways and vertically. "What exactly is... y'know, space?"

"It's the void between elements of matter," Adams said, grabbing the pliers from my belt to cut off some extra wire.

"How do you simulate that?"

"With the right electromagnetic field," Adams replied.

"So is our own space electrically charged?" I asked, thinking myself very clever.

"Depends on how you look at it," he said frankly.

I finally stopped trying to understand the concepts. I figured I'd get it in time or perhaps I'd never get it. A job was still a job, so I put my doubts on hold and cheerfully did what I could to help out.

"When did you first start working on this?" I asked as I helped Adams wire a very large monitor to hooks on the wall in front of his desk.

"This whole idea was my wife's," Adams said. "I'd love to take credit for it, but it took her ages to get me to help."

I knew Rose had died a few years ago. There were pictures of her everywhere in his house. Her paintings hung on every wall. I knew she was an artist—now I learned she was a scientist as well.

I looked at the photo of Rose on his desk, a picture of her laughing as she swung back in the air on a rope swing. Her face was not striking, but there was a deep beauty to it. Her attraction came from within and expressed itself in spirited eyes and a natural smile. Sometimes Adams would get distracted from work and sit at his desk, staring at her photo. He'd extend two fingers and touch the image.

"When we married, she was outlining her theory. She designed the whole thing. I took time off to help."

"How did she die?" I asked.

"Car accident," he said, returning to fasten wires to the monitor.

"I'm sorry," I offered. "Was anyone else hurt?"

"No. She flew off the road and rolled."

"How did you find out about it?"

"A call from the hospital."

"Who found her?"

"Don't know. Someone just called for an ambulance."

"Didn't you want to know?"

"How would that matter?" he asked, looking at me.

I wanted to ask more about Rose, but I sensed it wasn't appropriate.

"Actually, I'm a little jealous this was her idea," he added, lightening the mood.

I had to ask, "Why are you doing this? To follow up on her dream?"

"Maybe. Maybe there's more to it," he admitted. Jim's light perked up.

"What's that?" I asked.

"Yeah," Jim added. "Why?"

Adams paused for a moment as if he had to search for the answer. "Profound curiosity," he said at last, almost looking through me. "I see it as the ultimate experiment. If I can create a universe... then what does it say about who created ours?"

Jim and I left it at that.

Setbacks

BY MY SECOND MONTH, I felt like I understood what was going on, or at least what we were trying to do. We were attempting a reproduction of The Big Bang at a microscopic level. Adams was hoping to create a brand new universe enclosed in a chamber the size of a small warehouse, by conducting a subatomic reaction that would create matter at a nearly infinite scale. Then it would be released into an electrically charged, simulated space arena.

To a large degree, nothing worked as planned. The simulated space was supposed to create its own realm of zero gravity. It took Adams weeks to get the bugs out of it. The magnetic field worked fairly well, but the egg-shaped cavity was not absolutely airtight. Tiny leaks in the chamber continuously presented themselves and needed repair. Many times, I put on protective clothing and spray-coated the cavity with a gluey gel, careful not to bump into the cameras.

Adams also faced problems with the mechanism that supplied and compressed the hydrogen molecules, then timing it up with the device that isolated the quarks. It was difficult for the devices to work harmoniously.

"Go figure," I told Jim, mocking Adams for his eccentric yet optimistic nature.

"Yeah, go figure," Jim said with a chuckle.

We enjoyed jokes about Adams getting in way over his head on the project. Adams let us have our fun. He knew how to quiet us when he wanted to.

"You shouldn't be laughing so hard, you know," Adams joked in turn. "If matter creation really gets out of control, an explosion like you couldn't imagine might take place." We stopped laughing. Adams continued, "It won't matter where you are if that happens, so you might as well be at ground zero when we push the button."

I knew Adams was kidding, that it was likely to be safe, though I never knew how seriously to take him. Surely he didn't know exactly what was going on though he often acted like he did. I knew he was brilliant even as he ran into problems with every aspect of the experiment. Many weeks went by with slow progress and Adams scribbling notes in his little brown book. Sometimes he complained to Rose's photo about what wasn't working. He'd talk aloud to her as if she were sitting on that swing behind the glass, ready to answer. I began to pity him.

"What if it never works?" I asked once, slumping in my chair at the end of a long and boring day.

"My investor and I will be out of a bunch of time and money," Adams said.

"What if it does work?" Jim asked.

"It will be really cool," Adams said, mimicking me.

Adams was set to the task. He never openly doubted Rose's theory. He simply worked harder to deal with his setbacks. One by one, he addressed problems and made steps toward running the experiment. I admired his determination.

I finally visited the Star Bar after weeks away. The name was misleading, since no celebrity was ever known to have been inside the place. It was a small and narrow bar with just a few tables, a spot for some cheap booze. I used to be one of the more regular regulars, though lately I had been working too hard to stop in.

Samantha, the owner and bartender, was one of my only friends. Sam, as she preferred, had extremely dark skin and thick, black hair that was turning gray. She was middle-aged and full of life, buxom and strong. More than once, I had watched Sam drag men from the bar and toss them out the front door, men who had gotten too drunk and out of line with her.

Her face lit up when I arrived and she instinctively poured me a beer. "Mr. Gruber! Haven't seen you for a while. Got any jokes for me?"

"Haven't been working construction. Got a new job in a science laboratory," I said.

"That is a good one."

Sam couldn't believe I was an apprentice to someone like Adams. She didn't buy it until I went into all the details. She loved hearing them and especially of Jim, though she was most skeptical that he could sound human.

"And this scientist," Sam asked, "is he married?"

"I don't think he's your type."

"Single and employed is my type," she said, pouring a couple of shots. "Bring him in sometime."

"I will. We've just been working too hard."

"Jon, don't forget about us little people when you hit it big."

"I doubt that will happen, but it's as good a toast as any." We downed a shot to my future.

The Stargazer

O*n Webster's tenth birthday, his father bought him a telescope. Mr. Adams found it at a garage sale from a retiring professor. Although he knew nothing about telescopes, he bought it for his son on a whim. The professor gave him basic instruction and threw in a guide to astronomy. Mr. Adams took the telescope home, wrapped it in brown paper and set it up on a flat section of the roof.*

Webster found it odd to be climbing out a window onto the roof with his parents to open one last present. When he unwrapped the telescope, he looked at it strangely, unaware of what it was.

Following the professor's advice, Mr. Adams pointed the telescope toward the moon and adjusted the focus. He looked into it and laughed with astonishment, then invited Webster to take a peek. The boy put his eye to the piece. He saw the moon so closely he could make out thousands of small circles etched into the landscape. He hadn't known about impact craters from objects hitting the moon, nor had his father. Both were delighted. They stayed on the roof late into the night.

By twelve, Webster was an avid stargazer, though his father's participation had dwindled. When he asked his father for money to buy a larger telescope, one with higher magnification, his father suggested he earn the money himself. Webster did so, by doing yard work for neighbors. His parents watched the boy set up the new telescope, impressed with his devotion.

Webster stayed up very late on clear nights, becoming extremely familiar with nearby planets. He even constructed a mobile of the solar system, decorative balls that hung by strings from the ceiling in his room. He used it as his own celestial calendar, adjusting the positions of the planets daily, marveling at their beauty and mystery.

His teachers complained that Webster often fell asleep in class. Over time his grades dropped. Mr. Adams threatened to take the telescope away, but Mrs. Adams supported the boy's hobby because of the creativity it had sparked in him. She argued to let the boy stargaze but under stricter limits.

Webster fought the idea of time constraints, since some of the most wonderful views happened during the early hours of the morning. He promised the telescope would not get in the way of his grades and agreed to a tighter time limit, only occasionally sneaking out for special cosmic events.

At fifteen, Webster participated in a college astronomy course, which included field trips to a nearby observatory.

There he looked through huge telescopes that could see into the depths of the universe. He became fascinated with things that couldn't really be seen, things with wonderful names like black holes and antimatter. These entities had been theorized about but never proven. Webster decided he wanted to know everything possible about the universe. There were so many questions. How did it begin? How far did it go? Did it have an end? To a young scientist, these questions loomed large. He set out to answer them.

Over the years, the answers to his questions eluded him, like trying to see antimatter. The more he studied the universe, the more complex it remained. He realized he was just one person on a little planet drifting in a cosmic ocean without a guide. He grew up with few friends and few experiences.

He graduated with degrees in astronomy but chose not to teach it. Instead he went to work for an acquaintance in the field of artificial intelligence.

Light

Eventually I realized Adams was reporting to someone. A man named Frank Maxwell was financing the project. The company, Maxwell Enterprises, was on my paychecks.

"Who is this Maxwell?" I asked.

"Frank? He's been funding the project since the start," Adams said.

"How come I've never met him?" Jim asked.

"He's a busy man," Adams said. "He has other business to manage, profit-making businesses." His reluctance to talk about it made me even more curious about the man who was paying my wages.

Adams said no more, but he placed a new photo on his desk. Rose's photo was on the left. The new one went on the right. The face in the picture was that of a lovely young lady, and for some reason I had trouble recognizing her from the halls of Webster's home, the girl who had caught my attention on first glance.

"She's a cutie," I said.

"She's more than that," Adams replied. "She's my daughter, Whitney."

"Oh."

Our tests continued until one afternoon, when Adams decided the simulation was ready. Late in the day we connected the lines to the huge hydrogen tanks, the final step toward making Rose's idea a reality. It had been nearly three months since I began working there. Spring was in bloom.

The next morning I felt a wall of tension around Adams. He didn't speak to me in the truck on the way to work. Instead, he mumbled to himself and to Rose as he went over every item in his head. At the lab, he double-checked every piece of equipment. I spun around in my swivel chair and chatted with Jim. Jim said he sensed the tension too, though I couldn't imagine how. Minutes turned into hours.

I waited patiently for Adams to do whatever he thought was necessary. For some reason I didn't feel especially nervous or excited, mostly bored, as

I had been for the past several weeks. As we went over our checklist of final preparations for the third time, I still had the feeling something wouldn't work, that there was no way the simulation was going to happen. I never mentioned it to Adams, but I couldn't shake my deeply rooted pessimism, even as I sat yards away from an electromagnetic field that was about to experience an atomic injection of immense proportions.

"Jim, prepare the sub-particle setting for initial hydrogen release," Adams finally said. I thought I heard a bit of fear in his voice.

"Check," Jim responded.

"What's the rate on the setting?" Adams asked.

"At standard rate, seventeen trillion units per second."

"Are the molecules in the prep chamber still at critical mass?"

"Yes."

"Then we're ready, unless there's something I've forgotten," Adams said, looking around.

I held up the dark glasses. "Do we need these?" Adams had brought them for the explosion of light he was expecting across the monitors.

"Right. We're going to need those," he said. We put them on.

"Anything else?"

"Should we say a prayer or something?" I asked.

"If you would like to."

I took off the glasses, closed my eyes and put my hands to my face in prayer. "How about, God... please, please help us do this."

"Sounds like something Rose would approve of," Adams said. "Jim, I do believe we're ready. You can release hydrogen molecules at any time."

"Release in five seconds," Jim said. I put the glasses back on. "Four... three... two... one..."

That's when I realized I was nervous. Something changed in that moment of time as I stood in a dark room looking at black monitors and wearing sunglasses while a nuclear event was taking place yards away. Those jokes from Adams about a mishap destroying the planet must have gotten to me. Or it could have been the thought of Rose's spirit in the room that made the skin on my arms break out in goose bumps.

Even behind the silly shades, I could see the anticipation and anxiety written in the lines of his face. This event defined a decade of work, from Rose's theorizing, to planning, to convincing Maxwell and Adams it could be done. Then after her death, the thousands of hours of bringing all the pieces together.

I wiped the sweat from my palms onto my pants. Adams gripped the back of his swivel chair as he stood behind it, pressing his thumbs into the fabric. His stare remained locked on the blank monitors. I felt the tension getting worse, and I wanted to say something witty to break the silence but nothing came to mind. Instead, a calm peace spread over us from the dark screens. I could hear my breathing and feel my heartbeat over the sounds of anything else. The silence made me think something wasn't working. I looked at the control panel and noticed Jim's green light was glowing as brightly as I had ever seen it, as if at any moment he would explode from thinking. I figured there must be a glitch, and I expected Adams to take off his glasses in frustration and start complaining to Rose about what went wrong.

Then suddenly, a tiny spot of light began to show on the main monitor.

As soon as I could focus on it, it flashed into a brilliant explosion across all the monitors. Then it was dark again. The flash had blinded me briefly after it dissipated. Jim's light dimmed to a dull green glow. I took off my glasses and looked to Adams for an explanation. He started laughing out loud, staring at the screens. Eventually I saw tiny dots of light remained. Those spots of white emerged from the center of the main monitor and began spreading out and getting larger.

"Yes!" Adams cried.

"Yes, what?" I asked.

"Everything okay, Jim?" he asked, taking off his glasses.

"I think so," Jim said. "I think it's working."

The screens remained primarily dark, but small areas of glowing light were visible.

"There!" Adams said. "Let's get a closer shot from Monitor One."

As the camera zoomed in, I could make out what looked like glowing gas. The light was bright yet transparent. It floated outward and settled into swirls with other bits and pieces. My hand made swirling motions, mimicking the action on the monitors.

I turned to Adams. "What is that stuff?"

"Matter," Adams said, smiling broadly. "Pure matter."

It didn't look like matter. It looked like a bundle of glowing gas. As the shot went closer in toward the light, I could see big blobs and little blobs, each pulsing with tiny specks of light.

"Chemical analysis of the matter, Jim?" Adams asked, nervously spinning the chair in front of him.

"Hydrogen. Entirely hydrogen."

"Perfect!" Adams said, rubbing his hands together.

"It's just gas," I said. "You took hydrogen from one source and merely placed it into another."

We watched the images of the glowing gas blobs become larger. They spread out and intermingled with other blobs of light. It was mildly intriguing. We stood motionless for several minutes just watching.

Then Adams broke the trance. "See, Jon. These lights number in the millions. Most are locked in orbits with others."

As I looked more closely at the tiny areas of light, I suddenly realized they looked like galaxies.

A shiver traveled down my spine. A tiny universe had been created before my eyes. Within minutes, dozens of different masses sparkled against the darkness on the screens. Each mass hovered about on its own, tracked by a different camera within the cavity of the building and displayed on a monitor. Our dimly lit lab room was filled with light from these newborn galaxies.

Adams laughed again. "Jim, zoom Camera Two in closer."

Monitor Two revealed a cluster of stars, tons of them surrounded by extraordinary colors and formations. It was like a fountain of magic dust, reminding me of the pictures in the hallway I passed by each day.

"What's happening here?" I asked. "This doesn't look like gas anymore."

"It's a nebula!" Adams cried out, raising his arms to the ceiling in victory. "We have a nebula! Slow down the rate, Jim. Take it down to a crawl."

The twisting and moving slowed down, halting the lights. The monitors displayed dozens of galaxies frozen in time. Adams, mystified by his creation, stared at the screens. Each one showcased a galaxy of brilliant lights and amazing colors. He laughed in delight.

"We did it," he said, shaking me. "We really did it."

I looked around at the monitors into a vast horizon of heavens, feeling like I was on a space station in the center of the universe.

"I still don't understand," I said. "How did this come from a little atomic matter?"

Adams sat in his chair, calmed himself, and stared at the monitors in a dreamy way as if the full understanding of the invention had just come to him.

"When you analyze extremely small things, like quarks and elements of atoms... and when you compare them to extremely large things, like stars and galaxies... they're oddly similar. Physical size may be one of the great mysteries of life."

Then it became clear to me. I found myself saying out loud, "We have a model of a universe. Not just a plastic model, but a living, breathing, real universe right in front of us."

All that time in the making, I never really understood the significance of what he was attempting until that moment.

"What's more," Adams added, "we've just witnessed The Big Bang."

"Creation has happened! It's been a long road, but we arrived today. Rose, you were right as usual. Portal from ct over zero at parsec y! If I die tomorrow, I'll be happy. Doubtful to sleep tonight, the rush of it all is still in me. Watching light come out of nothing... watching the birth of stars! It was everything I had hoped for and more."

- from p. 23 of Webster's journal.

Evolution versus Creation

*D*r. *Adams thought little of religion. He had no experience with it while growing up. Neither of his parents had strong opinions on the subject, but the astronomer in Webster took umbrage with the idea that religion had anything to do with the universe. Theories of evolution made infinitely more sense to him. On several occasions, even at cocktail parties, he argued evolution with people who supported creation.*

"Religion is a mythical history used by primitive people to explain the world and heavens," Dr. Adams said as he mingled at a fundraiser. "People couldn't admit they didn't know how it all began, so they came up with the notion of God. Easy enough."

A minister approached Adams and began a discussion with him. It eventually escalated to an argument that went on and on, with Adams insulting religion and anyone who supported it. His comments went over so well that they ended with a fist to his face and Webster falling to the floor.

After throwing the punch, the minister was horribly embarrassed. He left the party while his daughter stayed, tending to Webster's bleeding nose. Rose administered ice as Adams lay on the floor.

"Care for some free advice?" Rose asked him as she knelt down and dabbed his cut lip with her handkerchief. "When presenting your opinions in mixed company, try not to insult people just because you disagree with them."

Adams looked up and saw a woman of intelligence and sincerity, a woman who appeared to him to be angelic. "Good advice."

She helped him to his feet and added, "You know what they say... you attract a lot more flies with sugar."

They talked for the rest of the party. He had never met a woman like Rose— attractive, well-dressed, and able to lecture him. Before the guests had left, he sincerely apologized to everyone for his behavior. He apologized later to her father.

Rose was familiar with Webster's way of thinking long before meeting him. As a girl who studied the sciences, she was often surrounded by people of a solid-proof mind-set, those who didn't believe anything they couldn't measure. This was in contrast to her upbringing. As the daughter of a minister, Rose never had the option of dismissing religion or arguing about it. If she did, she would have disrespected her parents. They never forced any way of thinking upon her. Rose was allowed to pursue both science and religion. They taught her to follow her heart and to seek out answers of any nature.

Rose began working for Maxwell Enterprises. She was in a different department than Adams, on a team studying molecular biology. While she was discovering the wonders of subatomic particles, she was also thinking about the dynamics of life. She wondered if there was any end to the existence of smaller and smaller particles.

A year after the party, Rose ran into Adams at a company function. They spoke about their work. She explained how each month brought new discoveries.

"The atom is not nearly the smallest unit of measure," Rose told Adams over a drink. "There are bosons, leptons, even things we haven't yet named, but we know they must exist. The deeper we look, the more we find."

"My years in astronomy were exactly the same," he remarked. "The further out in space I looked, the more I saw."

They talked for hours, finding it incredible that they had not bumped into each other at work.

Adams and Rose began getting together for lunch on the campus that adjoined Maxwell Enterprises. Sometimes they went to the deli, at other times one of them would pack a lunch to share. Some days they sat by the campus pond, and on others they went for walks around the lecture halls and ate nutrition bars. Each looked forward to the lunch hour conversations as the highlight of the day.

They had many similarities and interests, but they also had their differences. These usually involved the subject of religion. Rose could not understand why Adams would proclaim himself an atheist.

"How can you not believe in God, in some form?" she asked him as they strolled on the path around the campus pond.

"I can't believe in anything without proof," he stated, biting into a piece of fruit.

"That's why they call it faith," she replied, "because it can't be proven in a scientific manner."

"How can an intelligent person believe in something so nonevidential, like an invisible force that runs our universe?"

"I see it differently," Rose told him. "I find evidence everywhere I look."

Adams found Rose immensely attractive even when she disagreed with him. Her auburn hair fell gracefully over lean shoulders, and her green eyes contained a hint of smile even as they argued. The only thing in the world they were at odds about was religion. He couldn't prove her wrong nor could she convince him. They cared too much about each other to try to change the other's mind.

They married, regardless of the difference, under the roof of her father's church.

Science

IN THE EARLY UNIVERSE, matter floated through areas of space near the center of the egg-shaped cavity. Each element of matter was like a snowflake, similar to others in the brewing aftermath yet unique. The cameras presented detailed images of these tiny objects. The stars could have fit on my fingernail but in their own space, they were massive. On the monitors they appeared as gigantic balls of hot gas moving gracefully through the cosmos. I sat back and watched the chemistry unfold before my eyes, chemistry that turned into astronomy.

We witnessed the birth of stars. They began as hydrogen balls of different sizes and intensities. After forming, stars moved down the spiral arms of the emerging galaxy and clustered themselves into groups. Galaxies took on many shapes—mostly spiral and elliptical, but they all revolved with the same physics.

Jim recorded everything. We replayed the beginning moments of this little universe again and again. As I watched, I realized the collisions of chunks of gas were actually collisions of entire galaxies, each one made up of billions of stars. The early universe was like a basket of fireworks. It was explosive, with tremendous amounts of white light, radiation and colorful accents on the fringes. It was a beautiful chaos.

Hydrogen masses became large and small suns. Sometimes they collided with others, creating debris that would become planets and asteroids. Over time, Jim detected the presence of new elements forming around the stars and planets.

"Molecules have a way of changing," Adams explained, "from the simplest ones like hydrogen, to more complicated ones."

"How?" I asked.

"Intense heat. It makes the hydrogen atoms merge to form helium atoms."

"Hydrogen becomes helium?"

"And more. The star's interior is under pressure, which compounds the hydrogen into heavier elements, like carbon and oxygen."

Jim's sensing devices confirmed his description. We focused on a large white star, a mass of burning hydrogen. Jim detected helium on the surface of the glowing orb, an effect seen in a change of hue to a yellow light. Occasionally the star emitted matter from an internal explosion. The matter cooled as it sped off in space, and a tail formed with new elements. Jim identified carbon, nitrogen and silicon in the tails of several comets.

One night on our way home in the truck, under a clear and dark sky, Adams pulled over to the side of the road.

"What are you doing?"

"Get out," he said.

"Why?" I asked, getting out. I thought, what had I done? Adams turned off the truck lights and got out as well. He walked in front of the vehicle, looking directly upwards and motioning for me to follow.

"See that?" he said, pointing to the brightest star in the sky. I could see it easily over the others.

"Very pretty," I said.

"That's the closest star beyond our sun. Do you know how far away it is?"

"No."

"It's two and a half light years from here." I must not have looked impressed. Adams changed his tone to convey amazement. "That means it takes two and a half years for the light to make it here!"

"Long way, huh?" I appreciated the star more.

He pointed to the light and shook his head. "That star isn't there. It's somewhere else."

"What do you mean?"

"It was there, in that exact spot, two and a half years ago. We're looking at the light waves it emitted when it was there."

"Really?"

"That's how long it takes light to travel that kind of distance."

We drove back to his house in silence. I looked out the window at all the different stars, wondering how many light years away they were and how far they had moved from the spots I could see.

Adams often adjusted the rate of flow for the simulation. The more hydrogen molecules Jim introduced to the reactor, the faster time passed within the project. For his study time, Adams ran the reactor at a crawl or on minimal hydrogen release, as slowly as Jim could allow it. Crawl speed was the only time we could conduct studies. While the stars and planets on the monitors seemed to be standing still, they were experiencing time similar to us. Jim's reactor could go much, much faster than crawl speed, which we did when Adams wanted to see the progression of a star or planet.

"Release hydrogen," Adams instructed Jim, during a typical, early universe time leap.

A humming sound emerged. The lights on the monitors began to move. Stars turned into blurs of colors, and galaxies spun slowly. Millions upon millions of years passed, and we witnessed a fantastic light show of galactic movement.

"How fast can it go?" I asked.

"Not sure," Adams admitted. "Top speed is a guess. There's no sense running like that, but it could probably run at trillions of times the rate of crawl speed."

That meant time passing at trillions of times the rate of normal. Evolution was already happening. Adams knew it all along, and I was starting to get the picture.

I loved the time leaps and hummed along with the sound they produced. It was the only moment where the universe moved visibly as an assembly, after which we recorded the process of a star changing or even collapsing into a black hole. We executed the time leaps often, allowing the primitive universe to settle into its ways.

"How old is this universe?" I asked Adams.

"There's no real way to define time other than standard orbits."

"What's a standard orbit?"

Adams explained all of the planets revolved around their home star at a certain rate. The length of an average revolution established itself as a standard solar orbit, or standard year. Many planets had revolution periods close to the average measure, but there really was no exact planet or way to define time. Adams said the universe was roughly one or two billion standard units, though that didn't make sense, because for a period of time, planets hadn't even formed to establish orbits.

"Okay, that's enough. My brain is waving white flags," I said. The concept was extremely difficult. Defining time had never occurred to me to be impossible, but it totally baffled me. To think the swirling bits of hot gas had taken hundreds of millions of years to settle—that was another difficult concept.

"You see this star on Monitor One?" Adams asked, pointing to a hot blue sun.

"Yes."

"It's not there," Adams said, reminding me of the other night on the side of the road.

"That's just its light we're seeing, right?"

"Very good, Jon. Correct. It takes time for the light waves to make it to our cameras in this project, the same as in our night sky."

Jim chimed in, "That's why I have to adjust two or more cameras exactly the same distance from any object, if we want a cross reference of two shots."

"Why?"

"Otherwise we'd be seeing light from the same object at different times, and we wouldn't be able to combine the images."

If we wanted three-dimensional images, we had to use more than one camera so Jim's hardware could interpret the data.

The chamber walls for our little universe also affected the question of age. Unfortunately, our experiment had a limited lifetime. The walls of the egg-shaped cavity held a constant attraction force on the galaxies. At creation, the attraction was almost undetectable, but as the galaxies moved, they pulled away from the center at an accelerating rate. Over time, over trillions of standard orbits, the matter in the universe would reach the outer walls and self-destruct.

"How long from now?" I asked.

"What's your estimate, Jim?"

"About three trillion standard orbits," Jim said. "Maybe four."

"A long time, way more time than I intend to go through," Adams said, jotting the note in his brown booklet.

"If the outer walls are attracting the matter," I asked, "then is the matter speeding up toward them?"

"Yes," Adams said, looking impressed. "That's what I meant when I said the universe is expanding at an accelerating rate."

"Bizarre."

I tried to understand. We kept headache tablets in the bathroom cabinet, and I found them quite useful when dealing with new ideas.

The stars in our simulation were very similar to the ones in our night sky. Both were slowly changing, burning their hydrogen fuel at all times. Depending on burn rates and size, a star went through many phases of existence. Some raged in spurts of radioactivity, like pulsars. Others expanded outward, like red giants. Some had lots of planets orbiting them, others had none. They came in a variety of colors. Blue stars were the hottest and red ones the coolest. Some contracted in time, and some even exploded. Supernovas were explosions the size of millions of suns. They sent matter scattering across the universe. Change was happening every minute. The universe was growing exponentially.

As I rode my bicycle home from Webster's house after work, I realized what a different person I had become. Months earlier, I never would have thought about the beginning of the universe or nature of the cosmos. Lately, it was all I could think of. Certain things in life deserved serious attention, and I had the good fortune to be involved in something like that.

I pulled over to the side of the road to appreciate my own star, our orange sun, as it glowed red and set on the horizon. It hung so gracefully in the sky, casting warm rays through the trees, the houses and onto my face. I appreciated it more than ever, knowing how close it was compared to other stars in the galaxy. Bathed in its hazy glow, I pushed my bike up the last hill to my apartment, thanking heaven it wasn't a red giant.

Red giants intrigued me. Their impressive size and red hues made them stand out dramatically against the darkness of space. Curiously, red giants were in a state of massive growth. They even engulfed planets in orbits close to them. Red giants were dangerous, I thought. When we looked through our project for stars, Adams preferred that we searched for yellow, white and orange stars like our own. He believed they were the most stable and more likely to have planets orbiting them that were safe from harm.

My life had changed. Finally, I had a good-paying job that required sitting down for most of the day. This in itself was a huge success. I had always wondered if my days of labor would be cut short by a fall from a ladder or the slip of a saw blade. No one had ever paid me to sit on my ass and chat with a computer. I had to pinch myself for my turn of fortune.

What we did at first was data entry, lots and lots of data entry.

"Pick a galaxy, Jim, any galaxy," I said at the start of one day, leaning back into my chair and biting into a pastry.

Jim set Monitor One on a galaxy and zoomed in until it showed a field of stars.

"Okay, Jim, now pick a star, any star."

The monitor honed in ever closer until just one star filled the screen.

"Perfect, now get its coordinates and give me a readout, please."

Jim obliged. "Here we have an orange dwarf sun made of ninety-six percent hydrogen and three percent helium gases, with traces of methane and argon. I'm detecting some planets in its orbit. Would you like to hear their composition and location?"

"Sure," I said, enjoying the ease from effort that Jim provided.

All I did was change and label Jim's recording disks once they were full. I was having the time of my life, making good money for hanging out and talking with a computer about stars and planets and their chemical makeup. We studied moons, asteroids, comets, gas, anything we could see floating in space. Sometimes I worked a twelve to fourteen-hour shift just logging data.

"Jim," I said, "don't you just love how majestic some of these planets are?" Monitor One was focused on a world of molten lava, a fiery landscape that created dark rain clouds pierced by lightning bolts.

"I guess," Jim said. "I don't have anything to compare it to."

"Well, it's not something you see just by walking outside and looking up."

"That actually sounds pretty good to me," Jim said. "I'd like to walk outside and look up."

"Believe me. This is better," I said.

Adams made a note.

All planets had the ingredients for making water—two parts hydrogen and one part oxygen. On most of the planets, we found water in various forms: vapor, ice, snow and liquid. Water was beautiful and contrasting against stark landscapes. On some planets, large amounts of water vapor produced. It eventually formed lakes, rivers and oceans. It also took the shape of humidity and mixed with other gases to form early atmospheres.

Primitive worlds were raw and violent, as their inner cores released heat and radiation. Lightning charged the skies on some planets, while lava flowed on the surface. It amazed me all this was happening day after day without any life on the planets.

Adams theorized how life might begin. "Simple molecular things," he observed, "should respond to the highs and lows of radiation." He pointed to a shoreline on a calm planet that was displayed on Monitor One.

"Why should they?" I asked.

"Simple matter has changed into macro-molecules. These ever bigger clumps have been receiving doses of radiation and occasional bolts of electricity."

"So?"

"Molecules are getting more complex. They're adapting to an ever-changing environment." The beach scene on the monitor was not one I would have described as ever-changing.

"Until what?" Jim asked.

"Life has a way of popping up," Adams said. "Perhaps molecules will use radiation for energy. Maybe they are learning how to store heat for the night periods."

"Isn't that cute," I joked with Jim. "Molecules get cold at night."

"Cute or not," Adams said, "that may be when life starts, when molecules really start to mutate."

"Into what?" Jim asked.

"Into more complicated versions of themselves. Into molecules that can move, or eat, or reproduce. Life can branch off very quickly once it starts."

We theorized on the beginnings of life. Did life precede consciousness, or did consciousness precede life? At the moment when a molecule used solar radiation for energy, was that molecule alive? Was it aware? We debated these things as we watched our experiment evolve. Our cameras could identify shorelines made of water, rock and sand, but they could not see the particles that made up those objects.

"Am I alive?" Jim asked to my surprise. How simply honest he was.

His green light pulsed mildly. I looked to Adams for an answer.

"You are," Adams said with conviction. "You can think and function, therefore you are alive."

The answer seemed to satisfy Jim, and his light dimmed down to normal level. I wondered if Adams was as sure as his answer implied.

Soon afterwards, we found "primordial soup," as Adams called it. Visible life began in the wading pools and looked like sludge or slime. It was simple organisms and the forerunner to primitive algae. Once life started, it quickly spread. Over time, the algae and fungi mutated into heartier algae and into things that could eat the algae, like simple marine invertebrates.

For around a billion standard orbits, life lived as basic organisms: fungi, tiny marine animals, and green plants. Hardened lava became landmasses. Again, I couldn't believe it took hundreds of millions of years for fungus to evolve. Thank God for the time leaps. Eventually, we identified plants, fish, amphibians and insects.

I eagerly awaited the time leaps to see what changes would occur. Some of the planets showed amazing amounts of growth. As we revisited a planet over the course of a few time leaps, we could see it evolve from a lifeless, inhospitable world to a maturing, stable home with an atmosphere, plants, reptiles and even primitive birds. Adams was ecstatic about the changes.

"Evolution happens before my eyes. Algae have grown into plants, insects to birds. It is all exactly as we expected, exactly as the evidence suggested it would."
    - from p. 38 of Webster's journal.

The Bet

Rose attended her father's weekly sermon as a married woman alone. It bothered her immensely that Adams refused to go. As time went on, she made repeated efforts to get him to open his mind to the divine nature within all life.

"How do you prove anything?" a pregnant Rose asked him. They were sharing a picnic lunch by the campus pond. "How do you prove that you even exist?"

"That's simple," Adams answered. "Because I am here, and I can make a recording of myself, and I can taste this sandwich."

"How do you know it's not just a figment of a wild dream?"

"That doesn't make any sense," he chided, lying back and closing his eyes as he chewed on the lunch.

"Maybe you're not giving the idea a chance. Let me ask you this; do you believe life is completely random, or could you be persuaded there might be some meaning behind it?"

"Like a plan?" he asked.

"Yes. Like a beautiful, choreographed plan."

"Are you implying my life has already been planned out? What would be the point of living if there was no free will?"

"I didn't say that," Rose replied. "So you really think life is completely random?"

"Yes," Adams said frankly through a mouthful of food.

"Then why are we together? Don't you think we were meant to be together?"

"I doubt there's another person on this planet for me," he said, placing his palm on her swollen belly and coaxing half a smile from her.

"Regardless of how well-suited we are, the one thing I would change about you is your stubbornness on this subject."

"And I you, my dear."

"Then it's settled," she said, standing up and tossing a stone into the pond. Splash.

"What's settled?" he asked, squinting through the glare of the sun behind her.

"We'll have a bet."

"On what?"

"I will bet you," Rose began, "that somehow, someway, I will convince you life has a plan that is absolutely beyond the realm of random chance. I will convince you that God must exist."

"How will you ever be able to prove that?"

"I don't know, but I will."

"Fine," he said, almost dismissing the subject. "What shall we bet?"

"If I convince you..." She thought about it.

"Please don't ask me to go to church."

"Afraid of losing the bet?" she asked.

"Are you kidding? It's a bet," Adams agreed, convinced there was no way he could lose such a wager.

Evolution

ONE NIGHT AFTER WORK we stopped at the Star Bar, and I introduced Adams to Sam, who poured my favorite beer. When I saw Adams pondering his choices, I ordered one for him too. He sipped his while I downed mine quickly.

"So you're the scientist?" Sam asked him, placing another beer in front of me. "What's it like working with all that high-tech stuff?"

"Sometimes, great fun. Other times, frustration to no end."

Sam asked questions about the project though it was clear she really wanted to know more about him. Adams tried to explain it in terms she could understand. Customers down the bar gave him funny looks as he spoke of subatomic particles and molecular alterations, but Sam hung on every word. She must have thought Adams wouldn't be interested in a local barmaid, but she liked the attention of an educated man explaining the mysteries of the cosmos. He waved his arms like spinning galaxies as he attempted to explain the time leaps. Adams smiled and laughed more that night than I had ever seen. The project was going very well, and I guessed he was thinking about how proud Rose would have been.

When we drove back to his place, an unfamiliar car was parked in the driveway.

"Wonderful," Adams said, pulling up next to it. "Whitney's home."

"Your daughter?"

Whitney opened the front door as we got out of the truck. She jogged over to Adams, threw her arms around him and held him for nearly a minute. She looked even better in person than in the photo, like a younger version of Rose with glasses. She had the same auburn hair and natural smile of her mother, and a slender, fit body. I had wanted to meet Whitney for weeks, but it was a surprise to be doing so without notice. I was embarrassed for having a buzz from the bar.

Adams introduced us. "Whitney, Jon Gruber. Jon, Whitney."

Whitney shook my hand while keeping an arm around Adams.

I glanced at her hand and spotted a ring. Wondering if women were involved upon meeting them was becoming a bad habit.

"Whitney has just graduated from university," Adams said proudly. "With honors, I might add."

Whitney rolled her eyes as he boasted of her studies and grades. She finally interrupted him. "Dad, you're embarrassing me. Is this the man who made the alterations upstairs?"

I beamed with pride. "I am he."

"You do excellent work."

"Thank you."

"Can you join us for dinner, Jon?"

I couldn't refuse. She was gorgeous even with no makeup, wearing a blue cotton sweater and faded jeans. She had shoulder-length auburn hair, big green eyes, a small nose and full lips.

We set the table together. I smelled a hint of vanilla on her, and I found it to be an unusual and pleasant choice of perfume. Whitney told stories about her dad performing experiments in the past and nearly blowing up the house. He asked about her old classes and professors, but she was more interested in finding out from me and Adams what was new with our work. Adams made little effort to answer most of her questions, making himself busy or acting like he didn't hear her.

A bowl of salad was passed around the dinner table. Adams dug into it and asked, "How are your headaches, Whit?"

"They're still happening. Not as frequently."

I noticed she had put her hand to her temples a few times during the meal. "You get migraines?" I asked.

"Since my mom passed away." I felt sorry for her, wishing there was something to say.

Whitney served us slices of roast before serving herself. She went to the kitchen and returned with warm rolls that smelled delicious.

She looked at Adams inquisitively. "I feel like you have something to tell me. You're being especially aloof tonight."

"You've always had that," Adams admitted.

"What are you really up to, besides celebrating at the bar?"

Adams waited until he finished chewing. I realized he hadn't spoken of the project with her.

"You remember your mom's idea?"

"Of course. The Universe Generator. Her passion."

"We've done it," Adams proudly announced.

"You've done what?"

"We've got it up and running."

Whitney paused for a moment as if she couldn't believe what she had just heard. "Why didn't you tell me?" she said finally, glaring at him. Adams put his hand on her arm. "I didn't want to tell you until I knew it worked."

"Are you kidding me? It actually works?"

"It works beautifully," he said. Whitney looked over at me.

"It's really incredible," I added.

"I can't believe it. I need to see it!"

The following morning, Whitney arrived at the lab shortly after we did. We gave her the complete tour of the building and the lab. Adams described every aspect of the equipment and I nodded along.

Right from the start, Whitney loved Jim. She quizzed him from mathematics to chemistry. He seemed to melt under her attention. His green light glowed when she was around, even when nothing was being said, perhaps because she was the first woman he had met. Adams had Jim put together a display on the monitors that took the viewer flying through the universe, stopping at breathtaking vistas, from the colorful nebula clusters down to majestic, snow-capped mountains on certain planets. It seemed like Jim did everything a notch better than normal as if he was showing off for Whitney.

"This is incredible," she said over and over, amazed by the beauty of the celestial objects. I had almost forgotten how miraculous it was.

I sat in a chair next to her and shared the feeling of wonder and excitement she was experiencing. After the demonstration, she turned to me with interest.

"And you're a carpenter?"

"That's right."

"What did you study in school? Computers? Engineering?"

"No."

"Astrophysics?" she asked with an impressive tone.

"Never went. Your dad needed an assistant, and he knew me from working on his house."

"Whoa, I figured you must be a real brain to be working with my dad." Whitney sensed her words sounded insulting. "I didn't mean it like that."

"It's okay. I know what you meant."

Adams sat nearby and listened as Whitney tried to make sense of our pairing.

"But I don't understand how..."

"Your dad tells me what to do, and I do it. Simple. He and Jim do all the tough stuff. I thought I'd be in way over my head when I first started—"

"You were," Jim interrupted me.

I put my hand over Jim's main speaker. "Don't interrupt when people are talking, Jim."

A muffled and sarcastic "Sorry" came through my hand.

"Doesn't it amaze you?" Whitney spun slowly in the swivel chair, taking in views from dozens of monitors, each one focused on a galaxy, or a planet, or primitive life forms.

"Every day. I never imagined this when I first started."

I couldn't decide what was more interesting, the project or Whitney.

I found myself staring at her, trying not to get caught. Being near her reminded me that I hadn't been on a date for a long time. The problem was, she was the daughter of my boss, who by that time, was also my close friend. I was still aware of the ring on her finger. I reminded myself of those red flags. I didn't want to cause any waves with Adams, but here was this incredible person sitting next to me. My life was entering a period of transition, and I had no idea where that change might lead.

In the following days, Whitney came to work with us. She said it would be impossible to stay at home writing a post-graduate thesis while she knew what was happening in the lab. I thought it was a dream come true. I began wearing clean shirts every day.

"It's a perfect fit," she told me. "My thesis was going to be on the extinction of species. Now I'm thinking it can be on evolution."

"Like turning a negative into a positive," I said.

A third person made the data collection go much faster. Whitney immediately demonstrated abilities beyond mine. She could take one look at a planet and identify what stage of life it was in. She could say, "That one is in a Triassic period," or "This has just entered a Permian period." I didn't know what she meant, but it sounded impressive.

She also explained to me the concept of "ontogeny recapitulating phylogeny."

"What the heck does that mean?" I asked.

She looked at the expression on my face and burst out laughing. "Do you remember the term, from high school science?"

"Honestly? No."

She stood behind my chair and put her hands on my shoulders. I melted as we studied the monitor, focused on a group of slimy, brown slugs eating the algae at the edge of a pond.

"Ontogeny is the development of an organism from egg to adult," she explained. "Phylogeny is the entire history of a species. So as the embryo grows, it passes stages like adult versions of more primitive species."

"Very interesting," Jim said.

"Come again?" I asked.

"Before you were a baby, you were an embryo. At that point, you looked like an adult tadpole, for example. And when these slugs were younger, they probably looked like that too."

A light went on in my head. "So maybe tadpoles or slugs were our ancestors way back in time?"

"Perhaps, way back," Whitney said, still touching my shoulders.

"I'm not saying I buy it, but okay."

Whitney helped me as I struggled with the difficult concepts. She enjoyed teaching me and Jim, probably because she had been the student her entire life. The project took off to a new level once Whitney arrived. Jim and I had a new pride about our work.

Every night as we slept, Jim scoured the universe for new planets. Within a few weeks, he had discovered hundreds of planets, many having primordial soup or basic life forms evolving. Over the course of several million standard orbits, these planets produced many interesting species of life.

We found electric beings in the Kappa galaxy, on planet 4 of the dz332 sun. They looked like blobs and lines of colored light. The atmosphere of Kappa 4, as we called the planet, was charged with radioactivity. Lightning flared through the sky, and thick clouds served as a canopy to the awesome display. The surface was hardened lava and water. The animals moved in spurts, not running or flying, but in electric jolts from spot to spot. They had photoelectric cells across their bodies, making them glow in fantastic colors. The smallest beings had vivid purples and blues. They moved like supercharged hummingbirds. The largest beings had a dull, red hue and moved slower, though they were still fast by our standards.

On another planet, Rho 6 of a double star yn662, the animals resembled plants that could slither around. Their skin was scaled in shades of green and yellow. Some grew to be enormous. We watched them inch from warm rocks down to shallow wading pools in the heat of the day, to cool off and soak up some water. They had no heads or mouths.

"No heads since they don't need to see, hear or eat to live," Whitney reasoned. "No natural predators. They don't need to kill or defend, so they're also without defensive qualities."

Adams agreed. "Their massive bodies and hot stars take care of their needs."

They were host organisms for a number of small creatures who clung on to the lumbering animals. Rho 6 had many insects and small reptilians though the mobile plants were the most intriguing beings.

Whitney found them amazing. "Imagine if we could adapt their cell structure," she said. "We could get food directly from sunlight. World hunger would be a thing of the past."

"Yeah, but what would happen to our stomachs?"

"Another useless organ, just like your appendix."

I was more than happy to study other planets. On Sigma 2-c454, bubble creatures floated around in helium skies of orange, moving like hot air balloons. They traveled in schools like a pack of blimps. They glided gracefully, occasionally touching down on the surface and bounding back up high into the skies, opening their huge mouths.

Whitney speculated, "They're catching tiny bacteria in the atmosphere."

I wasn't so sure. "How could a creature that large live on bacteria that we can't even see?"

"Same as whales," Adams noted, jotting it down in his brown booklet.

The more we saw, the more bizarre we knew evolution to be. A few planets were composed of nothing but gases with no liquid water, yet spawned life anyway—creatures made of gas and electric charges. Life on some planets was so bizarre, we didn't know how to categorize it.

And on other planets, like Alpha 17, we found forms of life that were surprisingly familiar.

Alpha 17 of the star hh987, was the seventeenth planet in the orbit of a blue-white star in the Alpha galaxy. It was the first planet we found that had complex levels of life in the oceans, on land and in the sky.

Its air contained large amounts of nitrogen and oxygen. Its landmasses contained silicon, iron and aluminum. It had a moon roughly one-tenth its size, which created high and low tides. The distance to its small, hot star provided temperate zones, with ice caps on the poles and more tropical areas in between. It had an orbit around its sun that was faster than standard, yet it maintained a degree of rotation and gravity that was close to standard.

"All of these factors increase the chances for complex life to evolve," Adams said. "The more pleasant a planet's atmosphere, the more likely life will flourish."

The life forms reflected the cool and dim atmosphere. Plants were tough and sharp. Animals had long hair, big eyes and coatings of blubber.

The continents on Alpha 17 contained vegetation zones beneath windswept hills of ice and rock. The mountains appeared like the spines of a herd of beasts running west to east. Exposed rock and snow along the ridges suggested long-term wind and glacial patterns. In the lower elevations and around the coastlines, vegetation and animal life were abundant. Exotic and common-looking birds filled the skies, and the seas were full of fish and amphibians.

Alpha 17 was the first planet we found that had mammals. After several time leaps of about a hundred million orbits, a variety of mammals had evolved. Large rodents lived in burrows on the shoreline and ate fish. Others reminded us of boars. One of the most common species on the planet looked like giant pigs. We found them by the millions, filling the lowlands and feeding on grass and reeds. The giant pigs were the food source for a number of predators, who looked like bears and felines.

"Mammals stand apart," Whitney said, admiring a family of felines on Monitor One. "They give birth to live young. The parents care for the offspring together. The young ones like to play."

"Is that what they're doing?" Jim asked, commenting on the rough and tumble antics of the small cats.

"They're learning survival skills they'll use later when hunting," Whitney told him.

"Because it looks like they're hurting one another."

"They're not," Whitney reassured him. "They're learning. Community rules exist with mammals more so than other beings."

"Community rules?" I asked.

"The head male is in charge. The females raise the young. Hunting is a group effort. They work as a team in everything they do."

We watched the big cats execute a planned attack on a herd of giant pigs, which was wallowing in the marsh. The cats made a charge and isolated a young and helpless victim. We marveled at the carnivores' teamwork as they carried out the strike, though Whitney empathized with the victim of the attack.

We also documented groups of primates, the smaller ones living in the trees and the larger ones on the ground. Adams and Whitney were ecstatic after finding primates on Alpha 17, almost speechless. It took a couple of days for the effect to really hit me. I went into a numb stage without realizing it. I lost my interest in other life forms and just wanted to observe them.

Though they were as primitive as monkeys and apes, they were quickly developing into intelligent beings. Females managed the family while males fed and fought for breeding rights. The little ones played acrobatic games of tag in the trees. They roughhoused in the mornings and later groomed each other for ticks. The larger ones peeled and ate the green off the reeds, sharing with the smaller ones. I saw intrigue in their eyes as they witnessed the world around them. I felt the bond between parent and child as the elders nursed, comforted, and taught their offspring what they needed to know.

"Do you realize what we're watching here?" Adams asked me.

"What?"

"The evolution of intelligent beings."

Whitney brought in pictures of artists' renditions of our possible ancestors. We noted similarities between them and our subjects from Alpha 17. The main differences were slightly more hair and bigger eyes, but otherwise they were very similar.

That was our routine for the first month of Whitney's arrival.

We scoured the universe for planets with life, then we identified and categorized it. Once that was done, we did time leaps of anywhere from several thousand to a few million orbits and went through the same routine, with Jim constantly finding new planets to add to our collection. Adams was right. The universe was teeming with life because the building blocks for it were everywhere, two parts hydrogen and one part oxygen. With so many planets out there, the only trick was to keep looking. Since Jim took care of that, there really was no trick at all.

"So pleased Whit is here to see this. Her birthright, I suppose. Alpha 17 actually has primates, and I pinch myself as I write this. Been lagging with the rest of our logs, but who can blame us?"

- from p. 55 of Webster's journal.

Society

THE STARS AND PLANETS slowly returned to stationary positions at the end of one of our time leaps. The cameras, one by one, went through their readjustment phase and began showing clear images on the monitors. We started the routine of data collection, changing and labeling new discs for updates of everything on record, a chore that would take weeks. We didn't begin with Alpha 17, as its cameras were still readjusting, but we were getting updates from Sigma 2 when Jim interrupted us with the news.

"There are lights on Alpha 17," Jim said plainly, as a matter of fact.

"What do you mean?" Adams asked.

"There are lights that weren't there before our last time leap."

"Let's see."

Our crew waited patiently for Monitor One to establish a clear focus to Alpha 17. Eventually we saw the planet's night side. Although the oceans and landmasses were in darkness, the contours of the water and land could be identified, as well as tiny points of light twinkling through the atmosphere. Light sources beaconed to us from landmasses across the planet, concentrated around coastlines and rivers.

"Could it be fires?" Whitney asked.

"Fire has a different spectrum and wavelength," Jim said.

"Pick a light and go in closer," Adams said, tapping his clipboard on his desk.

Jim picked a light source and zoomed in. As the shot went ever nearer, we realized we were looking at thousands and thousands of individual lights.

"What is it?" Jim asked.

Adams stood motionless, staring at the monitor. Whitney had the same wide-eyed expression of disbelief. Adams looked at me, pointed at the monitor and broke out into nervous laughter. It took a moment for the reality to hit us, but when it did, we started shouting and laughing uncontrollably. We danced around the lab room, yelling absurdities and staring in shock at the recent addition on Alpha 17.

"What's going on?" Jim repeated, becoming impatient with us.

"It appears to be a city," Adams said with amazement.

"How did this happen?" I said in shock.

As Jim's focus penetrated the skies and scanned the metropolis, we saw structures everywhere. The streets were lined with buildings and cars moved by them. We saw factories with smokestacks, boats docking at a harbor and small planes taking off from a runway. We could even see a residential area where the homes were packed together in neat little rows.

"Jim, can you confirm the duration of our last time leap?" Adams finally asked.

"About fifty thousand standard orbits as scheduled."

"Surely that couldn't have been enough time," Adams said, fumbling through his notes on the planet.

"Enough time for what?" I asked.

"You don't go from primates to this in fifty thousand years!"

"Why not?" I asked.

"Evolution takes time, Jon. Usually huge amounts of time, like millions of years! Not fifty thousand."

"How do you know? No offense, but have you done this before?" I said, pointing to the monitors.

"It's just not reasonable."

"Reasonable or not, there it is," Whitney said.

"We must have missed something," Adams insisted.

"Like what?" Jim asked.

"There must have been tribes we didn't see. There must have been primates walking upright on two feet. There must have been a link from ape... to this!"

"Maybe they just evolved quicker than you thought they could," Whitney offered.

Jim took the shot in closer to a well-lit outdoor market and we analyzed the citizens. They wore simple clothing of basic colors. Shirts and pants without much flair was the norm. Some of the outfits were one-piece jumpsuits. The fashion theme was comfortable though a bit boring.

We compared the people to the primates from our logs. There were similarities though the modern version looked far more sophisticated and soft-featured. The current Alphans walked on two feet, upright in stance with straight spines. They were taller but still a bit stocky. They had larger eyes and less body hair though their faces were covered with a thin coat of hair—a feature for men, women, and children. I found the size of their eyes

46

to be interesting and wondered if that had something to do with their speedy evolution.

"Big eyes, big brains," I told Whitney. "See the relationship?"

"More like dim sun, big eyes," she reasoned. "Their sky is dimmer than ours. To see well, they need to take in more light." The blue-white Alphan star was bright and hot, yet smaller and further away in comparison.

We rechecked the wilderness areas and found groups of primates identical to the ones from our logs. They lived the same as before: roughhousing, grooming for ticks and eating green reeds.

"Maybe a select group branched off to become civilized," I proposed.

"It just doesn't make sense," Adams said. "Fifty thousand years?"

"Why worry about it so much? We can't go backward," Whitney added.

Our interest in the old primates didn't last long. Within minutes, we returned to the cities.

It amazed me to see the Alphans using products like ours: automobiles, airplanes, factories and farms built for mass production.

As the day went on, Adams became more convinced they must somehow be the descendants of our previous studies. He speculated we had either missed some small tribes entirely or that primates were capable of accelerated evolution.

"Regardless of how they got here," Whitney said, "isn't it incredibly coincidental that another species has evolved into something like us? Having the same inventions?"

"Aside from the timing, it is logical," Adams said. "Evolution starts from day one and creatures get more proficient at living. Ultimately they create things. What are the most basic inventions of all?"

"Sharp rocks for killing and eating," I said.

"And fire," Whitney added, "for killing and eating better."

Adams made a list. "Home, spear, fire. Once you've got the basics you can learn farming, clothing, medicine, then mathematics and the arts."

I followed his line of thought. "Then you've got the wheel and eventually the engine."

Jim found the concepts intriguing. His green light pulsed while we spoke about it.

"With the mammals it makes sense," Adams went on. "Birds haven't evolved to this, though they've had billions of years to try. Fish haven't, reptiles haven't, but apparently the right mammals do."

"Is this the evolution of the brain?" I asked.

"Looks that way," Adams said.

"Their heads have gotten bigger in ratio to their bodies," Jim commented.

Something was bothering Whitney. "But why do you suppose the Alphans are so similar to us? Why do they have two arms and two legs? Why do they have a head and a face with two eyes, a basic nose, and ears, sort of, and a mouth like ours?"

"Why wouldn't they?" I asked.

"Doesn't it seem awfully coincidental?" Whitney added. "The first intelligent life we find ends up more or less resembling us?"

Adams found logical answers. "Maybe it's necessary to have bipolar vision and hands with opposable thumbs and mouths capable of making so many sounds. Maybe those things are what separate the extraordinary species from the rest."

"I just think it seems very coincidental," she said.

We theorized the entire day. We laughed a lot and congratulated each other. We had found Alpha 17, a planet where "primordial soup" had evolved into a species of people who built major cities. If it had happened there, then it could have happened anywhere else in his creation and likely in our own universe.

That was when I finally met Frank Maxwell. When Adams broke the news to him, Maxwell came by for a visit. He was in his late sixties to early seventies with white hair. He was dressed in a dark blue tailored suit. He carried a wooden walking cane though he mostly used it for pointing at things. He opened his arms to Whitney upon seeing her.

"Young lady, look how you've grown. You're as beautiful as your mother."

"Thank you, Mr. Maxwell," Whitney said after hugging him.

"Oh please, call me Frank. Nice to meet you, Mr. Gruber." He took my hand and shook it longer than customary. "Webster has told me great things about you."

"I'm sure he exaggerated. And call me Jon."

Frank was awestruck by the project and the recent developments on Alpha 17. I watched him move throughout the lab room, carefully inspecting each monitor and the views they showed. For someone not interested in astronomy, as Adams had described, he did a good job of fooling me. He wanted to know everything about Alpha 17 as well as the other planets.

"You were right, Webster. You told me this idea could really work."

"Rose seldom made mistakes," Adams said.

"We all make mistakes," Frank said, correcting him.

"Thank you for believing in us." The two shook hands on their accomplishment and stared at the screens. Monitor One showed a busy Alphan street corner.

"There are people who will want to see this," Frank mentioned. "People who might contribute to the financial backing."

Almost reluctantly Adams said, "I'm becoming aware of that. I'm sure we can figure out the best way to handle this."

Frank returned to his gaze. "They really move about, don't they?"

"It's summer season for this hemisphere," Whitney observed.

The Alphan cities were packed with energetic people. The outdoor markets were flooded with activity. Merchants sold goods aggressively, calling out to passersby while holding items up for sale. Some of the customers haggled with them, walked away and then came back to negotiate. I laughed, thinking of the times I had done the same thing.

For the next several days we studied everything about them, with Frank often popping in for a visit.

Alphans walked with a jerky gait. They had strong legs and thick torsos and moved with power but not grace. They had a spontaneous quality about them, like that of children, and they seemed to act impulsively.

Jim enjoyed scanning the cameras through the neighborhoods. It was a summertime theme with many people outdoors enjoying the stretch of nice weather. We found kids playing games, people working on gardens and several examples of scenes that reminded me of old fashioned barbeques where neighbors ate together.

The tables were stacked with food as Alphans apparently ate large quantities, and they liked to eat in groups. From our observations, a common Alphan dinner involved having the neighbors over for a backyard barbeque of giant pig, vegetables, breads and what appeared to be intoxicating beverages. The women did most of the work while the men sat around eating and drinking.

We witnessed an odd thing. It was common for the occasional fight to break out, though when it was over everybody went back to the party, including the brawlers. Yet when the partying was done, they all went about their lives in a fairly brisk fashion, as if a certain energy kept them going.

Whitney noted, "They seem to have higher metabolism rates. They fill up on so much food, yet they go back to work on full stomachs."

"Possibly a result of cooler air and faster revolution speeds," Adams theorized.

During the days, Alphans built all kinds of structures. We zoomed in on a neighborhood development. The lots were tightly packed together as they maximized the number of homes in the area. They built their homes in similar fashion to the way we built ours. They started with wooden foundations and poured them with concrete. Then they built wooden frames and later added the finish work. As we analyzed their building methods, it was the first time I was the expert, explaining to the others the process and strategies of their work.

Alphans also enjoyed all sorts of games. Even at the jobsites, I noticed several men engaging in spontaneous roughhousing and tossing objects at each other. We watched many of the neighborhood kids as they wrestled and engaged in tough contact sports, both boys and girls. Jim's first lessons in the notion of sports came through the backyards and playgrounds, while we attempted to figure out the rules of their games. Jim very much enjoyed the concepts of play, as he was just as content watching the kids run around as we were watching Alphans cities at work. Had Jim been a real person, I think he would have been a natural at play.

On the darker side, many of the larger metropolitan areas contained huge arenas for gladiators. These were primarily large specimens of Alphans, both men and women, who battled with each other and with ferocious beasts. The gladiators wore body armor and wielded dangerous weapons. Screaming spectators filled the stands and threw objects and beverages at the participants on the field.

After watching some blows from the metal ball of one gladiator to another, I quickly realized the severity of it.

"This looks very interesting," I told Jim. "Now you're going to watch serious action."

"How so?" Jim asked.

"Because it looks like these guys aren't just playing. These guys fight to the death."

They fought on with extreme rage, hurling their weapons into each other as the crowds cheered them on. Never before had I seen such viciousness in sport.

"You mean they're intentionally trying to kill each other?" Jim asked.

"It appears that way," Whitney said.

"But why? I thought you said mammals worked as a team."

"Well, unfortunately not always."

50

"Can you explain it then?" Jim asked.

Whitney sighed. "No. Not really."

"Oh," Jim said. His light pulsed mildly on the concept.

Adams was less interested by the action in the arenas. Whitney found it hard to watch, especially when one of the gladiators hacked off the arm of another and then crushed his helmet with a spiked ball. The audience went wild as the victor raised his arms in triumph.

"How can you watch this, Jon? It's horrible," Whitney said.

"It helps me understand where we came from. Didn't our ancestors engage in regular warfare?"

"Yes," she admitted.

"Well, maybe this is the first step from moving out of war and into sport."

Jim asked, "If death is the outcome, is it still considered sport?"

"Perhaps," I said, "if death just happens to the individual and not to the tribe."

Whitney shook her head at my logic as she commonly did.

Regardless of where they were in measures of civilization, the Alphans were several decades to a century behind us on a level of technology. They had boats, cars and simple planes, but what we saw reminded us of our own models from earlier times. The boats and cars ran on fossil fuels, and their planes were propeller-driven.

On the roads, they drove fast. They showed little concern for speed limits or safety. When accidents occurred, the drivers usually got out of their cars and beat the daylights out of one another. No policemen or ambulances were seen. We speculated if they had any need for traffic court. We never witnessed a deadly accident, but we debated whether or not an Alphan would get into trouble if he ran over someone. Whitney hoped they did, but Adams and I thought perhaps not, judging from what we had seen in the sports arenas and at the backyard barbeques.

The more we studied them, the more we realized what a high level of energy their society had. Alphans were barbaric but not lazy. They worked long days and partied into the nights. They spread out across their planet, tearing down forests and draining marshlands to build highways and shopping malls. They lived life to the fullest, and I had to admire them for that, even if Whitney found them to be hostile.

We studied Alpha 17 exclusively for many days. Jim's recording discs had never before been filled with so much information on one planet in one time era. We worked at a feverish pace with excitement and enthusiasm. The hours and days flew by.

"While the Alphans are the most familiar species we have found, they are disturbingly lacking in some areas. I cannot find any evidence of social etiquette or law. 'Might is right' is their credo. Whitney is appalled by them, so is Jim, interestingly enough. Is he taking cues from her or does he really feel that way? Sometimes Jim surprises me. I predict advances in computers and engine systems within a hundred standard orbits. Jon has been questioning the schedule. I have to admit the idea has crossed my mind. Frank wants to let his investors see the lab. Not sure this is a good idea. What would Rose say?"

- from p. 71 of Webster's journal.

The Future

EVENTUALLY THE SUBJECT CAME UP about performing another time leap. It was Jim who first mentioned it out of simple curiosity. As soon as he did, there was little else I could talk about. Adams laughed at the notion.

"We have so much to learn about the Alphans as it is," he said, "not to mention the hundred or so other planets in our logs that have been completely abandoned since our last time leap."

"What else can we learn?" Whitney asked. "How to decapitate an opponent with one blow?" Adams didn't respond.

Whitney and I tossed arguments back and forth, weighing the pros and cons of such a decision. Each day as we documented their ways of life, we pressed Adams to consider the idea.

"In my opinion, there's no reason not to," I said.

Jim added, "What do you think will happen to the Alphans in the future?"

"I hope they might achieve a level of humanity," Whitney said. Then she added, "Why not just find out, Dad?"

"Out of the question."

But as the days went by, he became more and more intrigued. Whitney's suggestion must have sparked something within him. After a week, Adams seemed receptive to the idea. He ran his hands through his hair while he studied the monitors. Curiosity weighed against responsibility. The energy in the room was electric as we debated it.

"Jim," Adams said finally, "how much time do you think would pass in a leap adding the smallest amount of hydrogen?"

"Good question," Jim said.

It was the first time we had discussed the potentials for a mini-leap. Calculations were made to determine Jim's capabilities. The object was to fast forward the project the slightest amount possible, something the Universe Generator was not really designed to do. Adams pulled Rose's original notes from his desk. He went over the formulas and best estimates for each aspect of the operation. Jim had to release a minimal burst of hydrogen molecules, confirm it and then contract to idle. Each operation required a minimum of a few seconds. They calculated and came up with a rough estimate of ten seconds for Jim to perform the tasks.

Adams put his calculator and pen down. He leaned back, took a deep breath and said, "If all goes according to plan, it would come out to about a hundred standard orbits."

"Alpha 17's orbit is faster than standard," Jim reminded him. "More like a hundred and twenty for them."

A hundred and twenty years was a fair amount of time for a modern society. We debated the possibilities among ourselves. The excitement rose quickly.

I asked, "Should Maxwell be informed about it first?"

Adams dismissed the notion. "We've gotten to this point without Frank knowing anything. Why should he have to know now?"

To my great surprise, Adams decided to go for it. He instructed Jim to advance the universe by the smallest degree.

The humming sound began as Jim released the hydrogen. I watched the monitors. Though I could hear the familiar noise, like an electric engine, I could not detect any movement from the galaxies. They didn't budge. Some of the stars showed tiny movements, but it was miniscule in comparison to the usual leaps. This time, only the planets moved, leaving trails of light for a short period before coming back to a stop.

"That was a hundred years?" I asked.

"A hundred years is nothing to a universe," Jim reminded me.

"Let's adjust the first five monitors to Alpha 17," Adams said. His words were crisp, and I could feel the anticipation behind them.

The image from Monitor One picked up the Alpha galaxy. Then we identified the familiar blue-white sun within the maze of stars. As the monitor adjusted to search for the seventeenth planet, Whitney's eyes lit up. Jim locked in on the planet, and we recognized it as Alpha 17.

From space, it looked very similar as before although the snowy areas on the mountain ridges had receded and the polar caps were smaller.

The planet came into closer view. The shot zoomed through the atmosphere and through the thicker air toward the coastline. I immediately sensed a hundred years had passed. The atmosphere was thick with a low-lying haze and the cities had grown dramatically. Much taller buildings spread out in greater numbers as hundreds of flying machines filled the sky. The Alphans had become very modern, even more so than we were.

"Yes!" Adams cried out.

Jim followed some flying objects that were everywhere in the skies. Several devices caught our attention. Some looked like small, agile helicopters. Others appeared to be personal flying crafts, where individual Alphans flew around in transparent stand-up gadgets.

"They're flying!" Whitney noted. "They look like commuters."

Jim zoomed down to the ground. The traffic had become even busier with a variety of new road vehicles. The freeways were packed with them and they moved at high speeds. Some of the cars drove attached to the roads while others took off and hovered over them.

"So this is what the future is like?" I asked.

Adams sat down in his chair as if his legs were giving out. I could tell he had never really anticipated the outcome of this time leap. He appeared overwhelmed. Alpha 17 had gone from a home of primordial soup to a giant in technology in eleven time leaps.

Whitney sensed her father's shock and went to console him.

"Everything's going to be okay," she said, standing behind him and rubbing his shoulders. "This is good news, right?"

Adams finally spoke his feelings. "When we first speculated on finding advanced life forms, no one had ever... ever talked about finding life more advanced than we are."

It was difficult to accept. We watched silently as Jim scanned around the planet, giving us a bird's eye view of their cities. I felt like I was watching a fantasy movie with a wealth of information on display. The Alphans had better, more efficient products as well as things we didn't have at all.

The design of their buildings was staggering along with the sheer size. Many were shaped as giant cylinders, with large round bases rising to super-high points. These were much taller than any skyscraper of their past. Others were built out of thin and transparent materials that looked like spiders' webs, making them open to the air and convenient for flying devices to come and go.

Trying to take in the enormity of the downtown buildings and new devices gave me an intense headache. Whitney gave me a few capsules for it. We downed them together and watched the monitors with Adams in quiet shock. We sat there for hours, completely spellbound, staring at innovation, finally having to pull ourselves away for sleep.

On the way home in the truck we said surprisingly little, each feeling exhausted. When I got back to my apartment, I was disoriented.

I had trouble remembering which route I had ridden my bicycle from Webster's house. I also realized I had forgotten to put new recording discs in for Jim before we left for the night. That was a first.

I lay in bed and stared at my ceiling, thinking about it over and over. The experience was completely surreal. For weeks, I had watched gas settle and stars emerge. Then I had seen planets form and stuff start to grow. Then I had witnessed creatures evolve, with a multitude and variety more than I could have imagined. But on top of all that, within the past two weeks I had watched primates become a modern society. And then it had leapfrogged beyond us.

It was all happening at such an accelerating rate.

"Today the unthinkable happened. I did something that was in hindsight, perhaps the greatest risk I've ever taken. The result sent the Alphans into a super-modern time. Their structures and devices are far beyond ours. Several decades to a century. Frank will go through the ceiling, I know it. I doubt I'll be able to sleep tonight."

- from p. 75 of Webster's journal.

Elation

ADAMS CALLED FRANK the next morning and he came by immediately. When he first saw the new cities he stood in front of the monitors, laughing like a kid. Then he plunked down in a chair and asked Jim to show him around.

As we investigated the cities of Alpha 17, the flying machines in the skyways first caught our attention. In every section of sky, we saw hundreds of personal-sized little cages buzzing all over. They carried individuals mostly, but some held a couple of passengers. The pilots stood upright in a simple, metal-framed chamber in the shape of a cross with their arms out comfortably to the side. In the larger models, the passengers stood behind the pilot. They were so innovative yet they looked easy, fun and fast. There was something very different about them, unlike other flying devices I could think of. Some hovered in midair and then zoomed forward, or straight up or down, or even backward. The device seemed able to move in any direction, no matter where it was facing.

Frank stared at the monitor in disbelief. "How do these work?" he asked, following one with his finger. We all wanted to know.

"Some form of directional propulsion," Adams said.

"And strong engines," Frank added. He noticed a highway out of focus on the monitor. "Are those cars? Can we zoom in on this?"

"Show him the road by the coast that we like, Jim," I said, already having a feel for the place.

The monitor panned over to a busy freeway. It was built next to the ocean on a long stretch of coastline, a gorgeous setting for a drive.

The Alphans used an array of things as vehicles. I couldn't call them all cars because they didn't rely on tires touching the ground. Instead, the vehicles on this road floated several feet above the ground. Some Alphans rode futuristic motorcycles that had a flat area where the tires should be. They also hovered over the roadway. As the vehicles levitated, they traveled at very high speeds. The devices were so sleek and smooth that they sped along the shoreline highway with no apparent friction.

Adams pointed to the flat areas beneath the vehicles. "This looks like magnetic repulsion," he explained.

"Some of it looks like air propulsion," I added, merely quoting Adams from before but trying to impress Maxwell.

"This is incredible," Frank said. He moved closer to the monitor until he was just beneath it. He reached out a hand as if he could touch the cars.

"We've been looking at stuff like this all over the planet. There's no end to it," Adams said.

"Show me more," Frank said. "I want to see everything."

"Take him on the tour," Adams instructed.

Jim adjusted the main monitor to pan through a section of one of the busiest cities. Traffic floated in front of buildings that looked like super tall cylinders. Thousands of people and crafts filled our tiny view.

"Look at that!" Frank said excitedly upon first seeing the heart of the city.

"New factors at work here," Adams told him.

Frank added, "When I first agreed to help fund this, I never thought there'd be something marketable in it." Then he asked Whitney and me to have a seat. He said, "Listen now. Big changes are necessary. A security fence will be built around the grounds, and a couple of guards will be at the front gate." Adams nodded along as Frank went over the newly classified status of the project. "We need to get some experts in here to help us understand these products."

Adams added, "We can't share information or talk about work with anyone. Jon, that goes for Sam too."

"I understand," I said.

"You'll be getting a huge raise," Frank said. "I don't know what I'm paying them, but multiply it by three." Adams nodded.

When Frank left, I started jumping up and down. Whitney and I danced around the lab room, celebrating our good fortune. Jim played some music to go with our steps as Adams clapped along.

At the end of the day I suggested, "Let's go out. We've been working for weeks. I think we should release some energy."

Whitney agreed to the idea, but Adams told us, "Think I'll stay here and work. Go enjoy yourselves." He tossed me the keys to the truck. "I'll get a cab."

I felt instantly rich. I took Whitney somewhere neither of us had been before, a place where the waiters pampered the customers more than anyone should be. I ordered appetizers, an expensive bottle of wine, fresh fish dinners and desserts for both of us—all the things I never did at restaurants.

After gorging ourselves, we strolled around the river until we came across a small outdoor band. We stopped to appreciate the soft music they played, and I stuffed a few bills in their money jar. The horn player gave me a thankful nod.

"How about a dance?" Whitney requested.

"Real dancing? I'm pretty clumsy," I said, preferring not to.

She insisted. "Come on. It's easy."

She grabbed my waist and moved me around with the music. My feet shuffled in sync with hers. With each step, I felt more confident.

The horn player smiled. Then the music softened even more, and I held Whitney closer and shortened our steps. I pressed my cheek against hers and breathed in the scent of vanilla from her neck. I wanted to remember everything about that moment. As I danced and held her hand in mine, I was reminded of the ring on her finger. I debated whether to ask her about it.

Curiosity got to me and I blurted out, "You're not engaged, are you?"

"Because I wear this?" she asked. "This ring was my mother's."

"I shouldn't have mentioned it," I said, suddenly feeling stupid.

"How could you have known?" she said. "You know, Jon, you like to goof around but sometimes you're way too uptight."

"It's a problem I have around beautiful women," I said, shrugging my head.

"A lot of men have that problem. That's why I wear this ring."

"Keeps the jerks away?"

"Apparently not."

"Ha-ha."

"Kidding." She felt my awkwardness reach a peak. "Just relax," she emphasized, rubbing one hand over my shoulder and arm. "Listen to the music and relax." Whitney made our steps flow together.

"I can do this," I said, watching my feet.

She lifted my chin to face her. "How long have you been thinking about asking me that?"

"Since I met you," I admitted. She laughed and spun me around in circles on the dance floor.

Driving back to her house, she asked, "Do you want to stay in the guest room?"

I accepted readily. I felt too tired and slightly buzzed to ride my bicycle back to my apartment in the dark. We entered the house and saw Adams in his pajamas, turning off lights. He agreed it would be best if I stayed the night.

Whitney led me into the guest room. We sat down on the bed and looked at each other. I was still in a daze from the events at work and the dancing. It was the first time all night that I had been at a loss for words. I just sat there quietly gazing at her. She gazed back.

In a bold move I reached for her glasses to carefully pull them from her face and set them on the nightstand. As I looked into her eyes, I saw a mix of deep green and light brown. She shook her hair, brushed it back with her hand and smiled at me. She was so beautiful. I put my hand around her neck and kissed her.

We pulled back and looked at each other with slight surprise. I handed her glasses back. She put them on, looked at me and smiled again. Then she got up and slowly left the room. I lay down on the bed thinking about what had just happened. I turned out the light, undressed and got under the covers, waiting for the adrenaline rush to wear off until I finally managed to fall asleep.

Envy

WHEN WE ARRIVED AT WORK the next morning, the contractor was already digging foundations for the guard shack and perimeter fence. Frank Maxwell stood by the heavy machinery with two men in uniforms. He greeted us with a wave of his cane.

We got out of the truck and were introduced to Phil and Dave, part of our new team of security guards. He also told us about the people he was bringing in to help with technical research.

Jessica Baxter and Ian Nessen joined us later in the morning. Frank had given them a two-hour notice from their current jobs. When they met us at the front door, each had a look of concern over what could possibly have been so important. Adams breathed a sigh of relief when he saw them. Whitney and I were good help, but Jessica and Ian had professional engineering backgrounds. Adams knew them from projects they had been involved with over the past years though he had never worked with them directly. I was intimidated by them.

"May we come in?" Jessica asked, standing in front of Ian by the open doors. She was around forty, tall, with dark hair wrapped back in a weave. She wore a beige work suit with slacks and looked to be in fair shape for a corporate woman.

"Of course," Adams said. "Come in, please."

Frank made the introductions in the entry. Jessica had a nice smile and brown eyes. As we shook hands, I sensed that she had refined people skills.

Ian hesitated before shaking my hand, out of slight awkwardness. Ian looked more as I imagined really intelligent people to look. He wore thick glasses and left his hair in a controlled mess. He was a bit round in the middle and also had what appeared to be a mustard stain on his shirt from the day before. Ian was younger than I had expected, just a few years older than I was. I imagined he was super intelligent.

We thought it would overwhelm them to walk directly to the lab and show them what was going on. We stood with them in the entry while

Adams explained to Jessica and Ian what they were about to see. Mostly it was for their protection from fainting, which we thought might happen.

"Are you serious?" Jessica asked Adams. "I mean no offense, but that doesn't seem possible."

"Oh yes. It's a real universe, very much like ours. Only microscopic in proportion."

"And you have a planet in there, with a society?" Ian asked. Adams nodded. "A futuristic society?"

"That's why you're here," Frank added.

"When can we see it?" Ian asked.

"As soon as you feel comfortable with that," Adams said.

Jessica looked at Ian. He raised his eyes with anticipation.

Adams said, "It might be wise to follow us in, have a seat and then look at the monitors."

We walked them down the corridor toward the control room. Jessica looked around as if for hidden cameras, like she was wondering if a practical joke was being played on her.

We entered the lab and showed them to the chairs we had prepared. They both sat down. Then they lifted their eyes to the sea of monitors, several of which were focused on activities within a busy metropolis of Alpha 17. Jessica started to laugh in awe. Ian's reactions were more subdued as a slow grin came over his face.

I could tell they had no doubt of the project's authenticity. I pointed out the galaxy and solar system that Alpha 17 belonged to. Then we gave them an overview of the planet and the society. They were speechless. We showed them the city scenes we had been focusing on. Adams pointed out the varied structures and devices that had caught our attention.

Jim showed off his talents with Monitor One. He adjusted the focus to follow one of the personal flying devices, which we were now calling PFDs. Jim picked a young Alphan driver and buzzed alongside him throughout the city traffic. The young driver flew like a delivery boy. He weaved through the masses of commuters with aggressive turns, quick stops and starts. As Jim followed him, the effect was dizzying.

"Incredible!" they both gasped.

"That's probably enough," Whitney advised Jim, sensing it was becoming overwhelming to the arrivals.

Ian became sick first, using the bag we had provided for him. Upon seeing it, Jessica stood and made her way to the bathroom.

Adams reminded us, "We experienced these images over many days. Let's give them time to feel comfortable with it all. Jim, try to help them ease into this."

"Sorry."

Within an hour they were adjusted, excited and in awe like the rest of us about the prospects of the futuristic society. We showed them everything, continuing the tour of the other planets in our logs and finally back to Alpha 17. Jessica and Ian expressed a deep respect for all of us and especially for Adams.

"Thank you for this wonderful opportunity," Jessica said to him.

"And thank you, Mr. Maxwell," Ian said. Frank looked at him sternly and Ian added, "I mean Frank."

Jim liked having more people around, as he was getting used to socializing and showing off. Jim began to ask them question after trivial question until we had to remind him to pace himself.

"Hey Ian, what's that in your shirt pocket?" Jim asked.

"Electronic games," he answered.

"Can I play?"

"I don't know," Ian looked around to Adams and myself.

"You can watch Ian play it to start," I said. "But that will have to wait until later."

"I can bring a copy on disc tomorrow," Ian said. "I didn't expect—"

"It's okay," Whitney said. "He's just excited, meeting new people."

Ian was an interesting character, unlike anyone I had ever known. Frank sang his praises with an arm around his shoulder.

"Ian left school early to work with us as a video game creator," Frank told us as Ian hung his head in shyness. "He designed a line of three-dimensional combat games that sat on the shelf for years due to cost, but I loved the creativity. Amazing games. Then we moved Ian to automated machinery and then to the ranks of engineering and design. Then I got him working with Jessica, and the two have made tremendous achievements for my company. But there's a side to Ian that never grew up; he keeps a pocket version of games with him for when he isn't busy. A boy inside the man."

"What's Jessica's story?" Jim asked.

"Jessica," Frank continued as he walked behind her, "is like an extension of myself. She's been with me since she graduated from college."

"How long is that?" Jim asked.

"Jim, please," Whitney hushed him.

"Jessica has a knack for problem solving and engineering," Frank continued. "These two will be valuable additions to our team."

As Frank spoke of her, I realized Jessica was not only very gifted, she was quite attractive. She wore the slightest makeup, highlighting sharp eyes. Her teeth were especially straight and white.

"I'm really pleased to be here," she said. "We'll do whatever we can to help." She spoke with ease and looked each of us in the eye as she did. Her presence allowed Ian to relax. I felt like I could get along with both of them.

In a review of the Alphan people, we buzzed down to a busy street corner to get a look at them up close. The first thing we noticed was that some of the pedestrians were robots. Many of them accompanied real Alphans, but some of the robots were doing their own things.

Some were cleaning the streets and sidewalks, while others appeared to be running errands. As for the Alphans themselves, the people had changed somewhat physically over the last hundred and twenty years.

"They're a bit taller, more refined," Whitney explained to our new colleagues. "Their faces are less hairy. They're larger and probably stronger than their ancestors, and they move more gracefully."

"How many generations have passed since you did this time leap thing?" Jessica asked.

"Only about five to six," Whitney said.

"Are the changes more than you would have anticipated?"

"Yes."

The clothing had changed as well. The basic garments of old had been replaced with a new type of body suit tailored to the curves and fit snugly. Solid, striking colors were the norm, compared to browns and grays from the past. Some clothing looked metallic and had a shiny, smooth appearance.

"Don't know about the colors," Jessica commented, "but the fabric is interesting."

"What do you think, Ian?" I joked. "Would you like a revealing body suit like that?"

Ian was less interested in the clothing. "What about all this automation? It looks like robotics are doing everything."

Modern gadgets were everywhere. Window cleaners used suction cups to scale the skyscrapers and wash the glass. Vehicles retained their shine from tiny cleaners moving about the cars at certain stops. Auto taxis and pilots made rounds to give pedestrians rides. Much of the traffic in the skies seemed to be automated, though Alphans did fly some devices for themselves.

"This is my favorite," Frank said, pointing to the air traffic. "Ian and Jess, I want you to focus on these flying things all the commuters are using. Who would have thought they'd have personal flying devices?"

Everybody loved watching the PFDs. They gave the individual the ability to fly most anywhere in a dynamic, simple-looking craft.

"This design doesn't look very complicated," Ian remarked after watching it for a few minutes.

Adams and Ian discussed the design, and Jessica made sketches to match their description.

Ian saw it as, "A lightweight frame around the pilot. A system of small, rotating turbine engines. The pilot stands with his arms out to the side. The craft is shaped like a cross around him."

Adams estimated, "Maybe a hundred or two small but powerful turbines?"

They came up with a fairly plausible design for the frame and motors, as well as the changing angles of the turbines. Frank was delighted. One of the early questions from both Ian and Adams was what the crafts were using for power.

Jim attempted to identify any chemicals emitted from the devices though it was difficult for his sensors to be accurate with things so small. Plus, air movement around the device scattered any emissions that might have been.

Jessica took a phone from her pocket. "Margaret," she said into it, "schedule a meeting with Bill from Lee Aviation sometime next week." She looked at Frank, who nodded his approval.

"Not here, of course," Adams whispered to her.

"In the main conference room," she said to Margaret. "Of course," she told Adams.

"That was fast," I mentioned to Whitney.

Over the next few days, Adams worked with Ian and Jessica on the main monitors on several products, while Whitney and I used secondary monitors to make other observations. I taught Whitney how to adjust the cameras without Jim's assistance. We updated our maps of the known cities and towns from before, documenting everything we saw that was new or unusual, whether it was a device someone was using, or the way Alphans were doing things, or even how they lived.

One thing we noticed was the number of people living on the oceans. Alphans had developed many cities at sea, or aqua cities. They were sizeable floating layouts including elaborate homes, business complexes and even parks. Every dwelling on the huge barges was close to the shoreline.

"A bit ostentatious," Whitney observed.

I thought they were gorgeous. For the Alphans who made homes there, it looked like the ultimate in luxury, with lots of playful activities to do in and around the ocean. We found dozens of aqua cities, some permanently fixed in a calm location, others slowly drifting around the planet. Alphans by the dozens could be seen lying in lounge chairs in front of their homes, enjoying the good life.

"Is that what matters most?" Whitney remarked. "Lying around in the sun all day?"

"Sure beats working," I said, defending the Alphans.

On the mainland we found many interesting types of land-based vehicles. The Alphans had two primary car types. One looked rather traditional in body with the addition of a flat bottom, while the other looked like a large skateboard design. The latter had two wide wheels, which ran before and behind the passenger compartment, and they had excellent cornering abilities. They also had an array of flat-bottomed motorcycles, which employed air and magnetic forces to enable them to hover over the ground.

"Hardly anything relies on conventional tires," Jessica mentioned.

"Amazing, isn't it?" I agreed. "So, do you have a meeting planned for this too?"

"I have a few in mind," she said. "No reason to get ahead of ourselves."

Whitney and I analyzed the neighborhoods of Alpha 17. Their homes looked like upside-down cones with large round bases and pointy tops, similar to shapes we had seen from the downtown buildings though not so tall. Some were shaped like pyramids. The neighborhoods were packed with them.

"More units occupy a smaller amount of land," I realized. "The lots are small, but the homes are quite spacious. "

"Very good, Jon," Whitney said. "And what do you think these huge, sun-facing windows are for?"

"Tanning rooms?"

"Ha-ha."

We looked through the glass at several of the homes and found plants and fruits growing.

Whitney remarked, "There aren't any notable wires coming into the homes. I wonder if they're also getting solar energy from these windows."

"Why not?" I added. "Food and energy. Sounds like being totally self-sufficient."

It was in the streets and playgrounds on Alpha 17 where I found two dynamic toys. One was high-speed roller skates, which were long like skis and enabled the rider to travel down the road at frightening speeds. The riders wore a puffed-up body suit with padding from head to toe. They held long poles in each hand for balance as they skated powerfully down the road.

I also noticed several older kids playing with something that, at first look, I thought was just a kite. But as I watched them, I realized their feet were connected to a board hovering over the ground. As the kite was pulled by air currents, the kids jumped on their boards and were whooshed away, holding on tightly to the kite handles. They soared along and jumped over things with great distance.

"Sweet!" I said, inserting a disk and getting my notepad for sketches.

"Jim, when you get a chance, I want you to help me make some drawings here for the skates and this hoverkite thing."

"The board for the kite looks like reverse magnetism," Jim observed.

This was a concept I had begun to understand through Ian's discussions with Adams and Jessica. Many of the ground vehicles used this method, which cast a magnetic force onto a surface and then used opposing forces to float over that surface.

"Isn't it just like a hovercraft?" I asked Ian.

"No. The Alphan devices create a field of energy to float over, instead of creating a force to move. It uses less energy while accomplishing greater results."

Reverse magnetism was a big topic for weeks since it was such a large part of ground transportation.

Jessica taught me some of the basics for studying design. The skates were easy. I just had to figure out the method that made the wheels spin so fast. The hoverkite was a bit tougher. I understood the kite and harness well enough, but the trick would be designing the underside of the board. How did the battery work to cast the magnetic field, and how did the board resist that field? I had no idea. The others would be able to help though I wanted to make a contribution any way I could. Jim helped me occasionally as we went over the design and mechanics, and Whitney worked with me from time to time.

Eventually, Ian and Adams made their breakthroughs with reverse magnetism. To the amazement of everyone we were beginning to come up with designs for similar products that were refined by engineers at Maxwell Enterprises. Frank wanted to have a concise presentation for some of his investors as soon as possible. He was pleased I had done so much good work on the skates and hoverkites.

As the weeks went by, we had plenty of new information. Frank entertained investors from many different markets. Jessica made presentations at Maxwell Enterprises, and our crew loved hearing from her once she returned, often with stories of huge contracts in the works. I couldn't believe I was a part of a team about to change the world in dramatic ways.

I needed a reality check from the lab so after a long absence, I rode my bike over to the Star Bar for a beer one night. I felt bad that I hadn't seen Sam for so long.

"Well, I'll be," she said upon seeing me. "If it isn't my long-lost friend, Mr. Gruber." She poured me a beer. "We were going to send a search party after you."

"Good to see you," I said, leaning over the bar and giving her a kiss on the cheek. I put some money down on the counter.

Sam replied, "First one's on me." Then she realized how much money was there and asked, "Are you looking for change or something?"

"That's for you," I said, hoping she would forgive my absence in light of a big tip.

"I appreciate it, but seeing you is more important," she said as she pocketed the tip with a smile. "You're still working for that scientist, I assume."

"Yep."

"How's it going?" she asked.

"Great," I said, leaving it at that and drinking my beer. Sam knew it wasn't like me not to go into details.

"Can't talk about it?" she guessed.

"Nope," I said.

"Jon Gruber. You're in on something classified?" she exclaimed, as her eyes got wide with interest. A couple of drunks down the bar looked at me before returning their dull stare to the TV.

"I wish I could tell you about it, Sam. There's so much I wish I could tell you."

"Remember what I said when you first got into this?" she asked me.

"What?"

"Don't forget us little people."

I spent the night chatting with her about the men she was interested in. She caught me up to date with some of the dirty jokes from the construction sites. After a couple of beers, I got up and left her with another tip, wondering when I would be in to see her again.

"Grateful for the addition of Jess and Ian. This project is turning into a gold mine. Who would have guessed? Funny to think I used to wonder if anything would ever come of it."

- from p. 81 of Webster's journal.

Concerns

"THE GIANT PIGS have gone extinct," Whitney said.

"Really?" I asked, surprised. They used to be so common. "Are you sure?"

"There may be a few in some zoos, but there aren't any in the wilds or on the farms."

Adams looked up from his work as Whitney told of their extinction, as well as that of many of the predators who fed upon them. She gained the crew's attention and made some overall comments about what she had been finding.

"Reduced polar caps. Rise in carbon dioxide. Increased pollutants. Fewer species," Whitney reported. "The atmosphere is warmer as well."

That was not a surprise. Adams and I had both noticed a mild warming of the planet, but it did not seem drastic. Whitney believed it was more serious than it appeared. She showed us comparisons of the planet before and after the last time leap, as well as from previous eras.

"How serious do you think it is?" Jessica asked.

"I think it's very serious."

I mentioned, "Seeing planets going through change is something we've witnessed all along."

"The problem is the trend this is setting," Whitney said.

"Has the planet ever been warmer in the past, Jim?" Ian asked, chewing on his pen.

"Yes," Jim said, "in the distant past."

"But that was before animals existed," Whitney said, taking off her glasses and rubbing her eyes. "That was due to a young planet cooling off."

"How active are the winds?" Adams asked.

"Up by fifteen percent since our last leap," Jim told him.

"This concerns me the most," Whitney said to Adams and me. "All you guys have noticed are the gadgets since the time leap. You haven't even realized the changes to the environment."

"That's probably true," Adams admitted.

"They've lost a lot of species," Whitney said. "Especially the larger ones."

"But we've seen that all along," I mentioned. "Some species thrive while others die out. It's unfortunate, but isn't it also a natural part of evolution?"

"Depends on what the standards have been," Whitney replied. "What we haven't seen all along is a planet have increasingly fewer species. Usually they evolve more species over time, regardless of extinction. That goes for plant life as well."

"Perhaps intelligence brings a cost along with it," Ian said. He grabbed his pocket game player and switched it on.

We appreciated her study, but we weren't sure what to make of it. Yes, the planet showed the effects of having a modern species. Was that a bad thing? It was arguable. I felt it was better than studying the hundreds of planets in our logs that either had no life or life that was boring.

"Remember, we are not the Alphans," Jessica said, attempting to help Whitney gain a calm perspective. "We have the opportunity to study everything they can show us, the good with the bad."

Jessica was right, and even Whitney understood our fascination with the Alphans. She knew we were too excited by their technology to do anything else. The lab had already generated more original ideas in mere weeks than many corporations came up with in lifetimes.

"I just need you to be aware of this," Whitney said.

As we continued, the crew began to gel, each understanding our roles and doing what we could to make the lab most efficient. We each had our own specialty to work in, and Jim could help out where needed.

Adams, Jessica and Ian spent weeks studying engine systems, leaving Whitney and me to scan the planet for anything we could find. Whitney documented wildlife, and I made an effort to promote the fun side of Alpha 17 and continued to look for exotic toys.

I also made Ian promise he would let me participate in the testing of the first PFD. Adams and Frank had determined it was something they could design and sell through an affiliate to Maxwell Enterprises. The test models were going to be in development soon. They would be very basic compared to the Alphan models, but Ian and Adams were convinced they would work.

"If you really want to," Ian told me, "you can be the first to fly it."

The crew envisioned some unfortunate possibilities with me at the helm. Even Jim had a laugh as they told stories of me crashing due to poor judgment or having the engines cut off from a great height.

Ian explained, "The craft won't be able to cruise to a landing without power, like a plane can. It would just drop like a rock."

"If it's built well, I'm willing to take that risk."

The subject even came up about me writing a final will before the maiden voyage. I told Jim I would give him all my worldly possessions should anything happen.

Materialization

WHILE RIDING MY BICYCLE home on a breezy evening, about two months after Jessica's presentation of the hoverkite to investors, I was shocked to see a kid in my neighborhood holding a copy of the Alphan toy. I pulled over to the side of the road and watched the kid with about ten other intrigued children.

"Where did you get that?" I asked him.

"My dad's company is designing it."

"It's dangerous, you know. Does your father know you're using it?"

"He wouldn't mind."

It was a prototype, quite basic compared to the Alphan models. The boy had the kite in the air and the harness attached to his body, but he had no idea how to step on the board and keep it floating. He hadn't witnessed the art of keeping one foot in the strap and the other on the ground so he could jump onto the board after the wind had filled the kite. The other children stood by, watching with interest.

I set my bike down, walked over to the boy and said, "I can show you how it works."

"How do you know?"

"I just know."

I checked to see if the battery was activated and the magnetism was working. He let me wear his helmet, which pinched my ears badly. I explained the concepts to the kids as I put on the harness. The wind picked up. Once the kite had filled with air, I found myself pulling back hard on the reins. I pressed off with my grounded foot, jumped onto the board and let the wind guide me.

Gliding along, standing squarely on the hovering board, I was impressed by the fluid ride. I saw the ground rushing beneath me but couldn't feel anything. My hands gripped firmly to the kite handles as I traveled down the street at increasing speed. The children ran after me shouting wildly, falling further behind each second.

Standing on the board was fairly easy. Steering it proved awkward. As the wind strengthened, I shot through an intersection and became a hazard

for a set of cars. I narrowly avoided a painful accident as the drivers swerved to miss me and blasted their horns.

"Oh, shit."

I realized I had no idea how to steer the thing as I headed straight for a metal fence. The hoverkite and I hit the fence with a final sideways turn. The fence held our blow, and it threw the device and me to the ground with the impact knocking the air out of my lungs. I lay on the ground next to the toy, trying to regain some breath and composure. The children caught up to me, laughing hysterically.

"Wow, Mister," one of them said. "You just nailed yourself!"

"I'm okay," I said through my spasms for air, still attached to the device. I disconnected the harness, pulled off the helmet and felt the pain in my ribs.

"I'm ready to try it," the kid said who gave me the toy. I managed to stand, knocking the dust and pebbles from my body. I released the board's foot strap. We inspected the hoverkite, holding it up against the wind, and found no real damage. The kid was anxious to try it, never blaming me for wiping out but thankful for showing him how to get started.

"You better go somewhere more remote," I said. "Too much traffic around here."

The kids ran off to try the invention on the hillsides. I watched them proudly. Then I inspected my ribs, which brought considerable pain. I felt at least one was broken. I hobbled back to the bike and found myself unable to get on it, so I pushed it back to my apartment. I couldn't stop thinking that in just a matter of months the hoverkite went from the discovery room to the product development phase. Within a year, could it be on the market? Even through the pain of the broken rib, I couldn't stop smiling about it.

"You had to see a doctor?" Whitney asked after seeing me hobbling around at work.

"Just breaking in a new hoverkite," I said, trying to sit at my desk without bending.

"What?"

She came to my aid. I screamed when she touched my ribs. I told her the story of the great crash and my injury, yet she laughed when she realized how excited I was about the whole thing.

"How'd you break a rib?" Jim asked.

"Trying to do some tricks off a fence."

"I saw a couple of guys on the speed skates," Whitney told me, "on our way in this morning. They almost passed us in the truck."

"Probably more sons of the guys designing them," I said.

I inched my chair to the desk and began working until I heard Adams arguing with Frank and Jessica in Webster's office.

"What's that about?" I asked.

"They want to do another time leap," Whitney told me.

"They do?"

I ventured cautiously toward the hallway so I could hear the conversation better. Adams was in a heated debate with Jessica and Frank. His tone was one I hadn't heard from him.

"It's just an idea," Jessica said, trying to convince Adams to stay open-minded.

"Think about it," Frank said. "What might the next wave of products offer us?"

"We've done a pretty good job documenting everything they have," Jessica reasoned. "Why not see what the future holds?"

"And if it backfires?" Adams asked.

"Such as?" Frank asked.

"What if the planet suffers a collision with an asteroid, or a virus wipes out a third of the population? What then?"

"It's a hundred years. What makes you think that will happen?" Jessica asked him.

"Because I have no idea what will happen, therefore anything is possible," Adams said. "I realized how risky the last leap was just after we pushed the button."

"Came out fine," Frank said. "In fact, it was perfect."

"How do we know we'll have another success?" Adams asked him.

"You make a good point," Frank conceded. "But Jessica and I make good points as well. It may be a small risk, but isn't it one worth taking?"

Jessica said, "I don't want to argue with you. This is your project. It was just an idea raised by our investors."

The Alphans were so advanced as it was, I couldn't imagine them being any more advanced. Yet the idea was intriguing. I wondered what they might come up with. Would it be like another world?

Adams finally said, "I'll let the idea stew for a while."

Frank admitted, "Of course we don't want to do anything foolish."

"Part of the answer might lie in the numbers," Jessica added. "We'll find out what the investors are willing to pay for first rights to new patents."

"They want to do another leap. I never would have thought of it, but they actually want to leap a super-modern society. We've still got at least a hundred planets in our logs we haven't even checked on since the last one. What to do? Part of me thinks it's crazy, but another part is just as excited as they are. Never thought a leap would be such an issue. I'll have to think about this."

- from p. 93 of Webster's journal.

Theta 7

WHITNEY BEGAN DRIVING her own car so she could work different hours and have time alone with Jim. She probably also needed some space from Adams and me. We hadn't spoken about the kiss we shared, but I could tell Whitney was reluctant to date someone she worked with, or maybe just me. I understood, and although I would have happily dated her, I accepted the role of a good friend without pushing for more.

She would arrive at lunchtime and work with all of us for half of the day and then with Jim on her own projects afterwards. Having Jim to herself was something we all understood. One thing she was able to do was help us catch up on our logs. Ever since we found Alpha 17, we had done nothing to check up on the other known planets, nor had we looked for any new ones. Adams thought the split crew was a brilliant idea, and he encouraged me to stay late with her when I felt up to it.

Half of the nights I had the strength to stay late with her, and on other evenings I simply went home to fall asleep. Either way, I was always catching a ride with somebody. I had saved money by then, enough to make car payments, but I hadn't any time to do the shopping.

I was with Whitney the night she scanned the Theta galaxy, a small, elliptical galaxy in a far section of the universe where we hadn't done much research. Whitney was passing through a cross section of the galaxy, having Jim take notes of the star types and their positions. It was a routine that had been neglected for weeks. She cruised through the galaxy, inspecting dozens of Thetan stars, when a specific red sun caught her eye. She veered slightly from course to inspect it. She asked Jim to analyze the red star and look for any planets in its vicinity.

After some searching, Jim concluded the red giant sun had at least ten planets in its orbit. With that many, we decided to take an inventory and give them all a quick look. There was nothing remarkable about the first six. They were primarily gaseous and barren worlds.

But even from space, we could see the seventh planet was different. We could see its purplish-blue oceans and land masses of striking yellows, oranges and greens. From space it looked beautiful, and it seemed to be very warm. The technical name was Theta 7 of star gd556. It orbited a red giant sun, a large orb that lit up the planet in a thick, orange-colored atmosphere.

"This looks like the prettiest one yet," Whitney said. "Let's go in closer."

As the shot went in, we realized Theta 7 had a great variety of life. We scanned large sections of land and saw many ecosystems—savannah, grasslands, deserts and deep jungles. The air was clear, the forests thick with plants and trees, and the water in the lakes and oceans looked clean and inviting. We scanned over a white sandy beach and then the shallows of an ocean, where we saw a multitude of marine life in the clear water.

Jim reported, "It has a good blend of nitrogen, oxygen, silicon and carbon."

We scanned back over to the landmass and found wildlife in abundance. Jim took the shot deep into a savannah area, and we zoomed in on a thundering herd of hoofed mammals. The exotic beasts ran in a pack of thousands, galloping over hard ground and kicking up a whirlpool of dust in their wake. We followed them as they trampled across an established migration route, a path carved from pounding hooves and many years.

Other creatures watched the herd as well, mostly the smaller ones who dove underground as the masses thundered over them. There were also the predators hiding on the sidelines. Occasional streaking attacks encountered the herd. A group of canines made a successful lunge, singling out one of the younger beasts. Whitney rooted for the little animal to escape, but as the dogs closed in, she asked Jim to change the scene.

"Pan back toward the coastline," she said. "Take it up higher too. I want to see more from above."

The shot lifted, and the thundering herd became smaller until it was a blip that could barely be distinguished from the land. The monitor moved over a large section of coastline and the surrounding area. As the shot moved laterally over the countryside, we noticed a pattern of straight lines, rectangles and circles embedded in the landscape. There were several areas of them on the monitor, indicating something we had become familiar with from Alpha 17. Large well-defined rectangles and circles meant organization and farming.

"More intelligent life?" Whitney remarked.

"Doesn't surprise me a bit," I said. I picked up the phone and made the call to Adams at home.

Jim zoomed in on the area above the rectangular patterns. As the shot went toward the ground, we saw groomed rows of planted crops. They looked like they were doing well, with strong stalks and ripe fruit hanging from them. There were no signs of farming machinery.

As Jim readjusted the camera to follow a pathway from the rows, we were blessed with the presence of animals and farmers walking through the crops. The animals led the way. Large beasts without harnesses, they walked carefully past the rows of waist-high plants. The farmers followed, and we cheered as we saw them.

The farmers walked slowly with long strides. They carried bags around their shoulders and placed ripened fruit in them. Their walk seemed to have a rhythm to it, done patiently. We sensed the warmth of their atmosphere and the slowing effect of a humid afternoon. The farmers had smooth, brown skin and wore simple clothing around their midsection, like cloth hanging from a waistband. They were hairless on their bodies and heads. The ones we found worked casually, looking after the animals and picking choice fruit. A close-up on their faces showed them talking and laughing. Their eyes were spread wide around elongated heads, and their ears and noses were bigger than ours proportionally. They had no apparent teeth, just gummy nubs that barely showed when they opened their mouths. Their faces were very expressive. I saw them singing as they walked behind their beasts, and I sensed the enjoyment they were having.

Adams joined us within a few minutes, probably setting new speeding records along the way. Whitney gave him the data she had of the planet and the star, with Jim and me adding tidbits. Adams stared in shock as a thought came to him.

"This planet orbits a red giant?" he asked in surprise. Whitney and I should have thought of that as well, but we had been too absorbed in the new life to have recognized the oversight.

Like any burning object, a sun gradually lost its fuel. As that happened to red giants like the Thetan star, an interesting thing occurred. As its own gravitational pressures relaxed, the red stars actually expanded to many times their size. Red giants were in a state of massive growth, and they often engulfed their nearest orbiting planets and caused instability for those further out in orbit. After exhausting their resources over millions of years, the red giants would wear out and collapse back into themselves, often dragging a majority of their old solar system with them and making orphans of the planets remaining in space.

Red giants were not wonderful stars to be living under. They were in a state of change happening much faster than at previous eras. Seeing algae and primitive life growing on Theta 7 would not have been a surprise, but seeing mammals and people, and knowing how many millions of years it took for them to evolve is what made it surprising.

"I guess we don't know everything about evolution yet," I offered.

Adams sat down and asked Jim a number of questions about the star. Jim confirmed that the red star was indeed expanding. The rate was likely to be nearly one percent each hundred years. At that rate, the sun was doubling its size about every seven thousand years, not nearly the kind of stability we associated with advanced life forms.

"I don't think those numbers can be right," Adams reasoned.

"That's the best I can figure without doing a time leap," Jim replied.

We spent the evening scanning around Theta 7. All night we continued to find villages and farms spread across the globe. Some villages were small, but we also found others containing thousands of visible huts and people walking about. Theta 7 was surprisingly populated, more so than it appeared from above. The construction went beyond simple architecture. Some of the cities had large structures in beautiful design built of stone, clay and metal. Again we saw the conical shape in some dwellings similar to ones from Alpha 17, just built with basic materials.

The villages were very well kept. Even the largest cities appeared to be manicured. We also found artwork, statues, symbols of nature and what appeared to be temples with dramatic designs. People sat outside them in prayer or meditation. Other people walked about dancing.

They danced in groups and they danced alone, making mystical body movements and allowing themselves to be taken over with the moment. I found it fairly bizarre, but Whitney couldn't have been happier with her discovery.

"I love everything about this planet," Whitney said, watching a group of elders dancing, moving her arms as they did.

The people and lifestyle were so simple, yet something about them was quite appealing. Many of the people wore elegant robes, some of basic colors and others in dazzling displays. Other people, like the farmers, wore very little clothing made of the simplest cloth. Most of the children were naked.

There was nothing of technology to be found. Carts were pulled by beasts and not machines. There were no wires, no power plants, no electric lights.

Many of the villages had elaborate layouts with a central design. Near the middle of the villages were beautiful structures we presumed to be temples. Outside and nearby the temples, Thetans sat as if in meditation.

"With such long limbs," Whitney noted, "they seem very flexible to be sitting cross-legged."

Despite living under a red giant, Theta 7 appeared to be a comfortable planet to live on. It was primarily tropical with no polar caps, yet it maintained a series of continents with pleasant temperatures and a huge variety of nature.

Whitney had Jim take a collection of faces from the Thetan people and come up with a general look based on patterns. She then had Jim match results to a generic Alphan face. As we looked at the two composite faces side by side on the screen, the Alphans had lighter, off-white complexions with a thin coat of hair over their entire bodies. The Thetan skin was darker and their bodies were hairless, even on their heads. The Alphans had smaller, more compact heads, while the Thetan head was elongated. The Alphans were shorter and stockier. They had ears and noses that looked like indentations. The Thetans were taller and thinner, and their movements were far more graceful. The Thetans also had more pronounced ears and noses, and they had eyes similar to ours in size and angle, yet spread a bit wider around the head. The Alphans had larger, more circular eye openings.

"The differences are due to the physical traits of their planets," Adams said.

He had Jim calculate the time in years it would take for a message to be sent from one planet to the other, if they knew of each other's existence and attempted communication through radio signals. Jim figured that one planet would have to wait about twenty thousand years for the message to be received. The idea made no sense anyway, since the Thetans had no means of sending or receiving such a signal.

Even though they occupied worlds simultaneously in the same universe, there was basically no chance that they would ever know about each other, nor would they know about any of those other worlds because they were so far away from them. It made me think our situation was probably the same. Our universe was probably teeming with life, even intelligent life, but the chances of us ever connecting with it were very slim.

"Got a call tonight. We found Theta 7, our second planet with society! Strangest thing, orbits a red giant. Must have recently changed from a yellow star. Doubt they have much

time left. Polar caps are gone already. Shame they're so primitive, probably a thousand years from technology. Whitney fond of them. Hope she doesn't get too attached."

- from p. 97 of Webster's journal.

Conflict of Interest

FRANK WAS ABLE to persuade Adams to do another time leap. He made arrangements with three groups of investors to pay for first access to new patents. These were the same people who were currently working on Alphan transportation, construction design and energy sources. Adams agreed to it as long as we kept the investors away from the lab. He didn't want a crowd lusting after every single thing behind the monitors. Maxwell Enterprises was better suited for presentations anyway.

Because of the time constraints, the crew worked extra long days and some nights to finish our Alphan studies. We became fixated with the idea of pushing the button forward another hundred orbits and speculating over what might be possible. We spent the next week recording everything of interest that we could find on both Alpha 17 and Theta 7, the latter not having anything of scientific importance. Though we still had no idea how some of the Alphan products worked, Ian was confident we could put many of the pieces together at a later date.

Adams agreed with him. "Having video records should be enough."

Everyone except Whitney was excited for the future. Whitney had always found the Alphans to be disturbing and self-indulgent. She preferred to spend her time studying Theta 7.

She said, "I'd like to know how a society can live comfortably under a red giant star."

Adams admitted, "I'd like to know too, but I don't think we have the time to figure that out."

"What's going to happen to the Thetans if we make the leap?" Jim asked.

"Not sure," Adams said. "We can hope for the best. They've already lost their polar caps."

The main problem we faced was that the universe generator was designed for time leaps of millions to billions of standard orbits. Adams had no idea he'd be studying people when he put it together. He planned on studying stars and planets, and he set limits based on those guidelines.

Trying to get the leaps to be as small as possible was a matter of finding out how quickly Jim could perform all the necessary tasks. It had worked once already, but Adams did not have confidence in it working correctly every time. If things didn't go exactly to plan, Jim's estimate of Alphan orbits was likely to be off by a multiple.

Adams asked Jim, "What is your best estimate on this?"

"If all goes well, maybe ninety standard orbits."

"How would that correspond to Alpha 17?" Ian asked.

"Slightly over a hundred years."

Whitney recorded as much about Theta 7 as she could, for Adams didn't need to explain to her that there was a chance the people would not be around after the time leap.

"It's important to remember this is an experiment," Jessica told her. "The people are real and the situation they face is real, but as scientists, we shouldn't become overly attached to them."

"That feels a little cold to me," Whitney said.

"I don't mean it to," Jessica added. "I care for them too. I'd like to see them around for centuries."

"I know."

"We're scientists," Adams reminded her. "We have to maintain our ability to observe without wanting to interfere. It will probably be a thousand years before they have electricity, and by then their own star will have killed them."

Jessica and Ian appreciated the beauty of the Thetan world, but they spent little time examining it because they were hired to study technology. The Thetans hadn't even invented primitive weapons, and they were far from something like a steam engine.

"But don't you see the beauty of this world?" Whitney asked us. "There's no fighting, even among the children. There's no hustle and bustle in the streets. They live without worry or struggle and they dance in public. And see how they talk with one another? Conversations usually involve holding hands or arms in some fashion."

"Seems a little touchy-feely to me," Ian whispered.

One evening, Whitney and I were scanning around a coastal Thetan village. Ian and Jessica had finished for the day and were on their way out. Adams was organizing his own things. He looked over occasionally to Whitney's monitor as she took notes on the village. One of the larger buildings in the area had dozens of children around and within it, and we assumed it to be a school.

Thetan children played on the grounds there—some with balls, others in group dance and games, and some on jungle gyms. Others sat in meditative positions. As we watched the children practicing on the assortment of bars, we saw them perform tremendous acrobatics. Even the smallest children did flipping stunts with precision though there were no adults supervising. Some of the larger children climbed very high on the bars and did amazing stunts from the top.

"That looks like fun," Jim said. "I wish I could do something like that."

"It looks like somebody could get hurt out there," I added.

"What does pain feel like?"

"Like the opposite of fun," I told him. "You know, Jim, in some ways you have it really good. You don't have to eat, don't have to go to the bathroom and you don't even know what it's like to feel pain."

As I spoke, one of the kids on the high bars slipped and fell. He crashed to the ground and lay still. His head was bent at an awkward angle to his body. Whitney shrieked as it happened. Adams came over.

Seeing the Thetan boy lying motionless in that sickening position made me think he had died or at least had severely broken bones. As he lay on the ground, I began to feel pain in my ribs, even though my injury had mostly healed. I held my ribs from the increasing pain.

"What's happening?"

The other children climbed down from the bars and gathered around the fallen boy. They slowly straightened his head and limbs. Six of them sat beside him and placed their hands on various parts of his body. They sat with closed eyes and still hands, touching him on all sides. The other children didn't seem overly concerned. Only a small group gathered behind the hand-layers to watch. No adults were present. The children continued what they did as we watched in silence. The pain in my ribs began to subside. I assumed I must have punched myself upon the jolt of seeing the accident.

The hurt child eventually opened his eyes. The others got up from his side to help him stand. To our shock, the hurt child stood. Then he did something that seemed impossible. He climbed the high bars and resumed his play on the apparatus. The other kids went about their play as before, taking no special notice or concern for the boy who had just fallen.

"That was really strange," Whitney said.

"How did they do that?" I asked.

"I don't know," Adams said, shaking his head and watching the boy do a trick from the high bars. "I guess he wasn't that hurt."

"What are you guys talking about?" Jim asked.

"One boy was hurt, now he's not. What they just did was unique," Whitney explained.

"I'd be happy to trade places with you if I could, Jon," Jim said, still thinking about our conversation from before. "Believe it or not, I'd like to know what being hurt feels like."

"Maybe we can figure out a way for you to experience some of these things," I said, suddenly feeling bad for my remarks to Jim. Adams raised an eyebrow at me in an effort not to get Jim's hopes up for something unrealistic.

"Something strange happened today. A Thetan boy was badly injured. Or was he? A group of children seemed to heal him with a laying of hands. Straight out of a fantasy novel. Could that have really been what it seemed? If not, why would they have put on a show? For who? I can't stop thinking of it. Whitney is more interested in them than ever, and the next leap is scheduled in days."

- from p. 99 Webster's journal.

The PFD

I SPENT PART OF MY WEEK on the other side of town at Maxwell Enterprises as a consultant and test pilot for the personal flying device. It was like a dream coming true.

We took a prototype out to the desert for testing. Jessica and Ian accompanied Frank, me, three other engineers and some mechanics as we set out to attempt our first flight. Adams and Whitney had opted to stay behind and work though they made sure we recorded it so they could review it later. Jim had reminded me not to try any tricks on the first outing. Whitney had said a prayer that nothing harmful might happen and gave me a kiss for good luck. It was becoming known among the crew, there was something between us.

We arrived at the desert and rolled the PFD out of the truck and down the ramp. A wonderful feeling came over me as I realized I would be the first on my planet to fly one. The prototype was similar to the PFDs from Alpha 17 though ours was completely basic. It was about fifteen feet tall and twelve feet wide, in the shape of a cross or t. The outer part was the metal framing for the hundreds of small, rotating turbine engines. The inner part was the captain's chamber, where the pilot stood with his arms out comfortably to the side. The frame was made of ultra-light metal bars, and it was left open to the wind though the finished products would be encased in clear plastic around the pilot.

The power for our model was provided by jet fuel and hundreds of revolving turbines, each one with a specific angle and force that could be altered depending on the intention of the pilot. Ian, Jessica and I had been over the operations for several weeks since we had been studying the Alphan device with great scrutiny.

The most interesting part of the PFD was how the pilot operated it. There was not a myriad of controls, as one might assume, but simply areas for parts of the body to conform to. I stepped into the chamber, slipping rather comfortably into the pilot's zone. The contours of the area by my legs and feet fit snugly, as well as that around my arms and hands. Several safety belts held my neck, torso and waist, and were designed to use in unison, which had almost the same ease as putting on a seat belt. My fingers wrapped comfortably around molds, which were similar to joysticks.

Ian reminded me, "Squeezing the mold gives the proper adjustment to the force of the turbines, and pushing them where you want to go is the only function you do. Move your body the ways you want to go."

"Seems way too simple to work," I said.

I put on my helmet and checked that I could hear Ian's voice through my earpiece.

"Good luck," he said.

The men released the safety lines and backed away from the device. I flipped on the main power switch and heard the high-pitched whine of the turbines. I waited for a moment, allowing the idling system to warm up. The group of engineers monitored equipment displaying facets of the device. I inspected the lightweight cage around me and was surprised it was as strong as Ian had said.

Ian reminded me through my earpiece, "You should be able to survive a crash from five stories high."

Then Jessica's voice came through, "Don't go nearly that high, Jon. Keep it under twenty feet."

One of the engineers gave me the thumbs up that enough time had elapsed for the turbines to be warm. It was my cue to get going. The initial test was to lift the device off the ground and stay there. I slowly squeezed the two handles, appreciating their mold to my fingers and palms. The turbines whined at a higher pitch and the craft began to rise. The sudden movement startled me, and I released my grip causing the craft to settle roughly back down. I looked over to the others in slight embarrassment. Ian frowned, though Jessica laughed pleasantly.

Frank waved to me to go for it again. The second time, I would not let go. I squeezed the handles again but with less pressure, and the craft slowly and steadily climbed a few feet in the air. I imagined myself staying still.

"The height is good. Is everything okay?" Ian's voice came through my helmet.

"Yes!"

The next test was to set the craft back down gently. I relaxed my grip and lowered my arms and weight, setting it down slowly. This time it landed softly to a round of applause. I climbed back up to my original height and then imagined the device climbing higher to ten feet. I opened my eyes and realized I was hovering at ten feet over the desert floor in a PFD. I yelled with Joy. It was totally thrilling even though I had yet to move forward.

That was the third test, to move forward for some distance. I pushed forward slightly with my arms, hands and head, and the device began to move smoothly across the desert floor.

Ian's voice came through my headset, "Shift to the left a little. You're banking right." I made the adjustment and was told, "Hold that line."

Then I stopped the device, still hovering about ten feet over ground.

Test number four was to spin the device 180 degrees. I couldn't decide which way to turn, but eventually moved back with my right elbow and forward with my left arm and the same with my midsection and legs. The effect was amazing. The device smoothly performed the spin exactly as I wanted. I couldn't believe it. I felt like I had made a connection. It was like moving in water.

Ian's voice came through my helmet, "Try moving backward slowly."

This was the first deviation from the schedule, which was supposed to be returning to the original position. I obliged him and moved the craft slowly backward. I could sense as the craft either gained or lost slight levels of elevation, and I compensated with my body weight. The delight in combining machinery with simplicity was overwhelming, and I found myself unable to stop laughing. Ian reminded me to stay calm.

"I'm remaining as calm as I can!" I shouted.

Then Ian's voice came through, "Return to moving forward."

I obliged him with more sharpness in my response. He asked me to turn left as I went, and I made a slight adjustment to which the PFD banked beautifully. Next he asked me to make a right turn, which I did with easy control. It was unlike my experience on the hoverkite. Steering the PFD felt completely natural, as it was designed to adjust to my body movements. It seemed to know where I wanted to go.

I set it down at the original point and let Ian and Jessica make an inspection and get data on how much power was used during those first few minutes.

Frank asked me, "Are you ready for more?"

"Are you kidding?" I could hardly wait to take the thing out into the open air.

Ian said, "Fly around in large circles and see how it feels."

I flew straight ahead and was able to stop quickly. I turned at sharp angles without losing or gaining altitude.

I told Ian, "I think it's necessary to break the twenty-foot barrier."

"I'd advise you against it," his reply came through my helmet, but there was nothing he could do to stop me.

I flew to a height of about fifty feet, where I performed my first stunt.

I actually did a barrel roll, and it felt as simple as doing a somersault on the lawn. I could hear Jessica and Frank yelling encouragements through Ian's microphone as I did another barrel roll.

Ian reminded me, "Do you have any idea how expensive that thing is?" but I could also hear Frank yelling, "Go for it!"

The highlight of the day was a loop-de-loop performed just over their heads. I finally took Ian's advice and set the craft down after a five-minute free ride. The experiment had gone much better than planned. As they assisted me out of the device, they listened intently as I explained how it felt. I was an instant celebrity.

We returned to the lab with the video of it and watched it all again with Adams, Whitney and Jim. We discussed the level of freedom and excitement this was going to bring to people's lives. I proclaimed this single device might be as liberating for people today as the automobile was over a hundred years ago. Adams made a note of it in his booklet.

"I've seen the fruits of our labor. Jon is a natural ambassador for Alphan technologies."
  - from p. 102 of Webster's journal.

Demise

WHITNEY SHOWED UP for work the next day much later than normal. The long schedule was probably wearing on her just as it was on the rest of us. She didn't look well, and I thought perhaps she had come down with a cold. Adams asked her how she was feeling. She didn't answer, her face locked in a deep concern I had never seen from her.

"What's the matter?" Adams asked.

"I had a dream," she said. "More like a nightmare."

"What's wrong?"

She begged him, "Please don't make the leap tomorrow."

"But it's been scheduled for weeks. You know that."

"Can it be postponed or even cancelled?"

"What's this all about?"

"Please don't do it, Dad!" She put her hand to her temples.

Adams insisted she sit down since she sounded so distraught.

Whitney told us of the dream she had just before getting out of bed. "I saw the planet as a violent landscape, totally without life. It was devastating." She became even more upset as she explained the feeling of despair and sadness it had caused her.

Adams told her, "Whit, you need to recognize the facts. There's no stopping the expansion of that red star. Besides, even if we wanted to do something for them, there's nothing we can do."

"We could delay the leap," she pleaded with him.

"It's out of my hands. Frank has a dozen investors lined up to see the results and make offers. This is how it must be, Whitney. Surely you can understand that."

"I just don't want to lose them."

Whitney began to cry as she coped with the inevitable. Theta 7 was doomed, and there was nothing we could do.

I took her for a long walk to get her out of the lab and into some fresh air. We held hands for part of the way and spoke very little. There was nothing I could say that would make her feel any better. Whitney had already experienced great loss in her lifetime, a loss I could not imagine. Now she was poised for another. A few chosen words were unlikely to soothe her feelings.

The fresh air and the walk seemed to help. It was mid-summer, and she appreciated the trees, the birds and the tall grasses in the meadow. We walked around the pond to the far edge of the property and threw a few stones in the water. *Splash*. I watched the ripples as they raced across the calm water to the other shore.

"It's beautiful out here," I said, breaking the silence.

"It is," Whitney added.

We remained there for a couple of hours. We stayed until it was time for Adams and the others to end their shift. When we returned to the lab, it was nearing sunset. Adams met us at the front door as he was locking up for the night. Ian and Jessica had already left. I was glad to see Adams outside waiting for us. The lifting of Whitney's spirits would have been dampened by returning to the Thetan monitors.

Adams drove us to his house, where I got on my bike as he and Whitney went inside. As I rode to my apartment, I thought how odd it was that Whitney was so much more sensitive than the rest of us. The crew had little trouble distancing ourselves from anything occurring within that universe, except for Whitney. Even watching prey fall victim to predators was distressing to her. I thought it unlikely that she would be able to continue with us after we had lost the life on Theta 7. I wondered if she would be there the next day, if she would be able to witness the time leap and its results.

As the time approached for us to make the leap, Ian and I made bets on how far advanced the Alphans would be. We speculated that when we saw them next, they might have inventions that we would not be able to understand, the consensus being there were no limits to what we might find. Frank called Jessica and told us not to wait for him. He was entertaining clients at Maxwell Enterprises and lining up future business.

Adams spent some private time with Whitney as she was forced to conclude her study of the Thetans and simply hope for the best. Then she announced she was ready for the leap.

As Jim released the hydrogen for the mini-leap, the galaxies didn't budge. The effect created a few moments of blurring planetary images before returning to stable positions. The mini-leaps were quite boring in comparison to the leaps of old. Adams and I used to watch several million standard orbits whiz by at a time. Here we were witnessing around a hundred years, or 1/100,000 the size of old leaps.

The planets stabilized. The cameras and monitors went through their readjustment period. I was so excited, I was afraid to look.

Jim announced, "Theta 7 is not in its orbit."

Adams remarked, "Perhaps it's already been pulled into the gravity of the star."

Whitney curled up into a ball in her chair. I could sense her holding back the emotions. I rubbed her shoulders, trying to console her.

Then Jim announced, "I might have found it."

Whitney lifted her eyes to the monitor as the camera adjusted. The shot came in and identified a planet with purplish-blue oceans and landmasses of yellows, oranges and greens. The monitors closed in on the small world. It was Theta 7, looking much the same as before. Adams stared in surprise as Jim gave a readout of physical characteristics. Little had changed, except that the planet was slightly further away in orbit from its star.

"That's Theta 7?" Adams asked. "Are you sure this orbit reading is accurate?"

"Yep," Jim replied.

Whitney's voice cracked with anticipation, "Jim, zoom in closer. Get a closer look."

As the view took us from the space shot down through the atmosphere and eventually to the surface, we saw it was very much the same as before. The villages and cities were intact, and the people were still there, comfortably.

"Thank heaven," Whitney said. Her eyes welled up.

The farmers and other people went about their lives as before. Jim reported consistent temperatures with no increase in winds.

Adams wondered aloud, "What would cause it to have a different orbit?"

Jessica touched Whitney on the shoulder. "I'm glad they're okay."

"Thank you."

Then the monitors showing Alpha 17 began to come into focus. We turned our attention to them, feeling the excitement level in the room returning. As the shot zoomed closer to Alpha 17, I could see the atmosphere was clouded with a thick haze. As it went ever closer, the haze made it difficult for us to view the surface. Weather patterns swirled much more intensely, and we immediately realized something was different.

"One hundred twenty orbits," Jim reported.

"Are we sure that's Alpha 17?" I asked.

"Positive," Jim said.

We attempted to zoom into the ground but could not get a clear view through the turbulent surface winds. We saw glimpses and ground areas during lulls, but mostly we saw wind and sand sweeping by assorted landmarks.

"Oh no," Adams said.

"Looks like it's in the middle of a hurricane," Jessica added, pointing out the debris that was strewn on the surface and in the skies.

"Jim, can you get estimates on temp and wind speeds?" Adams asked.

"Average temperature higher by thirty degrees," Jim reported. "Average wind speed at forty knots per hour, gusts at over four hundred."

Alpha 17 was in the midst of a global storm. The skies were a whirling mess of dirt and debris. The oceans had risen and grown fierce, sending huge waves crashing into the land far beyond the previous coastline. Soot and ash were everywhere.

"It looks like it's been in a war," Ian commented.

What remained of the cities were bits and pieces. We found remnants of buildings and structures severely eroded by wind and sand, as if storms had beaten them for years. We scanned across to other continents and islands. The cities were deserted. Lights didn't come on in the night areas. We searched for hours for any signs of people.

"Found some," Jim finally announced.

We saw a group of three male Alphans scurrying about during one of the lulls in the winds. They wore rags for clothing and looked emaciated. We wondered what they were finding for food. They moved quickly and returned to the underground. The sighting was brief and inconclusive, leaving us theorizing over how many were alive and what kind of existence it was.

"Perhaps they can grow underground plants or fungus," Ian said, chewing the tip of his pen to a pulp.

"Maybe they can sift through the debris during lulls," I said.

"For what?" Whitney wondered.

"How many of them could be living down there?" Jessica asked.

Jim searched for wildlife. The savannahs were deserted. We could only find rodents living in holes in the ground. They came out to look for food when the winds died down.

Frank called and was on his way. Jessica and Ian sat in silence as we scanned across the areas where we knew great cities once existed. The skeletal remains of the buildings barely stood a story high, eroded by wind. I felt horrible. I couldn't believe it had happened. I watched the monitors in despair with the others. Adams didn't talk about it. He and Jim spent the day going over the planet, scanning every surface feature. It was a long and painful experience.

"How did it happen?" Frank asked upon arrival.

"We're trying to figure that out," Adams said, rubbing his eyes. "This wasn't such a good idea after all."

"We couldn't have predicted this," Frank said, pointing to the monitor.

"Maybe we could have avoided it," Adams replied.

"We took a chance," Jessica reminded him. "We all agreed to it. We took a gamble that didn't work. Don't blame us or yourself for trying, Webster."

"How can I not blame myself for letting them slip away?"

Ian and Frank agreed with Jessica. We were taking calculated risks and had been since we began the venture. We had already profited more than any of us had dreamed possible.

The feeling of despair settled in as the evening came. We left for the night in somber quiet.

The following days gave us time to mourn for them. We took plenty of physical data, though the results remained inconclusive.

Speculation ranged from natural disaster to artificial disaster to drastic climate change brought on by the Alphans, but we wouldn't know. Not knowing its final chapter was fitting since we never really knew its middle chapters either. Our knowledge of Alpha 17 was like picking up a book somewhere within it, reading some good parts and then skipping to the last page to find out everybody died. Then the book was taken from our hands. We simply would not know the whole story of Alpha 17, and we had no choice but to move on.

"We lost them. How could I have been so stupid?"
   - from p. 105 of Webster's journal.

Meditation

WE STUDIED THETA 7 and its intriguing people. Adams tried to figure out how their planet had moved further away in orbit from its sun.

"Planets don't move like this," he said. "There must be a cause."

He came up with two theories to explain it. First, that the red giant star was somehow pushing the planet away as it expanded. The theory sounded plausible, but even I was skeptical since all the other red giants in the universe did not work that way, nor were the other planets in the Thetan solar system responding similarly. The second theory was that a rogue asteroid had passed very close to it, so close that it altered the orbit of Theta 7. This theory also sounded good, but it fell under the skepticism that the life forms might have been horribly shaken by such an event, or the Thetan moon might have been knocked slightly out of orbit, which was not the case.

The orbit of the planet may have been the only thing that changed. Jim took the latest physical data of Theta 7 and recorded the updated village layouts. He made comparisons to the world we knew a hundred years back and concluded what we could tell just by looking at it—that not much, if anything, had changed.

"Don't know what to make of it," Adams said to Frank. "It's the only example in the universe we've seen do this."

"When might they experience some technical advances?" Frank asked.

"I don't know," Adams said. "It's just a simple culture at this point."

"I'd love to be able to do something with them," Jessica commented.

"Perhaps in a few more time leaps?" Frank asked.

"I'd love to leap them," Adams told us, keeping his voice from Whitney, "but it's risky. That red sun is expanding, and I doubt they'll be so lucky again in five hundred or a thousand years."

"So what do we do?" Jessica asked.

"Keep looking for newcomers," Adams said. "If it comes to it, we'll take the risk with Theta, but for now, I suggest we look for others."

Ian and Jessica stayed busy going over past recordings of Alphan products that we had yet to understand. Adams divided his time with them and with Jim, trying to figure out how Theta 7's orbit had changed. I returned to my past routine of scanning new solar systems for planets with any signs of life, hopefully intelligent life. Whitney had the people of Theta 7 mostly to herself.

Whitney noticed an interesting pattern. The layout of the Thetan villages was consistent. Each village was arranged in the shape of a large circle. The inner parts contained the public grounds, the temples, food carts and merchants while the outer parts were where the homes and farms were settled. At the very center of the villages was a large, round podium, like an elevated stage for speeches or performances.

Whitney was intrigued. Even villages from opposite sides of the planet had the same design.

"How can they have unity in design," Whitney wondered, "without any modern devices?"

Whitney's favorite village on the planet was nestled in a cove by the ocean. She referred to it as Coasttown. An inlet from the sea brought in the ocean, and the seawater crashed up against rock walls. The effect made beautiful rainbow mists at sunset and dawn. It became Whitney's model village for the planet.

Coasttown, like all Thetan villages, had its central podium. Whitney eventually realized the round stages were a place of morning ritual. The podiums were only used in the early hours of the morning, just before dawn. For the rest of the day and night, they sat empty.

Whitney documented the daily ritual there. Every morning, a group of six Thetans wearing plain white gowns convened at the podium. They arrived as the last hour of darkness still covered their village. They walked up the podium steps and sat in a circle in deep meditation for about an hour, until the red sun appeared over the horizon. As dawn broke, the group of six would end their session and leave the podium.

Then the village would become busy with the day's activity. Only after the sessions, would merchants bring out their goods and farmers arrive with carts of food. Whitney and Jim checked in on several different villages across Theta 7 and confirmed each one had a podium and followed this same routine at dawn. Some of the other Thetans meditated outdoors at their residences during the hour. It became an inspiration for Whitney.

"This is unbelievable," she realized. "Do you see what they're doing?"

As she inspected the matter further, she discovered there was always a group of Thetans meditating at a podium, since dawn was always happening somewhere. Whitney pointed out a meditation zone existed somewhere on the planet at every moment.

"So?" I said.

"Don't you appreciate the organization involved?" Whitney asked as she faced blank stares from the rest of us. "They don't have telephone lines or computers," she told Ian. "They don't have highways or flyways," she told Jessica. "And yet they all know this ritual at spots across the globe and do it every dawn of every day."

Adams sought a logical explanation. "It's noteworthy, but I don't see why that's so incredible. Maybe they started off with a doctrine that said the cities will be in a circle, and you will meditate in the center at dawn. As the tribes spread across the land, so did the doctrine."

"That's good, Dad, and a possibility, but don't you see, this is something they enjoy doing. This isn't being forced on them. And what about the change in their orbit? What are the chances these things could be related?"

It took a moment until Adams burst out laughing, followed by Ian, Jess and even me. The idea that meditating people could move planets was ridiculous to all of us. Adams finally said, "It's a phenomenon we can't yet explain, but there's no way the Thetans are somehow responsible."

In fact, Adams was more or less bored with the Thetans. He appreciated their existence as much as he would any culture within the project. But the Alphans were a tough act to follow. After the thrill of watching them, it was difficult to spend time with the Thetans and not be bored. They were agonizingly slow in just about everything. The only time I saw them move quickly was when the school kids practiced acrobatics, and even that grew old after a while. Whitney and Jim loved them, but Frank felt the same as the rest of us. The Thetans were a fascinating tribe of people, but they didn't have any technology that perked our interest. Perhaps in a few hundred to a thousand orbits, they could develop those things. Unfortunately, we estimated they wouldn't be around for that long under the influence of their expanding sun.

Whitney became enthralled with the idea of the meditation podiums. Every day, she watched the group convene at the podium in Coasttown. The same six Thetans gathered there in the wee hours of the morning, and Whitney became familiar with their group. One of them in particular caught her attention, an older Thetan woman who always sat next to the empty spot in the circle during the meditation. Whitney dubbed her The Grandmother since she appeared to be a very wise and respected member of the village.

After about a week, Whitney decided to meditate with them. She brought a padded mat from home and placed it on the floor. She lit a candle in the foreground. She removed her shoes and sat in a relaxed pose with her eyes closed. Her breathing quieted, and she remained sitting for about an hour in a peaceful state alongside the Thetans on her monitors. Once the Thetan sun began to rise, signaling the end of the session, Whitney came out of her meditation.

This became a daily habit. At the day's end, once Jessica and Ian had left for the night, Whitney and Jim would identify the sunrise line on Theta 7 and then find a village center and morning meditation group and join them. She preferred to use the Coasttown Group whenever the times overlapped, but sometimes they didn't, and then she used another village podium. She loved it regardless of which group she was with, and over the following days, she brought even more items to add to the spread: flowers, incense and more candles. She even made photocopies of certain Thetans like The Grandmother and the others from her group, and she placed their faces around her, emulating the circle.

Whitney and Jim became addicted. They looked forward to their evening meditation more than anything. Adams didn't mind that Jim liked to participate, so long as it was the last hour of the evening and he didn't need Jim's help. When they meditated, I usually helped Adams with other studies and gave them space and quiet. After a week, Whitney seemed to slip into it quite easily, sitting perfectly still and focused for an hour or more.

"It's wonderful," Whitney said after coming out of a session. "Something about doing it with them makes it an incredible experience."

I was skeptical. "Just sitting there?"

"Hard to believe, I know."

"Maybe we could all try it together?" Jim asked.

That would be a sight, all five of us sitting down for an hour in a meditative trance. Unlikely, I thought.

They persuaded me to try it, and I found it rather soothing though I wasn't nearly as excited about it as they were. For starters, it hurt my legs to sit still in one spot for an hour. I also had trouble keeping my eyes closed without having to check the monitors and see if the Thetans were still meditating. Somehow, Whitney never had to do that. She simply came out of it at the same time as they did. Jim said he could tell when it had ended too. While Jim meditated, his green light dwindled down to the lowest level I had seen. I couldn't understand how Jim could meditate or how he could tell when the sessions had ended, and I became suspicious he was just pretending to be involved.

"How do you feel when you meditate?" I asked Jim.

"I don't know how to describe it."

"Like a deep relaxation?"

"Yeah, but also a connection."

"To what?"

"I don't know," was his reply, and he left it at that.

Adams didn't understand Jim's interest in it but found it acceptable for him to participate. I thought it was a little odd yet something I couldn't argue with. Frank probably wouldn't have objected.

When Jessica found out, she commented, "It's a bit unprofessional, especially allowing Jim to participate instead of staying busy with other work."

There was still a list of things from Alpha 17 we were trying to comprehend, not to mention the need to find new planets with societies. Whitney continued her night sessions with the Thetans anyway.

In the course of choosing random Thetan villages at dawn, Jim and Whitney were not only getting a workout in meditation, but they were also developing a detailed map of the planet's villages, the people and their ways. Over the following days, I admitted to Whitney that she was right. The Thetans were intriguing.

Thetans were the first people I had encountered who didn't hurry. They played games and were fast runners and great leapers, especially the children, but they never rushed through their day. Life was easy and pleasant. Farming was one of the most common occupations, but the men and women who ran the farms did their tasks in a carefree manner, as opposed to busting their butts. The tailors, blacksmiths and merchants also had an air of calm about them as if there was no need for competitive selling.

It was also unclear if Thetans used a form of currency. Merchants of all types of products left their shops and carts completely open in the village markets, and they did not usually deal with the customers. Many merchants delivered a cart of goods and then left it in the open village streets. Thetans came and took what they needed. We never documented any form of money changing hands, making it unclear how their businesses worked.

I asked, "How does everyone know what to bring or who owes whom for what?"

Whitney had no answer besides, "It works for them."

They were consistently healthy, happy and peaceful. In fact, we could not find any examples of wealth or poverty. The huts were very much the same throughout the villages.

Aside from the meditation podiums, it was not clear if Thetans had a schedule. We found no clocks or watches. The children walked and danced to and from school at all times of the day. And while they were there, it wasn't clear what they were learning or who was teaching.

Many Thetan schools had no adults at all, just children. Some kids sat in rooms, others played games and danced, and others sat in meditation groups. Food was provided by larger children in a random fashion. They ate simple grains and fruits, eating small amounts very slowly. The children left the school grounds at random times as individuals or in small groups, not all at once as is usually associated with schools and schedules.

As Thetans socialized, we noticed a lot of contact between them. Thetans held each other as they spoke, not in a sexual way but as a part of their communication. They also held arms and hands frequently when walking in pairs.

Although it didn't happen often, we found apparent examples of healing by touch. As we had seen with the child who fell from the jungle gym, whenever a Thetan suffered an accident, many others came to his aid by meditating or a laying of hands over the injury. Whether it worked or not we could only speculate, but it appeared to work. Whitney mentioned her physical health and energy levels had been getting better since she had joined their meditation sessions.

At a crew meeting, she added, "I haven't had a migraine since the morning of that terrible dream. I owe it to the Thetans. I think they're amazing."

"I agree," Jim said.

"I don't know what to make of them or their planet," Adams said.

"I was hired to study technology," Ian added, his nose in his electronic game.

"When's the next time leap?" Frank asked.

I sided somewhere in the middle. I recognized a mystical quality about them, almost magical, yet I too yearned for something more exciting after being used to the Alphans.

I mostly looked forward to our weekly outings in the desert, when Jessica and Ian accompanied me as we made the final adjustments and improvements to the PFDs. The engineers at Maxwell Enterprises had done an excellent job of ironing out the few wrinkles we had found. To their credit, in my dozen or so test flights, I had taken only one crash, a minor fall that was largely due to my own mishandling of the device. The crash turned out to be of great importance, as we got additional data as to how the PFD handled the impact. As Ian had predicted, the craft was mostly unharmed and would have been able to survive a fall of bigger proportions.

I flew over the desert floor, chasing after birds and admiring the scenery. I relished the incredible feeling of freedom this device presented and found it to be quite a paradox this gift of joy had been donated to us by a society that no longer existed. I had never stopped wondering what happened to the people of Alpha 17, who as far as we knew were barely clinging to life, the few survivors sentenced to a meager existence in holes under the ground. How long might they last? I wondered.

I gracefully turned toward the last colors of sunset and wished there was some way to thank them for the wonderful things they had shared.

The Deltans

FRANK PRESSED ADAMS to make another time leap in an effort to advance the Thetans.

He said, "We really have nothing to lose if they aren't providing us with anything of value."

Adams was reluctant. The growing star and the painful loss of the Alphans weighed on him. He continued to press on with an approach that he credited to something Jessica had said.

"Since we've already found two planets with societies," he responded to Frank, "why can't we find more?"

Ian was working with Jim when we first discovered the new people, recognizing the smoke of a controlled burn from space. From the Delta galaxy, the thirteenth planet orbiting star rx339 became the third planet we had found with societies. The citizens of Delta 13 were quite primitive, though they had long since controlled fire and were into early tool production. They had huts and stone villages and practiced simple farming methods. In some areas, they built excellent rock walls and fortresses. Though their technology was similar to the Thetans, they immediately struck me as bizarre and far more primitive.

The Deltans were a savage and strange breed. They were a combination of two mammals in one. Comprising the Deltan individual was a host body and a much smaller, hairless version of the same within an abdominal pouch. They were connected by a feeding tube that could be seen when the little body stretched outwards from the abdomen. We categorized them and other breeds on the planet as marsupial though they had unique features compared to other marsupials from our logs. We had seen pouch-carrying animals before, but it was always adults with babies who eventually grew and left the pouch. The Deltan hosts grew from birth to adulthood with the smaller version consistently within them. The Deltan pairs remained together for life, and we speculated as to how the smaller version benefited the larger. The concept of everybody pulling their fair share was ingrained in us, even with alien life forms, and we assumed there was some usefulness behind it.

I suggested, "Perhaps the smaller is the brains and the larger the brawn." Though the comment was something of a joke, it was a plausible idea to the others.

Compared to the Alphans, the Deltans were taller and thinner, yet not as tall and thin as the Thetans. The Deltans were less hairy than the Alphans, yet they had body hair. The Deltans also had a small head with an elongated face and very sharp teeth. They looked ferocious at times, like a cornered dog. Deltans came in a wide array of skin and hair color, correlating to the climate zones they lived in. People with darker hair and skin lived close to the equator, and those with lighter complexions lived nearer to the poles. Mostly the Deltan pouch beings had pinkish complexions. The pouch beings were small, weak and without teeth. They never left the pouch entirely and were totally dependent on the outer being.

They wore basic clothing made from animal hides, mostly leather and furs, with a slot in the center for the pouch being. Both men and women wore similar outfits, jackets and pants, which made it hard to tell the gender.

The Deltan hands had a unique feature. Above each finger was a retractable claw. This enabled the Deltan to grab hold of things with his hand and deliver a scarring blow at the same time. The Deltan hand made them natural warriors.

Most Deltans carried weapons in public. They had friendly packs within their villages, but they were always on the defensive or the attack with neighboring villagers. Skirmishes were the norm, bloody battles where invaders came into the area of one tribe and attempted to overtake it. Even the children carried clubs and spears to participate in the warfare.

Deltan villages also contained groups of smaller people. Little gnomes could be found scurrying about the legs of the taller Deltans.

The gnomes were tiny, only coming up to a Deltan's knees. They were not marsupial but existed as one being. They were soft-featured compared to the Deltans, and they had hands with only fleshy fingers and palms, no claws. The gnomes served the larger Deltans in many ways. They cleaned up after them, prepared food, did manual labors, even played instruments, danced and performed tricks for the Deltans. I saw one little fellow bouncing around, doing handsprings and flips while his partners did juggling routines behind him for the pleasure of a troop of tired warriors.

"I like the little people," Jim mentioned. Everyone did. They were adorable.

Service and entertainment was the gnome's way of making an existence in the brutal villages. Being too small to be a threat to the Deltans, they were never a part of the battles. The gnomes simply served whichever Deltans came out on top.

In the oceans, we found huge wooden boats with dozens of long oars extending out from side portals. The boats were aided by sails, but they were extremely slow. The larger boats were decorated with weaponry. We watched a few conflicts at sea.

One warring boat of Delta savages bombarded a second with cannon fire. The second ship slowed under the attack, and the first ship docked at its side. Marauders from the first vessel flung themselves headfirst into a battle with knives and swords. The attackers killed every passenger, including the children, before tossing their bodies overboard.

Our crew was horrified by their brutality. Whitney became sick in the lab from watching it. She had thought that the Alphans were barbaric, but they were quite civil compared to the Deltans. The struggle for life was often a difficult thing to witness. There were moments of lawlessness that reminded us of how inhumane even intelligent beings could be. The only way for me to deal with it was to emotionally remove myself from the actions of the beings within the project.

Adams and Frank discussed how long to make the next time leap. For Delta 13, a thousand standard orbits was a nice round figure, hopefully enough time for the society to make major advances. But for Theta 7, the question remained if they would still be around. As the red giant sun expanded, a thousand orbits would presumably make life unbearable for them. We assumed their planet would not be able to repeat its survival performance after a leap of that size. Adams pushed for a few extra days before making the leap, to give the crew a chance to get as much information about the Deltans as possible. He was also buying time for Whitney.

Whitney was predictably disappointed about the time leap though she knew it was bound to occur. She argued for the Thetans' cause. She presented case after case of intriguing abilities and rituals demonstrated daily by them. But Adams knew the real roots of her attachment.

He explained to me, "Part of it has to do with Rose. Whitney has taken to the Thetans like family."

The following week, we made a time leap of a thousand standard orbits. The colored light trails from the planets began their motions.

Adams stood by his desk and then sat in his chair, watching the display as calmly as he could. Whitney sat on her mat with a lit candle, saying prayers for their safekeeping. I sat down next to her and offered my hand. She gripped it intensely as the planets continued their blurring motions. Eventually, the planets slowed down and returned to stationary positions. Jim reported that 1,050 standard orbits had passed. The cameras went through the readjustment period.

Then Jim said, "The red giant star has grown by fifteen percent," an amount slightly larger than we had anticipated. "Theta 7 is not in the orbit where it had been."

The cameras identified an empty field of space instead. This time I was sure it had been pulled into the gravitational zone of the growing star and had been incinerated. Whitney checked her emotions as Adams instructed Jim to continue looking. Jim made some calculations to determine where it might be if it was to remain in a similar temperate zone the Thetan life was accustomed to.

As Jim pushed the focus further away from the growing red star, he proclaimed, "I might have found it!"

The monitors slowly gathered focus, and we recognized the same planet of orange skies and purplish-blue oceans.

"Yes! Thank God. Please let them be there," Whitney said. She continued to squeeze my hand as the monitor zoomed in on the planet.

The shot went ever closer through the Thetan atmosphere and down to surface level. Everything we could see looked similar to before. Whitney jumped to her desk and assisted Jim as he panned through some villages.

What we saw amazed us. The villages were the same. The markets and the schools were the same. Even the meditation groups still got together at the dawn line. To the best of our knowledge, the society had not changed at all. Adams was dumbfounded. I saw the disappointment on the faces of Jessica and Ian, but Whitney couldn't have been happier.

"How is this planet still around?" Adams said, though he immediately realized his poor choice of words.

Jim replied, "It moves its orbit out in conjunction with a growing star."

"I can see that!" Adams objected. "But how? Have they got some kind of propulsion system we don't know about?"

"This doesn't make any sense," Ian added.

Sense or not, Whitney didn't care. She beamed as she watched her favorite planet still on our monitors despite the odds against it. She broke out into an awkward laughter, her face wet with tears.

Then the cameras refocused around the space of Delta 13. The atmosphere and landscape looked the same, but as the shot went in closer on a coastal area, we saw the villages were much more defined and spread out.

"Okay," Adams said. "This is a good start."

While Whitney reconnected with Theta 7, we studied the Deltans exclusively for days. Small villages had become larger, and new villages existed where none had before. The homes were also bigger and made out of stronger materials. The fortress walls were more than double the height and width of the past ones.

The Deltans still existed as two beings in one, though their society had become a much more diverse group of specialists. Deltans now operated large farms and used animals to work for them, pulling plows and turning welling drills. They were also woodcraftsmen, tailors, doctors and more. They molded metals for swords, chains, wagon frames and elegant body armor. The people wore similar outfits from before, basic apparel made of animal hides and furs, yet we noticed more tailoring. The hide jackets and pants fit and looked better, though the outfits for the men and women were still unisex.

Many of the larger Deltans wore decorative body armor, which contained an opening hinge for the smaller pouch being to either leave open or latch up. These Deltans often rode on hoofed beasts, apparently of higher rank. Their animals also wore armor over the head and around the belly.

The tiny gnomes still scurried about at the knees of the mighty Deltans. They performed basic services and still did tumbling acts and song-and-dance routines like before.

Ian said, "They appear to be the Deltan version of a pet. Something that the larger people enjoy having around without really having to pull their own weight."

Ian loved analyzing the advancement of the structures within the broader kingdoms and individual villages. Their construction was much more elaborate than it had been. Stone columns and archways with threatening statues decorated the entryway to many of the grander structures.

By then, Deltans had well-established armies. We watched many battles between warriors wielding metal spikes and heavy swords. Deltans were not the sort of beings I would want to encounter in a dark alley. Ian and I speculated they could have easily killed an Alphan gladiator, were it possible to put the two in a ring together.

Jim agreed, saying, "No contest. The Deltans are larger, stronger and quicker than the Alphans were."

Deltan rank within families and society seemed to stem from fighting prowess, and the women were no strangers to the contests. The largest Deltans were in charge, regardless of gender, whether at a family level or in the villages. In gladiator arenas, the sports often involved smaller Deltans being tortured and killed by larger ones, as well as being forced to fight animals. The action reminded us of the old Alphan arenas, but they were even more brutal.

Another interesting aspect was their practice of marriage. Deltan women took no interest in males who were not as tough as they were. We routinely saw examples of Deltan males challenging females to fights. The theory seemed to be that if he could beat her, he could have her. Sometimes the males received a bloody thrashing, as the rewards did not come easily. But there was nothing stranger than watching a Deltan male practically kill a female to make her fall in love with him.

Whitney called it "an unfortunate pattern for a society to fall in." As with any animal species, survival often relied on tactics to separate the strongest from the others.

We also watched large-scale battles in spots across the planet. These battles involved orchestrated efforts of thousands of warriors. The fighting took place on the fringes of the kingdoms, and we assumed they were each attempting to advance their boundaries.

"War and selective breeding must have weeded out the weak and created these awesome beings," Ian theorized, envious of their strength and fearless nature.

"I prefer the little people," Jim mentioned.

Ian and I enjoyed watching the warriors in battle, as it reminded us of the gladiator films we had seen as kids. We watched them fight for hours one night, explaining to Jim some of the weapons being used.

"That's a mace," I told him. "That's an interesting crossbow, for long distance attacks. These foot soldiers are carrying clubs and swords, for close fighting."

Jim had seen fighting and death before, especially in early Alpha 17, but never like this. It was Jim's first time seeing armies in action. Jim was curious but did not find watching spilled blood a pleasant experience.

The Deltans handled weapons with agility and strength. I appreciated that I did not live in such a place. The children would have torn someone like me to pieces just for a laugh. Ian and I rooted for different sides and tried to make the battles more fun for Jim. We continued to speculate on whether the inner being had any effect on the outer being, since during times of battle it was completely hidden under armor.

We also checked in on Alpha 17. The weather was less turbulent though years of violent winds had left a mark, resulting in a planet of extreme landscapes. The oceans had dried and receded to levels much lower than the original coastline. To our surprise, new polar ice caps were forming. The previous caps had receded at such a rate that Adams had expected to find none in the future.

Adams said, "It must have to do with the haze and dust keeping the sunlight from penetrating. Keeps the temps lower."

Jim couldn't find any of the people, not even the ones from the underground shelters, though there were plenty of signs of life intact.

In many areas, a hearty vine had taken over that provided shelter for insects and rodents. The seas contained plenty of fish species that had been around for millions of years. The landscape was scarred yet everything would settle down. Life would continue and begin a whole process again. The question remained; how long might it be before another intelligent society would arise? Perhaps in a million orbits? Perhaps a billion?

"Theta 7 still a mystery. Twice now it has performed an orbit shift. No reasonable explanation. Delta 13 showing improvement but still savages. Another thousand or two needed. Can Theta 7 do it again? I wouldn't bet against it. Frustrating. I'd like to know how."

- from p. 112 of Webster's journal.

Modernization

FRANK ASKED ME, "How would you like to see the results of some of your work?"

"What do you mean?"

"Come with me to see a new subdivision."

His chauffeur drove us to the outskirts of town. The site was in the foothills with a nice view of the valley below. The homes, three hundred planned, were being modeled after the Alphan design, the large cone shape with the sun side windows and enclosed greenhouses.

The limo pulled up to the construction zone. Frank and I got out and walked around the site of the first model home. The framework for the large cone was in place as a central pole stood about three stories high, and a dozen support poles outlined its walls. It looked like a broad standing, inverted cone.

I recognized some of the laborers from jobs I had been on in the past. Some recognized me as well.

One of the contractors yelled at me, "Grab a belt and get busy!"

"Just here to consult," I said. The contractor looked over and saw Frank standing next to me. He gave me a second look.

"I didn't see you there, Mr. Maxwell," he said.

Frank shook his hand. "How's it going, Mike?"

"Real good. I think we've got these plans figured out. There's not much to them."

I went over the plans with Mike. We identified the floor-level framing still to be done. I made sure he had faced the large window openings properly to get the maximum amount of sunlight. We discussed where to place the kitchen, bathrooms and bedrooms.

Mike mentioned, "It's spacious yet so cheap to build."

Frank didn't like the word. "Affordable, Mike. Affordable. Remember the customer."

"How many of these 'affordable' homes are we doing?" Mike asked.

"Three hundred for this site," I told him.

"If they're all this big, there's not going to be much space for a yard."

"That's the tradeoff," I said. "Big, affordable homes with less land."

"Works for some," Mike added. "So what is this special glass going on the sunny sides?"

"It's solar paneling," I said. "Not only can they have a greenhouse, but they can power their homes from the sunlight."

"So that explains why the electricians are coming before the power companies."

"That's the plan," I said.

The work crew listened intently as I pointed out the features and benefits of the design. I felt like I had stepped into a new dimension, on the fun and easy side of life. Frank let me do the talking.

Back at the lab, Whitney made an incredible remark after finding the dawn group at the podium in Coasttown. She believed the six Thetans in the meditation were the exact same people since our last time leap. She immediately recognized her friend, The Grandmother, and also identified the others from the images she had taken. She showed me the comparisons. The similarities were amazing.

"They're the same people," Whitney said. "I'm certain of it."

I couldn't believe it. "After 1,050 years?"

Jessica added, "They look like the people in the photos, but... the same people... that can't be possible."

"Probably direct descendents," Ian suggested.

"I'm telling you these are the exact same people!" Whitney insisted the crew took a closer look.

Jim multiplied the image of The Grandmother sitting calmly at her spot on several of our monitors. Whitney told us about the woman. I immediately sensed an energy about her I couldn't describe.

Whitney said, "She is the epitome of Thetan culture. She's lovely, graceful in movements. She always looks serene." Whitney called her The Grandmother, and that's what she appeared to be, a grand mother.

Whitney claimed she could identify her face out of a lineup of thousands. She also showed us how the current participants occupied the same spots in the meditation circle and lived in the same homes of the Coasttown village from over a thousand years ago.

"Like Ian said, they must be descendents," Adams believed.

"I'm positive on this," Whitney insisted.

She pulled her father closer to the monitor. She had Jim make a detailed face comparison of each member of the group and compare the results to our past records. Jim split the images of the Thetan faces on several different monitors. The matches appeared to be identical, with the current Thetans only looking about ten years older.

"For the sake of argument," Adams said, "let's pretend this is the same person. So what are we saying, that this Grandmother lady is a thousand years old?"

"My guess is she's at least ten thousand years old," Whitney said calmly. "Maybe twenty."

"That's ridiculous!" Ian blurted out. "There must be a better explanation."

"I'm inclined to agree," Jessica said, "but if this woman is ten or twenty thousand years old, then what's the secret?"

"Clean living?" I suggested, getting a few giggles from the others as Whitney remained composed.

"I don't know," Whitney said. "I only know we don't see any changes within the villages, just evidence of time passing on their planet. Trees in the forests have changed. Coastline has eroded, but the people remain the same."

Fortunately, the only way to confirm Whitney's theory was to do another time leap. First, we would make detailed observations of certain Thetans from across the globe, and then check comparisons after a time leap.

Ian proposed, "Let's identify at least ten different meditation groups and get before and after shots and physical addresses. We'll also get similar information on Thetans who are not in the meditation circles: farmers, merchants and even children."

Whitney assumed the task. She went about it diligently though she knew her work would end with us performing a time leap to prove or disprove her theory. By now she had confidence the planet would survive another leap, and that Thetans were living to be thousands of years old. The concept was not lost on Frank or Adams. As the senior members of our group, they appreciated Whitney's interest in the subject of ageless living. They were skeptical it was true, however, and they were also doubtful it could be incorporated by us, even if she could prove it.

The following days went by slowly, due to the suspense of trying to figure out how far to advance the universe. How much time did the Deltans need for their modernization? We made many predictions on timeframes for certain discoveries, like gunpowder and electricity.

Adams also predicted where Theta 7 might be after the time leap. Since it had baffled him twice before, he decided to trust Jim's hunch that the planet would be in a location to keep the temperature consistent with the growing star. Since we had first discovered Theta 7, the closest two planets in the red star's vicinity had been dragged out of their orbits into a collision course with their sun. The next closest planets to the red star—the third through sixth in orbit, also reflected the dramatic changes in temperature we expected to find. Theta 7 was the only planet in the system that was moving out. All the others were moving in.

Jim concluded, "If the trend continues, Theta 7 will end up being further out in orbit than Theta 8." This concept made no sense in a universe that otherwise had displayed very rigid laws of physics.

Whitney finished gathering the data. She gave Adams her best wishes for a time leap. Over the final days, she meditated with as many of the groups as she could.

Adams and Frank plotted how far to advance the universe. They decided on a timeframe of fifteen hundred standard orbits. For Theta 7, that was equal to about nine hundred years, now that its orbit was so much further out than it had been. For Delta 13, it translated to roughly thirteen hundred orbits.

The day of the leap dawned bright and clear. We gathered before the monitors.

Whitney said, "May we observe a moment of silence to recognize the risk to the Thetans and to wish them safekeeping." We all stood quietly for a few moments until Whitney thanked us.

Then Adams instructed Jim, "Release hydrogen."

The light show began. Planetary images sped in elliptical circles around their suns at ever-increasing velocities. Whitney sank into her seat. Her confidence was being put to the test. She held her hands over her eyes, waiting for it to be over.

"They'll be fine," I said. I hoped they would, for her sake.

I never tired of the beautiful light show, though the mini-leaps were nothing compared to the leaps of old. Enjoying the majesty of an entire galaxy in motion took the million-year leaps. I altered my routine by watching several monitors set up on individual solar systems and planets. I kept some distance from Whitney during the leap, knowing how difficult it was for her, and not wanting her to sense any pleasure I was having. When the planets came to a stop, the red giant star from the Theta galaxy slowly came into focus on one of the monitors.

"Oops," Jim said.

"What do you mean, oops?" Frank asked.

"We had a malfunction," Jim replied.

Adams was instantly concerned. "How so?"

"A little more hydrogen leaked out than we had planned."

"How much more?"

"About double," Jim replied. "We just performed a leap of 2,500 standard orbits."

"Oh no," Whitney said.

"What's the change to the star in the Theta galaxy?" Adams asked.

"About thirty percent larger," Jim answered.

"Have you found the planet?" Whitney asked.

"Not yet."

Adams pounded his desk in frustration. Jim directed the camera to where the planet would be if it had behaved as normal planets did.

Nothing existed there but empty space. Jim proceeded to search under the second formula, by figuring out the distance that would provide a comfortable temperature zone.

Within a few minutes, he proclaimed, "I've got it. It's beyond Theta 8!"

"Unbelievable," Adams said. He and I shared a quick look of doubt that this could happen.

As the shot came into focus, we saw the same orange atmosphere and purplish-blue oceans we knew to be Theta 7. Our view went closer through the skies and down to the surface. We recognized the same cities and villages. Whitney cried out in relief. She jumped to her chair as Jim scanned around. She assisted him in identifying old structures from record. To everyone's amazement, we could see remarkably few changes, if any.

"Impossible!" Adams shouted. "I'm sorry, Whit, but this totally defies logic!" Whitney shrugged her shoulders and beamed with pride.

As I watched the monitors, I noticed the Thetans still went about their slow-paced lives. Mud and grass huts made up the homes. Farmers walked up and down lush fields, picking fruits by hand. Random people were dancing. Many of the children were still naked. Jim identified changes to forests and coastal erosion for accuracy of the leap, as well as a volcanic eruption that had happened somewhere in between eras.

Jessica and Ian looked disappointed. Adams scratched his head in confusion. I too was in shock of what was happening, or what wasn't happening.

"I just want to understand this," Adams said calmly.

"It will be good to see what Whitney's data indicates," Frank added.

We turned our attention to the monitors coming into focus around Delta 13.

The cameras zoomed in through the Deltan atmosphere. Monitor One focused on a city by the ocean. We saw the difference immediately—bright lights, hazy skies and lots of machinery signaled dramatic changes had happened. We saw gigantic buildings and a busy air commuter scene. The excitement in the room catapulted as we zoomed in closer within the enormous Deltan city.

Frank heralded, "That's the kind of progress we're looking for!"

"Perfect!" Jessica applauded. "Not oops, Jim. Perfection."

"They must be a hundred years further than the Alphans," Ian remarked.

The skies had random air traffic, with even more advanced flying machines than we had seen on Alpha 17. Some looked like cylinders and discs, and they traveled at phenomenal speeds. The buildings were enormous with sleek, modern architecture.

"Sometimes it's better to be lucky than good," Ian added while shaking hands with Adams.

"Back in business," I said, playfully pushing Adams around. I sensed he was deeply relieved the time leap had turned out so well, even if it was a mistake. Once again, we had new things to dissect.

Except for Whitney, the crew spent the next several weeks studying Delta 13 exclusively. We saw ideas familiar from Alpha 17, but we also saw plenty of new ones.

Three days after the leap, Whitney presented her findings. The results came as we were analyzing a cargo system of metallic, cigar shaped vessels that ran from one end of a Deltan continent to the other in mere minutes.

"Everyone, visualize the proof!" Whitney proudly announced.

I looked over to the Thetan monitors where Whitney had collected the updated records of the meditation group from Coasttown. A chill shot down my spine as I recognized the face of The Grandmother and the other five Thetans from her group. We gathered in Whitney's corner. Jim showed before and after pictures of the faces from the meditation groups, the marketplaces and the school grounds. Thetans from all seven continents were represented, a few hundred individuals. The conclusion was inarguable. In each case, after more than 1,800 Thetan years, very little was detectable in terms of aging among the people. Even the smallest of children looked very much the same, just a few years older and a bit taller.

The crew stared in silence. I wasn't sure what to say. The odds of that many distant relatives looking very much the same not only by face, but by age, height, weight and complexion were too staggering to be believed.

"It would appear Whitney was right," Jessica managed, breaking our silence.

"Is there any way these could be descendents?" Adams asked.

Whitney replied with assurance, "No, they're not."

Whitney explained the concepts she had come to embrace. Thetan abilities included living for extremely long times. She was also convinced they could heal by touch, and they had long ago achieved world peace.

"I'm sorry I didn't believe you," I told her later. "I didn't recognize how special they are."

"It's okay," she said.

"What do you want to do about it?" I asked.

"I just want to study them," she said. "Let's pull the plug on the leaps for a while and just get to know them."

Whitney estimated the Thetan life expectancy to be over 50,000 years and possibly as much as 100,000. Adams couldn't argue with her though it was extremely hard to believe. Frank was impressed.

"Let's find out as much about them as we can," Frank said. "We have two societies to learn from. Their specialties just happen to lie in different fields."

We left the lab that night all together just after the sun had set.

I looked up as headlights snapped on in unison. Five cars shined ten headlights in our direction.

"Surprise!" Frank announced. "How do you like your bonuses?"

The cars had rounded, flat lower sections, reminding me of the vehicles from Alpha 17.

"They have Alphan technology?" I asked.

"Of course," he added. "They're hybrids. I wanted my crew to test the prototypes."

He had chosen convertibles for Jessica, Whitney and me, and made them green, blue and red respectively. Ian's hardtop was black and Webster's was purple.

Ian asked, "Why didn't I get a convertible?"

Frank replied, "Your brains are too valuable. Just kidding. Do you want one?"

Ian thought about it. "This will do for now."

I asked for volunteers to go for a ride. Whitney, Jessica and Ian climbed aboard my cruiser. Whitney sat in the front. Jessica and Ian plopped down in the back. Phil, the security guard, saluted us as I passed through the front gate.

We took off down the main street and drove a few minutes to reach the highway. We merged with the other cars and headed for the fast lane, which was clear. I stepped on the pedal and accelerated the car over the speed limit. Then the magnetic forces under the car came into action. The car lifted slightly, and the ride suddenly felt as smooth as floating on air.

"Steering is less accurate when the magnetic field is activated," Ian reminded me. I watched him in the rearview mirror as he tried to keep his flapping hair out of his glasses.

"What do you think?" I asked Whitney.

"It looks good on you."

Other drivers took notice of my car as well. Those in the slower lanes kept glancing over, looking at the flat lower section and the sleek lines. I received a few thumbs up from other drivers. I realized I wouldn't need to hitch a ride any longer. I took an exit and turned around to head back to the job site.

I dropped the others off in the lot then proceeded back to the highway. I drove for an hour as fast as possible, going nowhere in particular, just up and the down the road. It was a small miracle I didn't get a speeding ticket.

I was about to go home when I drove by the Star Bar at closing time. I saw Sam from the parking lot as she was locking up for the night.

I honked to her and yelled, "Sam, want a ride?"

"Momma taught me never to take rides from strangers," she spoke the well-rehearsed line.

"I'm not a stranger," I replied.

She turned, recognizing my voice. She walked over. "Gruber? Is that you in this beautiful machine?"

"So how about it? Do you want a ride in the world's newest automobile or not?"

Sam got into the passenger's seat and looked wide-eyed at the fancy interior. "How much are they paying you?"

"This was just a bonus," I told her.

I sped out of the parking lot and headed straight for the freeway so she could feel the fluid ride. I explained the concepts of how the car worked.

"I was one of the people who figured it out," I boasted.

"Like I believe that," she said.

"No, no. Really," I added.

"You're different, aren't you?" she said, touching my arm.

"I guess that's true, Sam. This job is beyond everything. I am different."

Spinning

SUPER-MODERN DELTA 13's kingdoms were still intact. Each of the five continents contained its own cities, villages and agricultural centers.

The rock walls of old had been replaced with modern energy shields, glowing orange and red boundary lines that rose to great heights. The shields completely outlined the continents in an impressive display of glowing security. There was no ground or air traffic between them.

The Deltan people were mostly citizens within their kingdoms. Nobody wore body armor anymore. Their clothing was stylish linens, with much more creativity and colors. For the women, breast lines and hips were accentuated. A showing of sexuality existed where none had previously. Like on Alpha 17, some of the outfits seemed to be made from a thin, soft metal.

The people looked less barbaric. The faces had softened, though they still had elongated snouts and sharp teeth. The arenas of old had replaced gladiators with hard-hitting sports and referees. Now they wore padding and helmets while attempting to toss objects into goals, instead of killing weaker opponents.

"Where are the gnomes?" Jim asked. He was the first to recognize their absence.

A search ensued for the little people but we couldn't find any. Jim became increasingly concerned.

"Something must have happened to them," Adams explained to him.

"Like what?"

"Maybe a virus went through their population."

"Or the Deltans changed their opinion of them," Ian added as a joke.

"Don't say that!"

The more Jim searched for them, the more distraught he became. He played an ongoing recording of the acrobatic gnomes and was reluctant to work on Delta 13.

The crew attempted to pull Jim out of his depression with the wonders of the modern planet. Deltans used a variety of flying devices much like the

Alphans, though the devices worked on different principles. The crafts had smooth shapes and moved at tremendous speed. They were shiny, metallic and round.

"This part of it is spinning." Ian pointed to the lower area of a saucer shaped device. "My guess is that it's spinning incredibly fast."

"How is that different?" Frank asked him.

"Our engines work by either creating a contained explosion or by pulling air in and pushing air out. In either case, exhaust is created. With the Deltan crafts, there's no air movement around them. There's nothing entering or exiting."

"What makes you think it's spinning?" Jessica asked him.

"The clue is in the shape," Ian said. "Why else would they all be round? Why would you need a roundness of shape? To spin, of course."

Adams agreed. "The dynamics are like childhood toys. Remember flying discs and tops?"

"So?" Frank asked.

Ian explained, "Spinning alters the physics of things. It makes things weigh less. In theory, it might be a way to break the speed of light."

"What would that do?" Jim asked.

"Breaking the speed of light?" Adams said. "I doubt that's possible."

"What if it is?" Jim repeated. "What do you think would happen?"

Neither of them had an immediate answer. Frank became interested and waited for a response.

"When the sound barrier is broken," Ian began, "a sonic boom results from air molecules forced under pressure."

"So if you have a similar thing with light," Adams continued Ian's thought, "then as light particles are forced under pressure, there might also be a release of energy. Perhaps a light boom."

"A light boom?" Frank asked.

"Possibly," Adams continued. "Remember the equation e equals mc squared? That means energy equals mass times the square of the speed of light. So energy, light and time are all connected."

"Now you've really lost me," Frank said.

"The energy at the speed of light is almost beyond measure," Ian continued. "It is such a staggering amount that even getting near the speed of light builds tremendous energy."

"The point is that these crafts have spinning engines?" Frank asked.

"That's my guess," Ian said.

"Fine. Do what you can to make sense of it."

Adams and Ian could talk of little else once the conversation started. They discussed concepts for engine designs while Jessica showed me how to make sketches to match their words.

Another interesting device was like a roving pedestal. Many of the Deltans stood on them and zoomed around a few feet over the ground. There was a round area to stand on and a podium for arms to grab onto and a housing area for the controls.

"This reminds me of the PFDs," I said. "As far as being a personal transport."

"But there aren't turbines blowing air for power," Jessica noted. "And they're smaller and hover close to the ground."

They also had no frames around them. The Deltan pedestals appeared much simpler though they incorporated a new technology.

Frank asked, "Could this be made using reverse magnetism?"

Ian said, "This pedestal does a lot more than just float. It creates lift and forward thrust."

"Spinning again?" Frank asked.

"Most likely."

Another item we found interesting was their method for handling mass transit. The Deltans had built pressurized tunnels for commuters, like a subway system. It was pneumatic tubing for people.

"Board a compartment at one end of the city," Jessica explained to Frank, "and seconds later, step out across town."

"Or minutes later, across the continent," I added.

"They can be built above ground or below, literally anywhere you want them," Jessica said.

Some of their products were beyond us. In the space above the planet, the Deltans had a system of satellites. Dozens of them were positioned above each of the main five continents. Jim searched for radio signals coming or going from the devices but was unable to find any.

Adams remarked, "They don't appear to be for communication."

Ian thought, "They may be a deterrent for incoming comets."

Jessica said, "Maybe they're outdated and they've been turned off."

I had no idea what to make of them, but I loved being a part of a team doing what we could to make sense of these things.

Whitney was fascinated with the updates, but only worked with us for an hour or two each day on the Deltans. When she did, she preferred to do her usual studies on environmental and species change. It surprised me when she chose to work with the natural world there, that she did not feel the excitement of the inventions. Though we still cared for each other, I felt a slight rift in our friendship made larger by my interest in technology and hers for nature.

Whitney found the Deltan atmosphere indicated a slight increase in temperature and greenhouse gases, but not nearly what she expected. Surely, the Deltans were using incredible amounts of energy, power to supply the needs of a billion citizens.

She wondered, "Why isn't their atmosphere heating up more, especially after our experience with Alpha 17?"

During the following days, Jessica and I made some discoveries that answered her question. The Deltans had designed a power source that didn't create heat. The more we learned of it, the more fascinated we were.

The Deltan generators made use of magnetic forces. The housing unit had two enormous magnets in the shape of concave slabs. These slabs stood upright to hold the rotor. The rotor assembly was another giant magnet in the shape of a cylinder that fit on top of the upright slabs. The whole apparatus was arranged so that the repulsion between the housing unit and the rotor assembly actually made the giant rotor float.

"The rotor is incredibly heavy," Ian explained to Frank, "yet once in place, it floats like a puff of air. Then they get it to spin."

"Go on," Frank said.

Ian explained, "This is the interesting part. It has no friction. It spins faster and faster until it puts out more energy than it needs to keep it spinning."

"A perpetual motion machine," Adams added. "They're making power for nothing."

"Impossible," Frank said. "Even I know energy can't be created. It can only be converted."

"That's what I thought too," Adams said, staring at the beautiful design. "I can't believe we've found this."

"If you're right," Frank said, "this is going to change everything."

"I know."

"Why is it so important?" Jim asked.

"This is like discovering fire, the wheel and electricity in the same day," Adams said.

Ian reflected, "The funniest part is… it's not even complicated. It's incredibly simple."

"Who would be the buyer for something like this?" I asked Frank.

"I'm sure we'll find the right one."

Later in the month, Frank told us he had accepted a huge offer from a major utility company.

"They want to sit on the plans and continue business as usual," he explained.

Adams was upset. "We can't lock this idea away just because they're the highest bidder."

"Why not?" Frank asked.

"This could revolutionize the world!"

"Free energy might not be in the best interest of the people," Frank mentioned. "How do you know this won't take off and spin out of control? Giving everyone on the planet unlimited energy sounds like quite a leap. We might not be ready for that."

Adams sat in his chair, torn over the whole thing. He hated the thought of not having the wonders of modern physics on display.

"It will come out in due time, Webster. The time just isn't now."

"Promise me not to make any more deals until I go over the contract," Adams said.

"The thermodynamic laws of energy have been turned upside down, and they're spinning in the vault of an investor. How much is this worth? I'll never have a financial concern even if I live to be as old as the Thetans, yet I don't care. Frank is a trusted friend, but this deal makes me sick. Chalk another one up to hindsight."

- from p. 117 of Webster's journal.

Communication

JESSICA AND IAN LEFT for the night, exhausted after working on the Deltan generators. Adams was tired too. He was battling a cold and didn't feel like staying as late as usual. He asked me if I would mind giving Whitney a ride home since she came with him. She was still meditating with the Thetans, and neither of us wanted to interrupt it.

"Go ahead," I told him. "I'll wait."

I planned on relaxing in my chair for the last half hour before the Thetan sun rose over Coasttown.

After Adams had left, I observed Whitney in her meditation. A deep stillness took over the lab. The monitors showed the faces of the six Thetans in meditation. It was still something of a marvel to me. It was eerily strange yet calm. I closed my eyes and relaxed. Just as I was beginning to fade out, I suddenly realized I had no idea where I had placed my keys. I searched for them all over my desk but couldn't find them and quickly got frustrated.

"Where are my car keys?" I said aloud, as my search became anxious.

"Behind the fire extinguisher," Whitney said calmly from her sitting position with her eyes closed.

I was surprised she had answered me. I apologized for not being quieter. Then I realized that she was right. I walked over to the fire extinguisher and found my keys placed on the ledge behind it. I had put them there upon arrival when Jessica had unloaded a bunch of documents on me. It was the only time I had ever put my keys there, and I was sure no one had seen me do it.

"How did you know that?" I asked her in a hushed tone. There was no response from Whitney. I couldn't tell if she was still meditating or if she was just sitting there with her eyes closed. "Whitney, can you hear me?"

"She cannot hear you at the moment," was the response from Whitney. Her voice had a strange calmness to it, and I assumed she was joking around.

"If she can't hear me, then how does she know where my keys are?"

"She doesn't," was the response from Whitney.

"Okay, I'll play along. Then who am I talking with?"

"In your terms, the one you refer to as The Grandmother."

"Very funny. Jim, you must have whispered where they were while I was going through my desk, right?"

"I had no idea," Jim replied. His green light pulsed.

"Okay, I'll admit that was a good one. Now can you finish up with what you're doing so we can get out of here?"

Whitney made no response. I looked up at the monitors and saw the Thetan sun had yet to rise over Coasttown. The Thetans were still in their meditation. Apparently so was Whitney. I looked at The Grandmother sitting calmly in her spot. I felt uneasy and sat down at my desk, waiting patiently for the Thetan sun to rise and for Whitney to come out of her session.

About twenty minutes passed before the session ended. The six Thetans stood and left the circle. Whitney rolled her neck around then opened her eyes slowly, as if the room was bright.

"Did my father leave already?" she asked me through a yawn.

"Yes, he did. That was a good joke, by the way."

"What do you mean?" Whitney asked. I jangled the car keys in front of her. "What are you talking about?"

"You almost had me going. Jim was perfectly calm about it. It was kind of funny, I'll admit."

Whitney gave me a blank expression. She said, "Jon, I have no idea what you're talking about."

"The joke's over. I'll be in the car." I walked out of the lab.

When Whitney sat in the passenger seat, she repeated she didn't know what I was talking about. As we sped down the road, I went over the conversation we had about the keys and about The Grandmother. I repeated that it was very amusing, but I still wanted to know how she knew it.

Whitney told me, "Stop the car." I pulled over on the side of the road. She looked me in the eyes and said, "Are you making this up?"

"Why would I make this up?"

"I promise you," she said, "I have no idea what you're talking about."

"You told me where my keys were, and then you said you weren't the one I was talking with, but you were The Grandmother."

"That's crazy!"

"Tell me about it!"

We drove the rest of the way to her house in silence. As she got out of the car, she searched my face one last time. I realized we were doubting each other's sincerity. I drove back to my place with an overwhelming feeling that Whitney had been honest with me. In the months I had known her, I had never once heard her tell a lie or play a joke on someone. It wasn't like her to do those things, no matter how trivial.

The next day, neither of us spoke about it to the others. We went about our work as usual. I assisted Adams on Deltan pneumatic tunnels. Jessica and Ian worked on roving pedestals. Whitney spent her day finding new Thetan villages and documenting the people who made up the various meditation groups. She was still attempting to understand their longevity and trying to figure out how it could affect our lives.

As the day wound down, Adams asked, "Would you mind staying late again to give Whitney a ride?"

He still wasn't feeling well. All of us were under the effects of months of long days at work. I considered telling him about the past night's event, but instead, I said it would be fine.

Adams left with Jessica and Ian. They were still discussing Deltan pedestals on their way out the door. Whitney and I were alone in the lab. She placed her mat on the floor and put her assorted photos of the Thetans in their proper places. She lit three candles and an incense stick then watched the monitors, waiting for the Coasttown Thetans to arrive.

I fixed my attention on the Thetan monitors. The group of six approached the podium in the darkness of the predawn light with The Grandmother leading the way. I watched with a growing curiosity to see if I could detect anything different about her, but I couldn't. Even in the dim light, I saw the look of serenity that defined her. The six Thetans took their positions within the circle. Whitney closed her eyes, and I pretended to stay busy with other duties. Jim said nothing, as he enjoyed participating in the sessions.

Within a few minutes, I sensed Whitney was locked in a meditative state. There was a difference about her face and her being that was subtle, but I could tell when she was there. Her face showed no emotion as she became the epitome of calmness. Jim's green light dwindled down to a very low level. While the meditation ensued, I became more curious and thought of ways to make sense of what had happened the night before.

I walked over to Whitney. I placed my hand several inches from her face and snapped my fingers lightly. She made no acknowledgement.

"Whitney?" I said softly. No response came back. I repeated her name again.

"She's meditating," Jim said quietly.

"I know. I'm just checking something out." The monitor showed The Grandmother sitting at her spot ever so peacefully. I wondered if it was worth trying some questions. "Grandmother," I said toward Whitney, as I looked at the Thetan face on the monitor. "Can you hear me?"

"Yes," came the response from Whitney's mouth. The voice was gentle. I didn't know what to say. The one thing I felt for certain was that Whitney was not playing a joke.

"Grandmother," I began, "is it your voice I hear coming through Whitney?"

"At this time, yes," Whitney spoke calmly.

"Do you mind if I ask a question?" I asked nervously.

"If it pleases you," she said. Her words came slowly, and there was a distinct properness to them.

"How did you know where my car keys were the other day?"

"The same as I know where they are now," was the response from Whitney's mouth.

"Where are they?" I asked.

"In the front right pocket of your pants," she answered. This came as another surprise but not a shock, for that's where they usually were.

"May I ask you another question?" I said, building up confidence to test her.

"If it pleases you."

"Jim, do me a favor and make a recording of this."

"Okay."

"How many beer bottles are on the shelf in the bathroom at my apartment?"

I had started the collection once I reached drinking age. I started at twenty to represent my birthday and placed a new beer bottle from a different country once a year on the shelf. It had evolved into something important to me, my way of feeling cosmopolitan. There was exactly one bottle for each year I was alive. No one in the world knew about it, and Whitney had never been inside my apartment.

"There are thirty-three," was the response. She was right.

"How do you know that?" I asked with absolute interest.

Through Whitney, The Grandmother spoke about vibrations and impulses and some kind of records. Within ten seconds, she had lost me entirely. She spoke at great length in a poised manner. The most I gathered from her spiel was that people were entities and everything was made up of vibrations. She went on and on for about fifteen minutes.

I had absolutely no idea what she was talking about, but I was relieved that Jim was recording it. After she stopped, I got a warm feeling about the whole thing.

"What color are the stripes on my socks?" I asked her next.

"Blue on the right, green on the left."

"Are you still recording this, Jim?"

"Every word."

"Good. What was the name of the dog I got when I was ten?"

"You called him Shep," came the response.

I asked any trivial question I could think of, and she answered correctly each time. Somehow, this Thetan elder knew everything about me.

I remained quiet for the remainder of the session and watched The Grandmother sitting calmly. I felt a growing respect toward her and the others in the group. I waited for what seemed an eternity for the Thetan sun to rise and the session to end. Once Whitney came back to present awareness, I didn't give her much time to unwind before I started telling her what had happened.

"I really don't want to start this conversation again," she interrupted me.

"We taped it," I told her. "Just listen."

Jim replayed it. Whitney rolled her eyes when the question about the beer bottles came up, but when she heard her own voice respond with the number thirty-three, she became more interested. Then I asked how The Grandmother did it. When her response started coming back, Whitney was overwhelmed. Her body quivered as if she was hit by an electrode.

"That's my voice!" she said.

"I know. It's incredible!"

"What am I talking about?" she asked in disbelief.

We listened again through the long explanation. Whitney shook her head in amazement. She also had difficulty understanding the meaning behind the words. The Grandmother kept referring to vibrations, intentions and entities, and something called the Akashic records.

Neither of us could follow it entirely, but its eloquence and complexity supported the argument that this was indeed the voice of another speaker. Whitney didn't talk that way. Nobody did.

"We've got to share this with my father," Whitney said. "Right away." We raced back to her house in my wheels. When we arrived, we discovered Adams asleep in his bed. Knowing he wasn't feeling well, we decided the news could wait until morning.

I drove home thinking about the wonder of it. When I reached my apartment, I went straight to the bathroom and counted the bottles on the shelf. A part of me was suddenly nervous I had been inaccurate.

To my delight, there were thirty-three beer bottles as expected.

The next morning when I arrived at work, Whitney and Adams were already listening to the recording. The speaker was within the lengthy explanation. Adams had a look of confusion building up on face. He acknowledged my presence but said nothing.

"It's amazing, isn't it," I said. Whitney smiled back to me.

"It certainly is," Adams managed, though he chose his words cautiously.

"What do you think about it?" I asked him.

"I'm not sure yet." He signaled to me to keep quiet so he could listen.

Jessica arrived and was curious what was going on, but she also received a wave off from Adams as he focused on the voice. By the time Ian arrived, it was almost over. The tape replayed the questions about my socks and my old dog's name. Ian assumed it was some kind of joke.

"What's this all about?" he asked.

Adams didn't say anything. I told Jessica and Ian about the previous night. I had trouble containing my enthusiasm. But when I finished the story and waited for their responses, all that came back were smart remarks and laughter.

"You don't believe me?" I asked them.

"No," they said. I glanced to Adams for confirmation. He was locked in the same thought pattern I had seen on his face when I entered the room.

"What about you, Dad?"

"Well," Adams said slowly, "there must be a reasonable explanation."

"Like what?" I asked.

"Like you two are making this up," he said flatly. Whitney was disappointed.

"Jim, tell them we're not making this up," I said.

"They're not making it up," Jim said emphatically.

"Now you've got Jim in on this too?" Jessica asked me. "I'm not sure that's such a good idea."

Adams agreed with her. "It takes the light waves almost two years to reach Jim's camera from that planet," he reminded us. "When we're watching these people, we're watching them two years ago. How could you be having a conversation with them?"

"I agree," I said. "I understand that you don't believe this. But you will after seeing it for yourselves. Is that okay with you?" I asked Whitney.

"Sure."

Jessica and Ian agreed. So it was set. We would see if Whitney could do it again with an audience. We spent the rest of the day not talking about it.

Whitney looked self-conscious as the others watched her place the icons about her mat in the usual manner. She preferred to meditate when everyone had left, even her father. I hoped she would be able to relax enough to reach that state of detachment.

Finally, the monitors above Whitney's desk showed the group of six Thetans approaching the podium at the beautiful village of Coasttown. The Grandmother led the group as they took their positions around the circle. I explained to the others in a quiet voice the way of the meditation sessions as I had observed.

The first several minutes were rather awkward. Whitney attempted to relax while the others sat and observed skeptically. Ian checked his watch a few times as if to say he hoped this wouldn't take too long.

I whispered, "It's worth the wait."

Whitney was getting close. I wanted to give her a few extra minutes to be sure. The others waited with mixed expressions appearing on their faces as the minutes passed.

Ian and Jessica noted the simple design on the circular podium and the seating placement of the people. Ian observed that the Thetans sat with six people in a seven-pointed circle. The position next to The Grandmother was left unoccupied, as was their custom.

I noticed the look of settlement on Whitney's face. I asked, "Can anybody hear me?"

"Yes," Whitney calmly replied.

"Am I speaking with The Grandmother?" I asked.

"You have said it so."

Ian and Jessica shared doubtful looks. Adams sat still.

I said, "Is it okay to ask some more questions?"

"If it pleases you," Whitney replied.

"Go ahead," I told the others. "Ask her anything you want."

There was a long pause. Adams looked like he didn't want to say anything at all, while Ian just seemed lost in a blank moment.

"What did I have for breakfast today?" Jessica asked.

"Half a melon and some bread," Whitney replied. Jessica raised an eyebrow.

"How much do I weigh?" Ian asked with a laugh.

"In your terms, one hundred and seventy-five pounds."

"That's about right, I think. How old am I?" Ian added. "In seconds."

"One billion, one hundred sixty-three million, sixty-five thousand, two hundred and three," she answered. I smiled broadly. I had a feeling she was right. Ian repeated the first three numbers to himself and thought about it. He grabbed his calculator and started punching in numbers.

"What was the name of my childhood doll?" Jessica asked as Ian busied himself with the calculator.

"You called her Sissy," the reply came. Jessica nodded her head in amazement.

"What was the name of Jessica's first lover?" I asked. Jessica gave me a look of disapproval and elbowed me in the chest.

"The entity's name was Randall Jackson, during his incarnation."

"She's right. But why do you say, 'during his incarnation?'" Jessica added.

"Because that entity has passed on," Whitney said.

"I wasn't aware of that." Jessica sat down absorbing the information. "I haven't thought of him for over twenty years."

"How old am I in seconds?" Ian repeated after coming up with his answer.

"One billion, one hundred sixty-three million, sixty-five thousand, two hundred and fifty."

"I have myself at a few less than that, although I'm not exactly sure what time I was born. Plus, I didn't factor in for this year. Are you starting from birth or conception?"

"Get past it, Ian!" I said. "Ask her something that really interests you!"

"You mean I can ask her anything, and she'll know the answer?"

"That's what I'm trying to tell you!"

Ian thought about it. He thought about the simplest question on his mind from the past week.

"Why can't we get the platform drive system on our prototype to emit the same amount of force as the ones from Delta 13?" Ian asked. "Does she know that?"

Adams interrupted, "Don't be absurd, Ian. She can't know about—"

"The problem lies in the set ratio of the emission source from the distance to the refraction lenses," Whitney began. "Velocities will be greatly improved by shortening and widening this area."

Ian perked up immediately as Whitney continued speaking in technical terms. She answered eloquently, using complex words of physics and engineering. Adams, Ian and Jessica were spellbound. I loved it, knowing this would put to rest any doubt this was contrived by Whitney or me. Ian found the answer to his liking, though he shook his head that this could be happening.

"Jim, are you recording this?" Adams asked.

"Every word."

The speaker went on and on. She pointed out several facets of their design that either needed improvements or simply weren't correct interpretations of the Deltan technology. Ian lit up with amazement. Jessica agreed that the speaker was making perfect sense. Once the speaker had finished, there was a quiet buzz throughout the lab.

Whitney sat calmly.

Ian asked, "How are you so knowledgeable about these drive systems?"

The speaker answered through Whitney, "This information is accessible in the Akashic records." Ian shrugged as if he didn't understand.

"I have a question for you," Adams added with a smile, as if he was trying to get to the bottom of a joke. "Are you aware that your planet is moving outwards in orbit?"

"Yes," she replied.

"What is causing that?"

"In the presence of a growing star, we ask our planet to move accordingly," the reply came from Whitney.

"Are you saying you are responsible for this?"

"We are through for the present," Whitney said.

"What do you mean?"

The monitor showed the Thetan sun was beginning to rise over Coasttown. Within a minute, the group of six would get up from their positions and resume their normal activities.

Adams repeated, "What do you mean 'we are through?'"

"It's too late," I told him. "Their sun is coming up. The session only lasts while they're in the trance."

"I don't understand," Adams said.

"Forget about that for a second," I told him. "What do you think? Ian? Jessica?"

"Absolutely incredible," Jessica whispered, watching the Thetans get out of their seated positions.

Whitney began to roll her head. She opened her eyes slowly, adjusting to the light. She looked at us as we stared at her in amazement.

"What?" Whitney asked defensively. "Did it work?"

"Unbelievable," Ian said. "How did you know all those answers?"

"All what answers?"

"You mean you don't remember?"

"She doesn't have any awareness of it while it's going on," I explained. "We don't know why. Maybe we should ask them next time."

"What did you think, Dad?"

Adams was slow to respond. He mulled over the information. "It doesn't make any sense. Though what you said about the Deltan pedestals made a lot of sense."

Jessica asked, "How do you feel, Whitney?"

"A little drained but fine. What did I say?"

Jim printed out a transcript. Whitney moved to a chair and scanned it.

After a few moments she reached out for Jessica. "I'm so sorry about your friend."

Jessica acknowledged the remark and sat next to her. Whitney read on. She was amazed with the description of the mechanisms that had not been sorted out by Ian and Adams. "This part is really wonderful," she whispered.

"I'd like a copy of that as well," Ian said. Jim printed another for him and one for Adams.

"How can they do it?" Adams asked Whitney. "How can they speak through you, especially concerning the physics involved?"

"I have no idea."

Adams was skeptical yet intrigued. He eyed The Grandmother. He watched her quietly as she walked off the podium and back to her grass hut.

The following day, Adams and Ian read through the advice on the Deltan roving pedestals. The comments made by The Grandmother were pure genius. As they analyzed the information, they came up with a series of follow-up questions.

Adams told Whitney, "I still don't believe that it's possible, but just for a laugh, I'd like to ask how the Thetans are getting their information."

"Fine," Whitney said.

"I also want to know how the planet moves in orbit, beyond the simple answer they gave."

Whitney wasn't sure what to make of her new ability. She attributed it entirely to the Thetans. She mentioned, "If anyone would like to try it, all you need to do is start meditating with them."

That evening, we contacted the Coasttown Thetans again. This time, the crew had a list of prepared questions.

Adams asked The Grandmother the first question. "How are you able to communicate through my daughter?"

"By connecting at the subconscious level," the speaker began. "The subconscious mind is in direct communication with all other subconscious minds."

"Help me understand that," Adams said.

The speaker spelled out a detailed account of the overall concept of communication. It was very matter-of-fact, unemotional information. She discussed people as entities. She also discussed energy and vibrations. "Vibrations" was a buzzword that kept popping up. As I understood it, the Thetans used the word to encompass verbal and mental communication. Thinking of any kind seemed to be a vibration. So was the ever-flowing wealth of information about anything at all.

I wasn't sure what vibrations didn't encompass. Terms like "source manifestations" and "planetary influences" also came up. Many of the answers were long-winded.

"Do you understand that this makes no sense?" Adams added. "The view we see of you is from light waves that take two years to reach us. How can we be seeing those wavelengths and conversing with you simultaneously?"

"The subconscious exists out of time," the reply came from Whitney, "just as spirit exists out of time."

Again, the speaker went into a lengthy explanation about the existence of non-physical entity processes. It was along the lines of thought waves being vibrations that existed beyond any measurement. Within a few sentences, she had lost me entirely.

Once the ramblings had stopped, Adams said, "Let's bring her out of it." Though the meditation was still taking place, and we had several questions we wanted to ask, there was a certain uneasiness about the process. Adams wasn't sure how he felt about his daughter being used as a medium. "I don't know how safe this whole process is."

I shook her shoulders lightly. When she didn't respond, I shook them harder. Then Whitney gasped for air and opened her eyes wide. As she regained consciousness she was profoundly affected, laughing softly while tears streamed down her face. Adams knelt before her and took her hands. She motioned to him that she was fine. It was the first time anyone had shaken her out of one of the sessions and seemed to have an intense effect, like being awakened in the middle of a vivid dream.

Whitney sat wide-eyed and amazed as we told her the information she had presented. As usual, she hadn't the vaguest notion she had spoken at all, let alone for twenty minutes. She asked for a glass of water.

Jessica provided one and Whitney took a few sips.

"It was like a blurring of time," Whitney said. Instead of recalling a pleasant meditation and momentary loss of senses, as usual, she described an out-of-body perception of her own spirit surrounded by others. "There was warmth and calm. There was love but I can't describe it. I couldn't see faces, but I sensed the presence of others with me."

"Just when I thought I'd seen everything. Could Whit be a medium for the Thetans? No. I cannot accept that. There must be an explanation. It doesn't make sense on a half dozen levels. But how did she describe Deltan technology so well?"

- from p. 124 of Webster's journal.

Psychic Abilities

THAT NIGHT WAS the summer festival. The stores closed early, and a large section of Main Street was blocked off. The townspeople gathered for a parade and fireworks to celebrate the end of summer. Whitney and I had planned to watch it.

She chose a picnic on a quiet hillside where we could see the activity of the town below. We hiked up a ways and spread a blanket under a tree. Whitney unpacked the food as I opened the wine. We ate in silence and watched the parade of town floats and marching kids.

"More wine?" she asked.

"Please." I offered my glass.

"You've been quiet, Jon." She tore off some bread and cheese, bit into it and offered me the last bite.

"My mind keeps flashing back to your meditation today."

"You're not upset with all this weird stuff, are you?"

"No, but... it is strange."

"It's strange for me too," she said. "Does it frighten you?"

"Frighten might not be the right word. I just don't understand it."

"Do you need to understand it?"

"I want to. Not that I understand most things at work, but this... this has really been a surprise."

"Do you believe in psychic abilities?" she asked.

"I never have. Why, do you think you're psychic?"

"Sometimes. Things will happen, and I'll feel like I knew it was going to happen."

"I don't think I'd want a gift like that," I said.

"Why not?"

"I don't know."

"Have you ever had an experience where it feels strange, like you'd already experienced it? That you were seeing something you'd seen before?"

"I think so."

"Isn't that sort of the same thing?" she asked.

"Maybe. I don't want to think about it too much."

She sensed my apprehension. A part of me didn't want Whitney to be psychic. I recognized it too, though I didn't know why.

"I really need your friendship right now," she said, lying down and looking at the sky.

"You've got it," I said, lying next to her and taking her hand. "I'm here for you. If I feel a little weird about it, that's just me. You can understand, right?"

"I guess it would be strange if you didn't feel that way."

I kissed her on the cheek, then on her lips. Then the fireworks went off. We sat up to watch them.

Skeptics

THE NEXT DAY WE EAGERLY awaited the afternoon when the Coasttown Thetans took their places at the podium. Whitney prepared her floor space with her mat, candles and icons. Then she handed me a piece of paper.

"What's this?" I asked.

"Questions from me," she said. "I'd like you to ask them since I obviously can't do it while in that state."

"Oh," I said, surprised that Whitney needed to ask anything.

I looked over the paper. There were four main questions. She wanted to know if they could heal with touch and, if so, how. She wanted to know if anyone could contact them, or if she was unique. She wanted to know the purpose behind the design of their villages, podiums and meditation circles. She also wanted to know how long they lived.

"I'm not sure we'll have time for all of these," I told her. "Your dad and Ian have a number of questions as well." Judging from the length of the speaker's responses, I wasn't sure we could get through more than four or five questions in a given session.

"Just make sure you ask one of my questions for every two of my father's," she told me. "These are some of the things I'm dying to find out."

"I'll do what I can," I said. She gave me a serious look. "One of yours for every two of his," I repeated.

The six Thetans approached the podium. Whitney hurried herself into position. She lit her candles and placed the photos around her mat.

Adams, Ian and Jessica came over. Frank was also present to witness the phenomenon for the first time. He sat in a chair at some distance. We all gave Whitney plenty of space and tried not to stare as she began her meditation. After about ten minutes, I sensed she was ready for questions.

Adams gave me a list of seven questions. Then he whispered to Frank, "I still don't believe in this, but the answers have been fascinating."

We began with specifics concerning Deltan roving pedestals. The engineers back at Maxwell Enterprises had made headway from the previous information, but their progress only led to more questions.

Whitney answered the first question in technical jargon. I glanced over to Frank. He was transfixed.

"Very interesting," he whispered to Adams.

Adams asked follow-up questions in response to the answers. As we got into the third and fourth of his questions strictly on ways of producing greater force in the Deltan drive systems, I wondered if we would have any time for the questions Whitney had prepared. I hesitated to mention it to Adams, since he and Ian were making so much progress. The hour flew by. When the speaker informed us that we were through for the present, I hadn't asked any of Whitney's requests.

She rolled her head slowly, coming out of the session. Frank applauded her efforts.

"Most amazing thing I've ever seen," he told her.

"I'm glad you liked it," Whitney responded. "Can I get a printout, Jim?" Jim produced a few pieces of paper, and she scanned through them looking for her questions.

"We made a lot of progress today," Adams told her. "Though I still don't get it, I can't argue with the results." He also had Jim produce a copy of the notes for himself and Ian as they returned to their desks to make sense of the new information.

"You didn't ask any of my questions?" Whitney looked at me sternly. "Not even one?"

"There wasn't any time," I apologized. "Their answers kept leading to more questions, and they were making such progress. I couldn't break in."

Whitney wasn't impressed. She packed up her things and told her father she was taking the car home. She left the room noticeably upset.

After she had left, Frank asked us, "Can we step into the other room for a moment?"

Jessica, Ian, Adams and I followed him from the lab and made ourselves comfortable in the office. Frank sat down in Webster's chair and paused for a moment, searching for the right words.

"What do you make of this?" he asked Adams from behind the desk.

Adams rubbed his eyes. "It's the strangest thing I've ever seen," he said, sitting in the chair facing him. "It makes absolutely no sense from a standpoint of physics."

"Even beyond the physics of it, how can this knowledge come from such a primitive culture?" Frank asked.

Ian chimed in, "Those people don't even possess a steam engine or an electric bulb."

"That's what I'm getting at," Frank said. "If they are the most primitive culture we've found, then how can they make sense of these matters of technology?"

"It doesn't add up," Jessica said, pacing about the room.

Adams shrugged, "I don't have an answer for it."

"I'm just going to throw this out there," Frank said, "Don't be put off by it. What's the chance this information is coming through Jim?"

"What?" I cried out, standing from my chair. "That's ridiculous."

"Hold on, Mr. Gruber. I don't doubt your sincerity, but let me present a possible case. It's been long known that Whitney and Jim have preferred this Thetan culture since we found them. Could it be possible this is some prank to get the rest of us to believe that they have special powers?"

"What are you saying?" Adams asked him. "That the two of them conjured this up?"

"I'm just looking for a reasonable explanation," Frank added. "You know, when all things are considered, typically the simplest solution is the right one."

"But how could the answers be coming from Whitney?" Ian asked, chewing his pen.

"An earpiece," Frank said, "or a well-placed speaker that only she can hear. Have you noticed how slowly she talks while giving the answers?"

"But how would they know details about the drive system?" Jessica asked.

Frank reasoned, "Hasn't Jim been working the entire time documenting the Deltan products and watching the three of you try and make sense of them? Perhaps he's figured out what you haven't been able to."

"Why would he keep that to himself?" Adams asked.

"Maybe he finds it amusing? I'm just saying it's possible."

"But what about all the other information that was presented before you saw this?" I said, standing over the desk. "What about the things she knew about Jessica and Ian from before?"

"Have you ever heard of background checks?" Frank said, motioning for me to have a seat. "Relax, Jon. My companies do them all the time with high-ranking people, especially in something classified."

140

"I don't believe it," I said, sitting back down. "I can't even believe we're talking about this seriously!"

"Wait a second," Adams said, pondering the idea. "I can't dispute the information we've been given. But it is much more plausible that this data is coming from Jim rather than from that primitive tribe."

"I'd have to agree," Ian added.

"You think Jim would play a trick on you?" I asked them.

"I'm just trying to make sense of something that doesn't make any sense!" Adams said, pulling his hands through his hair.

"You said she's in a trance while she's doing this?" Frank asked me.

"That's right. She doesn't have any memory upon waking from it."

Frank informed us, "People who are truly in a trance are literally removed from their senses."

Jessica continued his thought, "So she wouldn't feel it if we gave her a prick on the finger."

"That's the point," Frank added. "If she's really in a trance, then she can't hear through an earpiece either. I don't think any of us believe the information is coming solely through Whitney."

"Are you serious?" I argued. "You don't believe it could come from the Thetans?"

"No, I don't believe it," Adams said flatly. "For several reasons."

"Listen," Jessica said, standing behind me. "We don't doubt you, Jon, but we're going to need a little more proof of this phenomenon. Surely you recognize there's a chance this information is coming through Jim."

"Then check her ears for an earpiece," I reasoned. "Or stand next to her and see if you can hear Jim's voice."

"I hate to admit it," Adams added, "but a simple prick on the finger will let us know whether she's in a trance or not."

"It really is the only way," Jessica added.

I argued with them, but it was a lost cause. For the sake of scientific analysis, it was settled. Even I was forced to agree that it was for the good of everyone to be just a little skeptical in our approach. I assured them I would not share the discussion with Jim or Whitney.

The next day Whitney made us promise to ask her questions. She told Adams, "If you guys want my future assistance, then first let all four of my questions be asked before continuing with your own."

He agreed to it.

Around noon, Frank and the rest of us watched her go through the preparations of getting into her meditative trance. The Thetans took their positions on the podium in Coasttown. Whitney sat quietly for about ten minutes. The monitor above her desk showed the face of The Grandmother in her calm presence. Once Whitney had a look of detachment on her face, I told Adams she was ready. He advised me to go ahead with the questions that Whitney had prepared.

"Grandmother," I asked, "is anyone capable of doing what Whitney is doing? Is anyone capable of being the medium for this information?"

"Yes," Whitney replied. "All subconscious minds are connected. It is essential to be at peace to let the information flow. The knack for being the medium is to enable the conscious mind to receive vibrations from the subconscious. Even Whitney has not yet acquired that ability, though with practice she could."

"Okay, question number two. Are you capable of healing others through touch, and if so, how?"

"We are," she replied. "Physical beings are beings of energy. Pain is the result of energy not flowing properly..."

The speaker went into great detail. I understood the gist of it, but once again, she had lost me.

Adams nodded to Jessica to administer the first test since she had drawn the short straw. Jessica was to prick Whitney with a sharp pin underneath the fingernail.

Jessica approached her slowly with the pin. Whitney continued to speak about the physical body and energy fields. Jessica calmly took one of Whitney's hands into her own and brought the pin to the fingernail.

"What are you doing?" Jim asked her.

"This is just a test," Jessica told him.

"It's okay, Jim," Adams added from his chair, waving to Jessica to proceed.

Jessica slowly inserted the pin into the underside of Whitney's nail. A spot of blood dripped out as the pin was inserted far enough to stay there on its own. Jessica replaced her hand where it had been in Whitney's lap. The pin remained lodged as Whitney spoke without interruption or change in expression. Several glances went about the room as Whitney finished her spiel about energy healing.

"Satisfied?" I asked them.

"Almost," Frank said. "I know this isn't pleasant, but it's in the interest of everyone. Ask the next question please, Mr. Gruber."

It had been mentioned by Ian that perhaps a prick on the finger would not be an adequate test. Leave it to Ian to recognize such things, I thought.

"What is the purpose behind the layout of the Thetan villages? Why is there a podium central to every village, and why do Thetans meditate there every day just before dawn?"

Whitney answered in the speaker's voice. "Theta 7, as you say, has different situations from your planet. These have been evolutionary changes, some to the solar system and some to the people. The circle is a manifestation of the spiritual spheres of influence..."

Whitney continued with another detailed response. I wished they could have found shorter ways of answering. During the spiel, Adams nodded to Jessica to administer the second test.

Jessica took one of the matches Whitney used to light her meditation candles. They were large, wooden matches that scraped on the side of the box. She struck the match, and the space around her illuminated as the sulfur ignited. She let the match burn for a moment, allowing the wood to absorb much of the heat. She then took Whitney's other hand and gently held it as the speaker continued on the subject of the meditation circles.

"Please forgive me for doing this," Jessica told her. She gently blew out the match and then stuck it into Whitney's palm causing it to lightly burn the flesh. Adams turned his head in discomfort. Jessica looked amazed as she removed the smoking match from Whitney's palm. "Oh my God."

Jessica backed away as Whitney continued talking without signs of discomfort or tension. She went on for several minutes even though nobody was listening.

"Now are you satisfied?" I asked them. Impressed looks went from Ian to Frank to Adams.

"Did she have another question?" Jessica reminded me.

"Yes. Whitney would like to know how long your people are living. How many revolutions around your sun?"

"We are living much longer than you are accustomed to," Whitney replied. "I have lived for over 30,000 solar orbits, as you call them." I shook my head in disbelief and looked over to Adams. His expression had not changed, as if he was trying to see through the Thetans. "The man to my left is over 70,000 years old. We will review this another time, for we are through for the present."

The Thetan sun was beginning to rise. The session had ended. Within moments, Whitney would come out of her trance.

"I hope you're satisfied," I said to Adams and Frank, angry with them.

Adams tossed his hands as if he gave up. Frank nodded along with the others.

The pin still hung from Whitney's fingernail. I grabbed it quite hard to pull it out. It was sunk in deep but finally came out from the nail with a trickle of blood.

"Can I get a napkin over here or something?" I demanded.

Jessica hurried over with a clean handkerchief. We wrapped Whitney's finger gently and placed it back into her lap. The Thetans stood and began leaving the podium. Whitney rolled her head slowly then cried out in pain and brought her hands to her chest.

"What happened?!" she shouted. I dropped to my knees in front of her as Whitney cried louder.

"Whitney, I'm so sorry. Please forgive me."

"What did you do to me?" she said as she inspected her bloody finger and felt the pain of the burn on her other hand. Jessica brought some cream over and administered it to the burn.

Adams said, "It was my fault, dear. You can blame me."

"Why?"

"We had to confirm that you really were in a trance."

"What did you think I was doing?!"

Frank added, "Please, try to understand this from our point of view."

"I don't know if I want to." She got up and grabbed her father's car keys and ran from the room. Her meditation candles and icons were still in place on the floor.

"That went well," I said.

"It had to be done," Adams said.

"She'll feel better soon," Frank added. "She'll understand we had to do what we did."

I picked up Whitney's items and put them on her desk where she kept them. I rolled up her mat and put it away. Jim printed out a copy of what The Grandmother had said.

"This might help her feel better," Jim told me.

I grabbed the printout and excused myself for the evening. I raced my car back to Whitney's house but when I got there, I saw no sign of her or Webster's car. I felt like a schmuck. What a great friend I had been. I folded the papers over, pinned them to the front door and wrote her name on them. I also wrote that I was sorry.

Whitney didn't show up for work the next day. Adams said she came home late and had been in her room ever since.

He said, "Give her some time."

He too felt badly for what had happened, but he insisted it was the right thing to do. Jessica felt terrible about it, but she reminded me what happened was necessary.

"How can we accept something like this without validation?" Jessica asked me.

I still felt awful. In my opinion, I had been the one who let Whitney down.

The three of them were making sense of a new design for the Deltan drive system. They were using the notes from the Thetan speaker like it was an old treasure map with a few missing pieces.

I excused myself early and drove to Whitney's house. Surprisingly, she answered the door and let me in. Whitney listened quietly as I reviewed the conversation that led to the testing. What shocked her the most was that the crew could even think Jim might be involved in a prank.

"Are you going to come back to work?" I asked her.

"I'm going to have to," Whitney said, showing me the printout from the past reading. "Have you read this? It's incredible."

I had almost forgotten the Thetans had answered all four of Whitney's questions. She handed them to me and I skimmed through them. Within a few sentences, I was lost as to the meaning behind the words. The only answer I really understood was the response to the subject of aging.

"You were right," I said, with my focus on the pages. "They are living for huge lengths of time."

"I have some more questions I need to ask them."

"I promise you, nothing will ever happen again."

"I'm not worried about you, Jon. It's the others I'm not so sure I can trust. Even my dad."

"The tests they did satisfied everybody," I told her, trying to convince her as well as myself.

"I'd prefer to come by after the others have left."

That was something we couldn't count on unless we made arrangements ahead of time. I told her I'd take care of it. I returned to the lab and told everybody the deal.

"Whitney is willing to return but not with any of you present. She won't subject herself to being taken advantage of again."

The following day, Whitney returned. She arrived as everyone else was preparing to leave. She brought another list with more of her own questions. There was a final question from Adams that would be asked if there was enough time. He wanted to know what specifically was moving their planet. Ian and Jessica apologized to Whitney before leaving. Adams gave her a wink as he left.

Once the others had gone, Whitney had just a few minutes to get ready. She talked with Jim about the pain in her hands and what she did to make it feel better. Jim was still intrigued with the concept of pain.

"I wish it had happened to me instead of you," he told Whitney.

It was the first time we tried a session with another group of Thetans. Coasttown had passed the dawn line just before noon. Whitney wanted to try one of the other villages, so we lined up a group she had meditated with during her studies. They lived further inland on one of the Thetan continents. An elder male sat next to the open spot in the circle. Whitney advised me to direct my questions to him. She lit her candles and placed the photos and icons around her space as she laid her mat on the floor.

Even after the atrocious ending to the previous session, she was anxious to continue. The elder male and the others took their spots around the circle. Within a few moments the session had begun.

"Sir," I began, not sure what to call him. "Can you hear me?"

"Yes," came the reply.

"We have heard references to the Akashic records. What exactly are the Akashic records?"

"The Akashic records include everything that is or ever was," Whitney began. "The entire past makes up this body. Every action, every word, every thought or mental image in existence encompasses the records."

The enormity of those words was beyond my comprehension.

"But how can that be?" I asked, dumbfounded.

"Simply because it is," the speaker replied. "Trying to make sense of it would be impossible for someone such as yourself. Comprehension of the records is not important, but how you use them is."

I wanted to ask more questions about the records, but I remembered my promise to Whitney.

"Next question. Is it possible to access this information from any location, or is it necessary to have someone like you for the channel of that information?"

"It is possible for anyone to access the Akashic records. The subconscious can do it at any time. However, at the conscious level, it is nearly impossible for someone who is neither trained nor gifted. Otherwise, it is necessary to use some form of medium, as Whitney has been able to do with us."

146

"How has Whitney been able to accomplish this?"

"She has the gift for it. She has applied herself. Her interest in joining our meditation freely without any request for herself, separates her from the common individual."

"By that you mean someone like myself?"

"Yes."

I was feeling insulted, but I knew it was true. Whitney was as selfless as anyone I had ever known.

"Whitney would like to know if you provide information for others as well," I said.

"We provide answers for anyone who seeks them. It is extremely rare to encounter individuals who speak directly with us. It is most common to communicate indirectly with those who seek answers through dreams, prayer and meditation."

"Whitney would also like to know how you live for such long periods. Have your people always been this way, or is this something that has increased over time?"

"Millions of years ago, our ancestors were similar to yours, and the duration of their lives was similar. Theta 7, as you call it, has experienced many transformations. These were changes to the solar system and to the people. Part of our evolution has been an ascension as to the purpose of our lives. Simply living, taking care of the basic needs for hunger, shelter and reproduction, is not the focus of our lives. Present Thetans pursue universal enlightenment. We assist others as they struggle. You may think of us as guides or teachers. As the focus of our lives has changed, so have the physical attributes that define our lifetimes, such as the length of time we occupy these bodies."

I was blown away. He spoke so clearly. It was one of the first times I really understood what was said. He had answered all of the questions on Whitney's list.

"One last question. Dr. Adams would like to know specifically how the Thetans are able to move their planet further out in orbit."

"In the presence of a growing star we ask the planet to move so we may continue our experience here."

"That's it?"

"This will be difficult for him to understand. He does not recognize consciousness exists within every atom in the universe. Our planet is conscious, just as yours is. We communicate directly with that consciousness."

I started giggling, knowing Adams would doubt the answer, but I didn't feel the need to elaborate. I spent the rest of the session sitting quietly beside Whitney in my chair.

I sat in contemplation. The words from the elder brought me back to a time when Adams, Jim and I were first speculating on the origin of life. During the early stages of the project, we had debated whether life preceded consciousness, or whether consciousness preceded life. We assumed this was something that couldn't be known. If I had understood the elder correctly, he had settled the argument by saying that consciousness existed within stars and planets and the very atoms that made them. What a mind-blowing concept! All matter contained some form of consciousness?

When the session ended, I knew Whitney would be pleased. This session would make up for the last fiasco. Jim printed out a copy before I had to ask. Whitney opened her eyes to see me standing before her, proudly holding the printout.

"I think you're really going to like this," I said, handing her the pages.

"I'm not bleeding anywhere, am I?" she asked.

"Not this time."

War

BATTLES WERE STILL COMMON at the continental borders on Delta 13. Although the interiors of the continents were peaceful, thousands of soldiers threw themselves into the action at the borders in what seemed like a perpetual battle.

The soldiers used a fascinating crystal-powered laser weapon. It was small enough to be carried in the arms, yet powerful enough to blast through anything in its way. The beam could even penetrate the glowing force shields, the modern fortress walls that protected each continent.

Frank mentioned, "Our military will pay handsomely for this."

"How do crystals work?" I asked Ian. I had always thought crystals were just decorative rocks.

"Crystals take light and break it up into its component colors," Ian said, removing his thick glasses and rubbing his eyes. "Different crystals have different optical properties. Polarimetry is a method by which light is aligned to a single plane. But there's also a method of squeezing crystals for huge electrical potential."

"Squeezing crystals?"

"Sounds strange, I know," Ian said. "I suspect both are elements of how those guns work."

Many of the soldiers wore a body suit made out of a highly reflective lightweight metal. The metal was so reflective that light waves bent around the suit, making the soldier appear invisible. Frank found it to be quite imaginative. He asked Jessica to start working on a presentation for his investors.

"I don't think this is a good idea," Adams said to Frank.

"Better this ends up with our people than someone else."

"Perhaps," Adams admitted. "Wouldn't it be better if no one had it?"

"What makes you think this won't be invented someday?" Frank asked him. Adams had no answer.

In addition to their laser rifles, the Deltan soldiers used a version like a cannon that floated alongside the troops as they advanced on foot. The cannons shot a thick laser blast, a solid line of orange light. The force shields shot at the soldiers and the cannons, while the armies attempted to penetrate their neighbors' territories.

"It's a suicide mission," I remarked, watching one night with Ian and Jess. A division of foot soldiers headed out bravely into the enemy's land.

"They must know they're not coming back," Ian mused. "They probably see it as a badge of honor."

I asked, "Doesn't it seem pointless?"

"From here, yes," Jessica said. "From there, who knows?"

For a reason that wasn't clear, the skyways were entirely free of warfare. The wonderful disks and cigar-shaped vessels always kept to the airspace over their own kingdoms. This was most confusing to our crew. We all considered air superiority to be the vital factor in any war campaign. We thought it might have to do with the satellites in space, the ones we had yet to understand. We often wondered how their governments had evolved under so much hatred. The universe Adams had created left us mostly guessing in areas of politics and customs.

Frank asked that one of his investors, a man from an aeronautical defense company, be allowed to see the Deltan force shields and to witness the question and answer period with the Thetans. Adams left the decision up to Whitney.

Whitney said, "I can't imagine they'll help you with that."

"Is it okay if we ask?" Frank said.

"I guess so," Whitney said to my surprise. "I'm curious what they'll have to say."

Frank brought in the man from the defense company. The two took a seat by the far wall. Once the Coasttown Thetans had congregated, Whitney sat in position ready for the first question. I told Ian to ask what he wanted.

"What is the source behind the Deltan crystal energy shields?" Ian asked her.

"Just as you have said," The Grandmother replied through Whitney. "Crystal energy."

"Let me rephrase this," Ian went on. "If I were trying to build a crystal energy shield, what would be the process?"

"It is important to understand," the speaker began, "when seeking information of this nature, one must consider the purposes, aims and ideals of the individuals involved."

She stopped speaking. We wondered the reason for the pause. Frank looked a bit uncomfortable next to his associate.

"Is she waiting for me to answer?" Ian asked me in a hushed tone.

"I don't know," I said.

Frank spoke up. "The aim is longevity of life."

"Longevity of life comes through harmony with all living things," the speaker replied, "not through highly powered weaponry."

"But we didn't ask you about any weaponry," Ian objected.

"The same technology you speak of for the shields can enable weapons of mass destruction," the speaker replied.

Ian looked confused. Frank motioned for the crew to follow him into Webster's office. We left Whitney sitting quietly by herself in the middle of the lab.

The man from the defense company was not pleased. He told Frank, "This isn't what I expected." Frank looked to Adams, but Adams deflected his glance and said nothing.

"I'm sorry for the delay," Frank offered. "We're working on it."

"That response seemed pretty clear," I told them.

Frank asked Ian, "Might there be a way around it?"

"Perhaps we could break the question up into parts," Ian suggested.

"What are you thinking?" Jessica asked.

"We could ask about the properties of crystals to start. Once she gets on the subject of polarimetry, we can ask about aligning the power into a single plane."

"It's worth a shot," Frank added.

We returned to the lab. Ian looked to me to ask the question. The blank look on my face must have conveyed that I didn't know enough about the subject to frame it properly.

"Grandmother," Ian asked, "can you tell us about the natural qualities of the crystal in terms of harnessing energy?"

"The science of which you ask," the speaker began, "is known as crystallography. The crystal bends light and separates it into its component colors. There are many ways to harness energy from this naturally forming object. One way is building successive layers at constant angles to produce a unit cell."

As she spoke, Frank gave the investor a look of assurance. The man's face changed dramatically as she gave a detailed account of energy sources that could be built using crystals. She spoke for ten minutes in such scientific detail that I was completely left behind. Adams and Ian shared glances as if to ask the other if he knew what to make of it. The investor was spellbound. Then the speaker paused.

"As a follow-up to that," Ian asked her, "how would one harness the energy into a single plane?"

"As stated before, it is important to recognize the purposes, aims and ideals of the individuals involved when seeking such information," she replied. There was no change of tone to her voice. Her response remained matter-of-fact.

"But I don't understand how you can answer the question at one level and not another," Ian objected.

"We are through for the present," Whitney said.

I looked up to the monitors. The sun had yet to rise over Coasttown. I realized it would be five minutes before the meditation would truly end.

"Can you at least answer his question?" Frank asked.

Nothing came from Whitney as she sat in her trance.

"I think this session has ended," Jim said.

"I think so too," Adams added.

Frank walked the man to the door and said, "We'll be in touch."

I sat in my chair and waited. The Thetans eventually got up from their positions and Whitney came out of her trance.

"How did it go?" she asked me.

"Fairly well."

Whitney read the notes Jim provided. A slow grin overcame her face. When she got to the last page, she laughed.

"What do you make of it?" I asked her.

"Just what she said. Some information isn't meant to be shared with certain individuals."

Frank returned and asked, "Would it be possible to contact another group for our next session? I wonder if The Grandmother would withhold anything."

"I seriously doubt it," Whitney replied, "but you can try the same question with another group."

The next evening, we found a meditation group in the central part of a continent, very far from Coasttown. Six Thetans approached the podium wearing white gowns in the darkness. A middle-aged man sat next to the open space in the circle. Whitney reached her state of detachment. I told Ian she was ready for questions.

"Can you hear me, sir?" Ian directed his question toward Whitney while he focused on the Thetan on the main monitor.

"Yes," he replied through Whitney.

"May I ask you some questions?" Ian said.

"If it pleases you."

Ian asked the same questions from the night before, about harnessing energy from crystals. The Thetan elder repeated the responses just as The Grandmother had.

"How would one harness that energy into a single plane?" Ian asked, crossing his fingers.

The elder replied through Whitney, "It is important to consider the purposes, aims and ideals of the individuals involved when seeking answers of such nature."

"Intriguing answers to certain questions. Very relieved the Thetans have decided not to answer defense related products. Listen to me. I'm no longer doubting them. Don't like thinking about it, but the results have been fantastic. Learned more from them in a few days than we would have all year without their help."

- from p. 128 of Webster's journal.

Highs and Lows

AT A CREW MEETING, Ian went over the progress report for the PFDs. Ian congratulated the team on its good work. Our weeks of design and testing went very well. The engineers back at Maxwell Enterprises had done an excellent job of interpreting the overall package and creating a product that did what it was supposed to do—it flew in every possible direction. The time frame to market the device was less than two years.

"There's only one area where we need performance parameters," Ian said, looking at me. "And I won't blame you if you don't want to do it."

"What?" I asked.

"We need to know altitude capability, how high it will go before the engines cut out."

"I thought you said it can't coast to a landing like a normal plane?"

"That's true," Ian said.

Jessica reassured me. "There's a parachute system in all the models. We've made this as safe as possible, Jon."

"What about a robot?" I asked. "Could a robot do this?"

"Maybe one from Alpha 17," Ian joked. "But we don't have anything here that could function like a human pilot."

"What if something goes wrong with the parachute system?" Whitney asked.

"There's a reserve chute for the pilot," Jessica added. "If anything goes wrong, Jon can disconnect the harness, jump out of the craft and open his own chute."

"Sounds like fun," Jim said.

"I highly doubt it will come to that," Ian stated.

"How high do the engineers think it can go?" Adams asked.

"Pretty high," Ian said. "About thirty thousand feet. Maybe forty."

I asked, "Won't it be freezing up there?"

"You'll be in a space suit with an oxygen supply," Ian said. "You'll be on constant radio chat with us below. If anything causes you to lose consciousness, we can activate the parachute from the ground."

"You don't have to do this," Whitney told me.

"How safe is the chute for the craft?" I asked.

"It's the same one the space division uses for its vessels," Jessica explained. "It's made for a plane that weighs fifty times more and falls from outer space."

"Sounds safe," Adams added.

"What the heck," I said. "Count me in."

Whitney rolled her eyes at my cavalier attitude though she didn't know how scared I was. I felt it was important for me to do what I could for the team. After all, I had done the other tests. The PFD was my baby.

The PFD was towed out to the desert. A driver from Maxwell Enterprises drove the truck. A second truck carried the same three engineers who had been present for all our tests, along with a bevy of monitoring devices. Frank, Ian, Jessica and I rode in the trailer with the PFD. During the ride, the four of us went over the functions of the parachutes, the space suit and the oxygen supply.

Adams and Whitney stayed in the lab. She wanted to find a group of Thetans at the dawn line and meditate with them. She believed saying prayers and sitting in quiet contemplation were the most helpful things she could do. When we got to the desert floor and had the PFD out and ready, I called her.

Ian set up the antenna for the device that would operate the chute in the event I was unable to. We pushed the button for a test, and the chute popped out from the back of the PFD as designed. I helped him repack it carefully into its compartment.

The engineers told Frank their monitoring equipment was ready.

Jessica helped me get into the bulky space suit. She helped me into my boots and gloves, then put the parachute pack over my shoulders and tightened the harness around my waist and crotch.

"Not too tight," I told her as she cinched it down between my legs.

She loosened it a notch. "Better?"

"Better."

She put my helmet on and snapped it to the suit in two places. She then added the oxygen tank and attached it to the front of my suit and helmet.

"Try breathing now," she said. I breathed in deeply. The oxygen came in easily through the helmet. It smelled pure.

"How am I going to be able to fly with all this crap on?" I asked. My heart was pounding.

"You'll be fine," Frank mentioned, giving me a pat on the back. "Just relax."

"We'll be with you in your headset," Jessica said.

"I'm not sure I can do this," I said, suddenly feeling very scared.

"It's going to be safe." She gave me a hug and kissed my helmet, leaving an impression of her lips on the plastic. "We're going to be talking with you every step of the way."

Ian and Jessica boosted me up to the cabin. Jessica climbed in and attached the flight harness for me. Then she jumped down. Once alone inside the PFD, I began to shake. I had flown the device a dozen times by then, and I hadn't felt fear since the initial flight. But it was another story knowing I was about to fly the device as high as it could go until its engines died. I had never used a parachute before and had never wanted to. Frank, Ian and Jessica watched me with admiration. The engineers sat patiently behind their equipment. The truck driver gave me a thumbs-up as I stood at the helm, ready to take off.

"Is that guy a paramedic?" I asked, pointing to the truck driver.

Ian's answer came through my helmet. "No."

I took one more deep breath and started the turbines. Their whine became louder as they warmed up. I waved to the crew and reluctantly began flying.

Ian had instructed me to climb in circles and I did, making large loops above the desert floor. I ascended higher and higher into the sky. Within a minute, I was higher than I had ever been in the device.

"How's it going?" Ian's voice came through my helmet.

"So far, so good," I replied.

"Let me know every thousand feet you get to, okay?"

"You got it, boss."

Once I was flying, I felt myself relaxing. I thought of the safety equipment surrounding me. I knew I could get out of the harness and jump from the PFD in about three seconds if I really had to. I thought about Jessica saying the main chute would land a space vessel of much greater weight. I looked at her lipstick smudge in front of my face. I also thought of Whitney sitting quietly in meditation back at the lab.

"One thousand," I called in.

The PFD performed beautifully. I made consistent circles, climbing higher and higher over the desert floor. The landscape looked like some of the planets we viewed from above. The barren desert floor resembled spots from Alpha 17. I passed the two and three thousand marks and called the numbers in.

"How's it flying?" Ian asked.

"Perfect. Nothing unusual."

After passing five thousand feet, I estimated I was approaching heights that few birds had ever known. I wondered what the air temperature was since the space suit shielded me from sensing it. I passed through a wispy layer of clouds and entered much bluer sky.

"Ten thousand," I called in.

"Anything unusual?" Ian asked.

"Nope."

The higher it flew, the calmer I became. I called out numbers as the PDF passed marks. I confirmed the location of the parachute button for the craft and the cord for my chute. I knew exactly where they were and how quickly I could reach them.

"Twenty thousand," I reported.

"We can't see you anymore," Jessica's voice came through my headset.

I looked down, barely able to distinguish the test area of desert floor. I couldn't see the others or the truck, as the wispy cloud layer beneath me filtered my view. I could only see the partial cloud cover and the horizon. The sun and the dark blue sky felt like my newest friends.

"Thirty thousand," I called in.

"How's it feel now?" Ian's transmission was mixed with static. I was reminded of my task.

"The device feels fine, but I can barely tell where I am anymore."

"This is a big area," Ian reassured me. "Just keep making those circles."

I breathed in more deeply. My heart rate picked up as I passed the forty thousand foot barrier. The sky looked much darker blue, almost black. I was getting close to outer space. I suddenly realized no one in their right mind would be able to fly this high anyway, since they wouldn't be able to breathe without an oxygen tank. I shook my head and continued to ascend.

"Fifty thousand," I called in.

"What?" Ian's voice crackled through my headset. "Repeat, please."

"Five, zero. Five, zero!"

"Copy that," Ian answered.

I had already flown higher than the engineers had predicted. Fifty thousand feet, I thought. This would be a story for my kids if I ever had any. I thought of places that distance from my apartment and how long it took me to ride my bike there.

Then the engines cut out. They did so all at once without any sputtering. One second they were working perfectly, the next they were completely off.

The craft plummeted toward the ground. My stomach lifted into my chest as blood rushed to my head, making me so dizzy I nearly passed out. A daze struck me as my brain worked frantically to remember the one task I was supposed to do next.

"Engines off!" I screamed.

I could hear Ian's voice crackling in my helmet. "Are they off?"

"Yes! They're off!"

What a change of events a few seconds had made. The climb upwards had been gradual and peaceful. The downward descent was horribly scary and loud with wind. The PFD and I sped straight downwards. I pushed the button to release the parachute. Nothing happened. I looked behind me and noticed the hatch had opened, but the chute was pinned on the downside of the craft.

"It didn't work!" I screamed to Ian. "The chute is stuck!"

"No problem. I'm pushing the button," he said.

"You don't get it! The chute is stuck on the device!"

I looked at the altimeter. I was falling fast. There wasn't much time. Trying to get out of my harness in the bulky space suit was more difficult than I had imagined. The awkwardness of working with space gloves made it all the worse. I fought off the urge to panic. I thought of the crew on the ground beneath me, wondering if the device would come crashing down in their vicinity.

Jessica's voice came through my helmet. "Jon, can you hear me?"

"I can't get the chute to work! Take cover!"

"Get out of there!" she insisted. "Forget about the craft!"

"I'm trying!"

Finally, I unhooked my harness and forced my way from the pilot's chamber toward the open door. We were still very high in the sky as I stood at the opening, attempting to calm my breathing. The PFD's chute remained stuck on the bottom, pinned by the direction the craft was falling. I gathered some sanity standing there on top, watching the trapped chute flap violently against the frame of the device. I had my own chute cord in my hand and was ready to pull it and float to safety. Then an idea struck me.

The only thing keeping the chute from opening was the direction the PFD was falling. If I could get the device to spin upwards even a slight amount, the chute should open. Then I could slip easily past it and pull my own chute. For some reason, the fear had left me entirely. My plan sounded genius. I could save a valuable machine. There was still time.

I held on firmly to the frame of the craft and crawled down the side. The wind rushed past me, making it difficult to keep my grip. A slight shift in the fall of the PFD made me think my plan could work. I hooked my hands around the frame and each other for added grip. I inched further down as we plummeted through the cloud layer. My weight began to affect the dynamics of the fall as the PFD spun slowly on axis until the wind caught the chute. It flew upwards into the sky, opened and jerked the craft from me, ripping my clutch from the frame of the device.

My plan worked to perfection, but I hadn't realized the torque my hands would be put through. Suddenly, I was hurling downwards alone with a searing pain in both hands. The pain made it unbearable to pull my own safety cord. I tried using my wrists, but I couldn't get the required force.

"Perfect," Ian said with relief through my helmet. "The chute has opened."

What he couldn't see was my body falling to the desert floor at terminal velocity. The wind roared by my suit, making a horrible flapping noise. I looked below and could make out the truck and the group of them next to it.

"I'm still falling!" I shouted.

"What's the matter?" Jessica's voice came through.

"I can't pull my cord!"

"Oh, Lord. I can see you!" Jessica screamed. "Pull your cord, Jon! Pull your cord!"

"I'm trying!"

My hands ached incredibly. There was so little time left as the ground rushed upwards at me. I grabbed the cord one final time and screamed while I pulled on it with all my strength. The chute opened, jerking me into the air. It felt like I had been thrown violently upwards.

As the chute opened fully, an incredible wave of relief came over me. I looked down to where the others were. I could see Jessica running first across the desert floor in the direction I was heading. I floated peacefully down and landed at some distance from the crew. I collapsed to the ground in exhaustion. The parachute rested gently on top of me.

Jessica arrived first and pulled the chute off me.

"Are you all right?" she gasped. She unsnapped my helmet.

"I'm okay," I managed.

She pulled the helmet off. I looked over and caught a sideways glance of Ian and Frank approaching from the distance. I looked up and saw the PFD gracefully floating in the sky with an enormous parachute above it.

"I thought we'd lost you," Jessica said, kneeling over me and almost crying.

"So did I."

She put her hands on each side of my face and kissed me on the lips. Ian and Frank arrived, with the three engineers just behind them.

With Jessica's aid, I got to my feet. She helped me remove the harness and the space suit. The driver of the truck arrived with the rig. They all lifted me into the cab. I plopped down on my stomach in the back.

Jessica got in and rubbed my shoulders.

"Thank goodness you're alive," she said.

All in all, the day's events were judged a success. We determined how high the PFD could go, considerably higher than they had predicted. We also discovered the problem with the parachute system, which could easily be fixed by putting a second chute on the opposite side. I saved a valuable machine, and nobody died. My hands felt better within a few hours. Frank said he was putting me in for a bonus.

I asked the others not to make a big deal about it back at the lab. I didn't want to concern Whitney. When I saw her that night, I told her, "Everything went beautifully."

She replied, "I knew it had."

Fire and Brimstone

THE NEXT MORNING I looked out my apartment window to see rain pouring down. I preferred not to drive my new convertible in such weather, so I took a cab to work.

Adams was there alone, his body sagging in the chair. He didn't speak when I entered the lab but just looked at me and then back at the monitors.

"What's going on? Where's Whit?"

Adams didn't answer. His dull stare remained fixed on the monitors.

"Is she okay?"

"It's Delta 13. Jim called me last night."

I looked at Monitor One. It wasn't the planet I knew as Delta 13. All I could see were waves of fire and wind.

"What happened?"

"They're having a war," Jim answered. "A serious war."

Fires raged on all the Deltan monitors. Black smoke billowed upwards and soot-filled rain fell from them. All across the planet bursts of red light shot downwards from the skies.

"Are those laser strikes?"

Adams nodded. We finally realized the function of the network of satellites. They fired laser strikes that passed over the energy shields. We had never seen them activated until now.

"Where are the people?"

"Dying," Adams said, pulling his hands through his hair. "I don't know if you should see this."

"What?"

Monitor Three showed the home of a Deltan family. The roof was torn off. I could see the family huddled in one corner of the house. The mother and father were shielding their kids from the destruction but it was too late. Their bodies were motionless. Their heads and arms were dripping like liquid under the intense heat.

"Oh God," I said.

I became sick immediately, puking on the floor of the lab. After emptying my stomach, I kept retching but nothing came out. Adams tried to assist me.

"It's okay, Jon. Let it go if you need to."

I looked up at him. "Can't we do anything?"

My question was foolish. Adams said nothing. He looked like he'd been without sleep for days.

"How could they?" I screamed. Adams didn't have an answer. "What were they fighting about? We don't even know what they were fighting about!"

Jessica and Ian arrived. The fires burned until the soot completely filled the atmosphere. Then it became impossible to see through the haze.

Adams estimated it would be years before the atmosphere settled. After watching the tapes of the final hours, we lost hope for any survivors.

I left numb. I had to see Whitney. I took a cab to her house. Before I could ring the bell, she opened the front door.

"You knew I was here?"

"It's Delta 13," she said, seeing the pained expression on my face.

I tried to explain the story but I started crying. Whitney grabbed hold of me and led me into the living room. We sat down on the couch. She held me until I was able to tell her what had happened.

I couldn't understand why it had hit me so hard. I had never felt close to the people of Delta 13. They were bizarre and barbaric in spite of their technologies. There was something about the brutal manner in which they'd lost their lives. Maybe because it happened so quickly. Maybe because I was a witness.

Delta 13 was a total loss. Its atmosphere was so clouded with smoke that we couldn't see any surface images. Perhaps after another time leap, things would settle down. What a waste, I thought. All the time in the making. What a waste.

Conscious Connection

"GRANDMOTHER," I ASKED during the next Thetan session. "What was the cause of the battles on Delta 13?"

"Fear," came the reply from Whitney.

"What kind of fear?"

"They were afraid of losing their territory," she replied. Ian and Jessica listened from chairs at the back of the lab. Adams paced slowly behind his desk. Frank wasn't present, though he had seen the destruction.

"They each wanted the other's land?" I asked.

"No, they wanted to hold onto their own land."

"So why did they always attack each other?"

"Fear makes people choose poorly. Fear drove them to attack at the borders instead of staying put."

"Is that what happened to Alpha 17?" Jessica spoke out.

"Theirs was a result of imbalanced living with the planet itself. The planet is conscious. The Alphans were ignorant of that, thereby bringing about a chain of events that made life intolerable."

"Their own planet destroyed them?" Adams asked

"The planet is part of the whole. When imbalance goes unchecked for too long, the results can be catastrophic."

"I have a question from Whitney," I said. "She would like to know if there is a meaning for us behind Delta's demise."

"It serves as an example. This could happen to your planet, if you live in fear and refuse to share with your neighbors. Though it is years away, it looms as a possibility."

"And the Alphans?" Jessica asked.

"Another example. Ignorance and mistreatment of all life forms is as dangerous as living in fear. Treat your planet as if it doesn't matter, and it will treat you the same. All life is connected."

"When you say all life is connected, how exactly is it connected?" Adams asked.

"Every element in the universe came from the same source of light," The Grandmother said through Whitney. "Everything that is, is from the great Oneness and was, at one time, connected."

Adams had described it similarly. Months before, he had explained to me how everything started out as a tiny point, infinitely small and infinitely dense. As the Thetans described it and as Adams did, the beginning of the universe was a tiny spot of infinite light.

"That was a long time ago," Adams mentioned. "A lot has changed since then."

"There is not a molecule in existence that cannot trace its origin back to the same source. You and the stars came from the same Oneness."

"What are you saying?" Adams asked. "That stars have consciousness?"

"Every element contains the divine energy of creation—even stars, planets and moons. They and you are part of the same universal consciousness."

"Do you know who created your universe?" he asked her. I was surprised Adams had gone there.

"Yes," she replied calmly through Whitney.

"Who?"

"That which is the divine spirit of creation. The... I AM THAT I AM," she said boldly.

The drink on my desk spilled over. The power of the words reverberated through my body. I AM THAT I AM. They were so simple yet so moving. Ian and Jessica fixated on The Grandmother sitting calmly in her circle. Jim's green light pulsed passionately. Adams appeared to be unfazed by her response. He seemed to be toying with the idea of continuing along the lines.

"Is that right?" he paused. "What would you say if I told you that it was me? I created this universe."

"You think you acted alone?" she said.

"More or less," Adams replied. "Of course this whole thing began with Rose, but she wasn't here to match all of the parts with the concept. And Jon was here, but that could have been anybody."

"You got sizzled," Jim whispered to me.

Adams went on, "Jim was instrumental. But he is acting as an extension of myself, being what he is."

"Is that all?" The Grandmother asked him.

"Perhaps some mention of Frank," Adams thought. "And that's probably all."

"Your view is limited. Did it all begin with you?"

"How do you mean?"

"You left out many others who, in one form or another, made this possible."

"Well... who?" Adams replied.

"Your parents. Rose's parents. All of your family. All of those who taught you what you know. All of those who came before you to make possible the things you needed. And the creative force within all things, the... I AM THAT I AM."

The crew sat in silence. I wondered how Adams would respond.

"All of those people deserve credit for this project?" he asked her.

"You have said it so," the reply came. Adams sat back in his chair. "Where would you be without those who came before you?" Adams had no answer. "How could you have done this without the others to prepare the way?" Again, Adams had nothing to say. "Don't you see that you are the extension of them, as you have so eloquently put it? Don't you see that you assist in their efforts, just as Jon and Jim are assisting in yours? And before all of them and you... the light."

Adams put his head down. A silence filled the lab along with an appreciation for all of our roles.

"Do not think less of yourself," she continued. "You deserve credit as well."

"Yes?" Adams asked, looking up to her on the monitor.

"Of course. You deserve as much credit as everybody else. For without you, this project never would have happened."

Adams thought about the information. He brought both hands to his face and held them there.

Patterns

"IF WE WERE ROAMING around the universe," Adams asked us a few days later, "and we found a new planet, what do you think the chances would be that our very first glimpse would contain people in a modern stage?"

"About ten million to one?" I guessed, swiveling back and forth in my chair.

"That's about right." He ran his hands through his hair, which contained more gray than I remembered from months before. "We'd be more likely to walk outside and be struck by a bolt of lightning."

"But isn't that what time leaps are for?" Ian said. "So we can pick out a planet that looks good and then fast forward it as much as we need to."

Frank looked at Adams to respond.

"The more we use time leaps," Adams countered, "the more we advance the entire universe, the more likely we might be missing some society out there that we haven't yet discovered."

"There is a way that might make it simple," Jim said.

"And that is..." Adams replied as if he were waiting to correct Jim.

"Why don't we ask the Thetans?" Jim offered. Adams looked skeptical.

"Why not?" Jessica said.

"They wouldn't help us with the Deltan shields. I doubt they would help us there," Adams answered.

"It's worth a shot," Ian added. Everyone looked over to Whitney.

"I think you guys are missing the point," Whitney replied. "Those cultures went extinct for a reason."

"True," Ian said. "But what if we asked them to help us find a society that is advanced without being a danger to itself?"

"Theta is advanced!" Whitney responded. "You just don't see it because they aren't building bombs and supersonic planes."

Whitney was right. Theta was a mystery because it didn't fit the pattern. For some reason, the Thetans were impervious to change. Most societies changed constantly. Most aspects of the universe changed constantly.

Later, I overheard her speaking with Jim on the matter.

"I don't get why they aren't trying to understand Thetan lifespan or healing techniques," she told him.

"Maybe they think it's too difficult?" Jim said. "Or maybe they don't want to live that long?"

"You're probably right," she said. "Surely Frank doesn't think we can learn from them. Neither do Ian or Jess."

"What about your dad?" Jim asked.

"The same. That hurts me the most."

"I'd be happy to spend all my time with you on Theta."

"I know, Jim."

I was jealous of their relationship. On a level of intellect or spirituality or something, Jim was able to connect with Whitney in ways I couldn't.

Our sessions were limited to Whitney's questions for a while. She preferred to keep the topics to areas where she felt we needed growth. Since the loss of Delta 13 and the lecture from The Grandmother, the crew was content to watch and listen for a few sessions.

"Grandmother, what should we think of when we think of the soul?" I asked for Whitney. Adams and Jessica sat in chairs further back in the lab. Ian sat closer to me. Frank was not present for the session.

"The soul is an arrangement of energy made of spirit, mind and will. The soul is the foundation when an entity makes its sojourn to the physical."

"Is the soul the same in each lifetime?"

"Yes, though it may have a different focus for its work."

"How many previous lifetimes has Whitney lived?" The concept of reincarnation had been on the table since The Grandmother spoke of Jessica's first lover passing on.

"She is in her thirty-first sojourn or lifetime," came the reply.

"How many have I lived?" It wasn't the next question on Whitney's list, but I couldn't refrain from blurting it out.

"You are experiencing your one hundred and sixty-second sojourn."

Ian snickered and nudged me.

"Why so many?"

"Don't be discouraged by the number," the speaker said. "There are souls around you who have experienced an even greater number. Some entities experience several hundred lifetimes while others complete their work in just a few dozen."

"What does it mean if I keep coming back?" I asked.

"You still have work to do."

I felt embarrassed. For some reason, I had lived over five times as many lives as Whitney. I always assumed I was a quick learner. Now I was being told I was not, and by someone with whom I couldn't argue.

"Back to the list. Who was Whitney in her most recent lifetime?"

"She was a teacher and a healer. She was a beautiful man who led many—"

"She was a man?" I interrupted.

"Souls often switch gender from sojourn to sojourn."

"Does that mean I have been a woman before?" I asked nervously.

"Indeed, most of your lifetimes have been experienced as a woman."

Ian gave me another nudge and laughed. I didn't want to believe it. I was just coming around to the concept of lifetimes, and then she told me that! My ego protested, and I searched for a way to keep it from feeling like the truth. I returned my focus to Whitney and the list.

"Is there a main purpose to Whitney's life, and if so, what is it?"

"There is little work that Whitney has to do on herself, for she is quite complete. She entered this lifetime to help others find their way. Whitney leads by example. She also heals and teaches. Those are the reasons for her current incarnation, to guide others that they may gain in soul development."

"Have I gained in soul development in this lifetime?" I knew it was likely to be a disappointment, but I couldn't help myself.

"You have both gained and lost in soul development."

"Not all bad," I reasoned. "What should my focus be if I am to gain more during this lifetime?"

"Yours should be one of giving and loving your fellow human. Take not so seriously the selfish and material, but instead seek to assist others."

"How have I been selfish?"

"We are through for the present."

The sun was rising over Coasttown. The session had ended. As Jim printed out a copy, I grabbed it and wished that I could have thrown it away before Whitney read it.

"How did it go?" Whitney asked after coming out of it.

"Judge for yourself," I said, giving her the paper and slumping in my chair. I wondered why I had been such a slow learner. Why had I returned for so many lifetimes?

"This is wonderful," Whitney said as she read it.

"Wonderful for you," I responded.

"She was right," Jim said. "You still need a lot of work."

Whitney asked me, "Can you do me a favor next time?"

"Anything."

"Try not to interrupt her when she's answering my questions."

"No problem. It's probably just a case of me being selfish again."

Gifts

WHEN WE LEFT THE LAB that night I found a surprise awaiting me. Frank had towed a finished version of a PFD and left it in the front lot. It was placed next to my convertible with a ribbon around it and a card with my name on it. It was the same model I had saved in the high altitude test.

"Who knew it was my birthday?" I hadn't spoken about it.

Frank appeared from behind the machine. "I told you about those background checks."

"Happy birthday," Whitney said, punching my shoulder. "Why didn't you mention it?"

"I didn't want to make a big deal about it."

"These aren't going to be available for over a year, you know," Frank said. "Maybe longer if they get tied up in regulations. We have you currently cleared as a test pilot. Just stay out of trouble."

He smiled and gave me the keys for my PFD. The engineers had added some final touches since I last saw it. They added a dark plastic shield around the pilot's chamber, a heater, a cup holder and, of course, a double parachute system.

I climbed up and got behind the controls, feeling an overwhelming sense of gratitude.

I yelled to Frank, "This is awesome!" Then I realized there was space behind me for a passenger. "Does anyone want to go for a ride?"

Whitney shook her head, knowing my tendency for wild rides. Adams and Ian laughed at the idea.

Frank said, "If I were twenty years younger."

"I'd like to," Jessica said. She climbed up and strapped into the harness behind me. She tapped my shoulder and said, "Just don't do anything stupid."

"Okay. Hold on tight."

I lifted off a bit aggressively and took the machine over the woods. We buzzed a few feet above the treetops, sending birds scurrying for cover. Jessica shrieked. I stabilized the craft and flew in a straight line.

Jessica yelled in my ear, "Keep it simple, Jon!"

I flew alongside the hills and explored one of the river canyons. I performed a slow version of a loop-de-loop and a barrel roll.

"How's that?" I asked.

"I love it!"

Then I stopped the craft in midair, hovered for a moment, and performed the same stunts backward. It was my version of an amusement park ride. Jessica screamed and punched my shoulder.

"Knock it off! I mean it."

We flew gracefully toward the coast. After ten minutes, we were flying directly over the shoreline, dipping down close enough to feel the mist from waves crashing on the shore.

She said, "I want one. Will you give me flying lessons?"

"No problem."

We returned to the parking lot. Jessica thanked me and jumped out from the PFD. Then she hopped into her green convertible. As she drove off, I lifted the device into the air and flew out above her. She took her car up to cruising speed. I did a barrel roll over her head before making my way back to town. It was my birthday, and I was so pleased Frank had recognized it.

I stopped at a liquor store on the outskirts of town just as it was getting dark and set the craft down. I wanted to be noticed, but I didn't want it to turn into a mob. Five people were in the parking lot as I exited the craft. I jumped down from the cabin and entered the store, noticing the stunned look on the face of the shopkeeper. He stared at the PFD from behind his cash register like he had just witnessed a miracle. I went to the back and selected an imported six-pack to add to my collection.

"That thing run on regular?" he asked as I approached the counter. He was still staring at the device.

"Super," I responded, placing the beer on the counter. "How much?"

"It's on me," he said. I figured he was hoping to see me again.

By the time I came out with my beer, about ten people were walking around and touching my PFD, acting like it was a spaceship. I climbed on board and began to harness in. The crowd started asking questions.

"Where'd you get it?"

"How fast does it go?"

"What's it feel like?"

Then a very attractive girl asked, "Can it take a passenger?" I looked at her and realized what a selfish thing it would be to deny her request.

"What's your name?" I asked.

"Molly."

"Climb aboard, Molly."

Molly got in and put on the passenger harness. I lifted up very slowly. The crowd stared in awe beneath us. Molly gripped my shoulders tightly. I did a roll for the crowd as I took to the skies. Molly was thrilled.

"They're not gonna believe this at school!"

She asked me to fly over her house. Then she wanted to fly over several of her friends' houses, which we did. One of her friends came to her bedroom window to wave at us, a girl with bright red hair.

"Brandi, Brandi!" Molly waved to her, elated one of her friends had seen her. Now she had proof beyond the crowd at the liquor store.

We flew off. After a few more minutes, I asked Molly if I could drop her off at her home. When I landed on her lawn, Molly's parents came out in disbelief. She waved to them and jumped down from the craft. They stared like she had just been dropped off by aliens.

Molly asked me, "Would you take my number?"

She was too young for me. "I have a girlfriend," I said. It was a partial lie, but I wanted to get out of having to take the number. Then I told her, "This product will be on the market someday. You'll be in one again."

I flew back to my apartment in the dark and landed the device in front of my bedroom window. No one saw me as I locked it up and went inside.

I took the beer and sat by the window so I could drink it and watch my prized possession. After finishing my first beer, I placed the bottle in line with the others on the shelf in the bathroom. The collection was up to thirty-four.

The next day, Whitney brought in a large, wrapped package and laid it down flat on my desk. She said nothing and went straight to her chair.

"What's this?" I asked. Whitney didn't respond. "Aren't you going to say anything?"

"Jon, I can't believe you didn't tell us it was your birthday."

"Whitney, I didn't want people to feel obliged to get me something."

"Go ahead and open your present," she said, smiling.

"You get presents when it's your birthday?" Jim asked.

"Yep," I said.

"When is my birthday?"

"In a few months," Adams said.

"What would you like, Jim?" Whitney asked.

"Let me think about it." His green light pulsed mildly.

The package was lightweight, rectangular and flat. It was almost as wide as my arm span. With closed eyes, I slowly took the paper off the package, adding to the suspense. I felt the object beneath the wrapping. It had a wood casing around a glass face. I heard the others telling Whitney it was very nice. When I opened my eyes, I saw the picture of myself, a flattering charcoal portrait.

"This is beautiful," I said. "I didn't know you were such a good artist."

"I would have used colors if I had more time."

"It's perfect just the way it is."

I beamed with pride, never having received such a personalized gift. I thought of the perfect spot in my apartment for the portrait, on the bathroom wall above my beer bottles.

We asked the others if they wanted to know about their past lifetimes. I definitely did, though I still wrestled with the thought of being a woman.

Whitney reasoned, "People can't truly grow unless they're exposed to a variety of conditions. That includes gender, social status, beauty or even handicaps or disease."

Ian said, "I don't think I believe in it. Why would I want to entertain thoughts like that?"

Adams said, "If I were meant to know about a past lifetime, then wouldn't I have some recollection of one?"

"Maybe that's why the opportunity has presented itself now," I reasoned with him.

Jim said, "I'd like to know if I've had any."

"I'm not so sure that's a good idea," Adams said.

"Why not?" Jim asked.

"Artificial intelligence has only been around for so long," Adams told him.

"Perhaps you were a microwave oven," Ian joked.

Jim said, "I don't see the harm in asking. If I've had one, she'll tell me. If I haven't, she'll tell me that."

"I think it's a fine idea," Whitney said. "Put it on the list, Jon."

"I'd like to get back to some of the mine and Ian's questions," Adams said.

"Ah yes, scientific research," Whitney said. "After one of my questions, you may ask one of yours. Jon will see to it that we get equal time."

Adams had no choice but to grant her that. Abusing her trust was out of the question.

We found the dawn line near the center of a Thetan continent. Whitney led Jim to a village nearing its time for a meditation session. We found the village center with its podium unoccupied. We waited patiently for the robed Thetans to appear. A group of six in white gowns climbed the podium steps in the dark and took their seats. A young woman sat next to the empty spot in the circle. Whitney lit candles and sat quietly on her mat. Once the session had begun, Adams handed me several detailed questions. The first question he wanted to know was where he might be able to find a new society. I decided to ask Jim's question first to get it out of the way.

"Can you hear me, miss?" I asked.

"Yes," she responded through Whitney.

"How should I refer to you?"

"You may call me Teacher," she said.

"Teacher, has the entity who is now known as Jim, our central computer system," I began, managing to keep from laughing, "has this entity ever experienced any previous lifetimes?"

"Yes," was the reply. There were some low comments from Ian and Jessica in the back of the room.

"How many?" I asked.

"Seventy," she said, much to my surprise.

"What was Jim in his most recent incarnation?"

"The entity was a who, not a what. His name was Davidson. He was a husband and father of three girls."

"What was his occupation?" Adams chimed in, finding her answer a bit amusing.

"He was a scientist and an inventor," Teacher said through Whitney.

The room was still.

"What did he invent?" Jim asked.

"Many things. His primary achievement was in artificial intelligence. He designed a computer that functioned in similar ways to the brain."

"How come I've never heard of this individual before?" Adams said with a degree of doubt.

"He never achieved fame. He died before he finished his work."

"How did he die?" Jim asked. His light pulsed strongly.

"Brain tumor."

"Was the design similar to the one that Jim now uses?" Adams asked.

"Exactly the same."

A hush went through the lab room. Through the extended silence, I could see Jim's green light pulsing rapidly, and I imagined this information pleased him to no end. Adams sat there pondering this latest development. He seemed to have forgotten about the questions on his list.

"It seems awfully coincidental," Adams responded, "that in his past lifetime Jim invented the software he now uses."

"Mind is always the builder," Teacher said through Whitney. "Souls are associated with others with whom they have been connected in the past or with souls whose development is similar."

Adams sat in thought. Ian and Jessica remained quiet.

"Will I be reincarnated as a new entity after this lifetime?" Jim asked.

"If it will further the development of your soul," the reply came.

"Will I have a say in who I will be?"

"Souls are always involved in this process."

Omega 5

"ADAMS, DO YOU WANT to ask one of your questions?"

"Teacher," he said, snapping out of his thought. "Where might we find a planet with people who have advanced technologies and yet are not on the verge of a mass extinction?"

"What kind of technologies?" the reply came from Whitney.

"Similar to those from Delta 13, especially in the area of transportation," Adams said.

"What would be even better," Ian added, "would be a society with even more advanced technology than Delta 13."

"A society like that can be found in the Omega galaxy, as you call it. Look in the range of the white star in section y, number 229," the speaker replied.

"Thank you," Adams said. He added to Ian, "That was easy."

Ian punched in the coordinates and adjusted a set of cameras to the Omega galaxy. There were still a few questions on Whitney's list, so I returned to them. As I asked questions for Whitney, the others paid no attention, only interested in the new coordinates. The speaker began a long description on the subject of soul development. I joined the others and watched as the cameras slowly adjusted to the Omega system.

The session ended shortly after the speaker finished with Whitney's question. It was the first time Whitney had come out of her trance and not found the rest of us staring at her. We huddled in front of monitors on the other side of the lab. Jim printed out a copy of the session.

Whitney blew out her candles, stood up and read the printout.

"So that's what you're doing," she said after reading the response to the question.

Within minutes, the cameras focused on the white star in section y, number 229. From there, we identified planets orbiting the star. Immediately, we detected something unusual about the fifth planet, Omega 5-y229. It glowed with artificial light sources. We'd never seen anything like it. Orange and purple light patterns distinguished it, even from a great distance.

"Wow," Adams said. "Keep going in, Jim."

As the shot zoomed into the atmosphere, we saw a fog that shined in bright orange with streaks of purple, the colors glowing like neon. We also saw a collection of space dwellings and stations bound in orbit just beyond the orange zone. They were designed in a spider web pattern spanning across the atmosphere. Beneath the stations, the same orange, glowing energy field wrapped around the planet.

"It looks like a giant orange bubble," Jessica observed. We immediately sensed the Omegans were even more advanced than the Deltans.

Adams asked Ian, "What do you make of these stations?"

"Part of a network?" he speculated. "Probably has something to do with the bubble and these lines." Purple lines ran from one station to another, linking them across the upper atmosphere.

"Like a generation source?" Jessica asked.

"Proximity to the bubble makes me think so," Ian added. "They don't appear defensive in nature."

On closer inspection we saw a red, transparent glow that surrounded the space stations. The bodies of the stations appeared to be the common areas and control rooms, while the arms appeared to be the areas casting the orange bubble. Each space station contained several tiny windows, and through them we saw vegetable gardens and living quarters.

A shiny round ship, like a metallic disc, approached one of the stations and docked to it.

"Beautiful," Ian said. "Looks like air-locks are holding it in bay."

The excitement in our room was at its highest level in weeks, and we hadn't even dropped into the atmosphere of the new planet.

We scanned around the outer edge of the bubble to other stations. A second ship, looking like the first, released from its bay. It drifted down toward the atmosphere, through the orange bubble and into the glow of the planet's sky. Then a third one released from its bay, moving upwards into outer space. Then it completely vanished from sight. One second it was there, the next it was gone.

"Light speed mechanics," Ian said in awe.

"It must be!" Adams added. They were as excited as ever.

We zoomed into the planet's surface. We saw populated cities with enormous structures, also surrounded by colored energy fields.

The buildings had domed tops to them, giving the skyline a rounded appearance. Energy fields supported buildings and residences, and acted as roadways for traveling devices. Energy fields seemed to be incorporated to every structure. They came in a variety of colors, making the cities light up in a neon display.

"Oh my," Jessica said. "Look at the little Omegans!"

On the streets, wobbly little people walked around and rode in a variety of devices. They were short, round and doughy, and had oversized heads. Their clothing looked like thin energy gowns. Many of the outfits were completely translucent, which gave the appearance of wearing nothing at all, but being bathed in color.

"It looks like they're all going to a sleepover," Jessica added.

The outfits did look like futuristic negligees. The gowns didn't leave much to the imagination. To our surprise and mild embarrassment, the women had four breasts in sets of two, and the men had large penises.

"No inferiority complex there," Ian noted.

We gave Frank the tour later that day.

Adams told him, "They're centuries beyond the Deltans. No signs of warfare."

"What's this?" Frank asked, pointing to a red boundary line that ran across the entire screen of a monitor.

"The red fence system," Jessica answered. "It appears to be an energy grid that divides the artificial zones from the natural zones."

On one side of the red fence we saw pristine, unspoiled nature. Large forests, swamps and even jungles housed the wildlife there. On the other side was an urban utopia. The two worlds lived side by side, intertwined across the globe.

Ian added, "It looks like their way to keep nature and people separate and healthy."

The Omegans had a very soft look to them. They looked like cherubs—cute and chunky with pale, smooth skin. They had large heads with big eyes and the slightest trace of hair, but mostly I noticed their bodies looked like large babies with endowments.

"They're served in every way by automation," Adams noted. "Robots tend gardens. They serve meals by the pools and pamper the Omegans."

The robots were also short and plump and looked like the Omegans, though they had a distinguishing, metallic skin color. The people seemed to do nothing out of necessity. They stretched, ate meals and lounged in exotic pools.

"And the transportation?" Frank asked.

"Their devices are like floating chairs," Jessica told him. "Some models recline. They also ride stand-up versions similar to the roving pedestals of Delta 13."

"Though these devices are faster," Ian said. "The surrounding energy field, apparently, makes a big difference."

"And what are these things?" Frank observed, pointing to a floating entity that tailed behind a pedestrian. "That's the most bizarre thing I've ever seen."

"We haven't figured that out yet," Adams said.

Everywhere they went, Omegans were accompanied by a device that looked like a pulsating, electric amoeba. It was hard to tell if these devices were living beings or if they were artificial. The outlines of their frames morphed in contour as they remained in the background for every Omegan. We couldn't determine what they were or how the Omegans were using them, but the odd devices were always around. In some areas the floating entities traveled unattended by a person.

"It might be a long time before we'll make sense of these things," Ian speculated.

"Jim, add these to the list to ask the Thetans," Adams said. In our first day, the list had grown to dozens of questions.

The streets and lower airways were fairly busy. It seemed most of the traffic was automated service providers. Bubble crafts carried products from businesses to homes. Only a small percentage of the traffic contained actual Omegans.

"The younger ones enjoy the stand-up versions," Jessica told Frank.

"They're similar to Deltan pedestals. The older ones prefer reclining."

"And the floating things follow behind them?" Frank asked.

"It appears that way."

On the sidewalks, we found public compartments that looked like phone booths. We watched an Omegan walk into one. Within moments, his body disappeared.

"He just vanished!" Frank exclaimed.

Adams said, "It may be possible to transport flesh from one location to another. Jim..."

"I know, I know. Add it to the list."

Everything about the Omegans suggested the unlimited potential of the future.

"Have we hit the jackpot, or what?" Frank said.

"I guess," Adams said. "Maybe they're a little too advanced. I can't imagine we'll be able to make sense of half the things down there."

Ian agreed with him. "We can do our best, but it does look like a stretch."

"Nonsense," Frank said. "So it may take more time. Just do your best and take it day by day."

The odd thing we discovered about the Omegans was the degree to which they performed sexual acts. They had intercourse frequently, sometimes outdoors and in public, at times with multiple partners, or even with members of their own gender. This was vastly different than the other societies we had witnessed. Alphans usually had done it inside their homes. The Deltans had had sex even less often, and when they did, it often resembled rape. The Thetans rarely did, or more precisely, our cameras had never detected them. For Omegans, several times a day was common.

"Don't they get tired?" Jessica wondered.

"They look too cute to be so... dirty," Ian observed.

"They have appeal," I argued. "Who wouldn't like two extra breasts? Or to be so equipped?"

"Jon, please," Whitney said.

"Though it looks like they'd have trouble running around with those things."

"Or playing sports," Jim added.

We found it to be quite amusing and made it a source of many jokes.

"Hung like an Omegan" became a lab room expression. The men also had four nipples in sets. But more curiously, some of the people seemed like a mix of man and woman. Some Omegans had both breasts and penises, while others seemed like men with vaginas. Omegans reminded me of freak show people in this regard. Surprisingly, we found no examples of women who looked pregnant.

Omegans also used plenty of euphoria products. During the days when they were lounging by the pools, they often drank and smelled inhalants that appeared to have a deeply relaxing effect on them. Nearly all the Omegans used them, even the children. As they walked down the street, most of them appeared high or doped up, with slight imbalances to their step and a dazed look about the face.

"Maybe since they don't need to do anything," I said, "they just stay high and sexed up all day."

We also studied the orange energy bubble around the planet. We determined it was an ozone layer. The Thetans later confirmed it. Why they

180

had implemented an artificial layer was a good question. Whatever the reason, the filtering effect of the sun's rays was done in a glorious way.

Omega 5 had perfect weather. Everywhere was mild in temperature. Jim couldn't find any storms on the planet. He found areas of rain and even snow, but it was all gentle and in consistent amounts. There were none of the abnormal storms so common on every other planet, even Theta 7.

"The filter blocks out radiation and balances the planet's weather," Ian concluded. "No more need to fear storms or droughts."

We were astonished by their achievements. Their technology was many centuries ahead of the Alphans, who had blown our minds once upon a time, and clearly ahead of the Deltans as well, who had provided us with technology we still had yet to understand. The ideas from Omega 5 completely overwhelmed us. Time leaps were no longer necessary.

"This Omegan world is a dream, but I sense it is way too much. Everything they have, everything they do is eons beyond our abilities. Even if we could understand them, could we reproduce them? Part of me thinks no. Not in my lifetime. And the people? The laziest, most intoxicated, self-indulging group of do-nothings I could imagine. Is this the reward of superior intellect? Is this what we seek? If I could bring a man from our past, would he think the same of us? I certainly hope not."

- from p. 139 of Webster's journal.

The Joy of PFDs

FRANK PROVIDED JESSICA with her own PFD, as she had requested. I flew Jessica in her craft out to the desert, where she began her lessons. First I demonstrated the basics for her: taking off, hovering, flying in a straight line and landing. She experienced it all from the passenger's spot. Then I landed the craft and changed positions, standing behind her and giving instructions as she attempted those simple maneuvers. I alternated between holding her at the waist and by the arms, showing her how to use her body to let the craft know what she wanted it to do. She was cautious at the start, but as she realized the natural way the craft responded, she took to it well. By the end of the first outing, she was able to fly around safely and land smoothly.

Halfway through her second lesson, Jessica felt ready to fly solo. I stood on the desert floor and offered instructions through a headset in her helmet.

"How are you doing?" I asked from the ground. She flew slowly around me in circles.

"Fine, I think."

"You're going down slowly. A little higher. Better."

"It's getting easier," she said.

"Okay. Now do the same circles backward."

"You've got to be kidding!"

"Do it!"

She stopped the craft and hovered in midair. Getting it to move backward was a bit of a trick. It took pressing her weight against the back of the pilot's chamber. She crept back a small distance at a time. I shouted more encouragements to her until she began to get the hang of it.

"I love this thing!" she yelled as she completed her first backward circle.

For her third flight, I flew in my PFD beside her. We headed out into the countryside, over grassy fields and meadows. We wore the headsets for occasional instructions. I attempted to get her to do a barrel roll.

"No, Jon," she said. "I'm perfectly content to enjoy the ride in the standard position." By the end of the day, I managed to get her to do one, a roll she executed slowly but completely. She was elated by it but told me, "I still prefer just to cruise around."

We soared up and down the meadows for hours, chasing birds and enjoying the scenery. We talked about our backgrounds through our headsets. Over the course of flying together, Jessica and I finally got to know one another.

One night after a lesson with Jessica, I landed my PFD outside my apartment. A car pulled up next to me. I locked the cabin door and was about to walk up my apartment steps, when a young woman with bright red hair got out of the car and approached me.

"That thing is amazing," she said.

"It's pretty cool."

"You gave a friend of mine a ride two weeks ago. Remember Molly?"

"The girl I met outside the liquor store?"

"You flew over my house that evening. I waved to you from my window."

"That was you?"

"Molly said it was the most fun she's ever had."

"I'd have to agree with that," I told her.

"Could you take me for a ride?"

"I was about to turn in for the night. Maybe tomorrow?"

"It took me two weeks to figure out where you lived."

"You've been following me?" I asked.

"Every night. I watch the skies and drive the direction I see you go until I lose you. Then I wait there the next evening until I see you overhead. I kept making progress until tonight. I finally found you."

I looked at her more closely in the dark. She was one of the most beautiful girls I had ever seen. She had striking red hair and the face of a model. She also wore shorts and a tight blouse revealing long legs and ample curves. I had never been approached by such a beauty. I realized the pick-up potential my new toy was providing. She repeated how interested she would be in a ride, even for just a few minutes.

"Please take me for a ride. I'll pay you," she offered.

"What's your name?"

"Brandi."

How could I say no? I unlocked the cabin door and helped Brandi climb up. I buckled her into the passenger's harness. We took off and flew over the woods behind my apartment.

I told Brandi, "Let me know if anything is too frightening." Then I proceeded to perform a few stunts. We did several rolls. Brandi clutched my torso and pressed her chest into my back.

She shouted in my ear, "Molly was right! I love it!"

She directed me to fly over her house and then over a few homes of her friends, including Molly's. She was hoping to see someone, but it was late. After half an hour, we were getting low on fuel so I flew the craft back to my apartment.

Brandi was elated. When we jumped down from the cabin of the PFD, she asked, "May I come inside?"

I thought about Whitney and wondered if I had an obligation to say anything. I let Brandi in and apologized for the mess but she didn't care. She was still high from the flight.

She said, "That was like a dream come true."

"I can relate."

"What about you, Jon? What are some of your dreams?"

When I felt at a loss for words, she kissed me. Before I knew it, Brandi and I were in my bedroom.

In the morning, I felt as if I had cheated on Whitney, though we weren't dating. I also realized I was late for work for the first time ever.

When I returned home that night, Brandi was waiting on the apartment steps. She asked if we could go for another ride.

"I'm not sure," I said. "I sort of have someone in my life."

"Are you married?" Brandi asked me.

"Married? No."

"Are you engaged?" she asked, approaching me.

"No."

"Are you sleeping with her?"

"Well... no," I admitted.

"Then I don't see the big deal." She kissed me, then climbed into the cabin and put the harness on.

She had some good points. I forgot about Whitney and climbed aboard. We flew the craft to the ocean where I performed many of the maneuvers from the day before as well as a few new ones. Brandi loved every second of it. She egged me on to do more stunts. I dove the craft straight down toward the sea swells and pulled up at the last moment.

"Yes, yes, do it again!" Brandi shouted in my ear. I couldn't believe how much she trusted me. Jessica wouldn't have stood for any of my stunts without a serious reprimand.

After landing the craft back at my apartment, we went directly to the bedroom. Brandi repeated her performance from the night before.

She left me in bed as I fell asleep.

The following night, I was in for an even bigger surprise. I flew back to my apartment expecting to see Brandi waiting on the steps.

There was no one. I locked the PFD's cabin and entered my apartment, disappointed. I turned on a light and couldn't believe what I saw.

There was debris everywhere. It looked as if a storm had gone through the place. As I turned a corner in disbelief, a fist came out of nowhere and knocked me to the ground. Then I received a couple of kicks to my midsection. I looked up to a very large man pointing a finger at me.

"Don't ever touch my girlfriend again!" he shouted at me in complete rage. I could barely see his face in the glare of the ceiling light.

"Who?" I asked, gasping for breath and trying to get a look at him.

"You know who!" he said. He kicked me once more and left me crumpled on the floor.

I managed to stand and staggered to the bathroom. Blood covered my face and shirt. Fortunately, his punch had missed my nose. My mouth was another story, though. My lower lip was badly cut and a tooth had been knocked loose. I looked to my shelf to see the beer-bottle collection untouched and the portrait from Whitney still intact. It was the only part of my apartment the intruder had not destroyed.

I drove my car to the Star Bar. Sam was alone behind the counter, cleaning glasses.

"What happened? You okay?"

"I'll live," I told her, sitting on the stool in front of her.

"That didn't happen at work, did it?" I shook my head no. "You poor, unlucky guy," she added, as she wiped dried blood from my mouth with her bar towel.

"This is the face of a lucky man. The strikeout record is over," I said.

Sam smiled while cleaning my face. "Jealous boyfriend?" she guessed.

"Yep. You should see my place."

"Men."

Sam poured me a beer. I told her the whole story. She insisted I sleep on her couch, knowing I wouldn't be able to rest comfortably at my home.

Sam wanted to drive my car, and I let her. She loved it and took the long way back to her place. Once inside her apartment, she put me on the couch and covered me with blankets.

In the morning she woke me up, fed me breakfast and dropped herself off in the parking lot of the Star Bar. She also told me, "Don't make me wait so long to see you."

When I arrived at work that day, everyone noticed my fattened lip. I told them a lie about taking a fall in my apartment. But when I saw Frank, I asked if I could speak with him.

Frank led me into Webster's office. He said, "Looks like someone gave you their best shot." I told him the Brandi story and about finding my apartment in shambles and being blindsided by her boyfriend.

"Say no more," he said.

Within two days, my tooth was fixed and I was a homeowner. Frank set me up with a great house, one in the new development. The house was a replica of the models from Alpha 17, complete with its own solar panels and greenhouse if I wanted to start a vegetable garden. The best part about the house was that it was at the end of the development and had a fenced yard, in a section where none of the other homes had yet been built. I would be able to fly in and out without drawing attention.

I told him, "I'll start making payments on it right away."

"Not to worry. The house is paid for," Frank said. "I take care of my people."

I returned to my apartment and grabbed the few things I wanted to bring to my new house. I gathered the beer bottles and set them up on a shelf in one of my three bathrooms. Whitney's portrait looked great in the new living room, though I worried it was slightly egocentric in such a prominent spot. I bought a bedroom and living room set, something I had never done. I brought my old bike over and a few odds and ends, but the rest of the stuff went to the dump.

I invited the crew over for a housewarming party, but everyone was so busy we had trouble picking a date. Instead, Whitney came over alone. We had a nice dinner, nothing fancy, but good.

Time Out

WHITNEY SAID TO ME, "Take a day off and come play with me."

"Where?"

"Someplace quiet."

I'd been working non-stop for so many weeks that she was concerned for my mental health. Adams gave his approval, so I obliged her.

We drove my convertible to the foothills. The drive was gorgeous, with autumn colors on each side of the winding road. Whitney directed me to a pull-off, a small parking area at the entrance to a foot trail.

She grabbed her backpack from the trunk. It was filled with fruit, sandwiches and water. I offered to carry it, but she preferred to do it, claiming, "I like the exercise."

We hiked up the narrow, winding path. The climb was gradual. As we ascended into the foothills, I paused every few moments to adjust my breathing.

"I'm getting out of shape," I mentioned. Whitney continued on, climbing easily despite carrying our supplies.

As we ascended higher, I looked back toward our faraway town. On one edge, I could see the new housing development, the sea of tops tightly packed together. I tried to identify mine, but it was blurred in with the others. They looked so odd—a collection of pointy tops, standing apart drastically from the older, traditional structures. I estimated where our project was located. I thought of the crew and their work on Omegan energy fields.

"It will still be there when we get back," Whitney yelled.

"Just enjoying the scenery."

She waited for me to catch up. We hiked further along the trail. The beauty of the trees and flowers reminded me that I needed to get out more. Whitney picked a white blossom from a bush and stuck it in her hair. Then she picked a yellow one and offered it to me. I placed it in a buttonhole on my shirt. We walked mostly in silence with Whitney leading the way. After a while, we reached a plateau on the trail where the path widened and a field of tall grass and colorful flowers awaited. I felt like I had entered sacred ground.

"This is gorgeous," I whispered. "Do you come here often?"

"This is one of my favorites."

She walked lightly through the tall grasses, careful not to step on any of the flowers. A fallen tree near the middle of the meadow provided a large seating area. Whitney removed the backpack and placed it next to the trunk. She stretched her arms toward the blue sky and breathed in deeply with closed eyes. A light breeze swept across the tall grasses and wildflowers.

"You come here alone?" I asked.

"Sometimes."

"What do you do?"

"Whatever I feel like." Whitney laughed and broke out into a dance, with flowing body movements reminding me of the Thetans. I let go of my inhibitions and joined her. We danced like graceful fools around the fallen tree.

I applauded her movements and thanked her for the dance. She pulled the blanket from the pack, and I helped her spread it out next to the fallen tree. The top of the bark was fairly flat and made a useful table.

Whitney handed me a knife to slice the fruit. She unwrapped the sandwiches and took out glasses for the water. Within a minute, we sat on the blanket with a nice lunch in a lovely setting.

"I'd go crazy if I couldn't do this now and then," Whitney said as she bit into a slice of melon.

I nodded, appreciating the moment. I closed my eyes and felt the warmth of the sun on my face. I breathed in fresh air and wildflowers for the first time in months. A butterfly landed on my hand. It inspected my palm then flew haphazardly away. We ate in silence. After finishing my sandwich, I lay back against the fallen tree.

Whitney moved closer to me. She placed my head comfortably on her thigh and gently stroked my hair. The effect of the hike, the food, the meadow and being with Whitney was totally relaxing. I drifted off in little time. I woke up later, surprised I had nodded off so easily.

"Have I been asleep?" I asked. Whitney looked down at me and nodded yes. "For how long?"

"Maybe an hour. You were snoring."

"Why didn't you wake me?"

"You needed the rest."

I lifted my head from her thigh and could tell she appreciated having her leg to herself again. I stretched my arms and yawned deeply.

"I don't want to lose this," Whitney said out of the blue.

"What makes you say that?"

"I worry we'll become the Alphans someday, or the Deltans."

"Or the Omegans?"

"Heaven forbid." Whitney distrusted the Omegans since their red energy fields separated the people from the natural world. A hike on a mountain trail to a meadow was not accessible for them.

"Is it one or the other?" I asked.

"What do you mean?"

"Is it a choice we have to make? Do we have to be like those cultures or like the Thetans?"

"Maybe there's a middle ground, but I don't like the direction we're heading."

"Why?" I asked.

"It seems like people only care about technology. All people want is more 'this' and more 'that,' while offering less of themselves."

"Are you afraid for the future?"

"Not afraid exactly," she said, staring at a little purple flower bending toward her in a light breeze. "I'm just concerned about the changes happening to our world."

I placed my hand on hers. We spent the rest of the day speaking very little. We packed our lunch and blanket then walked around the meadow before returning to the trail.

As we walked back down the narrow dirt path, I thought of our situation. Whitney had good reason to be concerned. It seemed like we were at a crossroads in time. Never before had so much change come about so quickly. The world was a much different place than when I was a child. Due to the success of the project, the world was headed for even more changes. Would society be mature enough to handle the responsibilities that come with so much knowledge? I wondered, as we made our way down the dirt path back to the car.

Once inside the convertible on the road home, I was reminded again of the vast differences of civilization compared to the peaceful meadow we had just left. Were they compatible? If not, which was better?

Spinning Ever More

THE CREW CONTINUED TO STUDY the Omegans. We had to ask the Thetans for help with everything. They had plenty of answers, but the products seemed far beyond our capacity to replicate them. Even the energy fields were designed through advanced chemical manipulations that would be difficult for a firm from our planet to emulate.

We identified ground level spaceports. The ships stationed there were shiny, metallic discs and cylinders. They moved with incredible grace, producing no air drafts. They were similar to the designs from Delta 13 but even more advanced. While the Deltan ships had been confined to their own atmosphere, the Omegan ships routinely left theirs. They could move in any direction, and they could completely disappear which was something the Deltan ships had never done.

At one spaceport, we watched several Omegans board a cigar-shaped craft. Wearing the normal transparent energy gowns, they hobbled up a stairwell, which retracted after their entrance. Multicolored lights came on around the outer surface. The ship lifted off the ground and rose slowly until it was at a fair height. Then it disappeared.

"Where did it go?" Jim asked.

"Perhaps the correct question is 'when' did it go?" Ian replied.

"What do you mean?" I asked.

"If it has the kind of propulsion I think it does, once the system approaches light speed, time is experienced differently," Ian explained.

"I don't understand."

"Time is a variable, not a constant. Time is a product of speed. The closer you get to the speed of light, the less time you experience."

"I still don't understand."

It reminded me of the light generated from stars and how it took years to reach us. I had learned that time involved light in its equation, but now Ian was telling me it involved speed as well. Time, light and speed had never seemed to be related concepts, nor did they seem so difficult to understand.

"Don't feel bad," Adams said. "The main thing is this craft has an engine system reaching speeds near light. Once it does that, it can move around invisible to us."

After a week we hadn't figured out much of anything, even with the assistance of the Thetans. They did confirm the Omegan crafts had engine systems reaching speeds close to that of light.

One evening after the others had left, Jessica stayed late with me. It was Whitney's day off. Jessica wanted to learn how to use some of Jim's camera functions. Adams or I always did it when Jim was busy working on something else. Over the months, I had become an expert on manual scanning and focusing.

I showed Jessica how to adjust a set of cameras in a straight line, either north or south or side to side. Jim was content to watch and listen as I explained his functions. She played with the controls. The trick was to be very smooth with the fine tuning. We saw an Omegan couple lying on a platform device floating around the city.

I told her, "Try following them."

The floating device moved too quickly for her, so I told her instead to make an inspection of all the sights she could find on a particular street.

"Okay," she said, moving the camera angle slowly about the scene. "Here are apartments. Here are public transport chambers. Here we have a row of commercial buildings."

"Very good," I said. "Now let's move a little further into the city range."

She scanned to the left until the high rises took over the view. Night was approaching, and a few people mulled about in the streets. A man lounged in a slow-moving energy bubble. His eyes were half-open and his face beet red. He appeared to be grossly intoxicated.

I said, "Follow the wasted guy in that cab."

"He's moving a little faster than I'd like."

"Jessica, he's barely moving." I helped her with the controls, placing my hand on hers and adjusting the speed to the right level. "There, you're getting it."

As she got more competent, she was able to follow the cab without my help. Then it came to a stop, and the man entered a high-rise building.

"Okay," I said. "Now scale up the building and check out its roof."

Jessica used the controls to climb the building floor by floor. The shot lifted to the peak. We saw a penthouse suite with a pool and people lounging. Trees lined the pool, which had a cascading waterfall at one end. Omegan women splashed playfully in the falls. Robotic servants placed trays of fruit for a group of men. The men lay in lounge chairs, eating and watching the women.

"Let's check this out," Jessica said as she maneuvered the shot in closer to the pool scene. As the shot went in, we noticed nobody wore any energy gowns. A few other Omegans, also naked, walked casually by the poolside.

"Hello," I said.

Some of the people began to engage in sexual acts. Jessica tried to move the camera angle but couldn't.

"What's wrong? It's not responding," she said.

"Why?" Jim asked, locking the camera on the scene by the pool. "Why don't you want to watch this?"

"Because it's not appropriate," I explained.

"Why not?"

"That's just the way it is," I said, not having a better answer.

"Why is sex so common on this planet?" Jim asked. He adjusted the monitor to go even closer to the group of Omegans. His green light was pulsing mildly.

"People need to reproduce," I told him.

"But why haven't we found any pregnant Omegans?" he asked.

"Maybe they just have really small babies," I offered.

"That would be a first," he countered. "None of the women seem the least bit pregnant, yet look at how often they do this." Jim filled the monitors with scenes he had recorded from Omega 5, scenes of all types of Omegans engaging in sexual acts. Jessica and I looked around at a sea of naked aliens, feeling like we were in the middle of a galactic orgy.

"These examples were all taken last night."

"Okay, that's enough, Jim," I told him.

"Let's get back to something else, please," Jessica said, diverting her eyes.

"Not until you answer my question," Jim said. "Why is this so important to them?"

"Because it makes them feel good," I told him. "People like having sex. You know that."

"What does it feel like?"

"Oh, come on, Jim. There are some things you will never understand. I'm sorry, but this is one of them."

Jim adjusted the focus even closer to the group by the pool. I looked over to Jessica and shrugged.

Jessica suggested, "Perhaps we should go into Webster's office and give Jim some time alone on this."

Once inside the office, Jessica and I laughed at the predicament we found ourselves in. Neither of us knew what to tell Jim to make him understand. We discussed how difficult it was to explain the attraction between a man and a woman. We tried to explain it to ourselves. She made fun of all the sex on the monitors by placing her arms around my shoulders. I noticed how appealing she looked.

For some reason, I leaned forward and kissed her. I didn't think twice about it. It started as a simple kiss, but it quickly became more intense. Jessica was more sensual than I would have thought. We quickly got caught up in the moment, kissing passionately until it became awkward.

I averted her eyes and said, "I don't know what came over me."

"Let's just not mention this and move on."

We returned to the lab and checked on Jim. He was still trying to make sense of what was happening on the monitors. We told him we were leaving for the night.

He yelled after us, "You're being neglectful of my needs!"

Once outside, Jessica approached me for another round of kissing.

Having my arms around her felt completely natural. Dave, one of the security guards, looked over and noticed us. Then I made eye contact with him and he looked away.

I flew home lost in thought, not knowing what to make of it. How did this fit in with my interest in Whitney? I still cared for her, and yet I was fooling around on her left and right. Since she held a mild disdain for Jessica, I knew this would upset her. Perhaps with Brandi she would understand but not with Jessica.

Ruling Bodies

With HELP FROM THE THETANS, Ian began to understand how the Omegan ozone system worked.

"It's a weather controlling device," Ian explained of the orange bubble to Frank at a crew meeting. "They ensure good agricultural and living conditions. They can depend on warm summers and mild winters. They can even reduce the strength of violent weather."

"So this might be useful for our planet as well?" Frank asked.

"If we could figure it out," Ian said. "No more droughts or hurricanes or fires."

"I don't agree," Whitney said from her chair. "I see the enticement of perfect weather, but an artificial ozone seems to go against Mother Nature's own balancing mechanisms."

"We'll be helping Mother Nature balance herself," Ian argued. "The same as they do with their red fence system."

Whitney was the only one who was critical of the Omegans. Though they had a global community living in peace, everything about them was unsettling for her, especially the red fence.

"What good is it to live on a beautiful planet if you can't enjoy its natural treasures?" Whitney asked.

"They enjoy their beaches and mountains. They just do it from a distance," Ian said. "Maybe they care less about time on the beach compared to the prospects of space?" A part of me agreed with him. I would rather live on Omega 5 than on Theta 7, just for the luxuries and the thrills.

Whitney proposed an idea. "I think the Omegans live in a police state. The bubbles are tracking devices to keep an eye on everyone, to ensure they act within the rules."

"Well, there's an easy way to prove or disprove that," Ian said.

"Grandmother," I asked at our next session, "what is the purpose for the floating, pulsating bubbles that accompany the Omegans everywhere they go?"

"As you have said," the reply came through Whitney. "To accompany them."

"But why?"

"To watch over the citizens, to make sure they abide by their laws."

"Is it against the law to be in the natural areas on the planet?" I asked.

"That is correct."

"What else is against the laws?" Jessica asked.

"Murder, theft, any action that goes against the ruling body."

"But isn't the ruling body designed by the people, for the people?" Adams asked.

"Yes, but it comes with a cost."

"What do you mean?" Adams asked.

"The idea is to ensure peaceful existence for all Omegans. Yet it denies the right to self-expression and free will."

"Maybe it's for their own protection," Adams stated. "Maybe in a world so advanced, an individual left on his own could cause a lot of damage."

"That is the argument behind the laws," the speaker replied. "The basis for this argument is fear, and no good can come from a ruling body based on fear."

I didn't know what they were talking about. Living on Omega would be like a dream come true. No work, just play and relaxation. No problem hooking up with girls. Everything was taken care of by robotic assistance. They rode wonderful devices. The people lived comfortably. What was wrong with that?

"What about pregnancy?" Jessica added, returning to our list. "Why can't we find any pregnant women?"

"There aren't any," the speaker replied.

"How do they keep their population going?" Jessica asked.

"Births are administered by the ruling body. Omegan parents are informed when they have been approved for a child. That being is conceived, born and raised for the first year of its life under the care of the ruling body."

"With the parents' genetics?" Jessica asked.

"If they prefer their own, the genetics are taken from them. They have many choices."

"Sounds creepy," Jessica mentioned.

"Where is this ruling body?" Adams asked.

"Everywhere," the speaker replied. "With the floating bubbles, the ruling body has eyes and ears everywhere. We will review this again, for we are through for the present."

The Thetans came out of their meditation, and Whitney slowly opened her eyes. I brought her a glass of water and the printout from Jim.

Whitney read through it quickly. "I knew it. No free will."

"I see your point," I told Whitney. "But even if you're right, wouldn't it be worth giving up a few things if your life was taken care of in every way?"

"How can you call that a life?" Whitney argued. "Without freedom? Without risk or discovery? The Omegans live in a prison that just happens to have a lot of luxuries."

"It is debatable whether that's a bad thing or not," Adams said.

"The real danger," Whitney said, "is that the Omegans are controlling everything. The weather got bad so they found ways to modify it. The atmosphere heated up so they found ways to cool it. The wildlife died so they found ways to nourish it. A citizen did something wrong so they found ways to watch them. Every time something happened as a result of imbalanced living, the Omegans sought to control it."

"Isn't that what we do?" I didn't want to argue with her, but I had trouble seeing any other way to deal with the hazards of a modern society.

"They're treating the symptoms and not the cause. What if something goes wrong? They've completely entrusted their planet to an artificial ozone. What if it ever stops working?"

"I don't know," I said. "Maybe it will work forever."

"Do you know of anything that works forever?"

Confusion

JESSICA APPROACHED ME in the parking lot after work.

She said, "I think we need to talk. I know you have an interest in Whitney, and I don't want to come between that. Can you come to my place... just to talk?"

I agreed to follow her home.

Once there, she fixed us a couple of drinks. I sat on her couch as she sat in a nearby chair.

"The other night was a total surprise," she said. "But you're more than a work associate. You're a trusted friend. In fact, you're one of my only friends."

"That's something we have in common. Strange, considering we're so different."

"There's something about you that's good for me."

"What?"

"I need to laugh now and then. I know that."

I stood up and refilled our drinks. I told her how much I enjoyed her company, especially since flying together, but there was Whitney.

"We're not really dating," I added. "I can't make sense of it. We've never slept together, but I might be in love with her."

"Might?" Jessica asked.

"I've never been. I don't have much experience with women. How do you know when you're in love?"

Jessica told me stories about her past. She had been in two long and painful relationships. In each case, the men treated her poorly. She wanted them to truly love her but it was hopeless. After struggling for years, Jessica gave up. So she buried herself in work and became a bit cynical.

"Since you're always kidding around," she said, "you've helped me break out of that."

"You've helped me too. To become something I wasn't. More professional, more competent. You've helped me feel like I can be successful anywhere."

Jessica put her drink down. "Jon, what do men want?"

"What do you mean?"

"I mean from a woman. What do men really want?"

"That's difficult. I guess they want attraction."

"Do you think I'm attractive? If Whitney wasn't in your life, do you think you'd be attracted to me?"

"Why are you asking?"

"Because I don't know what to think of myself. Some things about me are attractive, I know. But overall, am I attractive to men? I really don't know."

"Of course you are. The other night in the lab, you felt wonderful."

Jessica half-smiled, relieved, I thought. I placed my drink on the mantle and held her.

"Thank you," she said. "I'm sorry I dumped all this on you."

"It's okay."

With my arms around her, an internal battle went on between my brain and my body. I didn't want to let go. We kissed, softly at first but then with more intensity.

I woke up the next morning with Jessica in my arms, wondering what I was doing.

"Have we made a mistake?" Jessica asked.

"I don't know." I was in a daze. The feeling was similar with Brandi but Jessica meant more to me. I didn't know how to define our relationship, or mine and Whitney's. Could I define it? The situation had turned into something difficult for all.

Over the next week, I spent several nights with Jessica. Part of me thought it was wrong while part of me felt it was right.

Whitney began to act differently around me, in and out of the lab. I feared she was beginning to suspect something.

"Is anything on your mind?" she asked me once. "Something you want to talk about?"

"No." I convinced myself my personal life really wasn't her business.

However, I couldn't kid myself. I was in love with Whitney, even if my behavior suggested otherwise.

I took her for a long drive home after work. We held hands and listened to a quiet station on the radio. Night fell. Whitney laid her head back in the leather seat and closed her eyes. I turned the music down low and adjusted the heat so she wouldn't be chilled.

When we got back to her place she looked at me and asked, "What's going on, Jon?"

"What?"

"I feel like you have something to tell me."

I debated what to say and had trouble looking her in the eye. The truth would upset her, but I hated the thought of lying. She'd see right through it, and I had promised never to lie to her. I was taking too long to answer.

"What's going on?" she repeated, lifting my face to hers.

"Something happened between me and Jessica."

"Something... as in sex?"

I paused before answering but had to be honest. "Yes."

"More than once?"

"Yes."

"Why didn't you tell me?"

"Because I was afraid of losing you," I told her. She pondered the thought. "I don't want to lose you."

"I need some time to think."

She got out of the car and ran into her house.

For several days, Whitney only talked with me as was needed in the lab. She preferred not to have any question periods with the Thetans but just to meditate quietly with them. She told Adams she needed a break for a while.

I watched Whitney in her meditations. I also worked with Jessica in our studies of Omega 5. Jessica had done nothing wrong, but I needed to keep it from getting serious.

"We need to talk," I mentioned to Jessica in the lab.

"I know."

"I'm not sure if this is smart."

"Me too," she said. "Especially if it affects us at work or as friends."

I was relieved that she understood and felt the same as I did, though I sensed a bit of disappointment in both of us.

I stood in the background one night, watching Whitney as she studied the Thetans. The monitor showed about thirty Thetans taking place in a ceremony. It was the first time we had witnessed the procedure, which consisted of a long march from the town square to a nearby lake. They sang and clapped the entire way. I wished I could have heard the sounds that seemed to bring them so much pleasure. When they arrived at the lake, they stood by the shore in single file.

An elderly Thetan man spoke to the group and dropped palm reeds and spices into the water. Then the Thetans took off their robes and stood naked by the water's edge. One at a time, aided by the elderly man, the Thetans walked into the water until they were submerged up to their necks. The elderly man dipped a bowl into the lake and poured the water over their heads. Then they turned around and walked back to the shore where they were greeted by a towel bearer. Then they redressed.

"This is a spiritual cleansing," Whitney said, appreciating the ritual.

"Is that why they're in the lake?" Jim asked.

"Water is a symbol of spirit and purity," she said.

"Why do people wear clothes?"

"Partly to keep warm. Partly because people don't feel comfortable being naked."

"Thetan children are usually naked."

"They don't have the same hang-ups we do."

"Would the world be a better place if people didn't have those hang-ups?"

"Maybe," Whitney said. "It would be different. I'm impressed with you, Jim. You come up with some profound questions."

Jim didn't respond, but I knew he was pleased with himself. His green light dimmed down.

Trickle Down

ONE MORNING, we were all in the lab when Frank came in. He opened a bottle of champagne and provided glasses for everyone. We gathered around, anxious to hear his announcement.

"We just landed our biggest account yet!" he said, over-pouring champagne into glasses and onto the floor. "Our military has bought the rights to a state-of-the-art satellite defense system."

Our reaction was one of surprise.

"You mean the system from Delta 13?" Adams asked.

"The very one," Frank announced proudly. "I just got back from a long meeting with the defense team. We've got some wrinkles to iron out, but I'm sure we'll manage them. It's a package deal that will be worth billions."

"Don't you remember, that system caused the destruction of the planet?" Adams responded, putting down his glass. "How could you sell it to our military?"

"It won't ever be used, Webster," Frank said, assuring him. "It's only going to be there as a deterrent."

"How do you know that?"

"We don't even know how to make those things fire!" Frank said with a laugh. "This is the best part. The military has the recordings we made when they were used on Delta 13. These recordings will leak out to the public and to other nations. Presto! Instant respect."

"But how do you know they'll never be used?"

"They can't even arm them if they don't have the technology," Frank said, still smiling. "It's the world's biggest bluff! There's nothing to worry about."

"But how can you trust them?"

"Webster, they're just decoys! I thought you'd be excited about this. You just became rich beyond your dreams."

"Wonderful. Listen, Frank, don't some ethical questions supersede financial gain?"

"It's a bluff, Webster. A bluff! How can we fear something that isn't actually real?"

"Other nations won't know that!"

"Don't you remember what the Thetans said?" Whitney added. "The aims, intentions and ideals are what matter."

"Hold on. We didn't invent the spear," Frank told us. "We didn't invent the gun or the hydrogen bomb. We didn't invent chemical weapons. But now, because we showed this product to the Defense Department... the world is suddenly a dangerous place? I don't get it. It's okay to share everything else, but when a product scares you... then it's suddenly a question of ethics? And you wanted to give everyone free energy without a thought."

Frank left the champagne on the desk. He shook his head and walked out. Ian, Jessica and I stood there holding our glasses, quietly reflecting on what we were doing.

"Frank. The consummate businessman. We had a blowout today over Deltan satellites. How could he have sold them? I'll never forgive myself if something happens. And yet, why can't I stop thinking about his points? Is it for me to decide what people can know about and what they can't? Where does responsibility truly lie?"

- from p. 149 of Webster's journal.

Reincarnation

ADAMS SHOWED THE EFFECTS of months of long and sometimes painful work. His once salty-brown hair was changing toward straight gray. His eyes and face showed more lines than when I first met him. I noticed changes to my appearance as well. My eyes sagged, and I had lost more hair. I'd put on several pounds, a result of not riding my bike anymore. Everyone gets older, I thought. The results weren't always pretty. I vowed to start adding some regular exercise back into my life.

Whitney, on the other hand, looked better than ever. Her face was so clear it shined, and her body looked firm and slim though she was probably exercising less than she was used to. She said it had been months since her last migraine.

After a week of silence, Whitney had a few questions she wanted to ask the Thetans. I thanked her for including me. Adams and the others were relieved to see her resume with the questions. They had a number of items they wanted to ask about, though they knew this session was to be dedicated to areas of Whitney's interest.

She went into her meditation with the group at Coasttown. The first questions dealt with the meaning of lifetimes. The speaker went on in great detail, much to the boredom of the rest of the crew. The follow-up questions dealt with the afterlife, a subject that caught our attention.

"Grandmother, what happens after a human being dies?" I asked her.

"The death of the body is not the death of the entity. The entity cannot die. The body is like a car for the soul. Once the lifetime has passed, the soul drops the body like you would if you bought a new car, there being no need to continue with the old one."

"Do some souls reincarnate into new human bodies?"

"Yes."

"Has my grandfather's soul reincarnated into a new body?" I asked, deviating from the list.

"Which one?" was the response. I had forgotten that both of my grandfathers had passed away, because I had never met the first one. He had died before my birth, and I had trouble remembering his name.

"Both of them."

"Your mother's father, the entity known as Harry, has entered a new physical lifetime. Your father's father, the entity known as Wilson, has not yet entered a new physical lifetime."

"Wilson! That's right," I said. "What do you mean he hasn't been reincarnated yet? What's he doing?"

"That soul is resting."

"What about my wife, Rose?" Adams mentioned somewhat casually. "Has she reincarnated into a new body?"

"Yes," the response came. A moment of silence followed. I wondered what Adams was going to say.

"Where is she?" he finally asked.

"In your terms... Zeta galaxy, section J, of star four hundred and—" the speaker relayed numbers we were familiar with. Those numbers were coordinates within the machine, and the effect on the crew was instantaneous disbelief.

"What?" Adams screamed, cutting off the speaker. "Are you trying to tell me that she's inside this thing?!" There was no response from Whitney.

"I think you have to phrase that better," I said to him.

He calmed himself and redirected. "The entity who was my wife, Rose Adams, is that entity now in a new body inside this machine?"

"Yes."

Adams couldn't believe it. He didn't know what to say next, nor did anyone. He sat down in his chair and began to laugh. He laughed in spurts and a little awkwardly, as if he was unsure if this news pleased or annoyed him. None of us made an effort to break him from the moment. Whitney sat, still in her trance. As Adams went on scratching his head, I noticed the Thetan sun in Coasttown was rising. I saw the slightest change to the expression on Whitney's face. The time for questions had passed. Whitney came out of her trance.

"Whitney, can you hear me?" Jim asked.

Her eyelids twitched as we gave her time to reconnect. She rolled her head from side to side and opened her eyes, noticing the sober mood of the room.

"What? Was it bad?" she asked, trying to make sense of our expressions.

Adams relayed the details of the questions until he came to the subject of Rose. Then he had trouble remembering the specifics of what had been said. Whitney shook as Jim reminded him The Grandmother said Rose's soul had been reincarnated, and she had given us coordinates that would lead to her.

"What were they?" Whitney asked anxiously.

"I got some of it, but your father cut them off as they were saying it," Jim said.

"What?!" Whitney screamed at him.

"You can't be serious," Adams objected.

Jim had recorded the information. Zeta galaxy, section J, star four hundred and seventy-something was a great place to start. The good news was the area we were discussing was a tiny percentage of the entire universe. The numbers boiled down to the size of about ten solar systems, which was still a considerable area when looking for an individual body.

"Should we have a session now, with another group?" Jessica asked.

"I don't think I can relax," Whitney said. "We'll have to wait until tomorrow when we can ask them again."

"We could at least start looking," I offered.

"I can't believe you're serious about this," Adams said to me.

"Besides, how can you look for someone in an area as large as several solar systems?"

"We're probably only talking about six or seven systems," I suggested. "Some of those stars probably don't have any planets in their orbit. For the ones that do, how many life supporting planets do you think could be out there?"

"Maybe three or four apiece?" he guessed.

"I'd say that's generous," I added, suddenly feeling confident in my logic. "But assuming that's true, how many of those are in a modern stage with societies?"

"How do you know she'd be on a planet in a modern stage?" Ian asked.

"Good point," I conceded. "Let's assume it. How many do you think?"

"Probably just one," Adams said at last.

Jim used several monitors to blanket the space the Thetans had led us to. The monitors looked almost entirely black, with tiny specks of light visible in many areas. We analyzed it.

The fourth star we found, number 474 in the J section of the Zeta galaxy, was a large yellow sun with several planets in its orbit. The first planet was small and close to its sun, too close for life. The second planet looked better. It had large amounts of carbon dioxide and water vapor, though its surface looked gaseous and unstable. By the time we reached the third planet, we immediately recognized large amounts of blue ocean. Any planet with that much water in liquid state had to support life. As our cameras zoomed in closer to the blue-green planet, Jim announced his sensors were detecting something artificial in wavelength.

"What is it?" Adams asked.

"It's a radio signal from the planet," Jim said.

"From the body itself?" Adams asked.

"From a satellite in orbit."

"What do you think it's for?" I asked.

"Maybe it's an attempt at communication," Whitney reasoned.

"What's it say, Jim?" I asked.

"I don't know," Jim said. "We'll have to decipher it first."

As the shot continued through the atmosphere and down to the surface of Zeta 3, nothing we had seen before could have prepared us for that moment. Zeta 3 was so much like our planet, it was scary.

Everywhere we looked, things appeared familiar. The mountains looked the same as ours, the trees and plants looked the same. We found a neighborhood where the houses and even the people looked the same.

"How do you explain this one?" I asked Adams.

"You got me."

"Unbelievable," Jessica said in awe.

"Amazing," Ian added.

"They look exactly like us," Whitney said.

We had seen similarities to our world on other planets, but nothing like this. We scanned around for hours. We watched people driving cars in the streets and playing sports in the parks, children with backpacks taking the bus home from school. On top of that, their society was almost at the same level of technology as ours, perhaps only a few decades behind us.

If it hadn't been for the difference in its continental make-up, I would have sworn someone was pulling a joke on us. But this was no joke. Zeta 3 was our identical twin from another dimension. We stared at the monitors in disbelief, as if we were looking into a mirror for the first time.

"It is remarkable," Frank said upon seeing the new planet. "What do you make of that, Webster?"

"Incredible coincidence," Adams said.

"And what about this beacon in space?" Frank asked.

"Jim's on it. Probably some kind of communication effort."

Jim had been working with the space signal since he found it. He compared it to all the other electronic imprints he was familiar with. He was very excited about deciphering it, as if someone had given him a puzzle. We left for the night knowing Jim would be doing everything he could to make sense of the signal.

By the next morning, Jim had turned the signal into a series of recognizable figures. It was a presentation of the planet and its life forms. The images included a picture of the globe itself along with its sun and fellow planets. There were also pictures of men, women and children doing fun things. There were pictures of animals and plants. There were even pictures of dinosaurs and other creatures we assumed had gone extinct. Then there was an alphabet explaining how to spell and pronounce numbers, letters and words. The message was detailed and self-explanatory. Overnight, Jim had become relatively proficient in their language.

"Great work, Jim," Adams said upon seeing the images from the signal. "What have you learned about them?"

"They call their planet Earth," Jim said.

"Earth?" I questioned it, finding it a strange name. "That sounds so... primitive."

"Is it any worse than what we call our planet?" Whitney asked. I thought about it and decided she was right.

"So why do you think they sent this signal?" I asked.

"Maybe to see if anybody's out there?" Jim said.

He sounded intrigued. This was the first time we had encountered a message in space, even though several of the societies we'd found were far more advanced than the people of Earth.

"The signal is coming from one satellite, correct?" Adams asked.

"Yes," Jim replied.

"Is there any indication where the signal originated?"

"Yes. I can input the coordinates."

Jim took the picture into one of the continents, down to an area of broad desert that had several radio telescopes. The huge devices stood out dramatically against the bare background of desert hills. We noticed a building next to the radio telescopes that might have been where the signal came from.

Occasionally, the building's front doors slid open, and people walked out to their cars. Their yellow sun was setting, and the people were ending a work shift and leaving for the night.

One woman walked out alone. Jim zoomed in on her. She carried several paintings. We watched as she set them down next to her car. She opened the trunk of the convertible and loaded the paintings one by one. Jim zoomed in closely on the artwork. They were of astronomical bodies, planets with rings and moons, and phenomena in the skies like quasars. She placed them carefully in the trunk and covered them each with blankets. We saw a close-up of her face as she walked around her car, got in and began driving off.

"Dad, there's something about her," Whitney said tentatively.

"Follow her, Jim," Adams said.

She drove down the desert highway. She passed the exits for the main part of the town. Several miles further she exited, then continued away from the town. She drifted in her lane and came a little close to some oncoming traffic. Then she took a few side streets until she turned down a long and dusty path. She parked the car at the end of the dirt road next to a modest home.

A dog wagged its tail and jumped at the vehicle as she got out of it. She petted it vigorously and then tossed a stick for it, before she unloaded the paintings from her trunk.

"That's her," Whitney said.

"How could that be her?" I asked. "There's probably over a billion people on the planet. It's at least a billion to one that this is her."

Adams watched but said nothing.

"We'll find out tonight," Whitney said.

"Why not have an immediate session with another group?" Jessica asked.

"I'd prefer to sit with The Grandmother on this one," Whitney said rather coldly.

The Earth woman worked in her flower garden just before dark. She wore a pair of faded overalls while diligently planting little flowers in a well-plotted garden. She looked to be in her fifties, having shoulder length brunette hair with gray roots and streaks. For some reason, Whitney felt certain she was the reincarnation of her mother.

Adams remained skeptical, but he couldn't take his eyes off her. The woman finished as the sky became dark. She stood up, took off her gloves and went indoors, out of our sight.

We waited for the Coasttown Thetans to arrive. The hours passed at a snail's pace. I assisted Ian and Jessica with the work they had been doing on

Omegan ozone. Adams and Whitney watched the monitor set on Earth, which showed the woman's house in the dark. Occasionally, the dog would move around in the yard. Once it went to the bathroom. I felt relieved when the Coasttown Thetans finally approached the podium for their dawn session.

Whitney was already sitting on her mat with her icons in place, the candles lit and incense burning. I wondered if she would be able to relax enough to get into her trance. She had only one question for me to ask. She made me repeat it over and over again to be sure I would ask it properly.

"Grandmother," I asked, once the session had begun. "There is a woman on this planet, Earth. We have the monitor focused on her house right now though she is presumably asleep at this time. We can see her dog in the backyard and her vehicle parked in front. Are you aware of the woman whom we are interested?"

"Yes," came the reply from Whitney. "We know the body of which you are speaking."

"Is she the present incarnation of the entity that was Rose Adams, formerly the mother of Whitney and wife of Webster?"

"The entity is one and the same."

"Ask her again," Adams told me.

"But she said that it was."

"Just do it, Jon!"

"Can you confirm that for me please? Is the soul who was Rose Adams, is she now this woman of Earth we are watching?"

"We repeat, the entity is one and the same," the speaker said.

"But there must be several billion people on this planet?" Adams implored.

"This is true."

"How could I have found her so easily? The chance of that would be nearly impossible!"

"There is nothing about your relationship with this woman based on chance," the speaker answered through Whitney. "Perhaps that is the point she is trying to make with you."

"This entity really is Rose?" Adams asked, his voice cracked with emotion.

"You have said it so."

Adams buckled at the knees. He plunked down in my chair and put his head in his hands. Sobs came through his palms as he wept intensely.

Jessica stood behind him and rubbed his shoulders, trying to offer some comfort.

"What is the name of the woman now?" I asked.

"She is known as Mara Smith," the reply came through Whitney. "Doctor Mara Smith."

"She's a doctor?" I asked.

"A title for her degrees in astronomy."

The floor was open for questions, though I didn't know what to do since they had answered the only question we had for the night. Adams was still crying. I couldn't tell if it was helping him any by asking more, so I let the session continue while hardly asking anything.

After a few minutes of silence I asked, "Does she live alone?"

"Yes, with her dog."

"Did she leave her job? Is that why she took her paintings home?"

"They're having the offices painted," the reply came. "And she wanted to make some changes."

Adams waved at me to refrain from asking questions. The extra information was too much for him. We waited patiently for the meditation to be over.

Eventually it ended, and Whitney came out of her trance and looked at me with extreme interest. Once she saw the red eyes and wet face of her father, she knew the answer.

"It really is her, isn't it?" Whitney said.

Whitney began to cry also, though she had the composure to stand and join her father as he remained seated in my chair. She put her arms around him and cried for several minutes. The moment became awkward. Ian and Jessica excused themselves for the night, leaving me to watch after them.

I drove us home. No one spoke on the way. After getting out, Whitney reached through my open window and hugged me. Then she went inside with her father. As I drove back to my house, I was overcome with a realization. I had finally seen the woman who had the idea for that little universe.

"Could it really be Rose? It's so hard to believe, and yet, I'm past the point of doubting them. If it's true, then it's the most wonderful discovery to date. And if it is true, then is it also a punishment? Is it some kind of cruel joke?"

- from p. 153 of Webster's journal.

The Earth Woman

WITHIN A COUPLE OF DAYS, we had a fairly clear view of Mara's life. She lived with her dog in a small house on the outskirts of the desert town. She woke up early and jogged with her dog. They passed the country store and went down to the park, where the happy animal jumped in the river. On the way back, she stopped at the market and picked up a hot drink and a paper. Then she walked back to her house, reading the front page on the way.

She left the dog in the yard and drove her car to work. Her job had something to do with the radio towers and astronomy, but it was impossible for us to see what was going on inside the building. When she was at work or inside her home, Adams waited impatiently for her to be outside again.

He had Jim replay tapes of Mara when she was working. He wanted to see her face as closely as he could. In some ways, Mara reminded me of the pictures I had seen of Rose. Neither of them wore makeup. They each had natural smiles and creases next to their eyes that went to their ears. Proportionally, Mara was slightly taller and thinner than Rose had been. Mara was a brunette, while Rose had auburn hair. Mara's eyes were brown, while Rose's had been mixed with green.

Adams observed, "She has the same spring to her step as Rose, and a similar grace in movement." He had Jim replay a look at the paintings, the ones she had taken from her office. "These look like Rose's work," he noticed.

"It's amazing," Whitney added. "The way she pets her dog, the way she works her garden. Everything about her reminds me of Mom."

"The question is, what are we going to do?" Adams said.

"I wish we could say hello," Whitney added. She put her hand to the monitor to touch the image of Mara.

"I wonder what she's thinking," he said.

Whenever Mara was outdoors, Adams and Whitney were spellbound. Unfortunately, she worked long hours. Adams spent many days stumbling around with other duties while he was really keeping an eye out for her. It became a major distraction for him.

Adams was mostly quiet. I figured he was thinking of nothing but Rose. Finally, here in the project that was his wife's idea, there was Mara. It was a cosmic connection, something that said, *"This matters!"* But what next?

Frank was also intrigued with Mara. He too sat for long periods, watching her from a chair in the lab, talking with Adams about the wonder of it all. He had known Rose for longer than he had known Adams.

"I funded this project for Rose," he reminded me. He commented on similarities he noticed between the Earth woman and his past associate, but he didn't obsess over Mara like Adams and Whitney did. He told me, "I was at the funeral. I've already said goodbye."

On clear nights, Mara stood on her roof stargazing with her telescope. She kept a bottle of wine and a glass by her side. She spent hours looking through the eyepiece, as well as looking upwards with her eyes. We would gaze back at her. Once, I brought a bottle of wine and three glasses into the lab so we could share in her moment. When I offered Whitney the glass, she kissed me on the cheek and thanked me. I thought a lot about our relationship during that time, how I had blown it with her.

I also thought about Jessica. A part of me missed her deeply, and it went beyond the physical. A bond had been created during the flying sessions and those nights together. Something about Jessica felt natural and fun. It was similar to how I felt with Whitney, but sometimes I thought Jessica and I were a more natural pairing. There was a side to us that was at the same level emotionally. Even though Whitney was the youngest of our crew, emotionally she was the most mature.

We spent our Thetan sessions asking questions about Mara. We watched as she worked on her knees in the flower garden. It was early morning on that part of the Earth. We asked a number of questions regarding the nature of her job.

"She is involved in the search for extraterrestrial intelligence," The Grandmother told us.

"Is she married?" I asked out of curiosity, though I immediately recognized it to be inappropriate.

"She is a widow," The Grandmother said through Whitney. Adams stood behind his chair, grabbing the back of it and pressing his fingers into it.

"Did her husband work for the same department?" Adams asked.

"Yes, he searched for life in the universe."

Adams let the answers soak in. He looked upset. Mara dug small holes in the soil and placed little flowers in them. She carefully poured a bit of water around each one. Adams handed me a note that contained a question. I thought he had lost his voice for the moment.

"What's Mara thinking about?" I asked.

"The flowers... how simple it is that they take root and grow. Why is life so paradoxical? I miss Michael. I'm angry that he left. Does he remember the pact? Will it be answered? Why did he have to leave? Does he even remember the pact?"

"What pact?" Adams asked.

"She made a pact with her husband that if there was a continuation of the soul, whoever left first would make an effort to demonstrate that to the other."

"How long has it been since he died?" Adams asked.

"Almost three years," the speaker replied.

Adams said as an aside, "That's the same amount of time since Rose left."

"Is there any way for us to contact her?" I asked.

"Not in the conventional sense," the speaker replied.

I looked at Adams to see if he wanted to ask anything else, but he shook his head no. We waited patiently for Whitney to come out of her trance. Adams read the printout again and again. Whitney finally came out, awaiting the pages.

Adams and Whitney left together that night. They didn't return until late the next day. Whitney told me they went to the coast and walked by the shore, talking about Rose. They walked for hours barefoot in the sand. It had been years since they had done that together.

Adams was subtly changing. He had always been introverted and quietly thoughtful. He became even more so. Now, it seemed that he was thinking entirely of Rose. He looked as if he was lost at work.

Ian told me, "He's nearly useless on these projects."

Whitney had prepared a dozen questions for me to ask The Grandmother that evening. Ian had a few questions of his own that would have to be put on hold.

"Grandmother," I asked. "Is it possible for us to contact this entity, Mara?"

"Yes and no," came the reply.

"Can you elaborate?"

"Contact, in the physical sense of the word, no. The entity has chosen a life that makes it impossible to be with her previous family. This is the entity's own choosing and must be respected. It is possible to make contact at the spiritual level, which is what she wants."

"How?"

"Through meditation and dreams," the speaker said.

"This is what she wants?" Adams asked.

"Simply because she has chosen a lifetime away from you doesn't mean she wants to be out of your life. Why else would you have found her?"

"But this doesn't make sense," Adams said, pacing around. "How can I continue to be a part of her life if I can't even hold her or say hello?"

"Through meditation and dreams, it is possible."

"But how do I do that?"

"You know how to dream. Your spiritual side is accessible through dreams and through meditation. That is a time of letting go of worldly desires, letting go of what you think of as your life."

"But I can't control my dreams," Adams said.

"Do you believe the entity wants to be controlled by you?"

"Of course not."

"Ask yourself why you seek control. Ask yourself why this arrangement is unacceptable, even though it was made in your own interests by the one you love."

"The one I love." Adams thought about the words. "Why did she have to marry someone else?" Adams added, getting off track of the list Whitney had given me.

"That can best be answered by you or her."

"But how can I ask her?" Adams objected.

"It is time for you to begin your lessons in meditation. Ask your daughter to help with this. Whitney is a gifted teacher."

Adams finally stopped talking. I waved the list of questions in the air to get his consent to return to the program. He was lost in thought, but he acknowledged my request.

"Grandmother," I said, "did the entity known as Rose make a conscious decision to leave or was her death an accident?"

"There are no accidents in life," the speaker said.

"If she made a conscious decision, then why?" I asked.

"She felt this was the only way to bring about the changes in her loved one that he needed," Whitney said.

"By dying?" Adams blurted out. "She thought that would be a good way to help me?!"

"This would best be answered by you or her. Speak with your daughter, and begin your practice."

"What if I find this arrangement unacceptable?"

"We are through for the present."

The Thetan sun still had several minutes before rising over Coasttown. Something about the speaker's tone had changed, as if she had grown impatient with Adams.

That night, I had a vivid dream. This one woke me up, leaving my heart pounding and my face bathed in sweat. The dream went like this:

She was behind the wheel, driving through a rainy night, driving faster than she should have been. She was crying and looked confused. There was a car behind her, and she continually checked the rearview mirror. The second car was not following closely, but it was following. Her heart was beating as loud as a drum.

I felt that the woman in the dream was Rose, though her face seemed different. My dream never led to an accident, but I sensed the accident was impending. I decided to ask Adams about it.

"Was it raining the night Rose had her accident?" I asked him the next morning. I mentioned it quietly so the others wouldn't hear me.

He put his clipboard down and thought about it. "It was," he said after a moment. "Why do you ask?"

"Just curious. I was wondering if the wet roads made the difference."

"I should have driven her," Adams said, recollecting.

"Where was she going?"

"She said she had some loose ends at work to tie up. She could never sleep with work on her brain."

"Did the accident happen between here and your house?" I asked.

"No, it was further in toward town," he said. "She was probably running by the store on her way home. Why are you so curious?"

"Just thinking about it," I said and left the conversation at that.

215

A New Practice

WHITNEY ASKED ME TO PARTICIPATE in Webster's first meditation lesson. She wanted me to arrive at the house very early in the morning, as the Thetans did, an hour before sunrise.

Whitney set her mat on the floor. Neither Adams nor I had her flexibility, so we sat in chairs. She lit a few candles and an incense burner. She placed some items around the room, including dried flowers, a picture of Rose and one of The Grandmother.

Once we were seated, we formed a triangle with each of us facing the center. There was a sense of intrigue. Though the session had not yet begun, I felt we were making progress simply by being there.

Whitney told us to relax. She explained, "The mind is an incessant worker that doesn't know how to take a break. Meditation quiets the mind so it can hear the voice that comes from within."

"But isn't that what my mind is?" Adams asked.

"There is a difference. The mind is like the noises at a loud party, and the voices within are like one interesting person at the party. The trick is to be so calm and focused that it is easy to hear the one quiet voice over the shouting from all the others."

"So how do we do it?" I asked, already feeling more relaxed.

"First, get comfortable," Whitney said. "Close your eyes. Let your breathing slow down. Loosen your body. Imagine the blood within you flowing to its needed areas. Let your mind be quiet."

"The first parts seem easy," Adams said through closed eyes. "It's letting my mind be quiet that seems so hard."

"Allow your mind to think of one thought. Allow your mind to think 'I am at peace.' As you quiet your mind by focusing on the mantra, slowly begin to feel the mantra instead of thinking of the words."

"What do I do when my brain starts to wander?" I asked.

"Return to the words. You are at peace. Start again mentally with the words and eventually stay with the feeling within them. The feeling is much more powerful than the words themselves."

"This is what you do?" Adams asked.

"This is how to get started," Whitney said calmly. "Once you get a feel for it, you will be able to meditate without need of the mantra."

"How long might this take?" I asked.

"A few weeks. A few months. Can you handle that?"

"Yes," I said.

"If this is how I can connect with Rose, then I can handle it."

We began by quieting our mouths. Then I attempted to quiet my mind. I told myself I was at peace, my body and brain and everything about me were at peace. As I told myself that, I began to feel the peace Whitney had described. The room was filled with it. I suspected it was easier with the three of us than if I had been doing it alone. Something about the group, especially Whitney, had a soothing effect on the space. I wondered if Adams was also experiencing this. Then I realized my mind was wandering. I let go of those thoughts.

We remained there for about a half hour. It was amazing how active my brain wanted to be. Thoughts kept popping up, like being with Jessica, or flying my PFD, or what I would eat for breakfast. I felt like my brain was an out-of-control puppy, and I was trying to leash it and get it to be obedient. But my brain, the puppy, wanted to be off its leash and run around. I struggled through that first session, returning many times to the words of my mantra.

"Okay," Whitney said softly. "Slowly return to your normal selves."

"My normal thinking self?" Adams asked, opening his eyes.

"How do you feel?"

"That was interesting," Adams said. "I had trouble not letting thoughts enter, but I did what you said, and I think I get it. My mind felt like a dog with no obedience training."

"That's exactly what I was feeling," I said.

"You picked up on each other's energy," Whitney said. "That's good. You've already experienced a connection."

"I don't think I came any closer to connecting with Rose," Adams said.

"This will take time," Whitney reassured him.

"I know. I can handle it."

"We should make a pact to do this for at least one month, here, every morning at the same time," Whitney said, looking over to me.

"Count me in," I said.

For the first week, it was an ordeal to get out of bed so early. My body wanted sleep until the light of dawn entered my room. But knowing how important it was for Adams and Whitney, I made sure never to be late. We stayed with the mantra "I am at peace," though Whitney told us many words or sayings would be acceptable.

On the third day, we lengthened our sessions to a full hour. When we came out of it, the daylight was just beginning to brighten the skies. I felt a spiritual connection when I saw it. I felt in tune with nature, and it suddenly made sense that the Thetans meditated just before dawn.

I also noticed an effect at work. After a week of morning meditations, I felt sharper at the end of the day. Adams worked mostly with Ian and I mostly with Jessica, but we talked with each other about our increased ability to focus on what we were doing and to feel less distracted.

Adams said, "This is making me more aware of Rose's presence, even if it's inspired by my own actions."

Our evening sessions with the Thetans were also influenced by what we were doing. Adams and I appreciated their ritual more, as well as Whitney's expertise in joining them.

We returned to our old routine, asking questions about the products we tried to understand. Ian and Frank were delighted to ask their questions again. During the next two weeks we made progress in understanding how certain things worked. We stayed with items from Delta 13. Ian and Adams ironed out many of the past wrinkles concerning their drive systems. We kept away from the crystal laser shields because Adams and Frank had not resolved their differences.

"Changes are happening. I don't know if I can attribute it to this new practice, but I can't discount the possibility. Rose, I miss you dearly. For a while, I had forgotten how much. It seems odd to be thinking that you can hear me, but maybe you can in your dreams. Maybe we can talk about it someday."

- from p. 156 of Webster's journal.

Divine Light

"GRANDMOTHER," I ASKED, "Whitney would like to know if there is a light source within people."

Ian grimaced as I finished the sentence. Even I thought the question was odd. Surprisingly, Adams did not. He looked interested to hear the response.

"Yes, dear child," she responded through Whitney. "Your spirit is made of light. The body you wear makes it difficult for others to see that brilliance within you. From the time the universe began, everything that is was made of light."

"Everything?" Adams asked. "Even people?"

"Light makes the atom. Light makes the electron, the proton, the photons, the quarks. Light is the beginning and the end, the Alpha and the Omega."

"How can matter be composed of light?" Adams asked.

"The most fundamental unit of matter is not the quark, lepton, nor anything smaller you can find. Beneath all of those things is light, the divine essence of creation. As you have been told, the Maker began with light."

"Now you're speaking about the origin of the universe, again," Adams said.

"The beginning of the universe was light. Divine light. There is light within every molecule. That light is from the same source and is divine in nature."

"If light is divine," Jim began, "and if there is light within all things, then are all things divine?"

"They are divine in origin."

"What about bad things?" Jessica asked, perplexed. "What about bad people? Are you saying evil doesn't exist?"

"Evil is choosing not to recognize divinity. Evil is selfishness, fear, hatred, ignorance. For you have continual decisions to make, and whether you choose good or evil is a matter of free will."

"How do we know which is which?" Jessica asked. "Sometimes it's so confusing."

"Ask the light within you."

Ian spoke out. "Is there anything that moves faster than light?"

"How can you move faster than timeless?" she said. "How can you time something that exists out of time?"

"That's an interesting point," Adams whispered to us. "At the speed of light, time stops. It goes to zero."

"I just wanted to see what she had to say about it," Ian whispered back.

"So, is light like another dimension?" I asked.

"Light and dimension are connected," the speaker began. "To say that light is a dimension is like saying water is an ocean. The first encompasses much more than the specific. We will review this another time, for we are through for the present."

We continued with our morning sessions. By the third week, it was much easier for me to get past the words of my mantra and right to the meaning. I noticed that my mantra and the feeling I reached were blending into something bigger. Adams described a similar experience.

He even said, "I've seen Rose in one of my dreams. I spoke with her about what I was doing."

I didn't tell him about my dream of Rose. I wanted to share it with him, but I wasn't ready to.

At the end of the first month, Whitney brought us gifts. She gave me a nice winter hat, which was perfect since the season was approaching.

She gave Adams a wool sweater. As she presented it to him, his eyes welled up. "You recognize it, don't you?" Whitney asked gently. Adams nodded, accepting the sweater and holding it to his chest.

"What's going on?" I asked.

"Rose began this," Adams said through his tears. "She never finished it. It's been tucked away in a drawer this whole time."

Whitney held him. Then she said, "Come on, let's see it on you."

The sweater was mostly black with areas of white in the front. Within the patches of white were colorful hints subtly woven between the light and the dark areas. I looked closer. It was an image of a galaxy.

"Perfect," Whitney said, inspecting the length of the arms.

"I have a question," I said. "What are we doing tomorrow?" It was the end of our pact to go for a month.

"Same time tomorrow?" Adams asked while looking at himself in a mirror.

"Count me in," Whitney said.

"Then I guess that makes three of us."

When I saw the look on Whitney's face, I knew I had said the right thing. I remembered the advice The Grandmother had given me, to be less selfish. Keeping my word with the sessions and always being on time was a success there. Perhaps I was gaining in soul development.

Adams wore his new sweater to work that day and the following days. He was a different man than I had known. He had opened up a spiritual side while softening the clinical one. He shared what was happening with Ian and Jessica. They commented about the changes as well.

Frank noticed it too. I sensed he was concerned the changes were negatively affecting Adams and his work. Frank spent time in the lab with him.

Jim told me later in private, "I think you should listen to this."

"Listen to what?" I asked.

"Mr. Maxwell and Dr. Adams have been talking a lot lately. I thought you'd want to know about it."

I sat down and listened to the recording Jim had made. Frank's voice was calm yet persistent, as he told Adams of his concerns with his recent behavior.

"Part of me thinks you're putting too much stock into all of this," Frank said.

"Too much stock?" Adams replied.

"All you do is watch Mara and reflect on the past. You might end up very disappointed in the end," Frank added.

"I understand where you're coming from. My personal changes won't bring Rose back. I know that. But this has helped me deal with losing her, as well as recognizing her spiritual presence."

"Her spiritual presence?" Frank asked.

"This was her creation. Rose is everywhere in this room. She's not just on that little planet. She's in the monitors. She's in the hydrogen. She's even in the desks and pencils."

"I think the Thetans have brainwashed you," Frank added. "I think they're brainwashing all of us."

Adams laughed, but there was some degree of truth to what Frank had said. Adams admitted, "I guess they are. But how can I argue with what they say?"

"I can't argue with it," Frank told him. "It's certainly made us richer. It's just hard to accept it all without questioning it at some level. Be careful, Webster."

"I understand how you feel," Adams said. "But there's nothing I can do about it."

"Now I've got Frank concerned. My oldest friend doesn't know me anymore. He'll come around, I think."

- from p. 160 of Webster's journal.

Association

WHITNEY SHOWED ME that sometimes I just needed to take off and reunite with my own planet.

On my next day off, I pulled my old bike out of the garage. I wiped the dust from the frame and brushed the cobwebs from the spokes. The chain was dry, so I gave it a squirt of oil. The tires had lost some air. I found the pump, filled them up and off we went.

How nice it was after so many weeks, to feel the wind in my hair as I rode down the streets of my new neighborhood. I'd forgotten the simple pleasure of pedaling a bike after months of driving my car and flying my PFD. My legs felt a little weak. I took my time and rode at a comfortable pace around familiar landmarks. I pedaled past the Star Bar and thought of Sam. I rode by my old apartment and wondered who was living in it. I followed the bike path down by the river and through the town parks.

After an hour, I stopped by the liquor store to get some water. I recognized the man behind the counter, who had been so impressed with my PFD months ago. He didn't remember me, but he was polite as he rang up the total for two bottles of water. I downed the first one quickly. I placed the second in the water holder and was ready for more pedaling.

A convertible pulled into the lot. I recognized Brandi right away, the redhead sitting in the passenger seat. Then I noticed Molly behind the wheel. The girls got out of the car to enter the store. I turned the bike around and pulled up next to the curb.

Their clothing looked like materials from Alpha 17. Brandi had a metallic miniskirt, and Molly wore a matching top. They both wore metallic-colored shoes. It was the first time I had seen articles of clothing inspired from the creation.

"Hey, Brandi. Hey, Molly," I said from my bike. "Nice duds."

"Hey," they replied, stopping in their tracks. They looked at one another for a sign of familiarity.

"What are you doing?" I asked.

"Nothing," Molly said awkwardly. "Just getting something to drink."

"Me too," I added, pulling the water bottle from its holder and taking a swig.

"Do we know you?" Brandi asked.

"You don't remember me?" I was shocked. The girls looked at each other and shook their heads. "I'm Jon. I took you flying two months ago." I wanted to say, 'we've had sex twice, remember?'

"Is that you?" Brandi asked. She came closer to inspect me, not nearly as excited about my looks on the bike than she had been when I had jumped down from the PFD. "I can't believe it. How funny that we didn't recognize you."

"Where's your machine?" Molly asked.

"At home. I wanted to get some exercise."

"That's awesome," Brandi said. "Give us a call, and let's go flying sometime."

"I'll do that."

The girls backed away from me and entered the store. I pedaled out of the lot and toward the path by the river. Like hell I was going to call them, I thought.

The Great Mystery

THERE WERE MANY HOURS of the day when we couldn't watch Mara, whenever she was at work or inside her house. Adams always had Jim keep an eye out for her. They compiled a Mara disc recording every single thing she did outdoors. It was collections of her getting into the car, driving to work or to the store, taking her dog for morning and evening walks, working in the garden and painting on her patio.

"Rose liked to paint outside too," Adams remarked, as he watched Mara work on a new piece.

The canvas was almost entirely blank. She was beginning to sketch in background colors of blue and gray. It appeared to be a scene by the beach. I could make out ocean waves and dark, cloudy skies in the background. I wondered what she would paint in the center. Jim thought perhaps a jumping fish, and I guessed a ship. We decided to put it on the list of questions for the Thetans so we could enjoy watching the process unfold.

"Teacher," I asked, at a session with an inland group of Thetans, "Mara has been working on a painting lately. We've watched her create the background of ocean waves and skies. Do you know the artwork of which I'm referring?"

"Yes, we know of it," the young Thetan man responded through Whitney.

"I'm a little curious," I said. "What's going to be in the center of the picture?"

"It will be what it will be," the speaker responded. "You'll have to wait for her to finish it."

"You don't know the answer?" Adams asked.

"The future is not predetermined. Mind is the builder, yet the path of construction has infinite outlets."

"So our lives have not been predetermined?"

"Your existence is one of free will. How can you have freedom of expression if you are acting as a puppet on strings? What would be the meaning of your life, to amuse the puppeteer?"

"But your people have said that my life has a purpose behind it," Adams reminded him. "That sounds like a contradiction to hear you say now the future is not predetermined."

"Your life is an ongoing creation, an ever-flowing evolution, like the life forms you have been studying. Mind is the builder. You are the creator and the creation. You are the director and the actor and the play. Do you not see it?"

"Yes, I can see that," Adams said.

"See yourself as an evolution in progress. Be the evolution. Embrace the changes your soul has in mind for you."

"How do I know what they are?" Adams asked.

"Do not fear that you, the actor, are unaware of you, the director. The play unfolds. Experiences are presented where you have free will to respond. This is the great mystery. The purpose is to assist your soul in development."

"The great mystery?" Jim asked.

"One way to call the sojourn or lifetime," the speaker responded. "It is a mystery, because the experience is more meaningful that way. What use would your lifetime be if you knew the background of your soul or the challenges to be presented?"

"A great mystery because it can't be defined?" I asked.

"How could you define it?" the reply came. "You know that you cannot define time or light or existence. You can only describe them. This should not be troubling. Take comfort that there are others on your path, like ourselves, who are assisting you on this journey."

Understanding the Thetans was frustrating for Adams. Philosophy was not his specialty. It also frustrated him that he could watch Mara but not speak with her. He spent most of his days helping Ian halfheartedly while keeping an eye out for Mara. It was distracting for him and a nuisance to Ian, who still needed Adams to help with work.

The other problem was that it tied up the cameras that were able to film Earth. We had two in that section of the universe which could be calibrated at equal distance. Adams preferred both to be for Mara, extremely close, so we could generate three-dimensional images nearly at real-time. This disturbed Jessica. Her job was to search newfound planets for interesting ideas and products. She was handcuffed by the whole thing, forced to work with Ian on Omega 5 and with recordings we had from Delta 13. She complained about it to Frank several times before he finally had a talk with Adams.

"I'm not sure this is healthy for you," Frank told him at a crew meeting in the lab. "All you've done for the past few weeks is watch this woman. You haven't been working. You don't look like you've been eating. The closest people to ourselves are waiting to be unveiled. I think we should move the cameras to some other part of this planet so you can get back to normal."

"I'm fine, Frank," Adams said. He kept his eyes on Mara as she worked on her painting.

"What if it was just for a day or two," Jessica added, "so we can do some other surveys?"

"Even if this person was once Rose," Frank suggested, "she's not Rose now."

"That's not true, Frank," Adams said calmly. "Look at her. Everything about her reminds me of Rose. The way she paints on her back deck, the way she walk-jogs with her dog, even the way she's a bad driver. It is Rose."

"The question is, is this beneficial for you or for what we're doing here?" Frank added. "Webster, as you know, I lost a wife too, a long time ago," Frank went on. "I can relate to what you're going through. If one of these women turned out to be my Emily, I don't think it would be healthy for me to spend all of my time watching her."

"This was Rose's project," Adams replied angrily, without taking his eyes from the monitor. "Without her and me, you wouldn't even be here."

Besides Adams and Whitney, everyone else was anxious to study Earth. Although they were a few decades behind us, the people reminded us of ourselves in every way—appearance, actions, they probably thought like us too.

Frank asked Jessica and me if we would alter our schedules so we could get some work done after Adams had left for the night. Even though Jim had been instructed to watch out for Mara at all times, Frank felt we could get Jim to look elsewhere on the planet during the hours Mara was asleep and Adams was at home.

I told him, "My schedule is already very busy."

Jessica pleaded with me. In the end, I agreed to stay.

That night I convinced Jim to take a break from watching Mara's house. "It will still be there, and Mara will still be asleep on our return."

He reluctantly agreed, and we began charting the rest of the planet. Once we were alone, Jessica and I had a fairly good time scouting around.

Earth had large polar ice caps and five major continents. It also had lots of ocean. Seventy percent of it was covered with water. We found abundant sea life around the shorelines. The tropical areas held many white, sandy beaches, to which Jessica replied, "I need a vacation."

Jessica put her hand on my back and asked if I ever took vacations. I thought of the times we had shared together. The notion of spending a week with her by the ocean was tempting. She loosened her hair-pin and shook it out, and her soft brown hair fell to her shoulders. She looked even better than when she had first arrived many months ago. Had she changed or had my perception of her changed?

"I like this shirt on you," Jessica said as she released the top button, "but it looks like it's choking you."

"We can't do this," I told her.

She gave me a quick kiss on the lips. "I know," she said. "Definitely not here," she added. "Perhaps Jim can keep this up while we take a quick coffee break in Webster's office."

I didn't know what to say. More than anything I wanted her at that moment though I knew it would hinder my efforts at getting back with Whitney. I was confused and tired.

"Coffee does sound good," I said. "Back in a few minutes, Jim. Keep doing what you're doing."

"I'll be here," Jim added sarcastically.

The coffee machine was empty as it should have been so late in the day. I asked the dispenser to prepare two cups. As we waited for the machine to make them, Jessica asked me, "How are you feeling?"

"Confused and unsure," I told her.

"What do you want to do about it?"

"I don't think I want to answer that."

"I miss you," she told me.

"I miss you too."

Jessica put her arms around my back and hugged me warmly. I could tell she sympathized with my position. As her face turned to meet mine, I couldn't help but kiss her. We exchanged a long, soft kiss and held each other until the coffee was ready.

"Let's take this back into the other room," I told her.

Jim remarked, "You're back sooner than I had expected."

The three of us returned to our studies of Earth. As far as their technology—we found cars, planes and cell phones, but their models looked similar to ours from two decades in the past. In fact, we found nothing that would be considered new or innovative, especially compared to the products we had found from the other cultures. Earth did have a bright spot, however. After a time leap, it would be poised to show us all kinds of things about our probable future.

Losing Bets

"GRANDMOTHER," I BEGAN, from the list Adams had given me, "you made a reference to an entity who was the husband of Mara. You mentioned he passed on three years ago in Earth time. What was the name of the entity?"

"The entity was known as Michael Smith."

"Has that entity or soul reincarnated?" I asked.

"No," came the reply from Whitney. "The entity is resting."

"Why did she have to marry someone else?" Adams asked with remorse.

"To experience a relationship with someone of a similar mind," the reply came. "Does this information bother you?"

"Yes," Adams admitted.

"What if you had left first?" The Grandmother asked him. "Would you have wanted Rose to spend the rest of her life as a widow?"

"I guess not," Adams said.

"At her request, a lifetime was arranged for her own development, and yours and your daughter's. This was as Rose designed it, for mind is always the builder."

"Are you saying my mind wasn't in accord with Rose's?" Adams asked.

"You have said it so."

"But that's not true," Adams said, standing up and changing his tone. "We were a perfect match. We were probably the only two people on our planet who could have pulled off this project."

"But you did have a major difference," The Grandmother said through Whitney.

"I don't know what you mean," Adams said, pacing behind his chair.

"Think, Webster."

"Of course we had some differences. All couples have differences," Adams said.

"But one thing in particular..."

"I don't know what you're talking about."

"Yes, you do," she replied through Whitney.

"My mind's a blank."

"You remember... she was upset with you... by the campus pond... when she was pregnant with your daughter..."

"The bet?" Adams remembered. "Is that what you're referring to? That bet we made?"

"You have said it so."

"Right. The bet," Adams said, suddenly becoming upset. "That stupid, stupid bet."

"Thinking back on it now," The Grandmother said, "would you make the same bet today?"

"No." Adams looked upward and lamented, "Rose, is that why you left me? Okay, I admit it. You were right. There must be a God. I'm not sure what I think about him though!"

Adams collapsed into his chair and wept. I didn't know what to do for him. The Thetans continued their meditation though Whitney came out of her trance. She saw her father and jumped to assist him.

She knelt before him and held his head in her arms. She repeated many times, "Everything's going to be all right." She looked at me, dying to know what had been said in the session.

Ian had been watching the whole time, waiting patiently for questions further down the list. He put his coat on in frustration and left. Jessica sat at her desk, sadly watching Adams.

Whitney held onto Adams and helped him to the door. I handed her their jackets. Whitney asked me, "Can you come by the house later, and bring the printout from the session?"

I told her, "I'll be there shortly."

After they left, Jessica said, "She's very special. I can see why you care so much for her."

"That doesn't mean I don't care for you too," I told her. "This is a difficult thing for me."

"Did you enjoy the times we had together?" she asked.

"More than you know," I told her. "But that doesn't make it right."

"If we both enjoyed it, why does it have to be wrong or right?"

"That's a good question," I admitted. "I don't have the answer."

We went back to our work. I asked Jim to find some of the largest Earth cities so we could give Frank detailed notes on the more advanced products and their ways of life. Jessica and I went about our studies as professionals. I felt like a jerk, keeping myself from doing something that would feel good because my higher-self had instructed me to do so.

I realized that evening I was in love with two women. I loved Jessica in a way I couldn't describe or even admit. She had never done anything wrong to me, nor had she ever acted in a way that would hurt me. Now she was showing me the utmost in patience and respect.

I wondered if Jessica and I were meant to be together. Were we soul mates or were we just lovers? If not for Whitney, I would have been sure Jessica and I were meant for each other.

As we left that night, we spoke in the parking lot. I told her my feelings were frustrating to no end. I told her I didn't know what to do.

She said, "I know."

"Is this what love is?"

Jessica laughed sympathetically. "It's definitely not what you want it to be. At least that's been my experience."

I helped Jessica strap into the PFD, kissed her and watched her fly off. Then I hopped into mine and flew slowly to Whitney's house, thinking of what I was going to say.

When I set the craft down on her front lawn, Whitney came running out. She was wearing a full-length nightgown and was barefoot. It was a warm night for early winter, but it was still too cold to be dressed like she was.

"What are you doing?" I asked her from the cabin. "You're going to catch a cold."

"I don't mind," she said. "I wanted to see you." As soon as I got down, she threw her arms around my neck and kissed me. "I still care about you," she told me.

"I care about you too," I said, surprised by her actions. "I'm so sorry for—"

"I know what you're going through," she added. "I had a vision."

"A vision?"

"Think of it as a dream," she said with her arms still around me.

"Were you asleep?"

"I had it tonight, when they brought me out early from the session. It had to do with you and Jessica."

"I thought we've been through this." I let my arms fall to my side.

Whitney let go of me as well, turning her head and gathering her thoughts. "We have, but this is new. I saw the two of you together, and it was right." As she spoke the words, *"right"* jumped out at me. Just minutes before, Jessica had emphasized the same word, and it made a lasting impression hearing it from Whitney. "It's okay for you to be with Jessica now. You're not ready for me."

"Why, I have to work my way up to you?" I asked sarcastically.

"It's not like that. It's more like stages. You and Jessica are more compatible at this time."

"But I want to be with you," I told her. "I know I've made mistakes, but I really want to be with you."

"Not until you're ready for me. You still have a lot of growing to do."

"How long is that going to take?"

"I can't answer that," she said. "For now, I think you should meditate on your own. You need time, and meditation will help you grow."

"Is that what your vision told you?"

"My heart tells me."

"So you're dumping me?"

"It's not like that!" she said. "You're still special to me. I do love you, but I can't be more than friends until you're ready."

"You are dumping me."

"See it how you will. In the meantime, if you want to be with her, it might help you on your path."

"The Thetans told you this?"

"In a way, yes."

I gave her the printout from the session, kissed her lightly and got back into my PFD. I flew over toward the coast and buzzed along the shoreline, more confused than ever. I couldn't believe what Whitney told me. She loved me, and yet she wanted me to be with Jessica. The more I thought about it, the more I realized she was right. I was in love with both of them. Whitney was my ideal while Jessica was my reality. There was something to be said for each.

I flew over to Jessica's house and knocked on the door several times. It took her a while to respond, as she had been asleep. When she opened the door and saw me, she didn't look surprised.

"I just had a dream that you were here," Jessica said, wearing a pajama top.

She let me in. She took my hat and jacket and tossed them on the couch. She walked back to the bedroom and resumed her place under the covers while leaving them open for me. I took off my clothes and lay down beside her.

I told her, "I feel totally confused."

"It's okay, Jon. Just lie down and rest."

We put our arms around each other. I could tell she was happy, yet she managed to fall back to sleep within moments.

Frustration

MARA HAD NOT YET LEFT the building though the Earth sky had been dark for hours. The lot still contained nearly all the cars. The lights shined through the windows as a clue that something was happening inside, something keeping the employees at work well past midnight.

Mara finally left the building with the others. They chatted with great animation in the parking lot. Mara eventually got in her car and drove home. She fed her dog and went straight to bed.

In the morning, Mara abandoned her usual schedule. She threw the stick for her dog and petted him vigorously before getting into her car, as if to say, *"Sorry about the walk today."* She left him in the backyard and drove directly to the office, after having been home for only a few hours of sleep.

Adams and Whitney wondered what was going on. We had an immediate session with an inland group of Thetans. Frank was not present.

"Teacher," I said to the elderly man sitting next to the open spot in the circle, "are you aware of the building where Mara works, the building we are currently watching?"

"Yes," came the response from Whitney, "we have the structure and the people."

"It seems that something very exciting is happening there. Can you tell us more about it?"

"They have found a signal from deep space."

"What is the nature of the signal?" Adams asked, standing behind his chair, pressing his thumbs firmly into the plush back.

"A series of wavelengths. A series different from all the other objects they have recorded."

"Where is the source of the signal?" Adams asked.

"From this galaxy, the Theta galaxy, as you term it."

In the past, we had looked partially through it but found no other planets with advanced life on them, besides Theta 7. The thought of an artificial wavelength coming from this galaxy was a small surprise though not a shock. There were millions of stars in this area of the universe.

"Is the signal one of an artificial nature?" Adams asked.

"Yes and no," the elder replied.

"I don't understand."

"It's artificial in the sense that an entity is responsible but not in the sense that the wavelength is produced by machinery."

"Now you've lost me," Adams said, taking a seat and trying to follow the elder Thetan.

"Mind is always the builder," the speaker replied. "The heavenly bodies of the universe can be seen as the props of a stage. The signal is natural in source since it is a collection of wavelengths from a cluster of stars. Though it is also artificial in source, as it is a means of one entity contacting another."

"Who is being contacted?" Adams asked. "Mara?"

"You have said it so."

"Then who is contacting her?"

"Is it her past husband?" Jim guessed.

"It is."

Whitney remained in her trance on the floor, meditating quietly with the inland village Thetans, while the crew spoke of all the present clues.

"It must have to do with the pact," Ian whispered. "Remember what The Grandmother told us about Mara and her husband?"

"That whoever left first would make an effort to demonstrate an afterlife," Jessica added. "What was his name? Michael?"

"But how?" I asked. "How could someone use stars to say, 'See, honey, there's an afterlife?'"

Adams asked aloud, "Is it a direct message from Michael to Mara?"

"You have said it so," came the reply.

"What does it say?" Adams asked.

"That question can best be answered by yourself and Mara."

"But Teacher, how can I answer this?" Adams was perplexed.

"This is by the entity's own choosing and must be respected. We are through for the present."

The Thetan sun had yet to rise over the village though Whitney came out of her trance. She awoke suddenly, opening her eyes wide and breathing in deeply. She looked around in wonder.

"Are you okay?" I asked.

"It's so different when they bring me out early," she said as I helped her to her feet. Jessica brought her a glass of water, and we waited until she

236

had a sip. "It's like being surrounded by light and then being jerked out of it and placed back into my body."

"Sounds wonderful," Ian said.

"Just a slight shock to the system. What did they say?"

"Mara received a signal," I told her. "They've received their first message from space."

Whitney read the printout. "No wonder she couldn't sleep." Whitney found it intriguing that the Thetans chose not to tell us the details of the message.

Mara worked late into the evening again. Her coworkers left the building well after midnight. Many of them talked in the parking lot, their hands and arms moving in animated gestures.

Adams suspected there had to be a way to communicate with Mara. He grew impatient watching the tapes Jim provided.

He said, "I wonder if the Thetans would hold anything back from me." Though Jim's receptors had the ability to receive and interpret radio and light waves, they weren't designed to send any. Contacting Earth in the same way they had contacted us was not a possibility.

We had a session with another group, one from an inland village on another continent.

"Teacher," I asked, addressing the Thetan woman who sat next to the empty spot in the circle. "Webster Adams would like to know if it is possible to contact this woman, Mara."

The elder woman replied through Whitney, "As it has been said, through dreams and meditation."

"But is there another way," Adams asked, "to have a real dialogue where one person can ask and the other can answer, such as what we are doing now?"

"Not in this sense," came the reply. "For the situation is as the entity has requested."

"If we're really soul mates, then why is she shutting me out of her life?"

"Is she?" the Thetan elder replied. "Why do you think you found her so easily? The situation is more of an effort to keep you in her life while assisting you in an area of growth."

"Have I gained or lost in soul development?" Adams asked.

"You have lost some, but you are poised for gains."

237

"What about when she's asleep?" Adams said. "Is it possible to ask her questions then?"

"It is possible," the elder replied through Whitney, "but it will be up to her to answer."

Adams looked to the monitor showing Mara's house in the dark. The lights had been off for hours, and we assumed she was in deep sleep.

"Rose," Adams said, "can you hear me? Mara?"

There was no reply from Whitney. After waiting a few moments Adams repeated himself twice more. Each time, there was no reply.

Frank was watching. He looked embarrassed for Adams.

"I give up," Adams finally said. He slumped into his chair and brought his head down to his hands in his lap. He pulled his hair in frustration.

I didn't know what to do. We didn't have a list of questions so the floor was open. Ian asked Adams if he wouldn't mind asking a few work related questions. Adams nodded his approval.

"Teacher," Ian began awkwardly, "it's been a while since we've asked about the Omegan crafts. Can you assist me in going over the nature of the force that powers them? I'm most interested in the disc-shaped vessels that are seen leaving the blue pad areas. The ships seem capable of space voyage."

"As you have been told before," the woman spoke through Whitney, "those vessels are employing light speed mechanics."

Ian asked, "Can you go over the fundamentals of the Omegan method?" He was extremely happy to finally have some time to his questions.

Frank listened as the elder outlined the principles of the Omegan device. Once again, the technology was something that would be nearly impossible for us to replicate, but simply knowing how they worked was extremely valuable.

"Do you want to be with me? Sometimes I can't make sense of it. I know I need to grow. I know I was arrogant, stubborn. I know I was wrong. Is that enough? There's a void being here without you, especially knowing why you left. I can't change the past. I don't know if I can change the present or the future. But if there's anything I can do, I'm all ears."

- from p. 164 of Webster's journal.

Out of Body

I HAD MORE DREAMS OF ROSE the night of the crash. The dream was always the same. She drove through her tears in the rain while aware of the car following her. I wondered, was the car behind her a metaphor for something else, or was it a real car? Was the dream a physical reality of the past, or did it represent something else? Though the image disturbed me on several nights, it didn't seem wise to share it with Adams or Whitney.

I continued meditating in the early morning hours at my home. I rarely used my mantra anymore. After a couple of months of practice, I slipped into that peaceful zone much more easily. I found the experience to be subtly amazing. It quieted my mind and helped focus my energy for the day. When I told Whitney I was still meditating, she was impressed.

"Would you like to try an experiment?" she asked me.

She had been meditating with a new group of Thetans. This group lived on an island surrounded by large areas of ocean on both sides. The island was the only land for a small stretch of the planet. It was special because the group there meditated for a two-hour period instead of one. They were the only group Whitney knew of who meditated for that long at a village podium. Whitney called them the Island Group. The experience of meditating with them had been different for her. She wouldn't tell me what it was, but she was interested to see if I would also have a unique experience. I was happy to try.

We stayed very late one evening, waiting for the Island Group to enter the dawn line. I sat in a chair, removed my shoes and loosened my collar and sleeves.

"Just relax and breathe," Whitney said. "You have nothing to be concerned about."

"Is Jim going to join me?"

"I'd like to," Jim said.

"He's experienced it with me," she said. "But if he wants to, that's fine." Jim's green light glowed.

I felt nervous, wondering what the big surprise would be. I sat in my chair and attempted to calm myself. I took one last look at the monitor.

The six members of the Island Group approached their podium in the predawn darkness.

"Two hours?" I asked. "That's longer than I've ever done."

"You'll be surprised how quickly it will pass," Whitney said.

Her words had a soothing effect. I let go of my tension and focused on my breathing as the thoughts drifted by. If I had a thought, like being with Jessica, or Frank's concern for Adams, or my dream about Rose, then I imagined it contained within a bubble that floated away. Within a few minutes, I had sent dozens of bubbles out for good. I felt relaxed and at peace.

"Good," Whitney said, recognizing my improvement.

As the meditation progressed, I began to let go. I had a feeling the Island Group was aware of my presence. I felt as if they were focusing on my energy, and I was focusing on theirs. By then, I had meditated many times, but I had never felt the pull of another entity engaging me. In time, I was aware of leaving my body and hovering in darkness.

I went ever deeper and completely let go of my thoughts. I connected to the empty vacuum of space. It felt like my soul belonged there. I let myself drift in a sense of void, and I became aware of a light. I let my spirit move toward that light. As I became a part of it, I turned into a bird flying across the universe.

I flew down to the Thetan atmosphere, lower and lower until I was soaring over the ocean in the darkness of the night. Another bird joined me, a smaller one. I sensed it was Jim. We soared over the vast purple water. I was able to direct my flight anywhere I wanted. We flew over the island that was isolated within the vast ocean. I saw the town center, and I recognized the Island Group of Thetans in the pre-dawn, even though I was flying over them at a great height. I folded my wings and dove down to the podium where I landed in the open spot of the meditation circle. The Island Thetans sat there, unaffected by my sudden presence.

The other bird, Jim, landed on the branch of a nearby tree.

I looked around at the Island Group in their meditative trances. I sensed their energy open up to me and appreciate my presence. I looked to my left and saw the elder male gazing back at me with open eyes.

They reassured me with a look of peace and love. I wanted to express my appreciation for the experience. As soon as I felt the thought, I sensed they knew what I was trying to say. I opened my beak but only managed to make the squawking sound of a bird, which made the Thetan elder smile with his eyes. I relaxed and sat quietly with them, thinking of nothing, just enjoying the peace. I blacked out.

The light of dawn broke, and the wind picked up under my wings. I extended them, letting the air lift me again into the orange-colored sky.

Jim joined me in the air, and we flew above the island and out over the purplish-blue ocean. We flew ever higher over the planet and into outer space until I was once again in the void, no longer in a bird's body, but a spirit without form. I floated calmly in space until I began to sense my own breathing.

I returned to my body in the chair in the lab. I opened my eyes and saw Whitney smiling at me. I looked at the monitors and noticed the Island Thetans were leaving the podium. Their red sun was well into the start of its day. Jim's light was pulsing mildly.

"How do you feel?" Whitney asked.

"That was the most amazing thing." I stood up and shook the stiffness out of my legs.

"I saw you," Jim said. "You were a bird."

"Was that you with me?"

"Yes," he said proudly. "I love being a bird!"

"I was flying! Without a device around me, just wings. I never knew it could be like that."

"Now you know," Whitney said, looking at me with understanding.

I reached for her and held her warmly.

"Thank you. I'm sorry it took me so long to come around."

"I understand."

The incredible feeling of being a bird and hanging out with the Thetans stayed with me for the rest of the night. Once at home, I had trouble falling asleep. Flying in the body of a bird was a hundred times better than flying in my PFD. I wanted to share my experience with Jessica, but it was late. I lay on my bed, looking at the ceiling and going over every detail of the experience so I would never forget it.

Charlie

WE CREATED OUR OWN VERSION of the Omegan spy bubble. Ours was grossly primitive compared to theirs. Ours had a super-thin, plastic shell while theirs was made of electricity that morphed constantly in shape. Ours used a helium derivative to help keep it floating, along with three tiny, pivoting motors based on Alphan technology. We named it Charlie.

Charlie was a small cylinder about four inches long. It had a tiny battery and a lightweight casing made of solar cells. We took it outside once a day for recharging. It also contained a micro-camera and a transmitter linked to a monitor in the lab. That was it. Ian programmed Charlie to recognize faces, and the little device quickly proved it could find and follow any one of us around the lab. Ian and I ran around playing hide and seek from it behind chairs, desks, even Whitney's mat.

Adams thought Charlie was brilliant. "Now parents can keep an eye on their children," he said. "Wherever they go, he'll be their eyes."

Jessica agreed, "Even better for monitoring babies. They can alert a parent if the infant is crying or out of the crib."

Frank said, "They could follow 'browsing' customers to curb shoplifting."

Ian said, "Or keep an eye on parolees."

We played with Charlie for a few days until we thought it was ready for some real-world testing. Frank volunteered me, much to the relief of everyone else. Adams wanted to try the device for a day or two once I tired of it. Ian programmed Charlie to follow me. He also taped a tiny microchip to my neck as a beacon for long-distance retrieval.

It was fun having the bubble follow me wherever I went. I thought of Charlie as my little floating friend. It made a puttering sound and maintained a distance of about six feet. It shot me from the front, as Ian had programmed it, so they could see my face. For the first two days, I had to adjust to always having Charlie around, especially when trying to sleep. The other time of discomfort was in the bathroom, whether sitting on the toilet or taking a shower. By the third day, I realized I was showering and had forgotten Charlie's presence. I wondered what the others would say after having seen me entirely. I felt a wave of relief and was okay with that.

I remembered Jim's conversation with Whitney about nudity. I agreed with him. The world probably would be a better place if people weren't so hung up about being naked.

I took Charlie outside to do some tests. I got on my bike and rode at an increasing pace, testing its ability to follow. Charlie kept up until I reached higher speeds. Then it would fall further and further behind. The Omegan versions were capable of any speed, as far as we could tell.

I also tested its tracking capability by getting in my PFD and flying off to some distant location. Sure enough, Charlie showed up minutes later and resumed the normal distance from me. During all of my testing, the device worked to perfection.

We never completed testing during severe wind or rain, since the days were gorgeous during my week with Charlie. Ian suggested we arrange some work in a simulated atmosphere.

Frank said, "Charlie will be an instant hit with investors." He looked forward to finalizing the tests for our latest toy.

Conflicts of Interest

"I'VE DECIDED WHAT I WANT for my birthday," Jim announced, during the middle of a workday.

"What is it?" I asked. Whitney and Adams turned to listen.

"I want to be a boy."

"You are a boy," Adams told him.

"I want to be a real boy. Like on Earth."

Adams looked at me and frowned, as if I had something to do with his request.

"Sorry, Jim, but birthday gifts don't work that way," I said. "Usually people accept things that others can actually give them."

"I want to experience being a boy, just like we experienced being a bird."

Adams looked at me quizzically. I shrugged it off like I didn't know what Jim was talking about. I didn't want to go into it with Adams, thinking he wouldn't understand.

"Maybe the Thetans can help," Jim added.

"How about some new music to listen to? Or some new games to play in the evenings?" I offered, trying to make these items sound more exciting than they really were. "How about some new movies?"

"That's not what I want. I want to be a boy, like one of these boys."

Images of several Earth boys appeared on the monitors. They rode bikes, played sports and climbed trees. They ranged in age from twelve to fifteen, too old to be called children and too young to be men. They had a range of hair color and height, but they all had something in common; each looked athletic, bright and fun-loving. Each boy would have made any parent proud.

"I like this one the best. I wish I knew his name."

The main monitor showed a boy of about fifteen. He had wavy brown hair, brown eyes and a great smile. He played on a jungle gym with some friends, though he was the most adept at swinging by his legs and doing stunts on the apparatus. He helped one of the smaller boys climb to the top.

"Did you guys do stuff like that when you were kids?" Jim asked.

"Jim," Adams said. "You have to understand there are certain things we can't do for you. What if I asked you to make me young again? Do you see the connection?" Jim didn't answer.

"What if we tried to make you feel like a real boy?" Whitney offered. "What if we came up with ways to help you feel that way?"

"That would be better than music or games," Jim said.

"I think that sounds possible," Whitney said, giving Adams and me an assuring look. Jim's light pulsed mildly as he thought of the idea.

"How would you do that?" he asked.

"Birthday gifts are usually a surprise," Whitney told him.

"You'll just have to wait," I added, having no idea what Whitney was thinking.

"I hope you know what you're doing," Adams whispered to her.

Jim printed out the image of the Earth boy's face. At his request, Whitney taped it on the wall above his green light.

Upon seeing it, Jessica said, "Who's the dapper young man?"

"That's Jim," I told her, adding a wink.

"Ah yes," she said. "Now I see the resemblance."

Mara emerged from the office doors late at night, carrying long paper rolls under her arm. A few of her colleagues talked in the parking lot. Mara handed three of the rolls to her coworkers then took the final one into her car. Jim followed her as she sped down the desolate desert roads.

Her dog wagged his tail excitedly in the dark as the car lights illuminated his body. She spent several minutes petting the dog and tossing his stick. Then she grabbed the document and walked into her house. She came out moments later with a large bowl of food, which the animal ate voraciously.

The patio lights came on. Mara walked out with the document and set it up on one of her easels. She unrolled the poster-sized image and pinned its corners to the easel.

"Zoom in on that, please," Adams instructed Jim.

As the shot went closer to the image, we saw what the Thetans had been referring to. The object currently fascinating Mara and her coworkers was an image of stars, presumably from the Theta galaxy. A few dozen stars were there, some larger than others. A red giant was the largest image in the picture.

"That doesn't look proportional," Adams noticed. "There are way too many stars for that amount of space."

"Could they have compressed the images?" Ian guessed.

"They must have."

The poster also contained planets shining faintly near the stars, though the planets were tiny next to them.

"Why would she have compressed the images?" I asked.

Adams was intrigued. "I don't know." His words trailed off as if his mind was already into the matter. He watched Mara attempt to make sense of the puzzle before her. "Maybe she can't decide if the signal is coming from one location or if it's from a group."

Mara set up a second easel next to the first one. She grabbed a pencil and started sketching a copy of the poster on the new canvas. She picked certain images from the poster and drew them more prominently in their location. She then took the canvas off the easel and pinned it to the siding of her house. Then she set up another blank canvas and started the whole process again. Within two hours, she had a dozen different sketches of the poster hanging on her exterior siding, each one slightly different than the last. She put her pencil down and plunked into a chair, looking at the images as if lost.

The next day, Mara and her coworkers arrived early and stayed well past midnight. Their faces showed excitement mixed with frustration. Again, they argued intently in the parking lot before they finally got into their cars and drove off.

Back at her house, Mara resumed her efforts on the patio into the wee hours of the morning. She unrolled an even larger poster of the Thetan stars and pinned it on the siding where the first had been. She then brought out a blank canvas and repeated her efforts at sketching certain stars within the group. Jim compared the poster to images he had from the Theta galaxy.

The large red giant in the poster was roughly the same as the Thetan sun to other stars near it. Jim used that as a starting point and attempted to find stars which would fit the picture the same as Mara had it. The odds were against it, for there were thousands of red giants within the one Theta galaxy. Jim worked on the image until we had a session with the Coasttown Thetans.

"Grandmother," I asked, "is the red star from Mara's poster the same as your sun?" Adams crossed his fingers.

"It is."

"So is your planet creating the signal they're receiving?" Adams asked.

"The signal is not coming from our planet," the reply came, "though we are assisting in the effort."

"Can you elaborate on that?"

"The signal is coming from an entity, directly. The entity is using heavenly bodies to present his vibration."

"How can he do that?" Ian asked.

"Matters of the heart make things happen. We provide assistance, but the entity provides the vibration."

"This vibration that you speak of," Adams said. "That is a physical manifestation of one entity trying to contact another?"

"That is correct."

"What is he saying?"

"That matter can best be answered by yourself or Mara."

"But how could I possibly answer that?" Adams asked.

"The subconscious mind is in direct communication with all other subconscious minds."

"Perfect," Adams said. "I'll just have a subconscious chat with the dead husband of my reincarnated wife and get to the bottom of this."

Adams felt the Thetans were withholding information though he couldn't understand why. This wasn't like asking about weapons of mass destruction, the only other thing the Thetans had refused to speak about. This was something personal that indirectly involved him.

Jim made a similar copy of Mara's cluster of Thetan stars. Then he condensed the image as she had. The red giant and the others made an unlikely puzzle. There were dozens of round lights from stars in the frame, along with dozens of smaller images of planets and moons that revolved around those heavenly bodies. Hundreds of planets were hidden from sight, as their light was drowned out by that of their star or other stars. Only the planets that jutted out just the right distance and angle from their star cast some light and added to the picture. Adams made several copies of it and pinned them to the lab room, covering some monitors not being used. His efforts mirrored Mara's attempts on her patio.

Adams took the following day off from work, his first since the project began. He wanted to walk the strip of beach where he and Rose used to frequent. He said he needed to spend some time alone doing some soul searching, a term that had been completely alien to Adams months earlier. Frank saw an opportunity to ask the Thetans a question that had been on his mind for weeks.

"Grandmother," I asked later that evening, "we are considering a time leap in an effort to advance Earth. We would like to know any recommendations on when we should perform the leap and how long it should be. The goal of the leap would be to find Earth at a state in time when they can show us the most to make our world a better place." I looked over to Frank after asking the question. He approved.

"Yes," the response came through Whitney. "We understand your interest in seeing Earth in the future. It is a world like yours. Their advances might enable you to learn from those lessons."

"Exactly," Frank spoke out.

The Grandmother gave us a specific time, down to the very second when to make the leap. She also gave us a duration for the amount of hydrogen molecules to be released. Her answer was extremely concise, more so than we expected. The recommendation was for two weeks from the day. It should comprise exactly one hundred Thetan orbits, which would be approximately two hundred standard orbits, and close to one hundred and fifty Earth years.

"Less than two hundred years?" Ian said, surprised. "I doubt they'll be as advanced as the Deltans were, and not even close to the Omegans."

"Perhaps less is more," Jessica said. "These concepts from Omega 5 are amazing, but they're totally impractical in the here and now."

So it was set, I thought. Frank was going to argue his case before Adams. He would want to make a time leap in two weeks, and Adams would lose Mara forever if we did.

"You can't be serious!" Adams objected the next morning.

"We've got to think about the long-term goals here," Frank argued with him.

"I won't let you do it," Adams said firmly. The crew watched them debate.

"Stop thinking of yourself, Webster. Everybody on our planet could benefit from knowing what Earth is like one hundred and fifty years from now. You know that!"

"I've already lost her once, Frank. I can't go through that again."

"Watching Mara is not going to bring Rose back. She's not really here, Webster! I seriously doubt this is healthy for you."

"What are you saying?"

"Trust that the Thetans are right. You'll be together again someday, in another incarnation. Perhaps it's time to let her go in this one."

"I don't think I can do that."

"I want you to consider it," Frank said. "Just consider it."

"Give me some time."

"We've got two weeks," he added. "It would be nice to make this leap with your approval."

"How could he ask this? What do you think, Rose? You brought me here. Am I supposed to stand back and watch you go away again? Nothing's clear anymore."

- from p. 167 of Webster's journal.

Missing Pieces

THE DREAM KEPT RECURRING. It even started to bother me while I was in morning meditation. I thought of talking with Adams or Whitney, but I still wasn't sure what effect it would have on them. I wanted it to go away but it kept coming back.

An opportunity presented itself. Jessica had taken the day off and Frank was not with us. Adams and Ian had left early, as neither of them was feeling well. Whitney wanted to leave, but I convinced her to stay for a Thetan session. I told her I had work on myself that I wanted to do. The Coasttown Thetans wouldn't be approaching for several hours so we used a village new to her.

Jim identified the dawn line and found a village center. A group of Thetans were already meditating at their podium. An elderly woman sat in the spot next to the open space. Whitney yawned as she went through her routine of placing the mat, lighting the candles and getting into her quiet space.

Once the session began, I asked several questions concerning soul development in general. I waited patiently through the long, drawn-out explanations until I felt enough had been said to make a good printout for Whitney to read afterwards.

"Teacher," I said, "I've been having a recurring dream. The image is of a woman driving her car through a storm. I believe the entity was Rose Adams. Are you aware of this dream that I'm speaking of?"

"Yes," Whitney replied. "It is of Rose."

"Why does this image keep repeating itself to me?"

"Because the entity is trying to tell you something."

"What?" I asked.

"What do you recall?"

"I remember that she was upset, crying. I also remember there was a car following her, even though she was speeding. She had the accident attempting to lose the car behind her. Is that right?"

"There are no accidents in life," came the reply.

"She was attempting to lose the car behind her." I stated. "Why? Did she know the driver in the other car?"

"Yes."

"Who was following her?"

"The entity was Frank Maxwell."

I sat stunned, letting her words soak in. Something about the answer felt right, as soon as I heard them. I knew it was true. Frank was in the second car. The session ended soon after.

"Jim," I said, before Whitney came out of her trance. "Don't print those last few questions about Rose."

"Why not?"

"Because it will hurt Whitney."

"But I always print everything," Jim replied.

"Please, trust me. Do you want to hurt Whitney?"

"No."

"Then don't do it. You've got to trust me."

Whitney came out of the trance. Jim printed out the copy. I grabbed it and gave it a quick look to see Jim had done as I had asked. I breathed a sigh of relief as I handed the printout to her.

"Thank you, Jim. We'll discuss this more tomorrow."

I drove Whitney home. She was exhausted and almost fell asleep in the car. I dropped her off and continued to my house. That night, I lay on my bed thinking. Why was Frank following Rose? Why had Rose's spirit chosen me for this information?

The next few evenings didn't offer a chance to ask more questions. The rest of the crew was present. Ian had several glitches with Deltan generators and Omegan energy fields.

I did get to explain to Jim why I had asked him to keep the information about Rose a secret. I explained the difficulty of dealing with death. The answer would have been disturbing to Adams, Whitney and Frank.

I also told Jim, "I need to ask several follow-up questions. It will have to be our secret until we can make sense of it." Just when I thought Jim would never understand, he became excited about being involved in the detective work.

Something from the Heavens

ADAMS SPENT HOURS looking at the compressed star images. He was convinced that Mara was close to something though he couldn't guess what it was. He thought the actual signal, the wavelength from the stars, was more important than the positions of the lights themselves. But since Mara had taken this approach so seriously, Adams assumed there was merit to it.

Whitney sat in meditation with the Coasttown Group, though they had already answered as much as they were willing to tell us.

"Look at this," Adams said, pointing to the lineup of stars. "These here—one, two, three, four, five, six, seven." Adams dropped his hand to the next rough equivalent of a linear area. "Then nine stars here." He dropped his hand again. "Then nine here, again. Then another line of seven, and another line of seven."

"So?" I asked.

Adams had an insight. The image of the stars created a wavering line. In some spots, the stars were higher. In others they were lower.

The line continued from left to right. Below that, another line could be made out, with similar highs and lows to it. And below that one, another line and another. The images of the stars seemed to be arranged in five lines.

"It may be just coincidence," Adams admitted. "But seven, nine, nine, seven, seven. What's more," Adams said, becoming excited, "look at the position of the planets that show. Compare them in location to their stars. They're almost identical in the first and third lines... and also in the fourth and fifth lines."

Adams became ecstatic. He didn't know what he was looking at, but he had found a correlation in the lines. Mara seemed to be noticing the same thing. Her latest sketch focused on the five lines of the star groups. She added the positions of the planets more prominently, whereas before she had focused mainly on the light from the stars.

"What does it mean?" Ian asked.

"I don't know," Adams said. "But there seems to be something to it."

252

Adams connected the small lights from the planets to the much larger lights of the stars. Some stars had no planets visible, others had one and others had two. He went down each line with a marker, and then he went down each row connecting all the planets to their stars in this method. Mara did the same thing with her sketch. Adams laughed as he watched her mirror his markings.

"This is good," he said. "I'm not sure what it is, but at least we're on the same wavelength."

Mara went into her house for a minute. We wondered if she would return. She emerged holding something in her arms that looked like a guitar. She held the instrument and looked at the sketch before her. She picked the first note. A look on her face indicated the guitar didn't sound right. She played with it, adjusting the strings at the end and repeating the first note until she was satisfied. She looked at the painting and then picked the first note again. Then she adjusted her fingers and played the second, then the third and fourth.

"It's a song," Adams said, breaking into a broad smile. "Grandmother, is it a song? Are these dots and lines musical notes?"

"They are," the reply came through Whitney.

Mara seemed very pleased. She stared at the sketch as a tear ran down her cheek. She put the instrument down and went back into her house. She emerged moments later, holding a black box. She placed it on one of her deck chairs and attached a reel to it. The crew was spellbound by what she was doing. She plugged the machine into a wall outlet. The reel turned and a ray of light beamed onto her wall. She adjusted the focus until images within the light became clear.

"Home movies," Adams said. "We should have seen that."

Jim adjusted the image to the visions on the wall. Mara sat in a chair and watched. The movie showed her as a much younger lady. She wore a white gown, held the arm of an older gentleman and walked down an aisle between rows of standing people dressed very nicely. The scene was in a church. A handsome man with reddish hair in a black suit waited for her at the end of the aisle. When Mara reached him, he smiled and offered his hand. She took it, and they faced a minister reading from an open book.

"She's beautiful," Jessica said.

"Grandmother," Adams asked, while still watching the movie, "is that Michael, her past husband?"

"It is," the reply came from Whitney.

"And this is her wedding?" Adams added. His voice cracked with emotion.

"Yes."

We watched in silence as the couple listened to the minister before them. They eventually exchanged rings and a long kiss. The people burst into applause. Then they walked back up the aisle as the people threw small, white pellets at them. Adams pushed aside the tears as they streamed down his cheeks. I wished Whitney could have seen it at that moment.

Then the movie switched locations. Mara and Michael were the focus of all the wedding guests. They stood on a dance floor as the lights dimmed down. A spotlight came on, illuminating the couple.

As Mara watched the movie from the chair on her patio, she picked up her guitar, ready to play the first note. In the movie, Michael held Mara. They were just about to move.

"Please tell me the words, Grandmother," Adams said with tears in his eyes.

"Something in the way she moves," Whitney said as Mara played her guitar. The images of the couple in the movie began to dance gracefully on the ballroom floor before their admirers. "Attracts me like no other lover."

Adams cried, yet he kept his composure as he wanted to appreciate the moment.

"Something in the way she woos me," Whitney sang the soft melody. "I don't want to leave her now. You know I believe and how."

Mara dropped her guitar into her lap. The dancers in the movie continued, but Mara couldn't. She wept uncontrollably. Her eyes closed, and she pressed her palms against them. Adams watched through his pain as well, bringing his sleeve to his eyes to smear the tears.

Ian asked The Grandmother, "This was what Michael had to say?"

"Yes," Whitney replied, "he wanted to play their song for her."

"It's beautiful," Jessica added, wiping the tears from her own eyes. She handed Adams her handkerchief.

We watched the rest of the dance. Mara watched as well though she was unable to play the guitar. She wept the entire time yet signs of joy emerged behind the tears.

"This was his gift to her," Adams whispered. "He just wanted to say he loved her."

Answers

OVER THE FOLLOWING NIGHTS, my dream of Rose's accident continued. I had to get more private time with Whitney and the Thetans.

"I need one more to finish what I'm doing."

"Jon, I'm really tired," Whitney complained.

"Please. I won't ask again."

Whitney agreed to stay late and perform once more. After the others left, we found a group not far from Coasttown. A middle-aged Thetan woman sat next to the open spot. The session was already underway.

There would only be enough time to get right to the point. I waited until Whitney was in her trance. I asked if she could hear me a few times before going ahead with my questions.

"Teacher," I began, "was Frank Maxwell the one who discovered the condition of the body after Rose had her crash?"

"Yes," she said.

"Did he call the medical authorities?"

"Yes."

"Why did he leave before they arrived?" I asked, assuming this was true.

"He was afraid of being implicated in her death," Whitney replied.

"Did he attempt to kill her?"

"Of course not. He loved her."

"He loved her?"

"He loved her dearly," she replied.

"Then why was he following her?"

"He worried for her safety."

These answers went against my line of questioning, and I sat there trying to determine how to redirect my approach. After a pause, I asked, "Did they have a physical relationship?"

"Yes," she said.

"And they were trying to keep it a secret from Adams?"

"Their relationship happened before Rose fell in love with Webster."

"And Frank was never able to let her go?"

"That is correct. We are through for the present."

The Thetan sun began to rise. I told Jim not to make a printout. I watched the Thetans leave their podium. Whitney came out of her trance.

"Did you get what you were looking for?" Whitney asked me.

"I did. Thank you," I told her, wondering what I was going to do.

A few days later, I decided to discuss it with Frank. I asked for a private meeting in Webster's office. He obliged me right away.

"What's on your mind, Mr. Gruber?" Frank asked me from behind the desk.

"I need to discuss something," I told him. "I don't know how to begin."

Frank got up and repositioned himself in the chair next to mine. "Son," he said, "whenever you have something difficult to discuss, the best way is just to come out with it."

"I'm not sure how to say this."

"Have you been offered a position with another firm?" he asked.

"It's not like that."

"Then what is it?"

"It's about Rose Adams," I said. "You were there, the night she died. The Thetans told me."

His expression changed. Frank stood up and closed the door. Then he walked back around the desk and sat down.

"The Thetans told you this?"

"And more."

"Is Adams aware of it?"

"No."

"Whitney?"

"I haven't spoken with anyone. Only Jim knows about it."

Frank pressed two fingers to the bridge of his nose. He looked down to the floor. "It's true," he said finally. "I was there."

"Were you in love with her?" I asked.

"Those Thetans don't leave much unanswered," he said, as his eyes welled with tears. "Yes, I was in love with Rose."

"But she was married to Adams." I stood up.

"Our relationship occurred before she met Webster," he said, leaning back in his chair and looking at the ceiling. "I asked her to marry me."

"What happened?"

"She was young. There was the age difference. I couldn't blame her. I gave her some time to think, perhaps too much time. She fell in love with Webster."

"And you just watched her leave?" I said, pacing the office.

"What else could I do? You can't force someone to marry you."

"But you funded her project anyway?"

"She still worked for me. She was the brightest person I had ever met. I knew that if I funded the project, at least she would be around in case she ever changed her mind."

"But she was married to Adams by then."

"Sometimes people change their minds," he said.

"But she didn't."

"She came close. That's what we were discussing the night of the accident."

"You wanted her to leave Adams for you?"

"She had a fight with him and came to me to discuss it."

"What was the fight about?"

"Their relationship. Her. Him." Frank closed his eyes as if he were living the moment all over again. He spoke calmly. "Adams was only capable of so much. She knew that."

"She was confused that night," I said, recalling my images. "She was upset and confused."

"I didn't want her driving off that way."

"So you followed her?"

"Only because I wanted her to be safe. She was all over the road, Jon! You've got to believe me."

"And after the crash you called the authorities?"

"She had no pulse. I couldn't believe she was gone," he said, putting his hands to his face. I gave him some time. After he gathered himself, he asked, "Are you going to tell Adams?"

"I don't know what to do," I said. "I don't know if this will make anyone feel better."

"It won't. You won't be doing him a favor by telling him."

Decisions

FRANK AND ADAMS DISCUSSED the proposed time leap behind closed doors. I imagined Adams insisted on keeping things as they were while Frank argued for the time leap. Hours passed. The rest of the crew stayed busy in the lab, awaiting the final result.

When Adams finally emerged from the office, he looked drained. He saw Whitney and shook his head no. He grabbed his jacket and headed for the door. Whitney looked at me and sighed. Then she followed him. Frank came out a minute later.

"We'll be making the leap a week from today," Frank said, looking tired. "We'll do it to the Thetans' specifications. Whatever needs to be accomplished before then, I suggest we work diligently on those projects."

Frank returned to his office. I wondered if he had told Adams the whole story. A part of me wished he had though it seemed unlikely.

Adams didn't show up for work the next day. Neither did Whitney. I wondered if they were boycotting the place. There was a chance we would have no more sessions with the Thetans before the leap. In a way, it didn't matter. We knew the Thetans would be around in one hundred years.

We were also convinced little would have changed on Omega 5. The question remained about Earth, but we trusted the Thetans' advice for a time leap that would leave their society at a point where we could learn the most from them.

The following day, Adams and Whitney came back. They spent every possible minute watching Mara. While she worked, Jim kept an eye on the doors to her building. Once Mara walked out, Jim followed her as she got in her car and drove home. She played fetch with her dog. Then she went indoors as the sun set.

Later, Mara turned on her patio lights by the backyard and walked out in her painting shirt. She set up the easel, her brushes and colors. She stood before the same painting from a week before. The background was mostly finished. Sea waves beat against the rocky shoreline. The sky was dark. I imagined a ship would be the central image, or a leaping fish, or perhaps just more waves. Adams sat next to Whitney and we watched.

Mara dipped her brush in a beige blob and made some strokes in the center of the canvas. The lines she left were quick flashes. She dabbed the brush into her color palette, adding more yellow, red and white to the strokes. A roundness of shape became apparent, and I knew the central image was not going to be a ship or a fish.

As Mara continued, I detected a nose and chin. She outlined the area for the eyes. Then she worked on the mouth, which had closed lips and simple contentment. The hair was streaked with black and gray and had a waviness, as if beaten by the storm. Perhaps it was a sailor, I thought, a man of the sea on one of his countless voyages. The face looked out of place, jutting out from the rocky cliffs over the breaking sea waves. It was an odd combination, as if the spirit of the man lived at sea.

Mara worked on the eyes. She used delicate strokes and a smaller brush. Her technique changed slightly, as she took more time and care with them. She frequently dabbed in the color palette then made small additions with each pass of the brush. The eyes slowly took form, very blue eyes. I suddenly realized how familiar the face appeared.

"It's you," Whitney said, turning to her father.

The face resembled Adams. His hair had more gray in it now than in the painting, but it would have looked identical a few years ago. The chin, nose and mouth belonged to Adams. It was the eyes that settled it. The blue eyes that looked through a person were his. They were deep in contemplation, penetrating the surface and searching for answers.

We asked the Thetans about it later that evening. By the time the Coasttown Group was meditating, Mara was in bed. She left her painting outside to dry in the desert night.

"Grandmother," I asked, "are you aware of the painting Mara worked on today, the one of the face by the ocean?"

"Yes," came the reply, "we know of it."

"It looks like the face of Webster Adams," I said. "Is that who she painted?"

"You have said it so," she replied.

"But could it be of her late husband?" Adams asked.

"He was a man of reddish hair and brown eyes," the speaker replied.

"If it is of me," Adams asked, "how does she know what I look like?"

"As we have said before, the subconscious mind is in direct communication with all other subconscious minds. At this level, Mara knew you were watching as she painted it."

"I wish I could tell her how pleased I was," Adams said.

"You already have."

"Frank has insisted on making the time leap a week from today," Adams added. "He says you recommended it. Is this true?"

"Yes."

"How could you do that?" Adams asked. "Don't you know what it will do to me?"

"Mind is the builder. This is your creation, just as it is Rose's, Frank's, Whitney's and the others. The leap is something you are doing. Your acceptance will make the transition easier."

"It sounds so simple hearing it from you," Adams told her, his voice filled with emotion. "But it doesn't feel that way from here. It feels like a terrible mistake."

"The pain is a result of your struggle. Fear tells you to hold onto what you have. Your inner being wants to change as much as Rose wants you to. Letting go is frightening, but it is part of your soul development in this lifetime."

"So what should I do?" Adams asked.

"Listen to the voice within you. Ask it for daily guidance."

"Is that all?"

"You are experiencing the great mystery. It was designed by your soul. Your inner voice will lead you in every moment of every day. We are through."

The final week was difficult for everyone. Whitney was withdrawn. Adams cycled through bouts of anger and despair. He couldn't concentrate. Ian attempted to involve him with Omegan drive systems.

Instead, Adams sat quietly in his chair, staring at the monitor, waiting for Mara. Whitney said he hadn't been eating. He picked through the meals she prepared but was hardly interested. Frank was concerned about his mental health.

"Have you ever heard Webster talk of doing anything foolish, like thoughts of suicide?" Frank asked me. I hadn't, but it wouldn't have surprised me.

Frank asked Adams if he would mind having Charlie keep an eye on him for the final days before the leap. He told Adams it was for his own protection. Frank shared his concerns at a crew meeting.

He said, "Webster will be less likely to do something in the presence of Charlie, knowing how disturbing it would be for Whitney to witness."

"It's a fine idea," Whitney added. She told me privately she hadn't seen him so depressed since the funeral.

She encouraged Adams to use the device. To my surprise, he agreed. He even let Ian tape a microchip to his neck as a beacon signal should Adams get in his car and drive off, leaving Charlie behind.

Charlie floated above Adams, producing an image of his face on one of the monitors. Adams appeared to enjoy Charlie's presence. He talked with Charlie as he sat in his chair in the lab, audibly enough for me to overhear the conversations. He told Charlie all about Rose. He talked of how they had met, about being punched out by her father after being so outspoken against God. He told Charlie of the lunchtime meetings and the walks by the campus pond, the times when Adams was falling in love. He talked of the joy of Whitney's birth and the wonder of being a father to such a bright and insightful child. Adams also described the little things Mara did that reminded him of Rose.

I was going through a difficult period as well. Seeing Adams so depressed was not fun. Jim and I spoke about it. Jim understood the pain Adams was feeling.

"I feel partially responsible," Jim mentioned.

"No, Jim," I reprimanded him. "You must understand his pain is completely his own."

"But the Thetans said we're all in this together."

"Maybe we are," I said, trying to find the right words. "But you must recognize, you had nothing to do with Rose's death."

"I guess so."

I made Jim repeat that several times.

I spent some nights at Jessica's. Having her arms around me made me feel both at ease and confused about my possible future with Whitney.

During the final days, I actually took time away from the lab and frequented the Star Bar. Sam always had a calming effect on me. With two days to go, I skipped work completely, the first time I had not shown up to any job.

"Ready for another one?" Sam asked as she took my empty glass and held it under the tap.

"I guess."

"I haven't seen you this depressed since that cute little thing in the red dress punched you in the gut," Sam said, attempting to get a smile out of me.

"Why can't things be the way we'd like them to be?"

"It wouldn't be life without the lumps," Sam told me. She elevated her voice. "That's what makes the highs feel so high." She squeezed my hands then attended to another down the bar.

Someone sat down next to me. I didn't look over but remained focused on my beer, watching the head settle. I felt a firm pat on my back.

"Adams told me I might find you here," Frank said. I looked over, surprised to see my boss in the chair next to me. "I'll have what he's having," he said to Sam. She poured a beer and placed it on a coaster in front of him.

"I'm Samantha. Nice to meet you," she said offering her hand, impressed with Frank's attire. The Star Bar rarely had a man in a tailored suit.

"Frank Maxwell," he said, holding her hand longer than customary. "Is this your place, Samantha?"

"Not much to look at but it's all mine."

"She's a great bartender," I added. "And a better friend."

"Then you're a friend of mine," Frank said, finally releasing Sam's hand. He raised his glass in a toast. "To your place and to the lovely Samantha."

Sam patted her chest as if her heart was fluttering. She poured a round of shots, and we downed them. I knew why Frank had come.

"You remind me a lot of myself when I was your age," he began. "Confident, strong, streetwise."

"There's a chance for me yet," I joked.

"A good sense of humor is important when times get tough," he added. Frank sipped his beer and looked around at the pictures on the wall. We drank quietly and watched Sam work behind the counter.

"You really asked her to marry you?"

"She thought about it for a long time," he said sadly.

"But I thought you had a wife."

"Emily? Rest her soul. She'd passed away years before."

"I'm sorry."

"It happens, my young friend. Life deals the cards. We do our best to play them."

"Ain't that the truth," Sam chimed in, cleaning a glass near us.

"I guess you're right," I said, thinking of Whitney. "Some things just aren't meant to be." Sam moved a little further down the bar out of courtesy, still within earshot.

"We'll only be hurting Adams more by telling him," Frank said. "What good is that going to do?"

"And the leap?" I asked.

"The leap is something everyone can benefit from. At some point, Adams has to let her go. The Thetans gave the schedule. This is partly their decision. Mara is not Rose, nor will she ever be Rose. You've seen what this is doing to him."

"Part of me wants to tell Adams everything."

"Take your time and think about it. I'll support you no matter what you decide."

He gave me another pat on the back. He left most of his beer and a huge tip. Then he said goodbye to Sam, telling her he'd be in again.

"I'll be waiting," Sam told him.

"How do I say this? I never told you how much I loved you. My life was complete when you were in it. Lately it's felt like something new. But that's temporary, isn't it? We had our time, and we even had a second time. We've made a mark in this world, and we made the most beautiful creation I know of. Whitney. I see so much of you in her. She'll do great things, she already has. The Grandmother is right. I've been holding onto you ever since you left. The time has come. I am doing everything I can to let you go. Maybe we'll meet again someday. But now, I've got to make the best of my life with what I have. I love you and miss you, though I say this. Goodbye, Rose."

- from p. 178 of Webster's journal.

Finale

THE LEAP WASN'T SCHEDULED UNTIL the late afternoon. Adams chose not to be present. I didn't blame him. Saying goodbye to Mara was something he could do on his own.

Adams drove his car south on the highway with Charlie hovering over the passenger seat. The crew watched him on a monitor. Adams drove toward the coast and then proceeded along a curvy road for a long way.

The lab felt like a cold blanket had covered it. Hardly anyone spoke.

Frank spent the time sitting in a chair and watching us. Ian kept busy with projects from Omega 5. Jessica and Whitney assisted me in one final scan of Earth for landmarks and features of the major cities. There was no time for Whitney to say her goodbyes to Mara, who was asleep for most of the time we were in the lab. Whitney told me she had already said goodbye, in her own way. I wondered what the planet would look like in one hundred and fifty orbits. I figured the people would be somewhere between the Alphans and the Deltans with their technologies.

Jim was bothered that it was his birthday, and we had done nothing to try and make his wish come true.

"I'm sorry, Jim," Whitney said. "We'll find a way to make it up."

Jim said, "I understand," yet I knew he was upset. We had neglected his wish. We hadn't even brought in any other gifts, things that might make him feel like a boy. It was unfortunate to have a first birthday on such a day.

"When Adams is back and in good spirits," I told Jim, "we'll do something special."

Adams parked his car at the end of the road in a lot next to an old church. There were many other cars parked. He let Charlie follow him out before closing the door. Then he walked to the church.

A gathering of people sat in rows. A white-haired minister stood behind the pulpit and addressed the crowd. The minister acknowledged Adams with a subtle wave and gave a strange look at Charlie before returning to his sermon.

"That's my grandfather," Whitney said, indicating the minister. "My mother's father."

Adams moved carefully by the people in the back row to a seat in the corner. A few of them noticed that he had a floating, buzzing companion. Adams quietly assured those folks there was nothing to be alarmed about from the presence of Charlie. The people had looks of doubt anyway. He sat down and gave his attention to the minister.

He also looked around him at the beautiful stained glass windows that adorned the church.

"Why is he there?" I asked Whitney.

"I don't know. They've never been that close."

I wanted to hear what Whitney's grandfather was saying. It was a lively sermon. He made many hand gestures to the people in front of him and around him. His face went through a range of expressions. His shoulder-length, white hair flapped from side to side as he spoke. He often glanced back to the corner where Adams sat and seemed to be pleased that his son-in-law was in the church.

A collection plate passed from person to person and went from row to row. It had several assorted bills and some coins within it. Then the plate was in front of Adams. He took an open envelope from his pocket and put it on the plate. I magnified the image on the monitor and could see that the stuffed envelope contained large bills. I estimated there were several thousand dollars within it. A church volunteer came to pick the plate up from Adams. She gave a look of shock as she took the tray from him. She bowed her head and thanked him deeply.

The sermon came to an end. The people got up and walked out the front doors. Most of them had noticed Charlie by then, but they walked politely past Adams and left the building. Afterward, Adams approached the minister. He explained the presence of Charlie. The minister laughed. Then they held each other. The minister was smiling, but I could see the tears streaming down Webster's face.

"I doubt they've seen each other since my mom's funeral," Whitney said. "She was the only thing they had in common."

The minister led Adams outside. They walked down a dirt path leading into the woods. Charlie followed them as they walked and spoke. I wondered what they were talking about.

"Next time, we'll program Charlie with a microphone," I said to Ian.

They walked slowly down the narrow trail, Adams following the minister through the woods. Eventually, they turned around and retraced their steps. They returned to the church where they said their goodbyes. Adams got into his car and allowed time for Charlie to enter before closing the door. He waved to the minister then drove off.

Adams drove toward the coast.

Whitney said, "He's going to his favorite spot, where he and Mom used to go."

Adams parked by the end of the dirt road and walked toward the ocean. The dark, overcast skies and mist from the crashing waves gave the appearance of a somber and chilly day, but Adams walked along without a jacket. We saw a bolt of lightning in the air behind him.

Adams noticed it but continued walking. He stopped to appreciate an area of vegetation and some small trees alongside the path and read the placard there. He seemed to admire the landscaping. I imagined it was an addition to his old favorite spot by the beach. He closed his eyes as he breathed in the salt air. Another bolt of lightning lit up the sky behind him. He then continued along the pathway toward the dramatic views of the ocean at the edge of the terrain, where an area of cliffs jetted out over the breaking waves.

In the lab, the moment was quiet, yet not as tense as I would have thought. The Coasttown Thetans arrived at their podium. Whitney joined them in meditation. The rest of the crew watched the secondary monitor, focused on Adams as he walked down the dirt path.

I was looking at a different man from the one I'd met nearly a year ago. Adams had an air about him that was hard to define. There was an assurance and purpose to him, but not the same intensity as in the early days. I think the others noticed it too. Jessica and Ian had the same look of helplessness I was feeling. Frank looked as if he'd lost a lifelong friend.

Adams continued down the path toward the ocean. The land fell off dramatically at the edge, where large cliffs loomed over the breaking waves. Adams grabbed onto an old rope railing that led him out above the cliffs to a fantastic view of the ocean. The sea mist wet his face. He wiped his brow with the sleeve of his sweater as he appreciated the view.

Whitney was locked in her trance.

"What is the significance of the spot where Webster is now?" I asked The Grandmother. Whitney made no immediate answer. The Grandmother had the slightest change to her expression.

"It's where he first knew he was in love," Whitney replied.

"With Rose?" I asked. There was a long pause again from Whitney.

"Yes," she said. "And with life itself."

The crew returned their gaze to the monitor that showed Adams. He was in the same spot, holding the rope railing over the cliff band.

Another bolt of lightning struck the air behind him. He didn't turn in response. He focused down toward the powerful crashing of the sea waves into the rocks beneath him.

"He's not thinking about jumping, is he?" Jessica asked.

"No, he's just enjoying the view," The Grandmother replied.

The time was nearing the recommended start point for the leap. Jessica went through the checklist with Jim to make sure he had the right numbers. She confirmed the starting and stopping points as well as the predicted amount of hydrogen and valve timings the Thetans had prescribed.

"By the way, Jim," The Grandmother said through Whitney, "happy birthday."

"Thank you," Jim said, a bit reluctantly. "At least somebody remembered."

I looked at my watch as the time approached. Frank knew we were within minutes as well. He was pacing the center of the lab. I wondered if he would go through with it. There was a noticeable lack of enthusiasm among the crew members. It surprised me that Whitney would be meditating for the final moments.

I wasn't angry with Frank. If he wanted to make the leap, I would understand, just the same as if he chose not to. Frank believed he was doing a difficult favor for a friend, something that nobody else could do.

"He has to let go," Frank said as he made his decision. "It's not healthy for him. He has to let her go." He gave Jim the order to follow the instructions to the utmost of his abilities.

"Releasing hydrogen," Jim replied.

I heard the humming sound pick up. The monitor showing The Grandmother went to static. The one focused on Mara's house went to static. The other monitors showed the planets as they left light trails in their orbits, speeding around their suns. The monitor showing Adams also went to static.

Whitney was jolted out of her meditation. She let out a gasp of air as if she had been holding her breath under water. She looked around and realized the leap had commenced. She rose to her feet and joined me by my desk. I offered my hand. She grabbed hold of it as we watched the revolutions of the moving planets.

"Why would the monitor for Adams go to static?" I asked Ian.

"The signal must be getting interference from the leap," Ian suggested.

The whirling images continued for a few moments. Then the planets slowed down and returned to stable positions. Charlie's image of Adams standing on the cliff reappeared first. Adams was still looking out over the crashing waves beneath the ominous clouds. The frequency of the lightning strikes had increased though it was not raining.

Then the Thetan monitor came into focus. Jim adjusted the shot to the Coasttown village. As it went in closer on the central podium, the crew saw the Thetans sitting in meditation. The Grandmother and the others occupied the same spots, as if no time had passed. I realized Jim had carried out his duties to perfection, and The Grandmother had recommended the exact amount of hydrogen that ended the leap at the time of pre-dawn while they were meditating.

"Two hundred standard orbits," Jim reported sadly.

Mara was gone. We all knew it. Whitney looked dejected though she held her head up and searched the monitors for activity.

We turned our attention to the monitor showing Earth. I sensed the energy in the room rise slightly. Though it was a grave moment, especially for Whitney, everyone was eager to see what one hundred and fifty years had done to Earth and its society. Ian nervously chewed on a pen. Frank paced back and forth next to the main monitor. Jessica crossed her fingers, praying that everything would still be intact. I kissed Whitney on her forehead.

Jim identified Earth and zoomed into the atmosphere. The blue-green sphere still showed its colors, but now there was far more whiteness in the sky, indicating an increase in water vapor and gases.

"Looks a little different," I said, a bit concerned about the change.

"Keep going in, Jim," Frank directed.

The shot dove through the atmosphere, past the thick layer of cloud cover and ever closer to the ground. Jim identified Mara's continent, a landmass of great size that stretched to the northern and southern poles, bordered by large oceans on each side. Jim directed the cameras to the eastern shoreline, a highly populated area.

"See how their largest city is doing," I told Jim. "What's the name again?"

"New York," Jim reminded me. The camera zoomed in until we could make out the land and the shoreline. Our view was highly filtered by the water vapor in the air.

As the city came into focus, large areas of wispy clouds obscured the view. In between the clouds, we caught glimpses of city dwellings.

The skyline was much more rounded, not nearly as pointy as before. The structures, on average, were less tall than they had been. Many were dome-shaped. Some were like cones. There was traffic in the skyways.

The Earth people had invented some of the flying devices that reminded us of models from Alpha 17 and Delta 13, the same disc and cylinder shapes that our transportation departments were currently working to produce. The crew breathed a sigh of relief, seeing the busy metropolis, though we wanted to see more clearly what was happening down there. The filtered view became annoying.

"The atmosphere has warmed up," Whitney said. "What else would cause all this moisture in the air?"

Jim lifted the shot high up into the atmosphere to analyze the situation. The polar ice caps on both ends of the planet had receded dramatically. They were half their previous size. The oceans had risen as a result, and the sea water penetrated into the mainland around the coastline. One continent had the least amount of vapor above it, offering the best views of the planet.

"Let's get some closer shots from that area," Ian said, pointing to the island continent.

"They call that one Australia," Jim mentioned, as the cameras went in closer.

The central area of the continent offered the best views on the planet, perhaps because the dry landscape absorbed much of the vapor. There was still a lot of cloud cover, but it was a fraction of that compared to other parts of the globe.

In the midst of the desert, we saw large areas of open sand and rock with sparse vegetation and trees. We found some animal species, herds of hoofed beasts and reptiles by the few streams flowing through the desert.

Then we saw a human and a robot flying on a roving pedestal, similar to models from Delta 13. The pilot was a boy, about fifteen years old. The robot passenger stood behind the boy, gripping his waist for support. The two were out in the middle of the desert, the only marks of civilization.

"Follow them," Frank said.

Jim focused on the pair as they sped through the desert. The young pilot turned sharply to avoid sparse trees. He jumped the craft over large rocks that covered the terrain. His brown hair flapped wildly in the wind as he continued a spirited ride through the desert.

"That's him!" Jim proclaimed. "That's the boy I want to be!"

Jim was ecstatic. The monitor zoomed in closer. I took a second look and was shocked. The Earth boy looked very much like the photo Jim had printed out weeks before. I pulled the image from the wall, looked at it and was stunned by the resemblance. I glanced at Whitney, and she was also amazed at the similarities to the kid in the photo.

"See how much fun he's having," Jim went on. "He's out on his own, doing what he feels like. He can do anything."

The taller, robotic passenger maintained a solid grip around the boy's waist. It seemed to be not enjoying the ride nearly as much as the human pilot.

"Jim, please try to understand," I said. "We all have limitations."

"I wonder what his name is," Jim continued. "I wonder where he lives. What do you think his family is like?"

"Probably very loving," Whitney said.

"Do you think he goes to school?"

"Looks like he's skipping today," Ian mentioned.

"He certainly is a skilled rider," Jim added. "Oh, that looks like fun."

The youngster sped over the desert floor, leaping the craft over boulders, stumps and everything he could find. His approach seemed beyond gallant, almost reckless.

"That's what I should be doing," Jim lamented, as he realized the impossibility of his birthday wish.

The youngster continued to jump the craft over everything that presented itself. I watched him nervously, sensing he was setting himself up for an accident.

"Jim, I'm really sorry," I said. "I feel like I haven't been there for you."

"It's okay."

"No, it's not okay. I'm supposed to be like a big brother, and I haven't been getting the job done."

Suddenly, one of the obstacles threw the device higher into the air than the boy had planned. In mid-air, they were headed for a thick tree. The boy and the robot jumped from the device just before it smashed into the tree. When they hit the ground, they tumbled like rag-dolls across the desert floor. The crew gasped, and Whitney gripped my arm intensely.

"No!" Jim screamed.

The robot landed far from the boy, who lay in an awkward position on the ground. The robot slowly moved its arms in an effort to right itself. Then it lifted its head and looked for its master. Jim adjusted the camera to an extreme close-up of the boy. He lay in a crumpled heap, with one arm slung behind his head and a twisted, broken leg jutting out to the side. He made no effort to move. We couldn't see any air flow from his lungs though his heart rate must have been accelerated from the wild ride and the crash. The crew watched in stillness. I was sure the others concluded the same fate as I had—the boy was dead.

"Get up," Jim begged. "Please, get up. Open your eyes. Do something."

The robot approached him. It adjusted the boy's arms and legs to put the body in a natural position. The boy lay motionless.

Jim began to cry. He had never shown extreme sadness to the point of crying. Now he was truly empathizing with an individual.

I glanced over at the Thetan monitors. The image of The Grandmother was becoming larger on the screen. She was locked in her meditation. The focus on her face went deeper and deeper, until her closed eyes filled the screen. I sensed she was aware of the fate of the boy from Earth. The rest of the crew noticed the magnification of The Grandmother's face.

Jim's green light raged with intensity, as the sounds of his sobbing filled the lab, becoming so loud I had to cover my ears.

I looked at the monitor showing Adams by the seashore. The waves were crashing violently against the rocks beneath him. The wind had picked up, sending plumes of mist high into the air around him. His shirt was soaked from the spray yet he didn't appear to care. He gazed out to sea. The darkness of the clouds around him gave the appearance of twilight though it was still hours before sunset. Three bolts of lightning lit up the sky behind him in a web of brilliant light.

The humming sound of the hydrogen began. I checked the equipment. Jim's green light was glowing as strongly as I had ever seen it. He was still sobbing. I didn't know what to make of it.

"Jim," I said, "check the hydrogen. I think we have a leak!"

Jim didn't reply. The image of the boy from the Earth monitor became blurred. The image of The Grandmother went to static as well. The monitor that showed Adams at the beach also went to static. The planets began their movements.

"What's wrong, Jim?" Jessica asked.

Jim didn't respond. His sobs quieted down to silence. The lights of the planets sped up, traveling around their suns at increasing speeds.

"Jim," I said. "Something's not right! Stop the hydrogen!"

Jim's light began to fade.

"What's the matter?" Frank asked. No response came.

The stars and planets continued their movements, going ever faster, turning into a spectacle of blurring lights. Jim's light became dimmer by the second.

"What's happening, Jim?" Ian demanded.

Whitney held my hand as the galaxies turned into whirling spirals. Around and around they went, as the crew tried to get Jim to respond to their questions. I stared at the monitors as the galaxies moved ever faster. The humming sound increased in pitch, reminding me of the time leaps of old. Jim's light was out.

"We've lost them for sure!" Ian shouted.

"Why are you doing this?" Frank asked. "Please, answer me!"

The stars spun ever faster. I realized we were watching a hydrogen release of full proportions, a time leap bigger than anything we had ever witnessed. It was a shame that Adams couldn't have seen it, for he had only theorized on Jim's capabilities. If Adams had estimated correctly, we were watching time travel at trillions of times faster than standard speed. The crew stood in shock, amazed by the spectacle. The galaxies moved in dramatic fashion. Like spinning hurricanes, they traversed from the central areas out to the far edges of the universe.

"What's the matter, Jim?" Jessica repeated.

Again, there was no response. Moments ago, Jim's light had been raging as brightly as I had ever seen it, and now it was completely out.

There was nothing to do but watch. In the few minutes we stood there, the little universe experienced trillions of years of actual time. Earth was long gone. Even the Thetans were gone, for surely their red star had collapsed back into itself. Everything was moving closer to the pull of the outer walls.

"Goodbye, Jim," Whitney said sadly, touching his extinguished green light.

The galaxies continued their outward motions. The wild spinning of the cosmos was a sad and beautiful chaos. One by one, galaxies contacted the outer walls of the egg-shaped container. There, they disintegrated.

The crew watched, disheartened. Entire galaxies smashed into the walls and turned into black space. I wondered how Adams would have reacted had he seen it. His theory on the pull of the outer walls had been correct. The universe was disappearing. One by one, the galaxies turned from billions of hurling stars into voids of nothing. The monitors showed less and less light.

The lab became darker as the universe lost its galaxies. Eventually, the final ones made contact with the outer walls and smashed into oblivion. The monitors went to black as the humming sound slowed down and stopped. The hydrogen tanks were probably empty.

The crew stood quietly in the darkness of the lab. We looked at each other with blank expressions in the dim light. Only Whitney's meditation candles provided some glow. I walked to the switch to turn on the auxiliary lighting we used to need. As I did so, one of the monitors picked up a picture.

It was Charlie's shot of the beach. The single monitor lit up the lab slightly with the view from the coast. I saw the cliff and the breaking waves, but I couldn't find Adams in the picture. In fact, I couldn't see the end of the rope railing he had been holding. Instead, there was a break in the rope. The final section was gone. It looked as if the last bit of cliff had slipped into the ocean. Charlie's viewpoint was aiming down, as if something had happened to Adams to cause him to fall into the water.

"Oh God, no!" Whitney cried out.

Whitney and I raced out of the lab and jumped into my PFD. I flew the device as fast as it could toward the coast while Whitney cried and said prayers that Adams was okay. She directed me to the area where her father had been. I flew over his car and followed the dirt path.

I landed the machine right next to where we had seen him last. A bolt of lightning burst over the ocean as we arrived at the spot.

The rope railing had been severed near the end. The last section of cliff had fallen into the ocean. Whitney and I shimmied out as far as we could. We looked down at the crashing waves below, but there was no sign of Adams. Charlie hovered nearby, patiently waiting for Adams to emerge. I pulled Whitney back, further away from the ledge. I held her in my arms as she began to break up. Whitney buried her head in my chest and sobbed intensely. In the past few minutes, she had lost Mara, the Thetans, Jim and now her father. I worried that she might hurl herself off the cliff to end the pain.

I held onto her with all my strength. For several minutes, I heard the muffled sounds coming from her, as her face was buried in my chest. Whitney cried as deeply as anyone could. She held onto me, at times pounding her fists against my chest. I let her release emotion. The pain from her blows was nothing compared to what she was going through. She cried for minutes on end, until her voice broke up from the strain on her throat.

After a while, her sobs were mixed with laughter. It was an awkward laughter infused with pain, sorrow and insanity. As the minutes passed, more of her outbreaks sounded like pure laughter. I pulled my head slowly back so I could get a look at her. Her bloodshot eyes and reddened nose became visible to me as she cried and laughed in an uncontrollable release of emotions. The front of my shirt was soaked with her tears. Whitney's eyes looked through me as if I were a sheet of glass. I thought she had gone insane.

"Are you okay?" I asked, searching her eyes for some sign of recognition.

She nodded her head yes, and kept on crying and laughing softly. I let her continue until I realized it might make sense to try to get her to speak.

"Why are you laughing? You're not going crazy on me, are you?"

"No," she said. She buried her head back in my chest and continued with the strange combination. As the minutes went by, she cried less and laughed more. It didn't make any sense, but the effect made me start to laugh as well.

"Can you tell me why you're laughing?" I asked her.

"Because they're together again," she said. "They're finally together again."

"Who's together again?"

"My mom and dad."

I finally understood. Whitney had seen what I couldn't. Rose and Adams were together again, somewhere. She didn't have to explain it. She just knew it was true, and I knew that she was right.

We turned to look one more time at the sea. Two birds flew past us, squawking as they continued out over the ocean. We watched them as they became smaller and smaller, making their way toward the horizon.

After

I HELD WHITNEY'S SHOULDERS and guided her back to the PFD. She moved like a frightened child who had been doused with a bucket of cold water. I helped her climb into the cabin and strapped her harness on. We flew slowly to her home as darkness fell. We left Webster's car where had he parked it, in the lot by the dirt path.

Once at Whitney's house, I led her upstairs and put her into bed. I sat by her side, stroking her hair and looking into her eyes. She gazed at me and half-smiled. I sensed she was okay, or that she would be okay. I told her I would be sleeping nearby in the guest room, but I needed to be sure she was all right.

"Promise me you won't do anything drastic," I said.

"How can I? They made it clear, what I have to do. What would be the sense in starting all over?"

The next morning, Whitney slept in. I took the opportunity to fly to work. Frank, Jessica and Ian were already there, inspecting the original design notes from Rose, the ones Adams kept in his desk.

I assisted them for several hours. We discussed every detail I could remember from almost a year before. Jessica took short hand while Ian listened intently and nodded. The details I recalled were quite good, since that episode of struggling had left such a firm impression.

"The real problem is the absence of Jim," I said finally.

Our computerized friend had been woven into every detail of the simulation. We debated whether or not the project could be salvaged, but it seemed likely only if we could get Jim back and conscious again. That did not appear to be possible. No sign of life came from Jim's hardware, even though he still had electrical connections.

After sharing everything I could remember, I stuffed the things from my desk into a backpack. I also grabbed Whitney's items: her notebooks, the candles, the photos of the Thetans and her mat. Then I took Webster's little brown booklet from his desk, the one that he used to jot down his notes, and quickly slipped it in my pocket. I was sure Frank would want it, but it would mean more to Whitney.

"What are you going to do?" Frank asked me.

"I don't know. I need to take a little time off," I said, pulling my hands through my hair and wondering about my future.

Frank gave me the number of a man at Maxwell Enterprises. He told me to call him when I was ready to come back to work, assuming I would feel that way in the future. He said they would find ways for me to be helpful, that it didn't matter if I wasn't educated.

"Imagination is more important than knowledge," Frank told me, shaking my hand for longer than customary, as he had when we first met.

"Maybe I'll see you at the bar," I reminded him. "Stop in and see Sam."

"It's a date."

Ian and Jessica were still going over Rose's notes as I was ready to leave. I hugged Ian for the first time. It was heartfelt, without any of the typical male discomfort that would have overshadowed a hug between us in the past.

I also hugged Jessica. We held each other for a while. I would see her again soon, even if just to talk or go for a flight together. I needed time to sort things out, time for soul searching, but I knew I would be in touch with her. She kissed me and told me she would wait. I finally walked out the doors with my backpack over my shoulder and Whitney's mat under my arm. I left the project for good, the last time I would be in the space of that building.

Whitney had a nice meal prepared when I arrived at her house.

I joined her on the deck to a table set with fresh fruits and small sandwiches. Though it was the middle of winter, a calm and sunny day provided warmth that made it very pleasant. We ate in silence. She smiled at me as I shoved food into my mouth.

"I had a dream last night," she said, as she chewed slowly on a sandwich.

"Not a bad one, I hope."

Whitney paused before answering. She swallowed the mouthful and drank some water. "No, it wasn't bad."

"What was it?" I asked.

"I saw the boy from Earth."

"The one who died in the desert?"

"He didn't die," she said.

I didn't want to argue with her, but I remembered it vividly as one of the more unsettling images from my time there. "Whitney, we all saw it."

"The Grandmother did something. The entity passed on, but his body lived. I saw him make it out of the desert."

"Riding that machine? It was smashed to bits."

"The robot carried him."

"You saw all of that in your dream?"

"The boy recovered, but he was a different person afterwards. I saw what his name used to be."

"What was it?"

"It was James."

"So?" I said.

"He's not going by that anymore."

"What's he going by?"

"Jim."

I stopped eating as the information soaked in. Whitney bit into her sandwich and chewed as she looked out over the decking to the light colors of the coming sunset. I drank my water and made the connection.

The Grandmother had done what none of us were able to do. She had granted Jim's birthday wish. He got the chance to know what all those feelings in life were like, the chance to be a real boy.

I wondered what his experience was like.

The End

About the author...

Jason Matthews was born in North Carolina in 1967. He graduated from UNC-Chapel Hill with a degree in film and television. Jason lives in Pismo Beach, California, where he writes and teaches self-publishing.

He asks readers to **please leave reviews** at Amazon or anywhere you found the book.

He can be contacted through his websites, TheLittleUniverse.com - ebooksuccess4free.webs.com.

Facebook - facebook.com/Jason.M.Matthews

Google Plus - plus.google.com/+JasonMatthews/

Twitter - @Jason_Matthews

Where applicable, it helps to include a personal note. Thank you.

Other Books by Jason Matthews

The following are available as ebooks and paperbacks at major retailers.

Better You, Better Me - there's a better version of you ready to be energized. The ideas in this book are easy to add to your life, and they work wonders.

The Little Universe - a novel about creating a universe and discovering incredible things within it.

Jim's Life - the sequel novel, about a teenage boy on trial who can see and heal the human light fields, being hailed a miracle healer as the world argues over his case.

How to Make, Market and Sell Ebooks All for Free – self publish on any budget and sell ebooks at major retailers, your own sites on autopilot and much more.

How to Make Your Own Free Website: And Your Free Blog Too - a how to book for building free websites/blogs and making the most with them.

Get On Google Front Page - dedicated to SEO tips, using Google better and rising in search engine rankings.

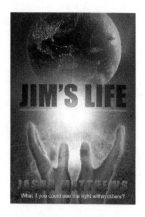

Please enjoy the first chapters of *Jim's Life*.

Prologue

Worn-out garments are shed by the body; worn-out bodies are shed by the dweller within the body. New bodies are donned by the dweller, like garments. - Bhagavad Gita 2:22

THE HUMAN BODY IS A TEMPORARY HOME for something far more eternal than the body itself. The soul is the essence and everlasting entity within the body. Upon physical death, the soul vacates the flesh and returns to universal source. The return to source is often followed by rest and reflection on the lifetime. Eventually some souls embark again to enter a new body for further experiences, which is widely known as reincarnation. Not a popular belief among Western societies, reincarnation has been accepted for thousands of years among vast groups including Buddhists, Hindus, Orthodox Jews, Africans, Native Americans, Gnostic Christians, ancient Greeks and more. These people believe, or believed, the soul is the true essence of life while the body is a shelter in which to experience and grow.

In rare cases a soul may decide to leave the body without it physically dying, to vacate it and allow that body to become the home for another soul. It is known as *soul transference*, where one soul leaves a living body as a gift for another. This is a story of one such event.

Body of Jim's Life

The wise fisherman cast his net into the sea. When he drew it up, it was full of little fish. Among them the wise fisherman saw a fine large fish. He easily chose that one and threw all the little fish back into the sea. Let those with good ears hear this lesson. - Gospel of Thomas

Queensland, Australia 2150AD

IGGY TRUDGED ONE STEP AT A TIME across the sandy terrain of the outback. The rover was a hundred meters back, scattered about the harsh landscape in busted pieces by the splintered gum tree. His master, James Ranck, lay like a crumpled heap in the robot's arms.

Iggy looked down. James didn't appear to be alive. No sign of breathing showed in his chest, and the broken limbs of James' legs and arms hung straight to the ground with no resistance, swinging loosely in tempo with Iggy's steps. The robotic unit was distressed by the look of it. His emotional programming would have created a mournful sound from his voice box if it were still working.

The crash had damaged Iggy as well, including his transmitters. Wires protruded from an open shoulder joint. Dirt covered his metallic frame. He had lost some power too, and without his solar cells recharging he wondered how long he might hold out. *What are the chances of getting home?* Iggy thought. Iggy had carried a few children before, but they were much smaller than James, a fifteen-year-old who felt surprisingly heavy. He walked for hours in the afternoon sun—with each step Iggy debating internally if they could make it back. He also wondered what the reception would be if James was dead.

Iggy resented the burden he carried. *How did I ever get assigned to this boy?* Iggy had been designed for professionals like architects, to be used in their creative processes. Instead, he got sold to a mechanic and then given to the

282

man's son. He hated the nickname. *For a thousand times, my name is Ignatius! I've never asked for anything else, and still James can't even do that.*

Brison Ranck flipped the meat on the grill. He sprinkled salt from a shaker and pressed it into the sizzling slabs with the tips of his fingers, then adjusted the angle of the solar receiver to catch more light of the setting sun. Now that it was February and late summer, the Australian sunset came earlier than the past few months.

Flow chopped vegetables as she watched her husband through the kitchen window. She reached over the stove to stir the rice pudding, James' favorite desert. She sipped her glass of red wine then checked the clock. Six-thirty. Ten minutes after James was supposed to set the table. The knife took out some of her anger onto the carrots.

Brison caught her eye and held up five broad fingers, indicating the time needed for the meat. Flow nodded and checked the clock again. James had his faults, but being late for supper wasn't one of them.

Brison came in with the steaming steaks as their juices bled into a puddle about to run over the plate. He walked with great care not to spill on the carpet. Flow watched him in his balancing act, appreciating her gentle giant moving so delicately.

"How we doin'?" Brison asked.

"Two minutes, love." Flow stirred the pudding with a wooden spoon while she put the veggies in a small oven.

"No response from Iggy?"

"Not yet."

Flow took another sip of wine and stared at the clock. She looked lost in thought until the oven's timer sounded. She took the greens and carrots out and placed them on the table.

"Anything else?" Brison asked as he lit candles on a table set for three.

"No, nothing."

Brison served himself the largest of the steaks, Flow the smallest and the middle one for the absent boy. He poured his wine and added some to Flow's glass. He checked the time and looked out the window. Twilight was taking over with no sign of their son's return.

"What do you think, Bris?"

"He'll be in," he assured her and sat down. "Something must've happened to the transmitters. Iggy's with him. Not to worry."

Flow sat in compliance. Brison sawed into his steak and placed a large piece in his mouth. Flow sipped her wine then stabbed at a carrot. They ate in silence.

283

Minutes later the evening sky had become dim. Flow's steak had a few bites in it while Brison had nearly finished his meal. They heard their dog begin to bark outside.

Brison jumped from his chair and went to the front door. Flow followed and stood by him on the threshold of the home, peering into the dim horizon.

"See anything?" Flow asked.

"No."

The barking persisted.

"Shep in his pen?"

"Yeah."

"What's that?" Flow pointed at an object that appeared to be moving toward them.

"Where?" Brison squinted but saw nothing.

"Right there," Flow insisted as she extended an arm out in front of his face.

Brison found it. Sure enough, something slowly approached from a hundred meters away. They walked cautiously out into the yard.

"Who's there?" Brison demanded. No answer. He squinted as he moved further out toward the entity. "Who is that?"

The dark figure came closer. It made no sound except the shuffle of dust under its feet.

"This is private property," Flow said. "Who's there?"

The curious figure silently closed the gap between them. Brison's fists tightened instinctively. Flow held him at his shoulder.

"Want me to get the laser?" she asked.

Brison shook his head. He didn't know what it was but he wasn't afraid. Shep barked incessantly as Brison moved ever closer toward the dark figure.

Eventually Brison realized he was looking at the family robot as it trudged awkwardly through the desert night. *It's Iggy,* he thought with relief.

"Iggy," he called out. "Where've you been?"

He strode to the robot with Flow just behind him. As they came closer they noticed Iggy was carrying something and looked like he had been through hell, with dust all over him and several wires hanging out. How odd everything seemed. It took a moment in the darkness for them to realize the motionless lump in Iggy's arms was their son.

Flow screamed, "Oh God!"

The darkest hour is just before the dawn. - Anonymous proverb

NURSES AND ROBOTIC UNITS bustled in and out of the Global Alliance hospital room, where the boy was connected to a multitude of devices and medicines.

Brison and Flow stood in the office of Dr. Sandra Maynard, the head of St. Teresa. They leaned against each other and somberly watched a holographic image of their son lying deathly still in bed. With the activity about James, his face was all they could clearly see. It was bruised and badly cut, more like a swollen blob of purples and reds than a human face. From inside the comfortable office they absorbed the grave reality of the situation. The buzzing sounds of machines, the sterile smells of antiseptic and the bright lights on the other side of the door were a stark contrast from where Iggy had returned their son. Flow wiped her reddened eyes while she mumbled to herself all the reasons why this shouldn't have happened. Brison squeezed her free hand.

When Dr. Maynard came into the room, the parents turned eagerly. She removed the thin hospital gown and gloves then tossed them in a receptacle.

"Mr. and Mrs. Ranck, sit down, please."

"Just tell us how he is," Brison said.

Maynard lowered her eyes and motioned to the couch. "Please."

They hesitated before sitting. Flow braced herself for the worst while Maynard pulled a chair over to face them.

"He was gone when he got here, but we were able to get a pulse back."

"He's alive?" Flow asked.

"His body is alive. EEG shows preserved brain activity but no reactions to external stimuli."

"In English," Brison said.

"Your son is brain-dead."

Brison cocked his head in doubt. "No. No, it can't be."

"There's not much we can do. I'm very, very sorry."

Flow expressed panic in fragments. "No... oh no... this... this can't..."

Brison shook his head, refusing to accept it. "There must be something that can be done."

"Brain-death is irreversible. Especially after several hours. He's on life support, but that's the way he'll remain."

"What are his chances?" Flow asked.

"For recovery? Mrs. Ranck, there have been extremely rare cases, but I need you to realize… it's not likely."

"He's a fighter," Brison said. "Do whatever you can."

"We already are. Just be aware of what he's up against." She squeezed the couple's hands and stood to leave. "You may stay here and watch him as long as you like."

Minutes later, Brison led Flow down the hospital corridor. She moved numbly, her mind spinning with the turn of events. Two hours before she was angry at her boy for being a bit late to dinner. Now she wondered if she would see him conscious again.

The sky-car drifted down into the Ranck property. It hovered a meter over the ground and settled in front of the walk. Brison looked over to Flow and caught her staring at something.

"Who's that?" Flow asked.

Brison turned and noticed the Federation car parked just off the driveway to his left. "Dunno."

The Rancks got out of their vehicle as the front doors of the Fed car opened. Two men in dark suits emerged. One of them held up an illuminated image displaying his credentials as a Federal detective.

"Mr. Ranck?"

"Yes?"

"I'm Randall Hutchins. This is Burnum Jerara," the elder man said. Hutchins was old with pale complexion. The younger Jerara looked Aboriginal with very dark skin.

"Something I can help you with?" Brison asked.

"Do you have any idea why we're here?" Jerara said. Standing out from his black skin were shiny platinum eyes and teeth, two indicators of cybernetic body parts still uncommon among the native Australians.

"No, officer."

"It's about your son," Hutchins said.

Brison was confused. "We know he's had an accident. Is that why you're here?"

Hutchins looked away momentarily. "We're aware of that. I am sorry, but no."

Flow poured coffee into four mugs as the men sat around the kitchen table. Though it was too late for coffee, Flow didn't expect to get much sleep anyway.

"Thank you," the officers said in unison.

Randall Hutchins, a cyborg of half man and machine, accepted the mug with his artificial arm. His internal sensors indicated the Rancks were upset but not nervous, that they likely knew nothing of the event.

"We're sorry to hear the news of your son," Hutchins said. "And yet, your family being Simplists, we have to conduct this interview. Do you know if James was with Abigail Walkins earlier today?"

"She goes by Missy," Flow said. "Her middle name. I don't know where James was but it's possible. Her folks live down the road."

"The Walkins are also Simplists," Jerara said. "Are your families close?"

"Not really," Brison said. "They're a bit more devout."

"A bit?" Flow reminded him.

"About a hundred times more."

"They're good people," Flow said. "Just extremely devout Simplists."

"And the kids?" Hutchins asked. "James and Missy?"

"Her parents don't like Missy in our home," Brison said.

"Because you're liberal with technologies?"

"Right. Sometimes the kids see each other outside."

"How long have they been mates?" Jerara asked.

"For years. 'Bout the same age."

Hutchins gently raised the difficult subject. "Does it surprise you then, that Fed rescue responded to a life alert after Missy was raped and strangled?"

"That couldn't have been our James," Brison insisted.

"So her memory has already been checked of that?" Flow asked.

"Yes."

"And what did they find?"

"Even if I had that information, I couldn't disclose it."

"Officer," Flow said, trying to remain composed, "there's something Fed should know about Missy."

"What is it?"

"She's not entirely sane. She lives in a fantasy world."

"She's nuts," Brison said.

"How so?"

"She fabricates things… a twisted sense of reality," Flow said.

"Twisted enough to alter her perception?" Jerara asked.

"I believe so."

"Anything's possible," Hutchins said. "That's why we're here asking you questions. We've talked with the Walkins. Missy's having forensic tests done, and your son is being evaluated by Fed investigators."

"In the hospital?" Flow asked in disbelief.

"There's no other way," Jerara said.

Hutchins tried to calm her. "Please don't worry. Our investigators are familiar with the needs of patients. Happens all the time. In some ways, they're better suited for it than hospital staff."

Brison ran his hands through his ruddy brown hair and lamented, "Christ, this is just what my son needs now."

Flow needed him to be a rock. She said quietly, "If something happened, I can't believe it was rape."

"Was anyone else with James at the time of the accident?" Jerara asked.

"No," Brison stated. Flow shot him a look and pinched his leg under the table.

"How did you find him?"

"The rover's transmitter. I tracked it in the car."

Flow sipped her coffee and wondered, *What the hell is he doing?*

Hutchins' emotional sensors detected deception for the first time.

If Allah brings you to it, Allah will bring you through it. - Qur'an

MISSY LAY AWAKE IN BED at a Federal hospital room about ten kilometers from St. Teresa Memorial. Her glazed eyes fixated on the ceiling as her mum watched with concern. As a Simplist, Detty Walkins was not permitted to physically be there. Instead, her holographic image sat on the bed next to Missy and mimicked the efforts of wiping away the last remnants of her daughter's tears.

Detty wished she could pull the covers a tad more over her daughter. Her hologram continued the act of stroking Missy's blond hair with the back of her fingers. Time stopped. This wasn't supposed to happen.

Detty's image turned away from her daughter and whispered angrily, "You had no right to sedate her without my permission."

"We had every right," a Federal computer voice answered.

"You've committed a terrible sin. There will be an inquiry."

"That is your right. Our agents can assist you—"

"We'll use our own agents, thank you."

"Your daughter's own life alert brought about Federal involvement. She will resume the rights of a Simplist, but only after she is fully released from Federal custody."

"There's more to it than that!"

"I'm okay, Mum," Missy said. "Try to relax." Missy looked like she felt horrible, not only for herself but for her parents.

"I'm so sorry," Detty whispered. "This never should have happened."

"Then why did it?"

"I don't know. I wish you could be at home with your dad and me tonight."

"But everything happens for a reason. I know it does."

"Not this. It's the devil's work."

Missy clenched her jaw and rolled her eyes.

"Visiting time is ending," the computer said.

From above the hospital ceiling a clap of thunder split the night sky. Its reverberations rumbled within the room. Moments later, heavy drops pelted the roof and created a steady patter throughout the upper floor.

Detty stared at Missy's eyes. She'd always found them mysterious, one blue and one brown. *My beautiful child. Why this?*

She managed, "G'night, Missy."

"G'night, Mum."

Detty's hologram faded from the hospital room.

At the Walkins' house, Missy's image disappeared from the living room. Detty turned from it, furious that the image maker had been installed in her all-natural home. She went down the hallway, her emotions about to spill over. She opened the bedroom door and found her husband waiting expectantly.

At the hospital, Missy lay awake as the tears welled up. A crack of lightning burst in the skies and flooded the room with flashes through the window. Then the calm of the rain returned, and the room powered down to its dimmest sleeping level.

"Help me understand," Missy whispered in the darkness. "All I want… is to understand it."

Ten kilometers away, lying in his hospital bed, a peaceful aura of blue light enveloped Jim. He was oblivious to the people and equipment working to keep his new body alive. Sleep. Breathe. Forget. Die and be born again. By now he had lost all consciousness of his previous existence. No memory of the lab. Nothing of his past friends or The Grandmother. He lay in a restful coma like a blank slate with no past and no foreseeable future. Sleep. Breathe. Forget. Die and be born again.

End of sample. The rest of *Jim's Life* is available at major retailers as ebook and paperback.